Sons of east Harlem

BY: ARMANDO RODRIGUEZ

This is a work of fiction. Names, characters, places, and incidents either are products of the author's imagination or are used fictitiously, and any resemblance to actual persons, living or dead, business establishments, events, or locales are entirely coincidental.

Interior Design by GhostwriterInc2016@gmail.com

Cover Design by GhostwriterInc2016@gmail.com

ACKNOWLEDGMENTS

To my Mommy, Barbara Rodriguez thank you for being the greatest woman to walk on earth. Thanks to my daughter, sisters, brothers, Aunts, uncles, nieces, nephews and cousins to make our family. We all look good.

I like to give a special thanks to Lynn Corvino, she is a force of many kinds and many talents. Everybody needs a Lynn.

Shout out to all of the real Sons Of East Harlem from that year 1990 and earlier who shot dice on the same corners as me and lived through the tale. J The Boss, Boo Harv, Macho, both Khans, KC, Lefty, Bump, Rubin, Raymond Santana, Whoodie, Dickwolf, Frost, Toy, Tanya, Bente, Wallyo, Johnny Fresh, Boo Black, Buddah, Steve Bo, Hutch, Ray, Binky, Joe, Gary, Vic, Donnell, Bam, Rudy, Kools, Moleik, Kenny High, Ashawnty, E, Alimo, Ben, Max, Otis, James bond, Green Eyed Tone, Jamel, Rich, Stagalee, Ron Jordan, Roger, Ricky, Vadar, Mike Murder, Juan, Gotham Rob, Bertha, Theo, Angel, Hampster, Charles, Carlos, Val the hundred more I know, and the thousand more I don't. Shout out to all the projects and blocks in East Harlem.

Great shout out to Marty, Rubin, Vinny, Gary, Manny and the entire Positive Work Force. WE PRESENTE UP IN HERE! OUR BACKYARD!

Everyone goes through hardships one time or another. Anyone can be cool when things are good. To be your best at the worse times will show who you are. That's what separates the strong from the weak.

Please post a comment on Instagram at sonsofeastharlem or contact me at sonsofeastharlem@gmail.com

PROLOGUE

The 1990s was an explosive era, illegal drugs influenced the entire country's way of life and the economy thrived. Money was exchanged then as easily as Emails are today. A study once showed that in the nineties, every person in the United States of America touched a bill in their lifetime that had cocaine residue on it. Everyone ate legally or illegally in a fast cash spending era because of Crack Cocaine.

Cash was plentiful now in the hoods on every scale. Millionaires were being made in the streets leading to more millionaires in corporate America. Many reaped the benefits of the Crack epidemic without the pain that came with selling it. Cash was so easily made it was spent freely. People that the hood identified with became more relevant now that the streets had money to spend.

Rap climbed to new heights, movie stars of all colors were becoming more popular and bigger in stature. Trends were created in the hoods and emulated through music into mainstream America. One way or another it all came back to money being made and spent from drugs and the popular money-making drug of the nineties was Crack. Either you sold it, used it or benefited from the exchange, whether you knew it or not.

Jobs were being created or expanded; products were sold more such as drug counselors, extra police officers, cab companies, barber shops, sales reps, fast food places, gold, cars, and clothes. Drug dealers spent money and gave it to be spent. The government created new jobs by the hundreds of thousands across the country. People's lives got better in some areas and destroyed for generations to come in others. Places with no economy now had one as Prisons were built in cities and towns that were doing poorly. People with no jobs prior to this explosion now paid taxes and had careers for themselves, and their families to come until this day.

A single prison created thousands of jobs, such as guards, medical staff, clerks and counselors but also including transportation services, food, food equipment, clothing, books and more. As more money was generated more taxes were collected.

On the other end of the spectrum was the demise of the people in the hoods who pushed the boom. Addicts were made, people were killed and placed in prisons. Incarcerated men left broken families and children fatherless, long sentences were given for crimes that were nonviolent many went to jail for years for the sale of a single crack or the false arrest of it. Police became the enemy as they caused more pain than order to the hoods across America.

What led to this was a combination of things, but it was definitely a government's success or failure. This book will tell the tales of East Harlem and the places it touched in the nineties. There were many hoods that all have identical stories. I will tell this one as a tribute to all those that have fallen to this explosion. This book is fiction and based upon the overall attitude of East Harlem in the year 1990.

CHAPTER ONE:
KEITH

"*A girl!*" I was still amazed by the birth of my daughter Ciera. Melinda was feeding her the bottle I'd warmed up while they laid on the Queen size bed. It was a surprise gift she saw for the first time four months ago after coming home from giving birth. Looking at them now I felt cheap and knew a change had to be made. Not cheap as in broke, because we had our needs and wants met. But cheap as in not good enough for them. I have to lead them to a better life, especially for my daughter.

The girls that grow up in these neighborhoods have odds already stacked against them. Drugs, early pregnancies, domestic violence, prostitution and more just waiting for them to choose one or the other or all in one. This was normal around here…*normal!* All this has become so normal to see and accept that it's not even shameful or surprising for young teens to go to jail in this era or area. Everyone is facing some type of force against them. I have to make a change for us and see to it that she will have options and opportunities and not a limited path. So, that her problems can be about peer pressure, clothes and girl stuff instead of pure pain and suffering.

"Keith…Keith!" Melinda was calling me. "Ju okay, Keith, ju look troubled?" she spoke with an accent although her overall English was pretty good.

"I'm okay, baby, I was just thinking about how beautiful you two look together," I said coming out of my daze.

Melinda was flawlessly cute like her creator did not take a chance on her being beautiful but extremely cute. She is Puerto Rican, short and thin with a curvy body especially her butt it was the biggest thing on her little body like it did not belong there and it ran in her family.

She looked tiny feeding the baby with all the space around them in the big bed as I smiled, she looked up at me. "Whaattt Keith?" she said smiling back.

At that moment, my beeper went off and the smile she wore faded, hiding her little white teeth behind small lips. The screen of the beeper showed my Uncle Scottie's number with 117-117-117 following it which means he was outside waiting on me. I went to the phone on the small dresser by the bed, feeling her eyes following me as I walked. I dialed the O-Jay cab number that I knew by heart.

"O'Jay cab company," he said on the phone.

"Yeah, this is Keith from one-hundred seventh street and Lexington can you send my regular driver to get me?" I said

"Sorry, Keith he's not here but I'll have a car there in ten minutes," he replied.

"That's good, I'll wait between Lexington and Park," I said.

"Okay, ten minutes." The phone hung up.

Knowing the base was in East Harlem seven blocks from us, I knew they'd be here quick. I moved in with Melinda and her family a little over a year ago and have been with her for two years. The apartment had four bedrooms and I made it comfortable by adding extra phone lines, the big TV and appliances.

"Ju, leaving now, Keith?" Melinda asked.

"Yeah, I won't be back until tonight. I'm going to take care of something important for us."

"Oh, your big surprise, just don't come home too late, Abuela is gonna cook."

"I'll make it back by eight, Mel. Save me a plate."

She took the bottle out of the baby's mouth and tossed it on the bed. As she carried Ciera in her arms, Melinda started using her feet and ass to inch toward the edge of the bed making low sounds while she moved.

"Uh…uh…uh," she said getting off the bed, then stood up placing the baby over her shoulders.

She was wearing a long robe with nothing under it. She walked back and forth patting Ciera's back attempting to burp her.

I went to the closet, took a pair of brown-and-white Uptowns from their box and slipped them on my feet. When Melinda walked toward me, she was staring into my eyes like she knew something I didn't. I then pulled out a brown-and-beige *Banana Republic* leather jacket and put it on. Melinda turned her back to me and started pacing. As she paced the floor turning her back to me, Ciera gave me the exact same look over her mother's shoulders.

Mel stood at the crib and placed the baby in it. I walked over behind them giving Ciera a kiss then Melinda. We paused as our lips touched and she held on tight closing her eyes. Her head rested on my chest.

"Baby, everything is going to be fine. I have major moves for us, okay," I said gently breaking away from her.

She looked up at me blinking her eyes. "Well, what's going on ju keep telling me ju got a secret for months. I don't need no bullshit going on behind my back, Keith."

I clipped a beeper to my pants, then put my family's beeper in the inside of my jacket pocket. I watched her watching me, seeing there was no real worry in her face, I continued getting ready so I could leave since I was already running late.

The element of surprise was hard to keep but we were in a good place. We loved and trusted each other deeply. Earlier in our relationship, we went through some rough stages on both our end but had gotten through it leading us to where we are now.

"Mel, I told you this is a long process. Just be patient you will love it and be major happy," I assured Melinda.

I got on my knees and went under the bed, grabbing a doubled plastic bag that held a brown paper bag, filled with one hundred thousand dollars in cash that she'd helped me count out last night. I looked to my right and she was walking toward me, plopping only her upper body onto the bed, facing down with her legs tiptoeing on the floor since she was so short. She then lifted her robe to the side showing her perfect tanned ass. I looked at it, then raised my hand and slapped it hard.

She yelled out, "Puneta!"

Holding the bag in my hand, I ran as she got up off the bed and chased behind me to the door. Once I was out, I closed the door and held onto the knob. I could feel and hear her trying to open it from the other side.

"Staaahhp…that shit hurts!" she screamed.

"Well, don't be teasing me when you know I have to go. Need anything sweetheart?"

"I got your, sweetheart, Keith! Open the door." She pulled hard on the door almost getting out.

"Do you need anything?" I asked again and she finally calmed down a little.

I knew Mel would try me again, but then the door stopped being pulled as I held on tighter.

She finally said, "Yeah, get me a smash ham and cheese with Mayo from my spot and tell Davi to get in here. He supposed to come home after school to do his homework."

"Okay, I got you baby. Anything else?"

"I want him in here Keith for real."

"On it, babe!"

Davi was her badass twelve-year-old son, that she had when she was sixteen. He was way too grown and advanced since he'd already seen too much for his age. I waited holding the doorknob with all my might, then came the strong pull from her end like I'd already assumed. I held on and it proved to be a failed attempt on her end, as I heard her stomp away cursing.

"Puneta, Keith, you're an asshole."

I walked into the living room where her sister was sitting on the couch watching a movie on the big floor model TV. Their mother came out of a room and Mel's sister Julissa got up. She was a bigger version of Mel and her mother was an older version of both Mel and Julissa. They all shared the same family trait…big round asses.

"Bye, Abuela," I said to Mel's mother.

"Aseguarate Y cuidate," Mel's mother replied.

"Sorry, don't speak Spanish. No comprendo, Abuela. See you later, you too, Julissa!"

"El vive aqui un ano Y toda via no sabe lo que yo digo…ha…ha…ha." Abuela told Julissa.

"What she say?" I asked Julissa.

"She said for you to be safe and that you've lived here for a year and still don't know what she's saying," Julissa explained.

I left with that note. When I got outside my uncle Scottie was chilling by the pay phone on the corner with two strong Pit Bulls. My uncle was five-ten, dark-skinned, weighed two-hundred and forty pounds and had a look that put fear in people all around, his bite was even worse. He was well known in East Harlem for the violence and things he'd done. He was respected even though he could not overcome his crack addiction.

He saw me and nodded it was around three-thirty. I walked over to him as I watched people outside hustling on both sides of the streets on the sidewalks in broad daylight, while others just walked along right past them as if nothing was wrong. Traffic was moving while crack was being handed to customers. This block had three different bosses on it, so the workers served customers with colored tops on the vials to indicate whose work it was, I owned Red.

Right on cue, Mama came running to see me as she usually does when I come out of the building. She was a beige colored, tiny woman, who looked old, but wasn't as old as you'd think. Yet she was everybody's Mama. Her voice was hoarse from the years of using crack with little or no sleep for weeks at a time. But her voice still had a feminine essence to it.

"Papa, list in." That's how she pronounces listen. "Mama seen the police out here watching everybody and nobody list *innnn…*" She dragged out the in.

"Mama, I'm in a hurry just watch their backs out here."

I went into the grocery store with her following my every move.

"Papa list in, Mama has to talk to you."

I quickly bought a Very Fine fruit punch juice and left back out with her on my heels to where Scottie and his dogs awaited looking silently and alert. The O-Jay pulled up, you could hear the inside locks pop open when it came to a stop in front of us. The windows were tinted on the long blue town car. The driver's side window rolled down. Scottie walked over to it, looked in and gave the driver a nod, then got into the back seat with the dogs.

"Oh, yeah, Mama here take this." I gave her two twenties for Mel's two-dollar sandwich knowing what she was going through. I take care of Mama and she takes care of me. According to her, she's in charge next to me. "Go buy me a ham and cheese smash with mayonnaise on it for Melinda at that store she likes. Then find that badass, Davi and tell him to get in the house. His mother wants him in now!"

Mama took the money and placed it where her bra was supposed to be in an attempt to hold it in place. Her breasts were so small and shriveled up from the nonstop abuse, the money dropped down to the bottom of her shirt. She shook it out, allowing it to drop to the ground.

She picked up the money and dropped it back in her shirt again. "Papa list in, when you coming back? Mama needs to talk to you." Her voice was going in and out like an audio button on a TV that was being flicked on and off as the money fell out again not being held by her breasts. She picked it up and dropped it back down her shirt.

I entered the front seat of the cab and gave the driver a dab. He looked ready to go but saw Mama standing right outside not letting the cab door close as the money fell out of her shirt again. She fumbled with it, catching it on her body with one hand before it hit the ground, her other hand held on to the cab door.

"Mama needs to talk to you, Papa." She put on what was supposed to be her sad face.

Her skin was clear and smooth except for the places where deep lines ran, and a small scar under her chin, a true war mark that came from an incident right here on 117th Street. Mama was tiny and tough, but sweet and loyal. She tucked her shirt in all around her with one hand. Then dropped the money in for the last time with no place for it to fall out. A look of satisfaction like she'd accomplished a big deed came across her face.

"Okay, Mama…okay, take care of everything. We will talk as soon as I get back, I promise."

"Papa, don't forget cause I'ma wait for you to get back, Papa."

"I won't Mama, see you when I get back." I leaned up and kissed her on the cheek, then sat back down as she closed the cab door and walked off real fast like she had important business to take care of, but it was the same ole normal everyday shit.

Scottie who's usually quiet said, "You gonna catch something messing with that old, bitch."

I laughed giving the driver the Long Island address as we pulled off toward the FDR. I placed a tape into the cassette deck player and Rakim's voice came to life blasting *Microphone Fiend.* I turned it loud, the heavy bass put us in a strong mood. I took out a large blunt of weed from my jacket and lit it up as the driver rolled up his window. Within minutes the car filled with smoke while we drove away.

CHAPTER TWO:
MAMA

King Papa, I love him. Keith was a real king and he knows I got his back. They all saw him talking to Mama before he left so now, they will listen to me. I was rushing straight to his crew.

"You bugging, Mama." Monk told me when I warned him earlier about T.N.T watching the block from 2nd Avenue. Monk is a nice kid and good to Keith so I'ma tell his ass one more time and that's it.

As I looked straight ahead, I was not taking my eyes off them. They were all the way at the very opposite end of the block today. Fats was counting money from a sale and Monk was yelling out Red tops to get a customer's attention. Fats thinks he's slick, but Mama knows what he be doing. I helped cook that batch up for Keith and that ain't the same batch. I know because I tried it earlier for my wake up. Wait till Keith finds out. He knows Mama tells the truth. There's no time to be wasting, Monk will get one warning and that's it. Then I gotta take care of Keith's business. T.N.T gonna roll today and I don't want Monk to go to jail, he lucky Mama likes him.

Welo's crew was across the street on their side, five of them spread out from corner to corner with the little ones overdressed in big coats and large boots. Once they start getting money and buying clothes on their own for the first time, they try to be bigger than what they really are. It's not even cold today and the snow on the ground was pushed to the side, melting. Yet they still wore them big coats and Timberland boots. Welo's crew had the youngest kids on the block doing the hand to hand mixed with some older ones that watched over them. Keith and Ray had two people each out today on the side they shared.

A skinny little boy about thirteen-years-old who started days ago, yelled out to me from across the street on Welo's side. "Mama…Mama, come over here and spend that money. Black tops is out…Black tops is out…Black tops is out!"

"Not now, Papa…Mama's busy." I squeaked out with my hoarse voice and kept rushing on.

He wore bummy clothes that let you know he's new. The coat looked cheap and tiny on him compared to his friends. By next week he'll be fresh from head to toe like the rest of Papa's workers trying to cop Welo's style. It was all a rerun for me.

"You know we got the best out here, Mama. Come get these Blacks!" he yelled as I was about to pass him from the other side of the street.

Then Tall-Tall Man who wore clothes that were clearly way too small for him copped off Little Kid. He wore a scarf and hat but no coat, his forearms showed as the sweater he wore did not even go down his wrists. I looked over to try and catch a glimpse of the crack vials being served but the cars parked on both sides of the street covered Little Kid from the shoulders down blocking the exchange. Tall-Tall Man put the bottles in his mouth as soon as he got them and walked off.

"Spend that money over here, Mama," Little Kid said putting away a knot of cash in his pocket as I could now see him in between cars looking this way.

I stopped completely leaning at my waist to get all the words out of me for him to hear. "Not now, Papa, Mama's busy!" I yelled at the top of my lungs and rushed on.

Two girls that I knew went to cop from him and a clear taste of crack smoke residue was in my mouth as I swallowed my spit trying to taste what was not there. The taste was strong as my mind pictured what they'd just bought. Welo's bottles are usually always so overstuffed that you would have to tap that little plastic vial on the floor to get the crack out. Plus, the quality was sometimes the best on the block. If not the whole East Harlem.

On our side, I was now passing Ray's people who were older teens that wore nice leather jackets. I envisioned the Green tops they had with hard white crack in the vial. When Ray's on he's on.

Them Greens be good but too small a lot of times. The one with the Eight-Ball jacket served the old man who lived on the top floor of Keith's building. While the other looked up the block for the police. That old man don't even smoke, he buys crack for sexual favors from women who get strung out and don't have the money to buy it. I slowed down a little as my curiosity got the best of me and wanted to see what the Greens was looking like. While Eight-Ball jacket served the old man, I picked up my pace. I had to handle Keith's business first.

As I walked up to Keith's crew Fats was leaning on a car watching me, and Monk was on the hood of the car looking at his beeper. Fats was about thirty, he was the oldest guy on 117th Street. He's been hustling on this block before Welo, Keith and Ray, and he's sold drugs for all of them. I can't stand him he likes to put his hands-on people and thinks he owns this block.

"How many you want, Mama?" Fats asked as I got closer to them.

I know what he be doing, wait till I tell Keith. Thinking about him getting over had me angry. In a low raspy voice that could barely be heard I spoke out without realizing it, "I know what you be doing. You think everybody stupid."

I was shocked when Fats replied, "Fuck you talking about, Mama? Get the fuck from over here before I slap the shit outta you!"

He came toward me, I jumped back quickly, then went into my panties and pulled out two glass pipes. One of them was broken at the tip and had a jagged edge. I held it in my right hand ready to swing.

"Try it, Papa…go 'head try it. Come on now, Papa, nobody's gonna hurt, Mama…nobody!"

Monk slid off the hood of the car so fast it surprised me because he was so chubby and got in between us. "Hold up, Fats. Chill don't be making the block hot out here with this bullshit," Monk said.

"I will kill her crack head ass with my hands. Tell her to get the fuck outta here!" Fats said.

"Ain't nobody gonna hurt, Mama," I repeated ready for his move.

He was not really interested in hurting me or he woulda pushed passed, Monk. I eased up keeping the pipe just in case. Fat's just wanted to yell and try to scare me.

"What's up, Mama? Let's go over here. What's up?" Monk said walking me a car length away.

"Papa, list in, I'm telling you to leave today T.N.T is gonna roll up and do a sweep. I'm telling you, Papa." My voice was going in and out I was thirsty for something to drink and thirsty to smoke crack. But I ignored that feeling, if I would have stopped to take care of the thirst, crack would have won, and I wouldn't get anything else done.

"You sure, Mama?" Monk asked looking dead into my face.

"Yes, Papa, Mama saw them. Please just go for now," my voice was getting worse by the minute.

Fats spoke out loud from behind Monk, "Fuck that old, bitch, she can't even speak."

A couple came to him and copped. I looked at him with a snarl and put my pipes away. I had things to do.

"Mama, did you see them yourself?" Monk asked.

I tried to talk and started getting really mad. So, I yelled out, "Papa the police are coming leave the block!" Then I walked off.

As I walked up Lexington to 119th Street, I saw people playing basketball in the schoolyard. It was packed with spectators outside and in the fence surrounding it. Girls had on big earrings, name brand clothes, and their hair was done up nicely. The boys had on gold chains, leather jackets, and new sneakers. It was one of those nice days in February that we didn't get too often, so they were out there looking their best.

Ray the boss was there with some boys.

"What's up, Mama?"

"What you doing over here, Mama?"

"Hey, Mama, what's up?"

People were greeting me everywhere I turned, I walked real fast, passing them saying, "Davi, has to get home."

Then I kept walking to handle Keith's business. I found a space on the fence and squeezed in next to a young girl.

"Hi, Mama," she said.

"Davi gotta get in the house now," I said and noticed how cute the girl was. "You look nice, your hair cute."

"Thanks, Mama," she replied.

I had my face close to the fence watching Davi dribble the ball on the court, playing with older and bigger people.

"Davi, get in the house now!" I yelled.

He instantly got distracted upon hearing me say his name. He turned his head to locate me. The other players saw his distraction and started rushing him, trying to take the ball. He threw it around his back then between his legs, avoiding the swipes of players and left them behind with his moves.

"Go, Papa…go, Papa!" I yelled, jumping up and down as I held onto the fence.

A kid older and bigger than Davi by at least five inches blocked his every move. Davi stepped back quickly and put up a jump shot that went into the basket.

I said out loud to no one in particular, "Papa, can play?"

"Oohhh!"

"Wow!"

"Did you see that? Shorty is nice!"

Roars from all around the crowd were heard. Suddenly I could feel the money in my shirt without touching it because I wanted to get high. I cupped my hands around my mouth like a bullhorn, yelling through the fence, "Davi, Melinda, said get in the house, right now!" Then I walked off as the crowd started laughing.

I searched my upper body for the money in my shirt. If I lost that money, Keith wouldn't believe me. My heart started speeding up as I got scared thinking about what Papa would think.

"Oh, here it is." My mouth moved but no words came out. I felt the money in my shirt and balled it up in my hand so I could be sure I wouldn't lose it.

I need one of them nice leather jackets everybody got so I can have better pockets. I'ma tell Keith to buy me one. Then it occurred to me after walking off that Davi probably did not hear me. I rushed back to the schoolyard, mad with my fists balled up, wanting to finish Keith's business. This time I walked through the gate, passing everybody to get on the court.

I saw a dealer I knew and said, "Hi Papa."

He tried to talk back but I moved through the crowd and onto the court ignoring all comments. I was directly under the rim as players ran down to the other end of the court with their backs to me.

I yelled out loudly while leaning forward with both fists clenched, "Daaaviiiiiiii!" I was so loud my throat hurt. Everybody stopped playing and looked back at me including him, The crowd was staring at me, too. "Melinda said get in the house, right now!"

I saw his mouth moving as he said some words with his hands up in the air. I stormed off with laughter and remarks from the crowd following me. I pushed through them hearing, "Mama don't play!"

"Oh shit!"

"Crazy bitch!"

"Your Mama!" I said causing loud laughs to continue behind my back. I then noticed Tall-Tall Man who copped some Black tops walking down 119th Street toward the Westside.

CHAPTER THREE:
TALL-TALL MAN

Once I scored to take the lead by one point the entire arena was on their feet and there was seven seconds left on the game clock. The crowd was going wild. The other team called a time out and we immediately got into our huddle with the coach.

"Don't foul play your own man," he told us.

I knew number 12 would get the ball, everyone else knew it too. He was their best scorer.

"Coach, let me guard number twelve?" I suggested.

"No, everyone hold your own man, now let's go!" Coach shouted.

We all repeated him. "Let's go!"

The five of us began shouting into the roars already being heard around us from the spectators in the stands. Thousands of people in the stadium screamed loud with cheers fit for an NBA star, either wanting them to score or us to stop them. The energy was intense and dreamlike.

I tried to focus on what coach had said, instead all I could think was, 'I've been through too much to get here and if we lose, I'd be forgotten. I'd spent three years on the bench, administration and the coaching staff knew my potential. However, they were constantly saying I made bad decisions off the court. Negative publicity was not acceptable for a Division One basketball player, so they kept me on the bench. Being one of the best players on the team made that decision difficult for me to swallow. Just to make it here from Harlem was a task alone. Escaping the lustiness that made life work in Harlem was the hardest part. The difference between Michael Jordan and one of the greatest streetball players ever, Earl Manigault was not their game, but that Mike did not fall to the vices of the streets. He was focused and disciplined that was the key.

First, I got benched for playing basketball back home in the Ruckus Park tournaments which is how I got money to support myself. Then I got arrested twice for shoplifting because I couldn't support myself. Those were the excuses along with other minor things that they used to keep me benched.

My parents were both deceased, I was living with my grandmother and little brother, so times got rough. I went through all the struggles, got through all the bad times and jumped over all the hurdles just waiting until my break finally came.

A starter in my position got hurt and I was able to start five games straight, winning all five of them. It wasn't just the fact that we were winning, but with me being a huge factor. I refused to lose. No longer could I be benched if they wanted me to be the goose laying their golden eggs. This win was important, it could give us a chance to make the March Madness tournament. I was playing for my life and it felt like I was playing for Harlem.

After breaking out of the huddle everyone went to guard their man. I pushed my teammate lightly toward mine and went to guard his.

I heard Coach in the mix of the all the cheers, "What are you doing? No, guard your man!"

The whistle blew and the ball went straight to number twelve and I was on him instantly.

"Defense!"

Boom! Boom!

"Defense!"

Boom! Boom!

The crowd was stomping, banging and yelling out to us, the underdogs in their house. We won them over! This game was supposed to have been an easy win for the other team. Number twelve was smaller than me and had a quick step with a knack to score or get fouled around the basket. Therefore, denying him from getting a good position was my plan. He was a somebody and I was a nobody, a close call would be given to him. That's why coach wanted my teammate to guard him, but I was not going to second guess myself now I had to focus. Harlem was rooting for me.

He hesitated with the surprise of having a bigger player that did not play his position defending him. I saw a smidge of confidence on his face while he dribbled the ball up the court, waiting to get in position for a good drive to the rim. A high pick came, and I fought through it, taking a chance like my instincts told me to. Full speed going forward I reached for the steal seeing the ball going in a downward motion. If he turned his back or put his hand out for any of the offensive privileges he had, a foul would be called. Then he would go to the foul line to shoot for the tie and possibly the win.

Instead, he did not expect me risking it all and turned his body only slightly as I got a clean steal and ran up the court for a hard dunk. The time expired and everyone ran to me from the entire stadium it seemed. White, black, Asian, women and men we were all the same at that moment, enjoying the upset that I'd made happen. Reporters sought me out through all the commotion on the court asking me questions on live television.

"So, what happened next?"

I heard the question as I looked at my surroundings. Seeing a filthy apartment with two males and a female looking and listening to me brought me back to the present moment.

"I came back to Harlem to celebrate after the win and saw this girl at Willie Burgers that I knew from one-hundred and thirty-second street on seventh. We went back to her house smoked and had sex. Only the weed had crack in it without me knowing, a Woolie she called it. Then she pulled out a pipe and we smoked all night with my money. When the money ran out, I sold everything I came with, sweaters with college logos, sneakers, my watch, even my gym bag. When there was nothing left, she threw me out. Now I'm here with you," I told them.

Three days had passed since that win and I needed to get home to clean up and get ready to go back and play in two days. All I needed right now was to get high one more time, then get out of Harlem and back to school.

She had a guy that helped me sell all my things when we were on a mission to get high, and that was him who I was talking to. He had a burglary lined up that was with a lot of climbing and I did it. I did one burglary to the next and my clothes got ripped up. Getting high had me all fucked up. I was lost wanting to go home and finally made it home to my grandmother's apartment last night and borrowed some money. It was late so I put on my little brother's clothes and went out searching for a hit. Now it all replayed in my head, how I came to this apartment on 119th Street on Lennox Avenue with people I don't even know but been getting high with for days.

I felt dirty and looked silly with these small clothes on with a chill of shame and sickness grabbing me. I thought about my grandma and wanted to just go home, clean up, then leave for school and put all this behind me. I managed a smile feeling like the Warrior trying to make it back to Coney Island. I pictured the Little Kid on the East Side wearing bummy clothes going hand to hand yelling out Blacktops. I just needed to get high one more time.

"I got an idea, let's go if yar want to get high."

CHAPTER FOUR: SCOTTIE

"This motherfucker! I'ma put my hand behind his neck and slam his face in the windshield until it goes through it," I grumbled to myself.

My eyes went to the dashboard searching for leverage that I could use for myself when I jumped over to his seat. Bad stood at attention while Luck was getting antsy, moving his front left paw, due to a tick he had. I started wrapping their leashes tight around my hand and asked him again.

"What the fuck did you just say?"

"I…I…I was just wondering how long we…" he answered and was cut off by me.

"No…no motherfucker you said what are we doing here that's what you said."

"No, I meant…" he tried to reply.

"No…no shit!" I repeated getting heated. "Fuck what you meant! I will beat the shit out of you and break every window in this bitch of a cab with your face."

"I'm sorry, Scottie, I…I…"

"Just shut the fuck up! And don't ever use my name in your mouth again. Shut the fuck up now!"

Luck barked then lunged at the small space inside the cab to get to the driver, giving my arm a jerk, but he fell short as I held onto the shortened leash. The driver flinched into the dashboard looking back frightened by the dog's attempt. I hit Luck on the head lightly, he knew better than to attack without command. Bad just kept his eyes on the driver.

"Good boy…good boy," I said patting Bad for waiting patiently.

I don't know why Keith just didn't use our regular driver? The fear in this jackass's eyes showed until he turned away from my stare. He sat in his seat but not all the way back, just looking ahead like a dummy. Fucking cab driver asking me questions, we just waiting that's it. Keith is too fucking nice with these clowns, then they get in your business and the next thing you know we in jail. He was still smart enough to not be driven to the direct address of the places we came for, leaving us in the cab walking to them alone. Nephew got a brain.

My mood dominated the cab and the silence was so clear I followed a car driving past us way down the street, hearing its tires roll on the tar as it made a turn at the light, while still staring at the back of the cabbie's head. The streets were quiet, clean and empty, I was not stepping out of this car in Long Island since I'd just pinpointed a car's location with my ears, me stepping out would be loud.

These pigs out here are foul, they won't have me in their jail, breaking my legs because they don't like the color of my skin. The dogs were tense and could feel my agitation as they moved around impatiently. So, I had to go outside and relax them even though, I didn't want to. My hand went to a small slit inside the black goose down, sending a wave of good feelings down my back knowing I did well for myself.

One night I stood up sowing a ripped T-shirt into little sacks then made a slit in the seam of this coat sewing a sack into its slit. That was a long night for me with the needle kicking my ass for hours. I was not trying to be arrested for Crack possession while I'm outside, especially here in the boondocks. Five Cracks were in there, right now. I was saving them because Keith didn't like me smoking around him. He kicked his fucking Coke habit and either didn't want to be reminded or didn't want the temptation of a hard high. Whatever the reason I respected it. I looked around, then took my gun out and hid it under the cabbie's seat, I was ready to get out.

I pushed the door as hard as I could trying to break the motherfucker open, it bounced back as I caught it and stepped out of the cab. An out of place feeling caught me and I knew I didn't belong there. When we got outside Bad's tongue was hanging out of his mouth and his big Pitbull head went back and forth from me to a nearby tree. Not used to this scene of houses I didn't even know if I should let them shit or piss around here. Bad and Luck was itching to mark this soft up for grabs territory. I dropped their leashes and they waited. I took a deep breath while they watched me, waiting for a command or rather permission.

"Go! Go!" I said.

Bad my first dog leaped and ran over to the trees. They both wanted to piss on it, Luck pissed on the cab then followed Bad to the greasy area.

Keith came back after two hours with a smile on his face like we'd won life or something. He was a pretty boy, who was six-one, light-brown skinned, with curly, low cut hair.

"It's almost done, baby. I like it…I like it a lot," he said shaking his head up and down, probably still seeing it in his mind as I stood quiet.

"I gave him my oral commitment plus some side cash to hold until the lawyers did the paperwork, putting it all in Ciera's name. The house is done we just waiting for the move in date either this month or next month. The vitamin store is next being only eleven blocks from the house. If we can maintain our life from the store's profit, I'll be finished with this drug dealing shit."

"Let's get the fuck outta here, nephew," I said feeling uncomfortable.

He passed me slapping my back in a good mood. Doing all this to leave the game wasn't going to be easy for him, but he'll see, once you taste some things others become too bland to eat. One thing for sure, I'm in this shit for life.

"Bad…Luck…in the car, let's go now!" I yelled, they followed my orders and we all got in.

I had to holla at Keith to get someone strong to take over for him when he leaves the game. These Harlem cats are soft, the older ones anyway and I can't do it. I have no patience for selling no drugs. Keith was sitting in the front seat looking at the quiet driver, then he looked at me and back at the driver.

"What's going on? Looks like a cat got your tongue," he said to the driver.

"Naw, a dog," I said catching the cabbie's eyes in the rearview mirror.

He looked forward and said, "Where to?"

Luck barked a nonviolent tone, to me he was saying pussy. Keith was starting to understand him just as clearly as I could.

"One sixteen and Lex, I'm hungry."

Keith pulled out a cassette tape put it inside the cassette deck on the radio, then pulled out a blunt, put it on his lap removing the tobacco from it, filled it with weed and started rolling it. The car was silent as we passed through this twilight zone. As we hit the exit out of the town and onto an expressway, the music was bumping, the car filled with weed smoke and we were on our way back to Harlem.

I did not smoke weed but the contact of it had me feeling mellow. As we reached 116th Street, Keith paid the driver and I got out of the cab as they said their goodbyes.

"See you around," I said to the driver while holding Bad and Luck's leashes in one hand, waiting on his reply.

He nodded, looking near me but not at me and said lowly, "Later." Then drove off.

King Corporal Chicken was one of our eating spots that were famous for the Snack Box, which we call the Crack Box for attracting all these fiends around here. Two dollars gets you two pieces of chicken, French fries, a biscuit and a cup of mash potatoes or coleslaw, your choice in a box. They were opened twenty-four hours a day and the chicken had a light, delicious curry taste to it.

Three people exited the store, I looked inside seeing two dealers from Johnson projects that I knew. We nodded at one another. Two fiends were crowded in there in the small waiting space. The servers were separated from the customers by a see-through bulletproof, hard thick plastic window. They didn't have to wait long, money was put into a revolving box, made out of the same clear hard plastic, as it spun to the cashier on the other side. He took out the money, replacing it with boxes then spinning it back to the customers to take out, they left the store and Keith went in.

I was feeling glad to be back home, lots of people were walking by. Luck stood up and started barking at a girl, startling her. I punched him on top of his head.

"Luck what the fuck…relax," I ordered.

He looked at Bad who sat calmly waiting. I looked around to see anybody who wanted to judge me. This was better than a dog biting someone, then they'd blame me. When I first had Bad as a little pup, he attracted girls. Now it takes a real dog lover for them to just ask if it's safe to pet them. Keith came out with four crack boxes in a bag and we started walking down Lexington Avenue towards my crib on 103rd Street. It was a good walk for Bad, Luck and me and the silence of it all was exactly how I liked it.

My nephew Keith was a lifesaver for me. He's gifted for making this money and I fit right with him holding him down. He probably could find another me, but I would never find another him. My life right now revolved around Keith and I had no doubts in him ever letting me down but leaving the game would not be the same for me. No matter what I got him more than he be knowing.

After about seven blocks Bad and Luck started whimpering and bumping my leg. This was something I did not train them to do, it began on its own. When they know the same people are walking behind us for more than two blocks or so they start that, Keith noticed it, too.

"Don't even say nothing," I said.

He always told me that I had them paranoid from smoking Crack with them near me. They were on point with this even when it meant nothing but just some people walking our same path behind us. I looked back seeing lots of people behind us walking down Lex. More than likely the group of young cats was the cause and the dogs whining was more than a trifle.

"Meet me at the crib," I said and made a right turn walking down 109th Street. Speeding ahead I turned left on Park Avenue and started walking slowly. Bad and Luck were pulling me to go faster and barking under their breath.

"Okay…okay," I agreed. "Just hold on Keith is coming, relax…relax."

Two blocks down Keith came into sight a block ahead of me, going downtown. Within seconds the crowd of kids appeared behind him.

Keith took off running and the kids took off after him. I pulled out my .38 Revolver wishing I had a different gun with more bullets.

"Get Keith…get Keith!" I ordered as Bad and Luck took off knowing that usually meant to go play with him. I shot once in the air making everybody look back.

The dogs were foaming at the mouth during a high-speed run with no sounds but their nails scratching the sidewalk and me running behind them. People froze in their skin, stuck in fear of the sight. Two big-headed, muscled beasts running with no restraints.

Keith's pursuers were teenagers, I did not recognize them but recorded their faces to never be forgotten again. The teens looking back at us turned off the sidewalk running fast, crossing the narrow street into moving cars toward Madison Avenue as horns blared at them. Bad kept going toward Keith and Luck stopped where the kids had ran. He waited on the sidewalk looking in their direction as his left paw tapped rapidly on the sidewalk, wanting to cross the street. But he knew the penalty for breaking my commands.

When I caught up to them, he barked. "I see them, good boy get em…get em…get em." Luck took off.

Blam! Blam! Blam!

"Luck, to me now… to me now!" I yelled as I jumped behind a car, hearing the gunshots. "Fuckin' little bastard shot at us."

I grabbed Luck searching his whole body while he squirmed impatiently in my grasp. He was fine, I had the urge to go after them with Luck waiting for my command. My face tightened up; I was undecided but knew what I had to do. Luck seeing my expression let off a defeated howl.

"We'll get em, Luck, don't worry let's go."

We had to let them go and get out of there. I woulda chased them but the description of me with a dog was too easy for the pigs to spot and pick us up. So, we left.

Keith was waiting in my crib patting Bad as we walked in. Luck stood by me waiting to be told he did well in front of Bad. So, I got out some treats.

"Good boys…good boys," I said as they ate, then I turned to Luck. "Good boy, no streets…no street. Good boy, listen to Scottie…listen to Scottie." I sat on the couch and Luck jumped on me.

"We got to squash that beef with them 106 fools," Keith said.

"How you know it's them?" I asked.

"Can't be nobody else."

"I seen them real good, I'ma go through there later."

"Nah…nah…nah, let's…"

I had to cut him off. "Fuck this soft shit, Keith. They laying on you, trying to catch you slipping and you always floating around making moves with money. This has to be dealt with!"

"That's Monk's hood we going to let him put a bug in their ears. Money and beef never go good together," he replied.

"Fuck this, Keith. You going to try and throw money or sense at this and they going to think we soft, sending others or having others hearing about it from their bragging. This is bullshit, if you pay 'em others will come. Nah, ain't no cash cows here. Remember this started over some beef about a girl and became something else. That's how shit escalates."

Keith looked at me, I could tell he was in deep thought. Bad was relaxing, he got up and ran to his room joyfully, while Luck was waiting.

"Play…play…play!" I said and he chased behind Bad.

"You right but let's sit on this, we going to have to set some type of example," Keith agreed. "But I want you to talk to, Eric." He went to the phone to beep Eric Rosario. "I want them to see that we got people and I'ma call over someone Brooklyn cats," Keith continued.

"Just tell me when," I answered.

"Here, this the rent money and another four hundred for you. Monk told me you took five bottles from him. I told you, Scottie, don't mess with that pack money; I always replace that."

I stood silent, that fat little fuck was corny as hell. Keith's crew on 117th was mostly soft. Eric Rosario didn't roll with him like that no more. He had potential but acted too young, Monk gets money but chases pussy all day. Guy was tough, but everyone else was not loyal.

"Keith want me to get, Mama? Me and her can handle this," I offered.

Keith laughed. "Scottie, stop messing with the workers. You're supposed to make them comfortable not scare them," he instructed.

"Yeah, okay, nephew. You got it, you the brains."

Keith got up and ran over to me. "And the muscle old man."

We started wrestling, then Bad and Luck came running to join in.

CHAPTER FIVE:
MAMA

The bakery was crowded with people waiting. I ignored them all and ran to Papa.

"Give me a ham and cheese smashed with mayonnaise. Papa, please hurry up Mama needs to go!" I said leaning on the display case.

I tried to hand the money over to him as I stretched my arm out as far as it could go, trying to reach him while holding it in the air.

"Papa you look nice with your matching white hat and apron," I said.

He just looked at me, then at my closed fist by his chin with the money in it and ignored me.

Papa was a hustler, a small Cuban man with moles on his face. He made a coffee, placed it in a bag, then grabbed a napkin and a straw and placed them in the bag too. Then he took the money and gave change from the pockets of his apron all in one swoop to the customer. He and his wife had been here forever making doughnuts.

He began serving someone else, so I spoke louder. "I'm right here Papa take this money!" I said dropping one twenty-dollar bill onto the counter as he still continued to ignore me.

He wiped a small workspace quickly, then put away the rag and returned to the counter. I waived my fist with the other twenty-dollar bill directly in his white face, and he got mad. "Mama slow it down…slow it down. I tell you before you get it out if you no stop it! You get it out!" He said making another coffee with a hot smashed bread and bagged it with everything, then gave change while watching me.

I dropped my hand. "Okay, Papa, but please Mama got to go, and you know you love Mama," I told him with a wink.

His wife at the register looked at me so I pouted my lips and rolled my eyes at her. She smiled back and happily, served a customer.

They made a nice couple, they were always speaking Spanish to each other while working and sharing laughs all at the same time, just like we did on the block. The Cuban coffee smelled strong and made me hungry. Food started jumping out to me from the display case, all the stuff Papa made looked nice. I was so hungry I started rubbing my empty stomach, as I stared at a long doughnut with yellow cream in it.

"I should buy one," I said to myself. "No, I should go to McDonald's and eat first." There would be enough money after I get Melinda's sandwich to buy six Treys and still have a twenty. "Wait, Keith is coming back, I could just use all this money, but that will be too late and Mama hungry now. Oh yeah, Eric Rosario is over there on a hundred and twenty-second street, he will buy Mama some food. He got his own work now, Papa's a boss. Let me handle Keith's business first, then I'll decide what to do…I'ma still have the money." My mind was racing, and I needed something to calm me down.

After today, I'm going to stop getting high for a while. I'm going to start eating good, go to a shelter and get cleaned up. Then come back to get some money with Keith and buy one of those leather jackets, with pockets for the money I make. Mama going to look nice, me and Keith going to make changes starting with Fats, he's slick and that's why Keith needs me.

"Mama, bente Aqui Ahora, it's your turn…Mama come on," he told me, then started making my order without me telling him what I wanted.

I'm telling you Papa was a hustler, with my hands on the counter and my chin resting on top of them. I watched as he went to work, taking out fresh Cuban bread, then he slit it open with a big knife.

"Mayonnaise Papa, mayonnaise," I squeaked out.

He stopped in motion with his back to me turning only his neck and gave me a stare. "A dios mio esta mujer esta loca. I know it, Mama…I know it." Then he took out the tub of mayonnaise and slapped some of it on the bread with a big knife. He put the tub away under the counter and came up with metal trays that had slices of ham in one and cheese in the other. He evenly placed the ham across the bread then the cheese, he closed it up and rolled the sandwich in a wax paper fast and neat.

"Papa da-me some agua please," I told him.

"Ella tiene todo este dinero Y no compra neda de tomar para ella," he said.

His wife stopped what she was doing and said, "Not funny." Then got me a cup of water and shook her head at him.

Papa put the rolled-up sandwich into the smash machine. The bottom was a metal, hot plate covered in aluminum foil. The top had a flat piece like an iron with a weight on it, covered in foil to smash the sandwich flat. He put the smash down on my order. It crisped the outside of the bread while heating the ham and cheese, keeping the inside warm and soft.

Papa took another order; he was hustling hard. I looked out of the window to see Tall-Tall Man wearing too small clothes talking with two people, more than likely scheming something. A nice-looking lady came into the store and the wife served her immediately. Papa took another order from a dirty man who left out fast. He took Melinda's sandwich out of the smash, then sliced into two halves and bagged it up.

A fuzziness came developed in my chest overcoming my hunger. I felt ashamed; everyone was looking at Mama. Replaying all the people Papa was serving, he wanted all of them out of the store fast. The dirty ones or smelly ones or crazy ones, Mama was one of them. I thought Papa liked me, looking at my clothes I didn't remember the last time I'd changed. People looked at me like the person they didn't want to be around. I wished Keith was there, all I wanted to do now was get high.

After I gave Melinda her sandwich, I came back out of the building seeing Monk and Fats were not there. I walked to Little Kid who was calling me earlier. He had three people waiting on him to be served. Two were leaning on the steel little fence that held plant life and dirt in front of the building. Little Kid's pockets were bulging, and a customer handed him a twenty. He pulled out a bunched-up ball of cash with ones and fives in no order from his pockets, he counted the change out slowly. Then handed the customer some Blacks that were stuffed to the top.

I was going to get on the line, but I didn't want to go to jail today and he was moving recklessly. "You going to jail like that, Papa. T.N.T. out here and you act like you got a license. Meet me in Keith's building and bring me six, Mama can't go to jail."

"Go, Mama, go ahead, I'll be right there! Who's next? Have your money ready or you don't get served," Little Kid said.

I crossed the street to Keith's building and went up the three steps to the stoop. As I looked over the block, I saw Tall-Tall Man on Lexington Avenue watching Little Kid hustle. I could tell he was up to something. At the other end on Park Avenue, I saw Guy one of Keith's good workers making a sale. I stepped down all three steps and wanted to warn Guy to be careful. I heard engines of cars coming fast and knew what was happening.

I went right back up the steps yelling out loud so everyone could hear, "T.N.T is rolling…T.N.T is rolling!"

At full speed from both directions on a one-way street, cars came onto the block. Little Kid was on his way to me already and started running. A van cut off the Park Avenue side making that screeching sound. I had to put my hands to my ears. Welo's older workers started walking off toward Lexington. Men were jumping out of the cars, running with guns drawn and pointing at anybody in their eyesight. Guy got handcuffed and thrown onto the ground. I ran into Keith's building past the first door, grabbing the second one that I knew was always locked, and it was. Papa came in behind me and we were trapped in between the doors.

I rung Melinda's intercom bell. "Mama please open the door. Melinda…Melinda open the door!" I yelled hoping she was listening through the intercom.

"Mama what are you doing? The door is locked…it's locked!" Little Kid said pushing all the buttons on the panel for different apartments.

The doors were made of glass and we saw all that was going on out there. Just a look our way by the cops and they would see us. Undercovers had their guns drawn, giving orders and people were lined up against the wall. I even saw the black man that goes to work in his bus uniform every morning against the wall. I bet he don't think he no different from us now. They all were going to be searched and all else would be sorted out later, T.N.T didn't play. Ray's workers were being chased. One was thrown on the ground roughly with the officer on top of him, placing a knee in his back. The other was grabbed up just a few feet away and pushed against the wall.

Two of the customers Little Kid had just served found themselves coming our way, trying to get into the building.

"Hell, no…no…no!" I yelled with my foot and body on the door. "Tell them, Papa, tell them or we going to jail. This Keith's building, they gotta go somewhere else."

"Yar get the fuck from here!" Papa said with a boy's voice as he held the door along with me.

They turned to leave, and a gun was in their faces seconds after they stepped away from the building.

"On the ground get down now!" I heard the cop's say.

"Who is it?" A voice said from the intercom. "Why you buzzing my buzzer like that? Mama, I hear you down there, stop ringing my bell!"

Bzzzzzz!

Someone finally buzzed us in, I pulled the door open quick before the buzzing stopped as the voice from the intercom continued speaking.

It was Mel's voice, "Mama is that you?"

We were already inside the building slamming the door behind us. We ran past the steps to the back of the building. I was opening a window that led to an open space one floor down. Papa stood at the base of the staircase holding the rail ready to go up,

Bang! Bang! Bang!

The entrance door was banged on. "Police, come open this door!"

Papa saw where I was going and rushed past me out the window. He hanged off the sill dropping himself down, falling when he landed. I climbed down behind him using holes somebody put in the rocks of the building just for this. As soon as

I touched the ground, I took off running. We went through an old tunnel with walls made of stone. It came into an opening leading to metal steps that went up to another building. Up the steps, he ran past me, waiting for me inside, looking lost. We were on the bottom of a staircase now inside a building on 118th Street.

"My stash, Mama I got to go get it." Papa was nothing but a little punk and panicking.

I should go find and take his stash, but Welo's his boss, and he don't mess around. That's why those men did not push the door in on us. As I walked up one flight, I knew he would follow me to the second floor.

"Papa, pull yourself together," I said with the little breath I had left as I breathed in hard, my heart was pounding fast. "I told you that T.N.T would roll. Worry about the stash later, just wait a minute before you go to jail," I schooled him.

He was looking like a scared lost kid, willing to do whatever I told him. Caught up in the game with harsh penalties, not like the TV life he'd watched. Papa was a kid and within weeks would grow into a hardened man.

"Fix yourself up, Papa, you can't go outside like that."

He took out a roll of money with a brown paper bag popping out of his pocket. It ripped open and crack vials fell all over the ground. I tucked my shirt in all around my pants tightly. He started picking them up, I got a paper bag off the ground and gave it to him quickly dropping vials down my shirt. We were picking up and placing the cracks into the bag he held. While dropping them in, I dropped two more into my shirt.

"Count them Papa and I'll tell you where to stash 'em so you can go get your other stash. This way you know Mama did not take anything from you," I told him.

He fixed himself up and put his big bills together in one pocket. He put fives together in another. He separated the ones in two knots into his sock. I brought six vials from him and he gave me two. He was no longer bulging with cash and left out to get his stash through the entrance of the building. I went back the same way we came through the alley back into Keith's building.

I rode the elevator to the top floor then walked to the staircase entrance. Opening the metal door, it slammed hard behind me making a loud noise. Everything was creeping me out. There were steps leading up to a landing that led to the roof and I went up there. A strong smell of piss hit me, and a dim yellowish light came from a fixture. It showed the stains on the small landing space and I calmed down feeling safe. Different colored tops and empty vials were everywhere. Used condoms, empty beer bottles, all added up to the rush and anticipation of what was coming next. *Me getting high*! I put my back to the wall untucking my shirt and shook the four Blacktop vials out. Then sliding down to the ground, I put them on my lap. I reached into my panties and pulled out both pipes, then placed one by my side and the other on my lap. Hearing silence all the way down to the first floor was a security system for me. As I settled in, I pulled out more Blacktop vials and a lighter.

Bang! A door was slammed on a lower floor, I froze. Kids were running up some flights and giggling. *Bang!* The exit door slammed, and silence came again unfreezing me.

I took two of the Blacktops from the bunch in front of me laying loose on my lap and emptied the crack into the mouth of the pipe, leaning my head back. I put my lips to the bottom side of it, brought my lighter to the mouth and lit the crack as it began to sizzle from the heat. It sounded like a can dragging across the cement floor but lower and less harsh. White smoke went through the pipe into my mouth and I tasted the strong cocaine with light baking soda of Welo's cracks hitting me instantly, my heart raced.

The smell was distinctive like no other. I could see myself and felt everything dirty change into clean. A brand-new leather jacket with my hair done up, all that is coming soon. I lit up again thinking about a house. Mama don't drive so I'ma have Monk drive me around. Getting money was not hard, my hands were moving around on their own repeating the process. It was automatic without me thinking but wanting and getting that high over and over. The pipe was in my mouth with the sound, then taste, then smell, and then hit. Eric was going to buy Mama some food later. Me and Keith is going to wear nice jackets, everybody loves Mama.

Graffiti on the wall read: ***Don't look now but here you are again! CYCO, Tone-Angie.***

I read other names and writings as I reached for some more vials to smoke as the strong smell of piss hit me. I panicked feeling like someone had stolen from me because there were only the empty ones around me. I must have smoked them all, I felt dirty again. Reaching and searching my body I found the other twenty-dollar bill and went down the steps. Hopefully, Little Kid hadn't left yet.

CHAPTER SIX
LITTLE KID

I was chilling, driving my green Suzuki jeep, bumping music down Lexington Avenue. Everybody was shouting me out as I passed.

"What's up, Cee?" Came from my left.

I nodded back at the kid, "Yo!" I nodded to my right.

"Holla at your boy, Cee."

"You already know," I said with my hand on the steering wheel. A Rolex hung on my wrist as I pushed my ride spitting Special Ed.

I'm kinda young but my tongue speaks maturity/ I'm not a child I need nothing, but security/ I get paid when my records gets played to cut it short/ I got it made…

I stopped in front of building 1990 where a bad chick named Stacy was standing, talking with other chicks, but she was the baddest by far. Everyone be sweating her. She wore a custom-made Gucci bag with matching Gucci boots from Dapper Dans on 125th Street. She was looking good as she came over to me. I saw people watching her perfect ass moving from an angle I couldn't see but my eyes were on her thick curvy thighs instead then they shifted up to her lips that opened.

"Turn it down…turn it down a little," she requested. "Let me holla at you, Corey. I see you getting this money now!"

Feelings came quick in my lower body, as I thought about the things, I'd heard she could do. I could only imagine that her body felt warm and soft. I'ma try and get a hug or something. As I turned the music down, I got some angry glances.

"They just hating on you, Corey. So, what you doing, right now?" she asked close up on the car.

Her hair was done in a Duby, she was wearing Door Knockers in her ears. Stacy's face was strong and womanly beautiful. I started getting hard, so I helped it a little getting there.

I pressed down feeling myself grow just in case she got in the car I'd be ready.

She leaned in and said, "Get the hell up and get ready for school, Corey."

My eyes opened and my mom's face was above me, zooming into focus. My room, the dresser with the small TV and the hanger attached for an antenna on top of it all came to sight.

"And stop touching yourself boy…that's nasty!"

She walked away shaking her ass in her nurse uniform. She worked overtime last night, so I figured she must have just come home. Having a good-looking young mother bothered me because my friends were always sweating her. That shit got me aggie. A roach ran across the ceiling while I was looking up from my bed and it froze like it knew that I saw him.

"Hurry up, I'm going to sleep and when you get back from school we need to talk. I heard you be coming in the house right before I get in from work…acting like you sleep. You think you slicker than your mom, huh? You're going to see, Corey. Now hurry your ass up!" She was loud through the whole house, getting me more aggie. She was way in her room, yet her voice stood all in my ears, traveling like she'd never left.

Not being able to help herself my dumb sister's voice came into my ears too. "Eww, mom he was playing with himself. I didn't even think he like girls the way he dresses."

"Shut up, Trina with your ugly face. You telling mom I don't be home at night? Watch how you gonna be sweating me when I start bagging your friends!" I yelled at the direction of the door still in the bed.

Her ugly face peeped in my room, "My friends like men with cars not boys with toys." She looked at my three G.I. Joe figures I had on the floor and continued running her mouth. "You can't even drive. You can't even buy nobody a real dinner, silly. Go somewhere!" Her head was gone.

"Chicken Head!" I yelled.

Then I heard my mother's voice again, "Stop talking to your brother like that and get your hot ass ready for school too, yar a mess."

"I get paid today," I told myself as I got out of bed.

I rubbed my eyes and lifted up the mattress seeing fives and ones laid out from my sixty dollars a day spread money, I'd been getting all week, that always seemed to come up short. I went to the bathroom smiling, then brushed my teeth with a ran down toothbrush and noted to buy a new one later, then I washed my face.

"There's some milk left for cereal and I boiled you two eggs. Come on, Corey let's go!" my moms yelled.

I get paid six hundred today, I'm about to get fly. Maybe after two more weeks, I can save some money for us to move out of here. My room was so small most of my stuff was stashed under the bed. I got an outdated Atari 5200; I don't even play with. I had to go to my friend's house to play Nintendo, I'll change that soon.

Welo be giving away his clothes and putting new stuff on right on the block. I'ma wear my bummiest stuff and throw them out when I get my new gear. As I looked through my clothes, I got aggie with all my things being bummy. That's okay though like I said things would change real soon. I put on a dirty Tee-shirt, some brown Wranglers with a patch on one knee and faded spots on the other from playing Scalees on the streets. A no-name brand sweater with holey socks then grabbed all my socks and underwear and put them in my book bag for the trash. I finished my attire with old Pumas and saw my toe come out of the hole on the right side. I couldn't wait to end this day. I grabbed a Levi Jacket with the white wool collar, I needed to cover up how I looked.

"Thanks, mom," I said in my head.

She'd bought me that, I was ready to go get paid. I get six hundred for the week and still get my sixty spread. That's double than what my moms make all week and after a month it goes up to seven a week. I usually worked from three to eleven after school, but I was skipping school today to work the early hours. Now I could shop, plus they told me Welo was going to talk to me about the police bust. I hope I ain't got to pay nothing that will be way too much and that bust was not my fault. Mama told me to say I saw Tall-Tall Man take the stash that was missing, and I did. She saved me that day over and over.

I left out of the door with my book bag and ran up the steps to the roof. I threw the socks and underwear over the side into a lot full of trash then hid my book bag and ran down the steps leaving my building heading to 117th Street.

The block was alive, people went in and out of that bakery with the Cuban coffee and soft bread, people were going in different directions. Most were going to the train station on 116th Street. Teens with backpacks, older people going to work, hustlers and fiends coming to the block, the movement was constant.

On the block, Welo's cherry red BMW was parked and he was leaning on it talking to people. As I walked past, I looked inside seeing two girls and a dude in the back seat.

"Get in the front. Wait you clean, right?" Welo spoke to me for the first time ever.

"Nah, I um…I mean yeah, I'm clean. I need some work though." I must've sounded like a scared fool.

"Just get in we doing something else."

"Oh, a'ight." I got inside the car and the kids in the back was definitely not from Harlem.

Seeing Welo up close he was a chubby, Puerto Rican who kept a smile on his face, but I knew he was dangerous. I was hoping he didn't tell me I have to pay for that loss in the bust. He was wearing the biggest link chain I'd ever seen, and a piece hung from it of a man and woman having sex while standing up. It was made of solid gold and the size of a Barbie doll. The piece could stand on it's on and move like it was having sex. He was also wearing a big wool Rich coat.

Welo's face shined with a smile. All his clothes were brand new, he seemed like a real-life superstar. People kept coming to him to talk, even regular people like women from the buildings and giving him kisses on the cheek. Sales were being made up the block on both sides. Druggem one of Welo's captains came over to Welo.

"I'm out…hold it down. I got Shorty's pay, beep me on the three-six-zero number. I'm not looking at the other ones," Welo instructed.

"Got you," Druggem agreed.

I felt good hearing I'ma get paid as Welo got in and we drove off. His beeper went off, he looked at it when we stopped at a light, then he placed it back on his waist next to two others that started beeping as well. He ignored them all.

He continued driving and looked at me making a face like something smelled bad. "What's up with you looking like a fiend. I can't even understand what you got on."

"Nah…nah, I'm just wearing this to throw away because I'ma buy new gear today."

"You look like an old wino from a flea market. Get that shit together, get money. All of yar get this shit together, get money. I don't want to hear no excuses, get shit done…that's it." He looked in the rearview mirror at the kids in the back seat, then at me and back on the street. "I got your pay and something extra we got some work to do okay."

"Yeah, I got you, Welo."

"You did good not getting caught and seeing Tall-Tall Man take the stash. That was the lookout's job. So, you did good, I reward my peoples. You're going to bottle up and get some extra paper."

I was happy inside not wanting to say nothing or sound stupid. He glanced at me then looked straight ahead. We pulled up on 122nd Street, Welo called out to this kid named Eric Rosario. He had bumps on his face but was fly as hell. He had the Forty-Below Timberland boots on, crispy blue denim jeans, and a tan hoodie with the same wool Rich coat Welo was wearing. He was also wearing a gold rope chain with a two-finger gold ring.

"Maybe they related," I said to myself. I'd seen Eric picking up my friend Tee from school before.

He took his time coming over to the car when he reached it Welo said, "Eric, meet me at the spot and bring two girls I got some B-I to bag."

Welo was ready to drive off when Eric replied, "You don't need me, Welo. Plus, I'm dirty with shit going on."

"Oh, word, you get a couple of dollars and too big for me now. You don't even holla at me for reup or nothing. Like you forgot me or something!"

"I ain't messing with you, you that nigga, Welo. Just doing me right now, trying to come up like you."

"I hear that shit, we going to talk. Do me a solid, right now, I need two or three people to come through and bottle up for me. You know I got something nice and I'll throw you a lil' something too."

"I got you…I got you. The same apartment in Taino from before, right?"

"Yeah, tell them to hurry up and get there like now. Who you sending?" Welo asked.

Eric called, "Yo' Tee!" A kid I know from my school came over from the cut in the building where he was hiding. They hustled more low-key than we did on 117th, Tee came with a slim girl walking behind him.

Welo said, "Yeah, they good." Then he drove off.

Going up in the Taino Towers elevator, I was a little mad I did not see Stacy when I was at 1990, I felt childish.

Welo spoke, "Right after this I'ma take yar back to Baltimore."

The kids from Baltimore seemed so serious. A war was out there in D.C. against Harlem, and Baltimore was part of that. Two men from my block on 119th Street went out there to get money and came back in coffins. That Alvin dude everybody be seeing riding on his motorcycle down 125th in the summertime, they say started all of it. But the truth was Welo and Ray was going out there with people and taking over blocks. Ray was just so silent, whoever did not know it would not know he and Welo were real close. Not even those on the block, but I see them do business.

I heard Alvin was from the East side but be messing with them Westside dudes hard because of their connects with bricklayers that have all the Coke you can handle.

After getting off the elevator we walked inside the apartment passing a kitchen that had an old Spanish man in there. He was cooking, a strong ammonia type smell came from it. It was the smell of a lot of Coke being cooked into Crack.

I followed Welo into a living room with two huge tables, one glass and the other wood with a mirror laying on it. Plastic chairs were in piles stacked against the clean wall. A burgundy couch was the only other thing in the entire living room facing the tables. It was far out against what looked like the entrance to a balcony covered in burgundy drapes. A boss probably sat there to watch the workers. There was a lot of empty room left all around us.

Welo took off his coat and went down three steps that led to other rooms. His beepers were making vibrating sounds on him. The others that came with me took chairs and sat at the two glass tables.

"Go over there, um…um Little Kid to the other table, grab three chairs," Welo instructed in a different tone, then disappeared out of sight into a room, the happy, smiling Welo was not here.

I took three chairs off the wall and over to the table. I sat down looking around trying to see where he went. I heard him speaking to someone, but didn't hear anyone respond, so I assumed he was on the phone. He came back five minutes later with a T-shirt and jeans on carrying sneaker boxes.

"When them niggas come from one-twenty second you watch them and tell them what to do," he said to me.

"I know Tee from my school," I said a little more relaxed.

"This real shit here, people get hurt fucking with us. So, whether he's your boy or not or you just happen to know him, you watch him. This is business. That kid shit is not for here, here is about this money. So, tell him what to do and watch his ass to make sure he don't steal from us."

Welo looked like he was ready to kill and no longer a star, he dropped boxes by the B-More kids and then three to me.

"I'm with you, Welo, I got it."

"And we going to get you some clothes after this. You looking like…bad."

The kids by the table started emptying packs of vials and the Blacktops into one box, then placed a box in front of them. I did the same.

"Here's your six-hundred." Welo came over giving me a look of disapproval, He dropped the money on the table, and I put the cash in my pocket. "Nah, nah that's your first mistake. I told you this not a game. No kid shit, you ain't no kid no more. This business, count that money up, make sure it's right. Make people respect you. You don't know if they trying you or if they made a mistake or whatever. You don't know, all you know is you want your cheddar, right?" All I could do is nod yes.

The Spanish man dropped a kilo of cooked Crack on the B-More kid's table and they began chopping away at it on the glass table. Chopping the Crack, placing rocks into the vials then topping it with black tops. The sneaker box was about to get filled. A kilo was placed on my table and I grabbed one of the new razors and was stopped by Welo's voice.

"No, you playing boss count their shit out in one hundred packs and keep the total count that comes off each brick." He came over and gave me a pen with *'Hello My Name Is'* tags and some plastic bags. "Keep track of what's made on each one and which table did it. All yar get down to your T-shirts. Tell them one-twenty-second street cats to do the same. Yo' Ramel bring me that." Ramel came out passing Welo a gun. "Here take this." He handed it to me.

There was a knock on the door as Welo handed me the gun, the 122nd Street kids came in and Welo left the living room. Tee was smiling and put his hand out. "What's up, Little Kid?"

I slapped his hand five. "This money," I said.

He rubbed his hands together smiling. "We about to get paid, paid, paid. You working with Welo, too, don't get bigger than that." He then noticed the gun in my hand, the girl with him did too. "Yep, I'm a boss, so let's get this done, Yar two strip to your T-shirts and underwear, grab the razor and bag up."

They started following my instructions. The girl did everything slowly. "Tee, I don't got no T-shirt," she said.

"Don't worry this is all business," I said.

She took off her shirt, her breasts were so small. I went to the couch and notice Tee wasn't smiling no more. I sat down and watched them work, I was a boss.

CHAPTER SEVEN
ERIC ROSARIO

Looking at the rows and rows of balconies that went across and up into the sky on the thirty-three stories high building of 1990. It stood alone on the block of Lexington Avenue, covering from 121st to 122nd Street. My eyes came down the building and I noted who was on their balconies paying close attention from the fourth floor down. At night there has been BB gun shootings, and we narrowed the bandit down to the fourth floor'

I just left from my crib on the thirty-first floor with four more packs of Blue top Crack for Chito to sell. Being that the block was clicking, him and Tee took turns and did six packs each in the last hour making me feel like, I guess, intoxicated with success.

Buying work from Welo and getting seven extra grams for sending Tee and his cousin to bottle up was a proper move for us even though I did not want to deal with Welo. The Work was good and the extra grams he gave me I used to overstuff the bottles made the block flow better than ever before. The timing was perfect for building up my Blue top clientele. Most people that hustled were inside today waiting for the fight to start and I took advantage of that. Momentum was building up for me.

It was dark out and a cop car passed us going down Lexington Avenue. Lately, they'd been parking and hitting us for random searches, so I was on point. I watched it cruise down the street until cars behind it blocked my sight of the actual police car, but the siren stood out above all of their roofs, moving further and further away. It passed 119th Street, that's when I noticed groups of people there leaving the schoolyard in a rush, Anxiety pumped in me.

Grabbing for my beeper, I saw I missed twos beeps from all this running around. It was my girl Tiff and Don Poe. I hurried to cross the street between two parked cars as the traffic continued moving on. I didn't even wait for the light to change, I timed a car passing me, and stepped directly behind it. The oncoming car slowed down as it saw me in the street. I ran across into the mid lane with that car and other cars passing behind and in front of me. I timed another car and did the same thing again. Reaching the other side of the street. This was an art I picked up from playing Man Hunt as a kid, it never left me.

In the store, I bought six forty ounces of Old English and four bags of different flavored chips to mix together. Then I rushed back out crossing the street carrying the two bags right into traffic. It was time for the fight. Chito had his back to the wall blending in with a brown leather jacket, black hoodie, and Cleveland brown hat. The indents of the brown building were blind spots for us from anyone watching the block from afar with no light coming from behind it. Not like 117th Street where you can hustle loosely, the cops run down on you regularly here because of a working class of people, building 1990 was always hot.

Three customers approached Chito and my eyes went to the oncoming traffic. T.N.T. was not out at night and ducking the Blue and Whites was easy if you're on point. Chito took their money and counted it with a glance, one by one going down the line and into his pocket than in reverse, hand to hand he was dropping Blue top vials in their palms.

Tee was by the pay phone on 121st Street's side of the block. I yelled out to him, "It's started…it's started, we out!"

Tee slapped a man five greeting him, but it was really a custie passing money. When Tee left the pay phone the custie went to it and picked up the Blue top vials he left behind.

Tee walked toward us quickly with his shoulders exaggerated, leaning forward with each stride he took. His jaw was moving from side to side mimicking a fiend name Joke. Me and Chito laughed, Tee was so skinny and did not care to dress. The older crowd here called him Dusty, but that was about to stop.

Pang! Pang! Pang! Pang! Pang!

As soon as Tee came near us, we were hit with pellets that hurt like hell. All of us ducked and started running. Tee tried to look up and was hit.

Pang! Pang! Pang! Pang!

"Aaahhh…fuck!" Tee yelled holding his face as we made it around the corner.

I touched the back of my head where I was hit, and my finger had a dot of blood. The big North Face coat I wore blocked everything else. I watched Tee move his hand from his face, he had a perfectly red circle above his eye which made me laugh.

"Seriously we gotta find out who's the BB bandit," I said.

"I think I know who he is but let me be sure before I say something. I just saw someone leave the balcony into the apartment, but it could be just that."

"Or just that," Chito said pointing to the shot on Tee's face that left a red spot causing me to laugh harder.

We walked around the corner and hit the intercom; Don Poe buzzed us in his building with Landlord catching the door behind us. He came into the lobby.

"Hold up, baby, take care of the Landlord or you will be sleeping in the streets."

Frustrated already I just wanted to see the fight and not be bothered with Landlord, who was an old, washed up gangster that was smoked out and tries to get over on people all the time.

"We out Landlord, that's it till later. We done for now," I said.

"Don't be fronting on me, come on, baby…it's the Landlord." With white thrush on his lips, he spoke.

"How many you want? I got a few on me, Eric," Tee said taking out some Cracks.

"You not talking to a punk on the street. Ain't no punk here, give me ten of them things." He moved swift and strong as he took money out of his pocket and held both hands behind his back. "I got to handle some tenants after this, I'm the Landlord baby. Here look at this." He took one arm out from his coat letting that side fall, then pulled up a sleeve on his sweater, and flexed a perfect muscle.

I was tired of people treating us like kids. Getting angrier I said, "That's why I didn't want to stop for you Landlord you always be holding me up."

"Holding you up…holding you up?" His voice was in a high-pitched tone as he moved back and forth.

"What! The Landlord don't hold nobody up, baby. Yar lucky yar not paying no rent for this here property you're on."

I got into my boxing stand that I learned as a kid and Chito was on point and ready. Tee spoke breaking my thoughts knowing the Landlord was about to get hurt.

"Let me get that money Landlord and no shorts."

Tee was the smart one out of all of us.

Landlord picked up on the tension, his face and tone changed, and he put a smile on his face. "Give me ten, baby, I'm just messing with yar, you know yar my people." Tee served him with the Landlord's eyes on the sale but watching us from his peripheral.

He left with a hard bop in his walk. "I'm the Landlord baby, you better ask somebody."

We waited on the elevator and everybody started counting out money. Tee was done with that last ten sale and I thought about how things were picking up for me and Big Willies noticing my progress. Yesterday when I was talking about Mike Tyson, Keith dared me to bet him two thousand on Buster Douglas and, Ray the boss jumped in it as well. They thought I wouldn't take it because it was too much for me, trying to punk me. I took the bet without backing down, shit this was easy money and nothin' to them but a come up for me. Tee and Chito handed me two hundred each and I placed it in my pocket. I had four-grand in another pocket so when Tyson knocks him out, I'm shooting straight to 117th Street to show them I was ready to pay, and I wanted mine.

We got on the elevator. "Happy birthday, Airric," Chito said in his distinctive accent and hugged me.

"To us," I said passing out a forty to each of them, we clinked our bottles chugging down the beer.

It was my seventeenth birthday on February 11, 1990. "This is our fuckin' year we going to blow up from this day on. Nineteen ninety is our year!"

"Get money!" Chito yelled.

"And more money!" Tee also yelled.

My bottle went to my mouth and I started drinking. Tee did a funny dance and said, "We about to start getting some of that good-good pussseyyy."

The elevator stopped on the fifth floor. An old, heavy, tough-looking woman with small, black moles under her eyes stood outside staring at us. Everything went silent, we all knew Ms. Carter and her daughter who went to school with Tee. She knew us and our mothers.

Tee said in a low tone, "Going up?"

She kept her gaze on us, pushing and holding the down button on the outside, knowing that if it was going down the doors would stay open. She stared us down the entire time which felt longer than the seconds it was. The three of us stood holding the beers in our hands stuck. The doors were closing with her eyes darting from one of us to the next until the doors closed and she was gone. I felt relief. We all laughed together, but I thought about what I was going to tell my mother later after Ms. Carter told her I had a beer in my hand?

Chito took a final gulp finishing his beer. He took out another one and began drinking it before the doors opened on the seventh floor. The activity was all through the hallway, weed was being smoked and the aroma was in the air. The guys with blunts in their hands were talking to chicks. Behind the exit door staircase, you could hear the dice shaking and being tossed, hitting the wall as bets were being called out. I knew that voice and poked my face in the window, looking in and heard the comments as they saw me.

"Bring that birthday money in here, or put that North face coat up, we'll take that."

The dice was thrown quickly, and their attention erased from me back to the dice as it rolled 1, 2, 3, he aced out and lost. "Yeah, keep fucking around with Eric Rosario, you gon' ace out again," Beefy said.

Everybody else went by nicknames, but I got locked up and made the Spanish newspaper at fourteen years old, The El Diario with my full name in it. That's how I was known by, Eric Rosario.

Behind us, Karate George came off the elevator calling out my name. "I need you right now, Eric Rosario. Ain't nobody hustling nowhere. And people are waiting for your work asking for the Blue."

"So, fuck you telling me for? We about to watch this fight," I said wanting to get inside already.

"Let me knock off some packs for you. I could knock off the packs while you watch the fight. Then bring you the money, I ain't going nowhere."

I was angry with all the bull that kept coming my way but speaking about work, I felt better because of how things were moving. Karate George likes to short the money three and four dollars there. Nothing serious but it adds up. However, I was about to win four grand and my work was in demand. I focused in on his face as my face tightened hoping he was not trying to play me. Crackheads don't be caring about nothing, but smoking Crack and he thinks we're just kids.

"Come on my man, I knew you since you was a kid. I did packs for you before. Don't do me like that," he pleaded.

I felt respected, Tee gave me a look as if it was okay and I gave him the two packs I had.

Karate George was my height and we both were taller than Tee and Chito. He could probably beat all three of us, really knowing Karate. He walked in a muscular karate way even wearing loose-fitting karate pants.

"Bring me back two-hundred," I said.

"Forty bottles in the pack, right?" he asked.

"Yeah, no shorts bee and I'm not playing," I replied.

He nodded but his look was not impressed with my speech. He took the packs and left down the staircase. The apartment door was wide open, and light shot in from the hall and most of the people inside were all around the big television. We all walked in.

It was dark with light coming from closed-door cracks and windows. The sound of beepers going off was followed by the screen being lit up and looked at. I recognized everyone except for two groups. A crew of five in the back was Westside cats. One of them been seeing this chick who lives in the building and some East River cats that's cool with Nigel and them from across the street. Monk was here, too.

Everybody had their coats on, and all the windows were open. The weed smoke was in the air with red dots being seen in front of faces, beers were being held by guys and girls. The cool air running through the apartment felt good. The living room furniture was pushed against the wall with a few people standing on top of it watching the screen of the big floor model. We walked up to the front saying what's up to everybody. Two girls whispered in Chito's ear. We were in front of the TV and the second round was starting.

Chito was finishing his third beer, I was on my second one and Tee was still sipping his first one.

"Nobody beating Mike…shit if your name Mike you can't go wrong, you're the best. Mike Tyson, Mike Jordan, Michael Jackson everybody wanna be like, Mike."

People were watching to see Mike knock out Buster.

"I got five hundred, he don't pass the fourth."

"Bet."

"I got eighty he don't pass the third."

"Keep that eighty foolio we on the fourth-round bets stupido."

People were all banking on what round Tyson would win, enforcing my confidence.

"Eric, you going to give me your half." Don Poe came looking down at me.

He was over six feet and skinny, still rocking a real afro. Referring to a three-way split of two hundred each that our crew, Nigel's crew, and Harv's crew said we would pay to use his crib to watch this fight on pay per view.

Giving him work would be better for both of us and since Blue tops were in demand, I knew that's what he wanted.

Don Poe pulled out his money as to add mine. "I can wait, or you can give me half in work when you get it."

"If you want some work, right now, go tell Karate George to give you a pack. He's downstairs with it."

His hands went up to his hips. "I'll wait for you to get it. I don't know why you just don't handle yar business? Mike is just going to lose tonight anyways."

"Shut the fuck up, you're in the way!" someone yelled from behind.

"You can get the fuck out my house faggot!" Don Poe yelled back.

Laughter came because everyone knew Don Poe was gay.

"You got Douglas the Buster?" I asked.

"Yeah, what you wanna put on it?" he asked back.

"If Mike wins, I get to use the room for two weeks straight free."

"And if he loses?" he said too gay for me.

"I'll give you…" I calculated in my head. "…I'll give you the four packs I got on me, right now." I exaggerated knowing Mike would win.

"Bet," he said quickly.

Me, Chito and Tee at the same time said, "Mo money…mo money…mo money!"

After the fight, I'ma give Tee and Chito five hundred a piece. Others started calling out to Don Poe wanting to get in on the action for the use of the free room to bottle up drugs and fuck girls.

"I got Cracks against the room for two weeks after, Eric Rosario," someone said.

"Bet," Don Poe agreed.

"I got Cracks against a week after that," someone else hollered.

"Bet," again Don Poe agreed.

"I got cash for cash," someone said.

Don Poe went into the kitchen and came back with a pen and pad, picking out his afro leaving the pick in it. He looked at all the faces in between the oohhs and ahhs and said,
"Bet…bet…bet…bet!" He pointed at every person he'd betted with, then walked away mumbling, "Toddler suckers.

Multiples comments followed:

"Get the fuck out the way for real."

"Seriously move!"

"Whoever can't pay I feel sorry for you. Yar know what he wants."

"He needs to kill himself that's what he really wants inside."

Laughter erupted and everyone focused their attention back at the TV. Mike wasn't looking good; he was taking big hits in the tenth round and his hard punches were being eaten by Douglas Buster.

I was in front of the TV in a fighting stance, shadowboxing and yelling at Mike. "Hook…hook him, Mike, now!" I was now throwing hooks myself at the air and Tyson did to landing it with Buster eating it up.

"Oohhh!" was heard in unison from everybody in the room, including me as Mike Tyson got hit and went down to the floor.

My stomach got a nervous tingle in it and the count started. "Get up, Mike…get the fuck up!" I yelled as he was down on his knees crawling on the mat looking for his mouthpiece.

I was into it I couldn't hear anything around me. Mike found his mouthpiece as he crawled on the mat. The ten count was ending, and it was over. Douglas Buster whoever he was had just beaten Mike Tyson on my birthday.

"Fuck!" I threw my beer down and it smashed on the floor. My face tightened; I couldn't believe this.

A blow hit the back of my head and I staggered. "That shit got on me!" the East River kid said and Roger from 1990 started swinging on him.

Chito immediately jumped in, knocking him down and kicking him soon as he hit the floor. I was hit again this time I reacted fast and started throwing punches until the dude fell. Tee came over with Monk and they stomped him hard. Fights broke out everywhere and it seemed that the 1990 and East River cats were the only ones against each other, but then I saw Nigel and his block fighting with the Westside people.

A kick in my back knocked the wind out of me and sent me flying to the floor hard. Pain hit my chest from the impact, I saw Nikes and Timberlands moving by my face. A bottle hit me on the head and bounced off not breaking giving me a different kind of pain. I got up with my face tightened and started swinging at an unfamiliar face as other faces started rushing in from the hallway.

The door was now opening and closing as the apartment lit up and darkened with people running in and out. I tripped backward and fell, then got up fast. I was feeling the effects of dizziness from the beer. Don Poe was being jumped and I grabbed a leg to a metal table that was turned upside down and swung it awkwardly at the people jumping Don Poe. I hit one kid and he stumbled backward. I got a better grip on the table leg and swung it again hitting a bigger dude.

When he fell, other dudes surrounding him moved back. The door opened and light came in over the guy on the floor as a dark liquid came from under him moving toward me. I stepped back, seeing faces staring at me holding the table legs. The door closed with a motionless silhouette on the floor.

Boommm!

I crashed to the floor along with other dudes. The gunshot rang inside the apartment. I knew it was time for me to go. I got up and pushed everybody outta my way trying to get to the door.

Boommm!

I pushed into the crowd so that if a shot came my way, it would hit somebody else. I shoved forward and fell out of the apartment. Tee was already by the staircase, so I ran over to him. Chito came running out of the apartment and fell then got back up. We all ran down the stairs and exited the building. Four men had guns pointed in our faces, it was the police in undercover clothes.

"Get on the wall!" one yelled.

"Turn around on the wall now!" another yelled louder.

They were shouting as others ran right past us. Blue and whites started pulling up with their sirens blaring, then started running to the building soon as they jumped out of their cars. I was good since the only thing I had on me was money. I knew Chito and Tee were clean. We were next to each other with our hands on the wall and grimaces on our faces. We all thought the same thing as we watched each other from the corner of our eyes.

The three of us followed their orders as people came down into the lobby then ran back up the stairs as the police watched through the locked door. Walkie talkie sounds were all around us while people were being searched. A cop got the door buzzed opened and cops immediately raided the building. The cop searching me pulled out my first stack and the four thousand dollars, then passed it to the cop behind him. He pulled out another stack, I calculated forty-four hundred, then the third stack. My face tightened.

"We got a rich one here, Vuggio," the officer said.

'Yeah, right,' I thought.

Another cop came over and took a good look at my face. "If he don't got I.D. take him in for a warrant check," he said.

"You got I.D. kid?" the first cop asked.

"Yes, sir my school I.D. is in my front pocket," I replied.

"How much money is this here?" he asked counting it.

"Five thousand seven hundred and uh…and uh." I was calculating exactly how much I had.

"What's it for?"

"My moms gave it to me."

"Yeah, whatever get out of here," he said handing me back my money and backed away.

"Gun…gun over here!" I heard one of the cop's yell.

I took my money, turned and hauled ass.

CHAPTER EIGHT
KEITH

It was close to seven at night as I waited outside for Melinda to surprise her. The block had a few people making sales with a small flow of customers walking through. I was trying to concentrate tonight on giving Melinda a good time and nothing else, but this life of the streets was twenty-four seven and hours after. Keeping my mind focused on the events or situations around here, staying on point and ahead of others near me was a daily life task. That's why I had to end this life.

Welo is always plotting and scheming, knowing he killed people for territory was not easy to ignore. I'm at the point in my life to soon exit the game while he's trying to dominate it. Fats playing me in obvious ways too hard was another thing I couldn't ignore. I have to take a step back from all of this, relax, and put my mind at ease. So, I don't make rushed or bad decisions. On that same note also show my woman a good time.

The beef, the vitamin store and the house in Long Island. I'm trying to cop even with so many obstacles in the way was my main focus. The block and my baby girl, Ciera nothing is to be forgotten and all has to be in order. So, I need to get a breather and evaluate all this on a relaxed mind. Then come back and handled it all step by step before it all blows up in my face.

I was dressed in clothes I'd bought earlier today. A light brown, shearing sheepskin coat and a matching hat with light brown Timbs. I purposely, let the ears from the hat hang down. I wore dirty clothes or construction clothes with Timbs purposely scuffed as I walked down the block to look like a working man. Making the police ignore me and put their attention back on those with the expensive clothing. But today I'm leaving the block so there's no need to elude them.

It was so cold out here even the custies were covered up. Well most of them, Mama was wearing the brand new *Pelle-Pelle* leather jacket I'd brought her today. Along with a white, Christmas hat showing off Santa's reindeer running across it with the ball on top. She was crossing the street at a fast speed toward a man wearing a heavy sweater and a light jacket. She pointed him to Guy and the custie switched directions going to cop Red tops. Guy quickly ran across the street to a lady she thought was a custie. Then recognizing she was not Mama she went back across again to a woman who was parlaying going right into a conversation. Mama was on her hustle today, back and forth running at customers, steering them to Guy, moving around fast.

One of Ray's workers yelled, "Ayo Bitch…stop flagging down my custies!"

Of course, Mama replied something that made him laugh. It was funny now but if it stays slow like this it could be a problem. I'm just staying out of this and letting it play out on its own. Four people out today had my work with instructions to see Monk for re-ups. Only Guy and Fats was making sales while the other two were shooting dice. The block was crowded with pitchers and not clicking hard with customers. My lawyer had just bailed out Guy and she wanted to hustle on the block. I told her to relax and that I would give her some cash. She refused, knowing she must have needed money I had Mama run her customers.

A dice game started ten minutes ago across the street with a group of five people, all with their backs to everything focused on three dice that rolled on the concrete floor as it came off the wall displaying numbers. Some had money under their feet being held as a bet. I guess they were going to get money one way or another as the block got slow. When I leave, I want to make sure Red tops stay out to keep a good flow. I don't have shifts or rules or none of that, I give work and you take yours and give me back mine. Depending on what my bricks cost or how my bread is, sometimes I give a dollar a bottle to workers like today when it's slow. So, they will stay out and hustle. That's the most they will get from anyone, usually, I give the going rate of fifty cents off every bottle they sell.

"Teddy up…Teddy up!" A loud call came for all to hear on the block.

Everyone doing dirt made a needed change to look legal. The people shooting dice put their money away pretending to talk to one another. Dealers walked away from stashes, continuing on like they were heading someplace and not just standing in wait. I saw one custie drop down to the ground behind a car. The police driving down the street could not see him. He may have had a warrant or even just did some petty crime. That was regular shit around here, it was the Yellow cab crew and they knew who they usually wanted to jump out on looking for guns. They cruised by slowly looking in everybody's faces. My back was to them just waiting, not seeing who they wanted they left. Immediately all went back to business as usual.

Scottie said he's going to come post up on the block. I told him to watch Monk's back. I'm going to warn him about the gun squad out today. A kid named Boisey is coming through to squash that silly beef from 106th Street going on. His street cred is up over there, one way or another it has to end. Eric Rosario is supposed to come through, but he was busy. At least he'd put me on to Boisey. That kid got a brain on him, hopefully, he will know how to stack that paper and get outta the game. Also, my Brooklyn people were coming that Scottie knows. This was enough to handle any beef without me being there.

Me and my baby Melinda were going to be out. I got her moms watching the baby. When I first came out here Mama was waiting to tell me about Fat's pushing his own work under my color again. I told her to tell Monk because he's the boss today and leave me and Melinda alone. She told me I looked nice and moved on looking for Monk as she checked her new jacket pockets that covered her down to her little legs. I thought of saying I heard from *Al Capone*, I expect you to steal just don't steal too much.

My mind had a lot going on inside, Welo was a murderous, slick motherfucker. So, I don't try and outdo him on the block. I could easily put more workers with higher ambition to get money as they get paid more by what they sell and not by hours or the work like Welo's. I could have bigger bottles with twenty-four-hour shifts, but he would have me killed or want me dead. Ahead of his thoughts I just make money off the block without outdoing him on this one.

Melinda came rushing out with a white coat and a hood surrounded by fur snugged around her pretty face. She had on blue jeans and white fabric boots, she was cute and stopped in her tracks laughing at me.

"What…you never seen me with a hat before?" I asked.

"You look silly…since when you rocking a shearing, Keith?"

"Oh, so I can't wear a shearing because you never saw me in one? You crazy, and you look like a little Puerto Rican snowman."

"A snowman don't got no ass like this negro." She turned showing her coat fitted on her butt, then tried to walk past me in a rush with her little self. When I stepped in front of her, she said, "I gotta go pick up mi tia, Abuela said so, and then get some…"

I cut her off by grabbing and holding her from behind, then kissing the side of her face. She pushed her lips to the side throwing kisses like she could feel my lips on hers.

"Nah, I told your moms to say that cause, I got a surprise for you for a couple of days. We going out just me…you and…and that ass."

She pushed back so I could feel her on me, and it felt good.

"You been with the baby ever since birth. So, we going to chill tonight. You deserve a break, baby."

She tried to struggle free. "Papi, I don't even got no panties…wait…wait…wait, let me just get some things." She squirmed to get out of my grasp.

"No…no, Mel, we out. Whatever you need is on your body or we will buy. And you not gonna need no panties."

She broke the hold I had on her and jumped her little body on to me. Her legs wrapped around me as we kissed then she put her head down on my shoulder.

I carried her toward the O'Jays as we walked past the dice games, there was now two going strong.

"Bet something, Keith! Let us get some of that Red top money you got," one of Welo's men said. He was not a pitcher but one of the higher-ups.

"Nah…nah, I got shit to do," I replied.

"Wait…wait let me shoot the dice! Let me shoot 'em," Melinda said.

I put her down and she looked Welo's lieutenant up and down like they had beef.

"Okay, cool. One roll, against my girl for a thousand. Win or lose we out," I said.

"Bet," Welo's man agreed.

"Let me get in on this my money good, too. I'm not here to spectate shoot something," a tough looking kid with a stack of money in his hand spoke. One of Jays Westside boys who didn't hustle here.

"Five hundred to you," I said to him.

Melinda grabbed the dice on the floor and put both her hands together, then started shaking them. A side bet was yelled out by a kid that grew up on the block, knowing Melinda.

"Bet she roll four and better," someone else quickly said.

"Bet forty she don't."

"Bet!"

The kid pulled out the money, others joined in with different amounts to the same bet. It seemed like the kids from here were betting on Melinda, hoping for beginner's luck.

Her little self was in the middle of the crowd and she held the three dice in two hands, then paused and looked at me. "Ready, Papi?" she asked.

"Do your thang girl!" I said.

"Come on baby…come on baby!" she said shaking the dice up in her hands.

I couldn't wait to tell her how out of place she looked later. She was bent slightly, in my mind, I was thinking she had no idea what she was doing. The dice left her hand with the three of them hitting the wall, bouncing off and rolling out. She jumped over one that came near her. Everybody ignored her looking to see the numbers that popped up. A three…four…and one.

"No…no…no!" she said, then picked up the dice and started speaking into her hands. "Big numbers baby…big numbers, come on!" She surprised me with her lingo and knowledge of the game to know that those numbers rolled meant nothing, it cracked me up.

She started shaking and talking to them with her mouth to her hand. She was all into this as she got ready to throw again.

"Baby don't move out of the way next time, let them hit off you ma. You're part of the game, let 'em hit you next time, okay," I schooled her.

She gave me a look and nodded. She was in a zone this was funny as hell. She started talking in Spanish and threw the dice. Two sixes and three came up, she jumped up and down excited.

"Yeaahhh, boy!"

She looked and bob toward me away from the crowd. I couldn't hold it any longer and busted out laughing.

"Que Pasa…que pasa, Keith why you so stupid," she said.

"You did good, baby. Just wait next to me."

All of the guys that bet with her to roll four and better paid their money. To those that bet against her on the roll, I saw how she looked and explained to her that the two big numbers was not the point but the three was. Welo's boy said too easy and grabbed the dice while I was talking to Melinda.

"Bet another thousand that both of you don't beat it," I said putting some pressure on him.

"Bet nigga, double up it's the only way." He threw the dice.

They landed, four…three…six came up. Side bets were being shouted out across the game with him in the middle surrounded by bettors.

"Bet he roll four and better!"

"Bet he don't!"

They called out waving money in their hands as people confirmed the amounts.

"A hundred on an ace."

"A hundred on heads."

"Bet."

"Bet."

Bets were made in the crowd, he threw the dice again and it was nothing, five…three and two came up.

"Watch your face when you ace," said a better that went against him.

"Shut the fuck up nigga. You betting a little hundred on this. I got two stacks on it lil' nigga bet something," he was speaking to one of Jay's pitchers that pulled out a pile of money.

"After she's gone this is my first bet against you, Big Willie. I bet on my wrist for real cash," he said.

"Cool," the dice holder said.

He threw the dice and a five…two came out with the third dice still spinning.

Melinda started yelling, "Ace out…ace out!" A term she musta heard before so many times around here while walking past the game.

The kids from the neighborhood gave me a little smirk not to embarrass her as there was no ace to be made.

The third dice finally stopped spinning and was a five.

Melinda said, "Them!" with a sad look on her face.

I laughed. "We won, baby!" I told her as the loser passed us two thousand dollars and the next dude stepped up to role.

"Let me show you how to do this son. Who don't like me bet something," he said.

Taking the three dice in his hand, he shook them above his head, as he held money in the other hand. I gave him five hundred before he rolled.

"You won," I told him, then grabbed Melinda and walked off.

The O'Jays were moving, Melinda was in a separate cab directly ahead of me mouthing the words, "Where are we going?"

I kept saying, "What?" with my hands up in the air from the front seat of the cab I was in.

She caught on and got mad then disappeared from the window's view. We were still in the city but driving fast on the FDR she popped up in her bra and stuck her tongue out at me, then disappeared down into the cab once again.

Her two feet came into sight, she wiggled her tiny toes then was gone again. My personal driver Thomas was laughing. A good moment went pass, then she positioned herself to what was to be a quick moon to us and flashed her pretty shaped ass with no panties. Her cab hit a bump suddenly as she tried to quickly pull up her pants and fell forward with her ass out in our faces, then out of sight with her feet in the air.

I wished I woulda recorded that, that was one for the books. Her face came into view and she had an '*I hurt myself*' look on her face.

I yelled out in my cab knowing she could not hear me but understood. "That's what you get!"

I was feeling horny and I knew she was, too. So, I took off my coat and held it in my left hand so that the driver couldn't see me and pulled my dick out for her and she gave me a fake long-distance oral through the cab window as I put it away. She kept her hand in motion and her mouth open, going deep with it. I gave her the cut it out motion with my hand under my neck, she gave me the middle finger.

We were in Pennsylvania now pulling into an area full of outlet stores. As soon as the cabs stopped, Melinda was out of hers and running to mine. My door flew open as I tried to exit, she pushed me back in and I fell on my back.

"I'm so horny, Papi! I need a little bit now just a little bit." She laid over top of me, stuck her hands inside my pants and started jerking me.

I responded fast as I grew to her touch and it felt so good. I tried lightly to get her off me, but she strongly held her little body weight on me and when I tried to talk, she spoke over me.

"Just a little bit, Keith!" she begged.

"We out in the open Mel, we have to shop real quick…I got shit planned." I tried to push her off me once again.

She looked to the driver and said, "Thomas pull up in the parking lot and leave." Then turned back to me. "Papi, just a little bit…come on," she whined and never stopped moving her hands or her body. "I'ma take it, Keith. Just hold up…just wait!" Her voice was as much as a turn on as everything else.

The driver had pulled us into a lot and stopped the car. I'd forgot that he was even driving until I heard his door open, then close. I looked up from where I laid on the seat, his figure had left, and we were between other cars now secluded. Melinda was on top of me, my pants was unzipped, and I was out of my jeans. They were pulled down just under my balls. She was rubbing her bare ass on me with her pants off and down on one ankle. I laid across her, wanting her so bad. She guided me in with a hand on the bottom of my shaft. She had the other hand holding onto the edge of the front seat balancing herself, while she squatted over me. She wiggled me around inside of her as I touched her walls and rotated in a circular motion. Then her hand left off me and she turned around holding me in her hand again and dropped down on me. I was all the way inside of her now.

It was warm and wet, she bounced up and down, not going too high off me and was moving fast. Every time she was all the way down, she slid back, and I could feel my tip come all the way out of its foreskin from her tightness as much as it could. Seeing the line come down her ass that separated her two cheeks while disappearing inside of her in flashes excited me. My arm stretched out touching the back of the front seat. I grabbed the top of the one we were on letting her do her thing. It was too much to see and feel all at the same time.

Her voice came slightly in low noises.
"Uh…unnhhh…um…aahhh!" That was the sound of actual penetration of wet sex being pulled in and out.

I felt pleasure shoot through my whole body and pushed up as she held onto the front seat with one hand and the other hand was under her ass, not losing rhythm she kept me inside of her until I came over and over again. Then pushed all the way inside of her till there was no more to give. I slipped out of her as I came down to the seat and she came down with me winding her cheeks on me. I was still hard when I pulled out of her.

She kissed me. "Damn, your zipper was hurting my ass, but it felt too good to stop. Papi let's go…come on we gotta go shopping now." She started fixing herself.

We bought lots of clothes of all name brands for ourselves, Davi, Julissa, Abuela and of course I got Mama a lil' something. We packed the cab and my personal driver Thomas drove it back home to Abuela's with the things that we were not going to use for the next three days. Soon after we arrived at the Poconos resort where I had a two-nights and one-day reservation for us. It was a fun day already and the night was still young.

We had long exhausting sex in the room. It felt good to be able to walk around naked, not worrying about who else was in the house. We went swimming, the pool was filled with other couples all into their own passion. This was what it was all about. We ate at the buffet, then played videos game together. She was so fun and made everything five times better than it already was. Like the horses' trail we walked on, the actual horse ride was planned for tomorrow, but we walked it in the pitch black of the night enjoying the freedom of the streets.

There are no days you can walk in the city without people around. Instead of smelling the concrete jungle there was real pine aroma that did not come from a bottle. Back in the room as I laid in the comfortable bed feeling so relaxed, I looked up at the ceiling and felt her warm mouth slowly covering me as I grew inside of her until it was too long for her to keep it in entirely. She bobbed her head up and down. I pictured it instead of looking at the real motions being made. I opened my legs and stretched out my arms while she continued with the only sound in the room being short, sucking noises in a rhythm timed on the upstroke from the suction as her mouth held me firm.

She used no hands only her mouth, she held the bottom of it and jerked me real fast keeping me in her mouth as the bed rocked under me. I felt out of control and came into her letting go of everything. For a moment it seemed like all my problems were gone. I was so relaxed afterward I don't remember anything or any actions except falling into a calm, relaxed deep sleep.

I awoke to find her out of the bed butt naked. I crawled out of bed and stood over her feeling her ass. It was nice and soft then I touched her nipple lightly and moved to her entire breast. Covering her back up with the sheet I looked around the room. Our new clothes were still in boxes and bags in a corner not unpacked. The bed was huge with nice, fresh bed sheets and the bathroom was nice. I took a warm shower, then walked around naked and sat down on the single chair in the room. I could not resist and got my two beepers from my pants.

I put both of them on vibrate and walked to the bathroom so I wouldn't disturb Melinda. I turned them on and instantly they started buzzing and the red light flicked. My spot on 119th Street on Lennox showed up a couple of times, some weight customers hit me up and my biggest concern was what I saw next: Scottie's number.

CHAPTER NINE
FATS

The dice game was big, so many motherfuckers came from all up and down Lexington Avenue that it had to break into two games. I had to get in on it and finally got my chance when Keith left. I'd betted up two-hundred and eighty dollars if I didn't come off big after this, I would hustle my work all night. Then re-up with the Dominicans in the morning on a hundred and Fifteenth Street on Broadway there's all kinds of ways that weight is being sold there.

Keith's pussy ass gave me a dollar a bottle incentive like I'm one of these little niggas or something. Like I'm going to be out here hustling for him when it's slow. I did a hundred of his bottles and my PC was eighty-five dollars, that's good considering how slow it was with them custies, playing on the situation looking for bargains. Fucking Mama was running that dike bitch Guy all the customers. This shit was crazy! Doing three hundred of my own work, money was made today.

Now all the chicks were posted up on the block, it was going to be a good night. I'ma slide up in one of them little bitches after shooting dice. First, I needed this easy bread. I'd been saving cash to cop me a whip for the summer with sixty-five thousand put up. I learned to never spend all your money on anything, plus I planned on going out to Poughkeepsie New York with half a brick to get this money, fuck Harlem.

The kid holding the dice was hot, I'ma wait till his hand get a little weak and just take some four better bets on him.

"I got fifty on his four and better."

"Bet!"

A kid name Pee Wee took it as I looked over at the girls across the street. The little cute one named Tarsha, with the ass saw me staring at her and gave me a dirty look like I was some lame.

"Fuck off my block you bum bitch, before I kick you in your back." I had a side bet with the dice rolling so I couldn't go check her. "Nobody wants that doorknob pussy you got."

She turned her back with ass out making me think of a way I could get that by talking nice to her later. A few laughs came from the dudes surrounded in the circle of the dice game. They shot comments about how good her pussy was. Two others agreed and she acted stink to me and gave me her thing out like that. I'ma get that ass, she was used to fucking these little dick niggas, but I'ma hurt that. Fuck that, once I'm finished here if she's still there and don't give me no play, I will run her ass off the block and not give a fuck who don't like it.

"Bet a hundred you weak wrist lil' nigga," I said.

"Bet a hundred to you, Fats." He took the bets from everyone around him.

"Fifty…fifty…seventy…fifty and a hundred to you. You got eighty, fifty and forty." He pointed with a hand full of cash to the faces he'd taken bets from.

Then he threw the dice that came up four…four…and six. Heads cracked we all lost; he collected the money in the same order going around.

"Fifty…fifty…seventy…fifty and a hundred Fats." He shook the dice.

I called out, "Two-fifty.

He went around, "Two-fifty, a hundred, sixty, eighty, forty, fifty…" then he pointed at every face that bet and rolled the dice.

Someone yelled, "I got eighty!"

"No bet to you!" he replied quickly and aced out paying all of us in that same order. I knew he was due to ace.

It was cold outside, all the big coats made us feel more crowded than we already were. Gold rope chains hung off some of the dude's necks, along with others adorned in rings and gold teeth. There was tens of thousands here to be taken on just jewelry and clothes if a robbery was to take place, right now. Easily about five or more guns was around just for that purpose.

I looked back and saw the girls leaving. I had some luck going in the game up about eight hundred. A kid adjusted the gun on his waist before he threw the dice. Hearing smaller bets being made in the other game from the other side of my eye, I saw the female wearing tight, blue jeans, a small brown coat, and dirty sneakers coming up the street and crossed to the other side of the block. Then realizing who it was, my dick grew hard as I turned to leave the game. I walked over to her before she went to cop from someone else or the old man from Keith's building gets her.

I heard someone say, "Thirsty!"

I ignored them; she saw me slowing down as I passed Keith's building.

"You got Reds, Fats…the real Red?" she asked.

"Yeah!" I nodded. "What's good, how many you want?"

"I only got two-dollars, right now. I'm trying to see who going to look out for me you know," she replied. "I'm good for it."

"Yeah, you good for it. You know what's up, I got you keep your two dollars. Meet me on the roof."

She walked off fast in her dirty coat while others watched. So, many had used her before they were probably thinking about the next time, they'd get a turn. Her head game was serious, and she was cute as hell at one time, now she looked plain, but not ugly. She was getting dirtier by the day and her beauty was fading. I followed her up to Keith's building.

Up on the landing right before I got to the roof it was dim and reeked of piss. I gave her three bottles. "Suck that shit good!"

I knew I could have given her one, but I wanted her to go in on it. She pulled out my already hard dick. Some girls can't even fit my dick in their mouths, but she was special with it. She got down on her knees and her hands went on the back of my ass. Her mouth opened wide, she directed it over my dick, took it into her mouth, then pushed me using her hands on my ass to take more deeper down her throat. I started hearing sucking noises like a plunge, my whole body was moving forward and backward from her pushing and pulling on my jeans. As her head tapped my stomach, I lost it and came quickly.

"You good?" she asked.

I looked at her with contempt, seeing her dirty clothes and her face up close looking fiendish caused me not to acknowledge her, knowing I was really mad at myself for not fucking her with a condom since I came too fast. I wiped my dick on my underwear and prepared to leave.

"Let me get that two dollars," I said taking out a bottle and handing it to her.

As I left the building my beeper went off and Monk's number flashed across the screen with 117 behind it which meant he was right here. I told Monk to get me two-hundred packs earlier, the crack I be having is so weak I have to mix it up. I was serving Keith's good shit so that I wouldn't lose clientele. I counted out two hundred for him so I could keep his work on me.

They were grouped earlier with people I'd never seen before and had left the block a half an hour ago. Some commotion was going on suddenly. A kid had punched a grown man in the face not fazing him physically, but angered he fought back. He should have run because shortly after that a crowd of teenagers came running and started beating on the man right before he tried to run, but it was too late. Druggem dropped him with a punch, knocking him out cold to the ground for a moment. The younger teens kicked him until he came back to, and Druggem finally stopped and allowed him to get up. He was delirious as he raised from the ground, with Druggem's blessing he staggered away.

I looked up the block for Monk and didn't see him nowhere around. So, he must have been on Park Avenue. I walked to Park Avenue, turned left toward 116th up the hill under the overhead train tracks and saw Scottie leaning on a car. I hated dealing with this motherfucker. Yet, and still, I went over to him, he had his gun pointed down, relax in his pose.

"Fuck is that you selling it or something?" I questioned.

He smirked not answering but kept his eyes on me.

Then looked around quickly and that's when I felt my nerves go through my back like cable cords. I felt nerves all through me and froze.

"What…what the fuck Scottie, what's up?"

"You're up you fuckin' piece of shit. Keith ain't no fuckin' punk and you motherfuckers took him too kindly. So, now you have to pay the piper."

I hated Scottie before but now, even more. Let me just get through this shit then get the drop on him. He's going to pay for this shit, were the thoughts roaming through my head

He raised up off the car.

"Here…nah, bee here's two-hundred I got for Monk and another five for you. I'm not even going to play on your intelligence. I was just getting money that's all, shit ain't that serious," I said.

He snatched the money and pointed the gun low toward my stomach.

"Scottie hold up…hold up…come on Bee, here…here…" I took out another knot of three hundred dollars that I had inside of my coat.

He snatched it but kept the gun aimed. I took out the dice winnings and he snatched that as well placing it in his coat pocket.

Then he looked into my eyes. "Where the work at?"

I took out two hundred packs from under my arm and gave it to him. I also gave him a loose pack as well. I patted myself down to show him I had nothing else. Then I heard what seemed like that loudest gunshot I ever heard in my life. I fell to the floor scared, then pain began to register, it was hot and burning in my side. Scottie started laughing. I was too scared to move, too scared to breathe. I think I held my breath and it hurt like hell.

"Bitch ass nigga!" I heard Scottie say.

I wanted to tell him to please wait or something, so I looked up. "Scottie…"

Two more flashes came with the sight of him in between. The sound was deafening, and the pain took away my other senses. Realizing I'd been hit, the sounds came back and was stuck in my ears. Then the sound, the flash, the pain, I was shot again. I closed my eyes, I seen the bullet wounds and then darkness. My body was not making sense. All I could do was hope that help would come soon.

CHAPTER TEN
MONK

The eight of us was waiting on Scottie by a hundred and sixth street on Park Avenue. One block away from the people we came for. One of my two cousins lived in these projects and had told us the main cat, Calvin who has a longtime beef with Keith was not there at the moment, but his people were. Come to find out the beef started over Melinda then escalated when they bumped heads again over a block Keith ended up leaving. Ever since then it's been an ongoing problem.

I started searching my pockets for a lighter wanting to smoke the blunt I'd just rolled up, then looked on the ground. The blunts insides that I'd dumped was spread out on the cement next to empty Crack vials but there was no fuckin' lighter. I must have been staring hard onto the ground when I heard Boisey.

"You looking like a fiend. Monk, probably had some cracks up in that last blunt."

A little bit of a chuckle came then ended by a Metro train passing us on the overhead, making loud noises. There was a moment where everyone was quiet not trying to talk over it and lose. The train was on top of a stone-built wall that had probably been around for hundreds of years. I'm glad I did not say that out loud or they woulda really roasted me for that shit. I was still feeling a good buzz from the weed earlier.

I pulled everything out of my pants pockets and placed it on the hood of the car. Tokens, AA batteries, a bag of rubber bands, dime bags of weed from the bus stop, a Phillie blunt, three dice and a ripped piece of a brown paper with a number and the name Cindy written on it from a girl I met today. I put the number in the air and started bragging.

"She bad none of yar can bag that…none of yar!" I paused inspecting their gear as they all looked at me.

I had confirmation after my assessment and put the paper in the air again. "Ugly ass niggas can't see me when it comes to these bitches bet that!" I went back to my search.

"You fat, brown-skinned baby bear…anything you bag I can bag and fuck on the same day," Eric Rosario taunted.

Three Brooklyn cats that were Keith's people were drinking forty ounces of Saint Ives now, so they were lightly high.

"Brooklyn ass bums yar dress like old school Cooley High characters and can't bag nothing…out here looking like a reject crew."

"What?" the youngest one replied. "This sweater is Aeriole Postale yar Harlem fools don't know shit about this."

"Right we don't and we don't wanna," my cousin said with the Harlem part of us laughing.

I felt my gun in my inside coat pocket knowing it was not next to that. I searched my hood finding six greasy, dirty dollars separate from the rest of my money. It was from that sale I'd acquired earlier. The fiend was so dirty if the police was watching the block, they woulda watched him, so when I served him, I snatched his money and hid it quickly. I put the paper in the air picturing Cindy.

"Nobody…" I repeated.

"Get the fuck outta here."

"You, fat, butterball looking, like where's Thanksgiving ass nigga."

"You no money with a big tummy ass nigga. Have to pay a buck just to fuck…brown ass nigga."

"What the fuck is, Monk, anyway? You look like that statue shit with the robe and belly out."

"You, lucky crack came out so you can get pussy…you pussy ass nigga."

The jokes kept coming, while I searched myself.

"Fuck all of yar," I said and pulled out a pile of cash, showing them as I shook my head looking at their faces.

"Yeah…yeah, get money niggas this PC right here."

"Yeah, right, that's work money nigga for, Keith," The older Brooklyn man said and put the cash away.

I pulled out a bunch of neatly counted rolls, wrapped in rubber bands and almost too much to hold in my hands from my front coat pockets.

"That's work money all prettied up nice for that Brooklyn native, Keith. Us Harlem cats like it free to go out and double up," I schooled him.

The lighter fell out of the cash onto the ground and everybody started clapping.

"That's because you ain't used to no money. You token having, train riding, Monk."

I put everything away, leaving the dice out and started shaking them over my head. The sound got everybody's attention. Boisey looked at his beeper giving me a look like '*I don't play, I rob them game*' and he does. He'd robbed plenty of them even when people knew who he was. I grew up around his bully ass and he'd been big since he was ten years old. He weighed two hundred and sixty pounds, was six-feet-three and only twenty-two years old.

Eric Rosario said the famous words… "Bet something!" And that was all it took.

Fifteen minutes later, we were in full swing of the dice game with loud small, friendly bets of five and ten dollars, more beer was opened and both of my blunts were smoked by five of us. I sent my cousin to see if Calvin was out there. When he left the distinct, bulky figure and hard walk of Scottie was coming toward us from the other way. He looked ready for tonight, he was dressed in all black clothes, boots and a Goose down coat. We stopped the game, those that hid their guns under car tires went to get them so we could go. He had a blunt in his hand and after sharing my two blunts I could use a push to get where I wanted to go.

He reached us and I inhaled deep to see if he had some of that exotic shit Keith be smoking. My face turned from that stink ass Crack smell all the way up in my nose, it was all on him too. The motherfucker had changed my entire mood. Others showed their reactions openly to the sudden unwanted smell coming from Scottie and started looking uneasy knowing that one of our homies was smoking Crack.

His eyes were bloodshot red and crazed looking. Boisey walked off a car length away as my cousin moved back looking angry.

"You're scaring me away and we on the same side. Smelling like you been smoking death all night. Did you handle that shit?" I told him to tell Fats he couldn't hustle on the block for us or nobody after those last two packs and he'd collected the money.

Scottie doesn't follow what I tell his ass. I'm trying to show I Keith can run this block after he leaves. He got somebody for his other spots but not 117th. Fats had to get off the block, every time he sold his own work, it was less PC for me. I get eleven or twenty-two packs at a time from Keith always getting a dollar a bottle, plus a free pack for myself after every ten packs was sold. He does this so I will keep someone pumping for me at fifty cents off the bottle or even the rare dollar when he tells me, but I always got some PC. Fats wanted the dollar and if he was doing his own work, I didn't get shit.

"Yeah…yeah, he gone," Scottie said out of his dry ass dark lips.

He pulled out a mound of money that was in layers of knots and had the smelly blunt of death in his mouth. He squinted his eyes from the smoke, he put away the mound and kept one of the knots while counting it out slowly. Money was not Scottie's thing all he wanted to do was get high and create violence. Keith takes care of him to the point that he's dependent on Keith. That's something I have to learn how to do. Scottie doesn't respect me as his boss, somehow, someway I have to change that.

He handed me the money. "That's Fat's two-hundred."

I looked at his hands as he passed me the cash. This crazy ass nigga had on new, black leather gloves. Suddenly I felt fear coursing through my veins. I counted out the money fast and placed a rubber band on it. Scottie don't be fronting or wearing gloves for no reason, I hoped he didn't do no dumb shit.

My cousin came back after I'd sent him to see if Calvin was around.

"No, Calvin, but like five guys and six girls. They got music blasting…"

"Are they serving customers?" Scottie asked cutting him off.

I took the last pull of the blunt and tossed it away. The smell was strong, my cousin had no clue who Scottie was, so he gave him a strange look.

"I asked you are they serving…are you deaf or retarded motherfucker?" Scottie got closer to him.

"They doing packs Scottie they been hustling since earlier," I said stepping in and taking charge to make sure this went right.

"Keith, wants us to talk this out first. If that don't work, then we handle them right there."

"Yar strapped?" Scottie asked Keith's people.

"Yeah!"

"Of course!"

"Uh-huh!" They all replied nodding their heads.

Scottie ignored the rest of us and told them. "Yar enter the projects from the hundred and fifth side and take whatever they got." Scottie turned and looked at me and my cousin. "If anybody runs out the projects, that's where you will be waiting on Madison Avenue. Then you can talk to them."

The Brooklyn dude busted out laughing.

"I'm going with you Scottie, yar two wait on Madison."

"I'm out baby, I'll see you on the block. I'ma do some packs they know my face."

"I'll wait on Madison," the other one said.

"Cool." Scottie had no words for anybody else.

Eric Rosario and Boisey walked off together seeing where this was going. It was dark and silent outside just like Scottie. We walked into the projects and saw two teens pitching and a little further down was a group of dudes sitting on benches with girls in their laps or in front of them drinking beer, blowing smoke, as music played from a radio all while chilling. The other half of us entered moving slowly.

"Wait here once I get a good drop on them go to Madison," Scottie said and changed his walk as he moved to the kid waiting on a sale to be made.

He approached Scottie. "How many you want?"

All of it asshole." Scottie's gun was already in his hand.

He cocked his arm way back and smacked the kid in the face with a strong blow, sending him to the ground. The kid laid there not moving. Scottie pointed the gun at the kid near him making a sale to a customer. They both put their hands up, then Scottie told the customer to go and he hauled ass.

"Over here." He laid the dealer by the unconscious one.

"Don't move!" I heard Scottie tell the guy and I walked backward watching the group on the benches get up. They looked our way as the Brooklyn cats waited. "Every fuckin' body on the floor now!"

All the girls quickly went down to the ground, the guys on the benches put their hands up, except one who started running and like an affect the others did too. Shortly after shots were fired and the last guy running was hit. I saw Scottie empty the unconscious person's pockets. The girls on the ground were being stripped of their Gucci bags, gold earrings, chains…even one that read: *Number One Mom*! I felt bad because I knew her. After watching our people go in every pocket. I was gone, as I made it to Madison Avenue, I heard another gunshot then saw my cousins.

The group that left the projects saw us and the next thing I heard was…*Boom! Boom! Boom!* I ducked as my cousin took out his gun. It looked like they were going to go at Scottie. They were getting a better position on him, but we threw them off and were now running to 5th Avenue. I wanted no parts of this, the fucking crack head had me mixed in and had this shit all figured out.

"Let's get them," my cousin suggested.

"Hell, no, let them go…we gotta go!" I refused.

We walked away…this shit had gone all wrong.

CHAPTER ELEVEN
SCOTTIE

As soon as I entered my apartment the dogs could feel my blood rushing through me. They started barking and circling around before I could sit down.

It was as if they were asking me…

"What happened to you?"

"What have you done?"

"Whose fear did you snatch?"

"Why you ain't take us?" They smelled it all over me.

"Go to your room now!" I ordered not in the mood for their nosey asses feigning to get the scents.

I was probably followed, so I went back to the door and stuck my head out looking both ways. Seeing nothing I ducked my head back in, then stuck it back out quickly. There was no one around so I went back inside. I closed and locked all three locks on the door then slid the chain on after. I went and got a broom from the kitchen and leaned it against the door. I lived only a few blocks away from them, but they don't know that as far as they know I'm from 117th Street. Soft ass Monk just froze up like a bitch and let them get shots off. You don't give them no sense of room to feel they have power and you have to overpower their every strength, snatching their every idea of any chance to even match you. Defeating their minds before the actual encounter, to ensure that they lose before it even begins.

"Who the fuck knows if they followed me home?" I asked myself.

A combination of nerves and energy was busting through me. I dropped down all the shades covering the windows in the dark apartment. I took off my coat, sweater, boots and socks, afterward, a pile of clothes rested in front of me. I stayed still not taking a breath and suddenly heard a noise. Quietly I took my gun from the coat on the floor and walked to the bathroom where the noise was coming from…somebody was here.

I paused by the door to hear where exactly they were, everything was quiet again. I pushed the door in and looked seeing the stillness of my shower and toilet, I turned the lights on! Seeing all the white tiles around the bathroom awoke my senses. Hold up, I slowed myself down, I was getting paranoid, so I lowered my gun. As I stepped out of the bathroom, Bad and Luck both stuck their heads out of their rooms. I saw only their noses and a fast glimpse of their faces poking.

"Get in, I don't wanna hear shit from, yar," I ordered.

Whimpers came to my ears then silence as they went back into their room. As I headed back to the living room, I had to pull myself together. I emptied all my pockets from my clothes onto the table. There was money in different rolls. I had no clue what money, was from who. Instantly I started feeling aroused thinking about how I made Fats give me all of his money before I killed him.

Seeing the fear in his face…in their faces when they saw me and how it changed their entire aura was such a rush of power that I loved. The power of seeing a man weakened from being faced with physical harm was intoxicating and shot through my body with empowerment. A natural law I mastered was that fear can be born from fierce courage the same way out of chaos comes order. Different faces from the day flashed before me and I felt my heart slowing down. I needed to roll something up to relive it all again. I pulled out Red top and Black top packs of crack and dropped them onto the table in front of the two-seat couch. I took my T-shirt off and stripped down to just my underwear, wishing I had something warm and wet to stick my dick in.

I unlocked my apartment, leaving the door wide open with all the money, drugs and gun on the table and walked down the hall. Three apartments down I knocked on the door knowing that Shirley would be home…fuckin' ugly bitch. I just needed my dick sucked while it was hard. I banged on the door and she answered, with her heavy voice from behind the door, that matched her fat ass.

"Who is it?" she asked.

I banged harder and harder then I heard a man's voice.

"Who the fuck hitting your door like that at this time of night," he barked.

"Who the fuck is it?" she yelled.

I kept banging on the door, I ignored their requests for me to speak, fuck them. She finally snatched the door opened with force and an attitude to match.

She was big and an even bigger, fat man was behind her trying to see me but couldn't over her fat ass being in his view. I looked directly in her face and wanted to just punch the shit out of the man behind her as I felt my body tense up. I was ready for some action. I was seeing right through her to him. She had on some big ass jeans and a long button up dress shirt, looking like a fat, slob, crack head. When my focus came in directly in front of me, I hated myself then started hating her. Looking at her juicy lips I remembered what I wanted her for and focused on them. She looked at me and a quick change came over her face, her eyes went to my underwear since those were the only thing I had on. Then her eyes were back up to my face.

"Scottie…Scottie, what…why you here?"

The man behind her spoke, "What's this?"

"Just hold on…hold on, I will be right back," she told him closing the door behind her, but it opened back up slightly.

He finally got a look at me as she left the apartment removing her big ass out of his way.

"This shit don't make no Goddamned sense," he commented angrily from behind the door.

"Come on, Scottie, with your crazy self. You tweaking right now. Come on let's go to your apartment. You know you ain't got no clothes on, right?" She closed the door noticing it did not close all the way the first time.

The man yelled out, "Shirley, I'm not gonna be waiting here all night!"

I grabbed her fat ass and said, "Come on bitch, take me inside and suck my big dick."

"Shut up, Scottie," she replied then yelled back to the man. "Just get in I'll be back with something for you later."

I stared at her big tits, started feeling horny and thought about squeezing them until I made her hurt.

"Let's go, Scottie," she interrupted my thoughts.

I pictured me all the way in her mouth as she led me down the hallway back inside my apartment. Once we were inside, Shirley pushed me down onto the couch.

"Get yourself together, Scottie. You got shit all laid out," she chastised.

Bad and Luck came into the living room and she quickly got up and went behind the couch. "Scottie…Scottie!"

I could hear her calling out to me, but all I saw was me running and the niggas I robbed. Then I heard shots making me jump up into a sitting position. I pictured the face of all of them so I would not forget any of them, not even the females. Too many people slipped just from forgetting a face.

"Scottie…Scottie!"

My neck went backward, I looked up hearing her loud ass voice. "Shut the fuck up before I slap you, bitch!" Her big titties and face was over me behind the couch. The dogs were in front of me by the crack bottles, gun, and money. "Now come around and suck my dick, put those lips on this, be useful and don't play wit' it."

"I ain't doing this with them dogs out, Scottie." She must have been trying to rob me.

I looked at her, then at Bad and Luck as they were ready to attack her fat ass even though they'd seen her a hundred times before. The bitch must have had some evil intentions to get me that they knew of.

"Wait by the door and watch the door." Both dogs were attentive and happy for a command, so they went by the door and waited. "Sit down and don't move you hear me!" They sat by the door as ordered.

Shirley came around the couch and looked at me with that thirsty wanting to smoke look. I told her, "I don't wanna hear your fuckin' voice that shit gives me a headache! Just use your mouth to suck my dick that's it and don't fuckin' say a word. I'm not playing…shut the fuck up!" I eyed her to make sure she understood exactly what I was saying. "Go ahead smoke and take some crack, but if you say a fuckin' word I'ma have Luck rip your ass apart." She took out her pipe ready to get high. "Smoke all you want but you better not take shit back and you better not say one fuckin' word, you fat bitch." She took a hit.

She's been through this with me a hundred times. I don't like that she's not afraid but as long as she listens, she's okay.

"Take all your clothes off too fat bitch, so you don't steal shit." I felt horny and my dick was still hard.

She started taking off her clothes, and I slapped her big ass so hard she almost fell. She gave me a look as if she wanted to say something. "I dare you to say something!" She continued to undress until she was fully naked. "Look at them fuckin' rolls! Come over here and suck my dick before you smoke again."

I laid out on the couch as she dropped to her knees taking my whole dick into her mouth and started slobbering all over it. Spit ran down the sides of my dick after only a few gulps from her there was no feeling of anything except suction. I wanted to talk shit but concentrated on the sloppy and wet feeling, her big head was going up and down like a crack head which is better than a porn star or any prostitute. My underwear was wet around the slit my dick was sticking out of from her saliva.

I pushed her head all the way down and her face was into my lap. She still did not miss a beat, she kept banging her face into my laps not missing any rhythm, continuing to go up and down. I held her head and she sucked me off with a choking sound every time I hit the back of her throat. She kept doing that until I smacked her before I would come.

"Don't fuckin' say a word!" I snapped and she didn't. Her mouth was wet with spit around it. "Turn your fat ass around," I ordered.

She did as she was told. "Scottie go slow, I didn't…" She got on all fours and I placed myself behind her, ignoring her. I rammed my dick in her ass. "Awww," she said.

"Shut the fuck up," I said, as she whimpered.

When she started making noises of pain again, I went harder and harder and she got louder and louder each time. Feeling her tightness grab on me when I backed out of her, she started pushing back at me taking my dick's full-length. I couldn't help myself and came into her big fat ass. I felt cum drop inside of her.

"Grab you ten bottles and get the fuck out!" I'd had enough of her.

She took the bottles and counted them slowly so I could see, then she put her clothes back on quietly and quickly left. I got up, went to the kitchen, grabbed a Phillie blunt, some weed, and a razor out of the drawer, then a plate out of the cabinet. I took it back to the living room and sat down on the couch. I slapped the money off the table not knowing what I would do with it anyway. I grabbed six bottles and emptied them onto the plate, then started chopping it into dust. I cut the blunt open, dumped the tobacco contents on the floor, broke the budded weed up into the blunt and sprinkled the crack dust over it, then rolled it up whole. Later, as I retreated to my room, I was smoking in the dark finally relaxed with Bad and Luck next to me on the bed.

Somebody was eavesdropping by the door, Bad and Luck was not even on their job.

"Go the fuck in your room now!" I yelled causing Luck to bark. "I will fuck you up, now go!" They both went.

I grabbed my other gun from under my bed and headed for the front door. Quietly I opened it and stuck my head out, looking both ways then ducked back in. I quickly stuck my head out once again and looked both ways. No one was there, I closed my door and locked all three locks, then slid the chain on and leaned the broom against the door. I was no longer in my apartment I saw that guy falling to the ground unconscious after he was hit with my gun and the girl's crying because of their property being taken and them niggas running from me…running from Scottie.

I then felt her next to me sucking my dick and her nasty fat ass and ugly face. Why the fuck did I let her put that nasty mouth on me? My dick was getting hard again as I thought of her doing it. I thought I heard a noise and saw a face in front of me, but I knew it was not there.

I went and got my sewing kit and a jacket to start sewing my secret pocket into it. After, I went to my dresser and opened it getting out shorts and sweaters and started putting secret pockets in all of them. Sewing was relaxing me, it was a good safety measure, too. I took some cracks from the living room and placed them in the new stashes I'd made. After about forty-five minutes of sewing, I smoked again. Then I laid on the bed and heard another noise. Fuck I'm getting paranoid, then again and again. It really was the door, I got my small shotgun out of my closet, I went to the door and opened it. Shirley's fat ass was coming straight to the couch without a word on her knees and that made me hard all over again.

CHAPTER TWELVE
TALL-TALL MAN

"Let me take the last shot," I said to no one opening my eyes.

I was still sleepy, but I saw a familiar face cleaning outside the doorway of the small room I was in. I closed my eyes to go back to sleep, not wanting to be up and she was gone.

What seemed like only seconds later, I awoke smelling the fresh scent of lemon cleanser. My eyes opened but my body did not want to move. I just looked over at the cleaned mopped floor that was still wet. I knew more time had passed then what I thought. As the scene was different in a someone picked up some kind of way. Exhausted physically and mentally, I went back to sleep with ease away from reality. The movement was around me for what seemed like a long period of time. At that moment, I heard a door slam and was wide awake. My mind was telling me to shower, get to the gym and shoot some practice shots. That's how I usually get through things, but this time was different.

My heart felt low this shit had to stop. I didn't even know what time…or what day it was. I was past starving and tasted a mix of I don't know what the fuck in my mouth. I needed a toothbrush bad I could taste the foul order just by breathing. I looked around the apartment like it was my first time. I knew I'd been there for days. It seemed like it was not me here, like I was here doing everything but watching it go on, making the decision seeing the outcome but now realizing the outcome was real.

I wanted to go back to sleep not to face this, but I slept too much. So much I was wide awake and alert. I have to get through this, some people sleep their whole life away, then wake up wondering where it all went. There's no way that was going to be me. I had to wake up and take the steps needed one by one to fix this thing, if not for me for my grandma at least, who always believed in me. I got up and looked out of the small room, the place was clean and definitely poor. Everything seemed worn out past its use from the broom with missing bristles against the hall wall. A wall that had stains that were cleaned but not erased all the way.

The table was covered with a clean cloth on top, probably an evenly ripped bedsheet. It stood with three chairs of different origins around it. I walked out into the living room and saw the TV that had a metal coat hanger with aluminum foil wrapped around the tip of it for better reception, but I never saw it on since I'd been there. I heard her in the bathroom, running water, so I went back into the small room.

The apartment was kept up as much as it could be in a place that had no income coming in. She had good habits for a user, I hoped I used protection. The idea of one of the many things she could have was scary. Her name popped into my head…Sly. Her nor the girl before her did I use protection with. We smoked most of the time and had been getting high ever since the lick I'd caught. I sat leaning over and put my face into my hands thinking about this past week and all I'd been through to get somewhere special in life just to throw it away now. I fell into a trap I was warned about as a kid not paying attention to it.

I'd been sleeping for hours, resting and waking up at moments just to go back to sleep from being so tired of the multiple days of no sleep at all, just being up, chasing a high and doing all types of things to get it. This last lick was a wild experience, I'd taken over six-hundred bottles when the police raided the block, we smoked it all and more. Since it was me that did it, I was like a boss to them. The others were going in and out hitting small licks, contributing to the stash to stay high and we did until the very last bottle was gone. Now, I wasn't feeling high, nervous or anxious.

"I gotta get myself together…this shit gotta stop!" I told myself.

I'd been wearing the same clothes for over a week. I smelled and had been on the Eastside of Harlem trying not to be recognized, but a few people did, and they made me feel shame and anger, but some showed love with a handout or a stay strong comment. A phone was on the floor by the bed, I picked it up and a dial tone came to my surprise. This would be my positive start toward my future. I put my fingers in the holes and spun the rotary around quickly knowing the number, I used it more in life than any other number and called my grandma.

"Hello!" my grandma answered.

"Hey, grandma," I replied.

After hearing my voice my grandma started talking as she usually does when she's excited or shocked. As she rambled on, I tried to speak over her, after a while neither of us was able to hear one another. I needed a lot done to get back on track and she had things to say too but I was able to finally speak up and get her to hear me.

"Grandma…Grandma, I'm fine. I just need…" I was cut off by the raising of her voice.

"You're not fine…just be quiet and listen. I talked to your coach yesterday. He asked why you missed practice and why you were doing other stuff? I told him you sprained your angle bad…"

"Grandma did…" I cut her off trying to justify her words, but she cut me off once again.

"Shut up, boy, and listen!" she yelled. "You just got to listen, right now," she was adamant, so I did exactly as she said and listened. "So, I told him you went to the hospital and I was admitted for my heart and that we'd just hit bad times," she spoke calmer this time. "Now your cousin done came to the hospital for a fractured ankle. I made him get a paper from the hospital and yar have the same last name, so I had my neighbor who works for welfare put your name on it and fax it to your coach. Pretending like it was you and all is okay. As long as you get yourself together. He said he will call you tonight at eight because he needs you," she said then everything suddenly went silent.

I wanted to cry Grandma had held me down past what I could ever believe. We stayed on the phone not talking for a moment both of us feeling the sadness to all this after as many sacrifices.

"Okay, Grandma." I agreed grabbing all the strength in me to not let my voice break. "I will be there."

"I love you, son, just remember from the day you were born until you ride in that hearse things ain't never too bad to be fixed. And things will never get too bad that I won't be here for you. Baby get yourself together before you lose yourself. That is all I have to say about that. Now I sent your little brother out and got you a whole outfit. No sneakers though so when you get here forget all that mess and…and remember that I love you. Take care, baby!"

Just like that, she was gone. I heard the dial tone it was a warning signal and I slowly hung up the phone. As I wiped the tears from my eyes, Sly entered the room.

"Morning I got oatmeal if you want it." Her smile was cute, and her voice was girly and nice.

I only saw a crack addict before but after hearing my Grandmother I saw a woman who'd fallen on hard times and lost herself.

"Everybody left and did not come back after you started sleeping. You held us all together and we were all doing things until the crack ran out." She stood quietly as I just stared at her not saying anything. "You promised to take me away, talking about being some big basketball star and I believed you. But all I want if you can, is for you to get me out of here into a real program with some real help if you make it."

I became horny all of a sudden and did not know why. My urges and yearns needled me, she looked like she was waiting for me to tell her what to do and she would do anything I asked making me feel sad and useless, emotions ran through me. I started getting slightly aroused just because she would do whatever I asked. I knew to ignore my lower desires, seeing her was not an attraction only lust of power, I felt nasty. My mind was working off urges to get high with thoughts I had nothing to do with crossing my mind. All I could think about was hustling up some drugs or even having her go perform sex to get a quick couple of bottles so I could get high one last time. I knew then that was a lie it was the carrot being dangled over a donkey's face by the man on his back.

I washed up as clean as I could, staying silent for a moment before finally telling her, "Never change your number. I will help you soon just never change your number."

"Okay." Was all she said as she watched me leave.

Without a penny, on me, I began walking towards the Westside of Harlem not stopping for nothing on my way home. Outside of her projects, people were doing their everyday living and on the move. Me leaving this place would be forever and never for me to come back. It's funny how I wanted nothing more than to be back in Harlem before. Now I just wanted to get back to school. It was a good twenty-five-minute walk if I hurried. As I walked people looked at me, being over six feet was enough already, but the clothes I wore were too small and ridiculous which caused a great deal of attention.

I walked faster hoping they would forget me before they saw me again on TV if they didn't get a good look. I started speed walking, even taking some shortcuts along the way. A smile came over my face knowing this was all over with and my life was about to take a fantastic turn. Never again would I do this bullshit. Not thinking while moving so fast, I was passing down 117th Street between Lexington and Park Avenue. A lot of people were out, the little old lady Mama was wearing an expensive leather jacket rushing away as always, except now something was odd. I felt wrong as she tried hard not to look at me, I thought it was nothing. I kept going halfway down the block thinking of a Biz Markie song and started singing it out loud as I continued to walk.

"On and on and to the break of dawn and when you buy food cheap you need a coupon," I sang, and became relaxed then relieved to be headed home.

However, instincts made me look back and I saw the kid I'd stole from running fast behind me. The song in my head stopped and I sped up.

"Hey, Tall-Tall Man!" I heard him calling out to me. "You a crazy motherfucker for coming back around here. You shoulda went back to college stupid ass!" he hollered as he kept running.

"Damn they recognized," I said to myself as I speeded up my pace.

"Yo' hold up!" he yelled, then I heard him yell to someone else. "That's him…that's him, right there!"

He caught up to me and hit me with a weak hook.

"Stagalee!" he called out.

I grabbed him easily and threw him on the ground. At least four people ran toward me from the direction he'd come from and another from across the street. The whole block came alert. I ran a few steps and a person leaning on a car suddenly just hit me in the face, causing me to fall. I got up and was surrounded with punches coming at me. I threw a few punches back and was kicked in my back sending me to the floor. As I tried to get back up, they came from behind me, something hit my leg it hurt like hell and dropped me to my knees. I realized it was a bat causing me agonizing pain. I started swinging with all my might, hitting the swinger of the bat causing him to stumbled backward and fall. That gave the others caution in their attack.

"I gotta get the hell outta here," I mumbled to myself. I knocked another kid to the ground hitting him hard.

I was hit so hard in the back of my head I fell flat. *'I can't be defeated,'* I thought as I got up quick and started throwing wild punches to keep them away. I saw the kid I'd knocked down get up and start running away.

"He's probably going to get a gun…run," I told myself.

As my thoughts ran rampant someone else picked up the bat. I couldn't let nothing stop me. I focused on one kid and started hitting him with a couple of punches, at the same time I was being hit by others. I saw blood on his mouth, then the bat hit me again in the same leg but a different spot causing more agonizing pain.

I focused like I'd done during hard training on the court and started pushing in one direction to get away. If I get into a sprint none of them can catch me or keep up. Another kid hit me in the face before I broke through them and I held onto him with all the blows I felt. Not being able to rush anymore and unsure of how many people were delivering the punches I was taking. I was swinging like a wild animal attacking them.

"Stagalee…Stagalee…" I heard as direct punches came at my face.

On the Eastside, knocking out fiends was a game they played. A kick in my back sent me to the ground and I scraped my hands.

"He that basketball college dude…I'm telling you," someone said.

"He ain't gonna be playin' no more," another replied.

I felt my leg being stomped on, it hurt like hell. Just as I looked up after closing my eyes from the excruciating pain, someone jumped and landed on it, I heard the loud snap.

"Aaaahhh…aahhhh…motherfuckers!" The pain was too much for me…the beating continued.

The bat hit me in the shoulder causing new pain. I curled into a ball, I badly wanted to run.

"Fuuucckkk!" I couldn't go anywhere as powerful punches came at my face.

I could not do anything but feel it, not wanting to hurt anymore my body moved wildly and started rolling and twisting trying to escape the painful punches, kicks and the bat that kept coming over and over again.

"You killing me…stop!" I pleaded, they ignored my pleas, I could no longer make out anything anymore except *pain…pain*!

Uuurrrnnnnn! The buzzer sounded. "Boooo…booo!" The crowd hated me I couldn't make a shot in the basketball arena. Why was my uniform so small and why was I hurt? That faded and my sight saw punches now and felt pain in my leg. It hurt…I hurt, I did not want to be here, I could not take it.

"Coach take me out!"

Suddenly though my prayers were answered it seemed as a raspy voice yelled interrupting all the commotion, "Papa, stop yar gonna bring the police round here. That's enough…Papa tell them to stop!"

A male's voice followed behind hers, "Drag him off the block."

'Is this real?' I thought.

It all stopped, I got up the best I could and tried to run. Then tried to walk. I was confused but moving, someone grabbed me underneath my arms and was dragging me backward. The pain was so bad on my leg, shoulders and all over it seemed that it didn't even matter anymore. I saw someone from the side wind their fist up for a punch and boom.

"Ref, ref where's the foul!" I screamed then felt my body continuously being dragged as another fist came.

I saw it but did not feel it as the sound of the buzzer came. *Urrrrn!* A foul was called, finally I was shooting a shot as the crowd in the arena cheered.

I heard Mama, "Papa stop hitting him you a punk."

My eyes opened seeing the bottom of a brown boot with a tree symbol coming dead on and a whistle blew.

"Foul!"

"Booo…booo…booo!" Boos were all around me.

"I didn't do nothing ref!" I shouted I was being dragged and kept feeling my leg, my eye, my shoulder in extreme pain.

"Fuck that Westside, nigga!" someone commented.

As we stood in the huddle the coach said, "Guard your man and no one else. No hot stuff either that's why this is happening to you."

I started yelling back, "Fuck you…fuck you…" Waking up yelling I felt myself conscious and calmed down. I was in the hospital.

I could feel the pain around my body. As I tried to focus the pain was in my eyes, it hurt as I squinted to see. I saw my grandma along with my little brother over in the corner holding brand new clothes that I knew my grandmother had bought for me. I closed my eyes tight feeling tears leave them. Everything hurt.

CHAPTER THIRTEEN
DETECTIVE VUGGIO

"He has on a blue large Goose coat, buttoned up with the hood over his head, black jeans, black boots and he's walking down Second Avenue, getting ready to cross toward Taino Towers. It's a positive visual," Detective Blanche's voice came over the radio like the sounds from an intercom.

"Copy, car two we're on our way," I replied.

He and another plainclothes officer were waiting in a blue, unmarked car outside of a building in Wagna Projects. We had information that a homicide suspect lives there with his girlfriend from time to time. I was parked on Paladino Avenue on the other side of the projects with my partner where the suspect's mother lived. These people don't go too far from their hoods, they're like territorial or something, I looked at my watch it was 3:30 PM.

"Call in for back up, crowds of school kids will be out. God's willing there won't be any shooting."

We took off fast down the street, weaving through cars and got stuck in traffic.

Whoop! Whoop!

Cars moved and we inched up when the talkie spoke again from between my thighs.

"Suspect has looked back at us he may know we're on to him…he's walking at a faster pace. He's fumbling under his coat. Officer is out of the vehicle and pursuing downtown on foot from a distance."

I visualized exactly what was going on with my hands on the steering wheel. "Here we go." Putting out the siren on top of the yellow cab roof, he used the car's radio calling us into base. "Special team five to base we are in pursuit of a possible armed Felon wearing a blue coat, black jeans. Male six-two is a homicide suspect possibly armed on one twenty-third street and second avenue plainclothes officers are at the scene."

We inched our way into oncoming traffic. *Whoop! Whoop!* We moved passed cars that turned out of our path responding to the sounds.

Over the cars radio immediately came back a female's steady voice, "Felony pursuit…Felony pursuit of a possible armed suspect on One twenty-third street and Second avenue. Black male, six-two, wearing a blue coat and black jeans. Plainclothes officers are at the scene on One twenty-third street and Second avenue."

An oncoming car slowed down as I sped in front of him passing quickly and the radio continued to talk.

"Be advised the suspect is wanted for questioning on a homicide, back up is required," the female's voice was from Rosie she was always professional.

Our car was moving fast in spurts, I picked up the radio and spoke to our other unmarked officer. "Car three cover from the Westside of Taino Towers the suspect may flee in that direction."

"Copy car one, car three is advancing up third avenue now. We are parked between second and third waiting. One officer is out the vehicle," the radio barked again.

"He's crossed through traffic heading toward the towers, officer on foot is in close pursuit."

"Make the arrest…make the arrest! Car two we don't want him going into those thirty-something storied buildings disappearing!" I yelled into the radio, driving through traffic placing it back between my thighs.

Our sirens and lights came alive, as we swerved through cars. I visualized the response knowing the officer in the car would turn his siren on to signal the pursuing officer on foot to make the arrest and seconds after the radio barked.

"Team two officer is chasing suspect on foot. He's running, car two is in pursuit." Seconds away from them, I heard their sirens go on in continuance then saw the chase of the suspect running with an officer behind him and the car catching up.

We sped up behind car two.

"He's in-flight…he's in flight, tossing something under a green Sedan between One twenty-second and one twenty-third street. He's reaching again…turning toward Third avenue on one Twenty-second street."

"Everyone apprehend with caution let's be smart people. Car two…car two we are directly behind you pursuing the suspect. You retrieve the object you observed being tossed," I replied into the radio.

The cars radio was answering with response, "Unit seventeen is at the scene on Second Avenue."

"Unit twenty-two is out on foot on One twenty-second street." As blue and whites were responding we trapped in the suspect, car two pulled over to the side in front of us passing him as we hit traffic and jumped out running.

"Car three is in position waiting, suspect is running our way, he's insight," came over the radio in my hand, I saw the officer chase the suspect crossing right in front of him to the other side of the street.

I was breathing hard controlling my pace, blue and whites were behind me, cars were at a halt and the people inside looked out to see what was going on. Car three was going up the wrong way and stopped the traffic on a one-way small street.

"He tossed something under a red Sedan right before he crossed the street. Officer has contact with the suspect, he's resisting arrest."

I saw him toss someone to the floor and he ran another few feet with an officer, tackling him against a car, he would not go down. I yelled out from a distance nearing the scene as civilians gathered in groups.

"You're caught, it's over get down on the floor now!" My gun was out of the holster for the suspect and to maintain crowd control. I was surveying the scene for any possible interferences as the spectators grew with excitement.

He wrestled with two officers, a third came and helped grabbed ahold of him, but he would not go down. At this point his hood had come off his head.

"Corey…Corey Johnston, it's over don't make it worse. Get down on the floor now!" He started fighting hard, in the midst, he tossed one of the officers to the ground.

I lifted my radio over my head and brought it down on his head as hard as I could. Then he fell to his knees instantly, holding his head, as blood flowed through his fingers. I kicked him in the stomach as he fell to the sidewalk. He curled up in a groan and officers were on him now able to control the situation. Then he was placed on his stomach, down onto the pavement, and his hands were behind his back as they cuffed him.

The officer that he tossed to the ground during our pursuit kicked him in the face. The suspect's face turned red from the force and snapped back to get a look at who did it. More officers arrived on the scene.

"Officers control the scene," I said to the blue and whites and they approached the bystanders moving them back.

"I retrieved drugs from the place where he tossed it," Detective Blanch said coming onto the scene. "I went to the car where he threw something a second time and retrieved a loaded nine-millimeter weapon."

I put my gun away and the suspect was still on the ground, cuffed and faced down.

Detective Blanch went through his pockets. "Guess we don't have to tell you what we want you for huh, kiddo?"

"Fuck all you bitches," he replied.

"Put him in the car," I said.

They lifted him by his cuffs and threw him in the back seat of the unmarked car that came onto the sidewalk. I surveyed the crowd to see any familiar faces or new ones that were pointed out by my snitch and saw only a few dealers that I was not interested in. The streets even know I only wanted the guns and violent ones off the streets, I called over a blue and white.

"Back track the route taken by the suspect and see if he tossed anything else. These people can be crafty." I was known in the precinct for my good work. It was me never underestimating these people and not having arrogance like many other officers do thinking they're all dumb, so I proceeded with good results.

The next day we had a lot installed for us as we listened to the captain give us our new broken window comp stat strategy that starts today. As crimes that have been taking place in our precinct has been connected to crimes in the 23rd precinct district in high volumes. Last night I was awakened and told of a shooting death on 117th Street and Park Avenue directly two blocks from the precinct. Even though, I was exhausted from the homicide bust I still had to visit the scene last night.

Everyone was seated and focused on the captain's words. Commanding officers and their lead detectives or officer that belonged to any task force in our precinct were there. The room was packed this was good for our profession. It would assure that we didn't miss out on vital information known by police officers that wasn't shared in a timely manner or at all to ongoing operations causing lots of late arrests that could leave a violent criminal out to commit a violent act. As well as lots of early arrests by other precincts leading to missing opportunities to make larger busts resulting in taking bigger quantities of drugs off the street even shutting down an entire drug gang.

The high man DEA of Manhattan, Thomas Morgenthau himself has set the protocol of sharing information in a timely manner of great importance. God knows I agree with him, we have centered the Technical Narcotics team, also known as T.N.T here in the 25th precinct with us having the highest drug rate in East Harlem. More officers and A.D.A.s were hired, the pressure to make arrests were on all of us and we were given quotas to attain. I don't like the fact that we allow quotas from big wigs not on the streets to estimate the among of people we need to arrest.

Because of rookies and officers trying to come up feeling forced to make lots of arrests, some being bogus just to keep up with their quotas. Although most people that lived around here for that matter are guilty of something. I would still like to believe we are arresting people for crimes and not quotas.

After the meeting, I walked out with my commanding officer to the break room as my team waited for me. Two detectives and three officers, plus me made up the Special Unit Five known as the gun squad. The newest member officer Bengal would be the only person affected by this new initiative. It's as if God answered my prayers for us to unite against this wave of crime. Some of them are smart people and others are slick. So, I pray one day that

I will be in position to trap off these animals in groups instead of individually.

My commanding officer posted his six-two, two-hundred-pound, muscular frame against the wall as I began talking to my unit.

"So, I've been updated on the situation of changes and it will not be any harder police work just more information for us to get the guns. Officer Bengal?"

"Yeah, boss," he said alert and looking calm as I continued.

"During roll call, you will write down all new names and areas we are going to cover and relay the new names or targets we have. Then get them to the desk sergeant the same way we do for T.N.T. But now that will be cross-referenced with the twenty-third precinct and you will pick up any relevant information to share with us as well," I continued with the protocol for five minutes then moved on.

"So, men it seems there has been some violence that may connect between districts on the same night by the same persons or group of persons. Our job is not Narcotics, of course, we want the guns and violence, but it seems as if a struggle is ensuing or the retaliation that occurred last night maybe over a drug beef. No matter the cause we need to make arrests."

"The homicide happened in our district on one-hundred and seventeen street on Park Avenue and the retaliation or shootings on a hundred and six on Madison there was witnesses that saw one or two people being shot, but none showing up in Manhattan hospitals. Detective Blanch will visit Bronx hospitals seeking our shooting victims."

A Spanish detective entered the room. "Here is detective, Hernandez from T.N.T to share some intel." He walked in facing everybody. "Our linking evidence gentlemen is the description of a suspect seen by two eyewitnesses on Madison Avenue running and ducking as another person was being shot at. He was also seen the same night by my officers a half an hour before the homicide on one-hundred and seventeenth street. The same male was at both places at the times of incident. He is a dealer of interest to us by the name of, Monk."

CHAPTER FOURTEEN
KEITH

Four hundred thousand was stacked in one pile and forty thousand in another, with a loaded Uzi lying between them on the bed. Holding Ciera in my arms centered my mind on everything I ran from. A sense of fear came having that kind of money in sight, although I try to share love and money with people, it's never enough for them to not want more. I kissed her tiny face and smelled the scent of new baby all over her body. Ciera depended on me in every way of life.

Warm sensations ran through my back as my mind spoke saying, "Love her…teach her…protect her!"

"Papi, you want Mofango and Salami with egg or you running out this morning, Keith?" Melinda yelled from the kitchen.

"Mel, come in here I don't want to yell while holding the baby," I said with my face turned away from Ciera as her little hands held my chin.

Melinda came into the room and stood by the door looking cute in little red shorts showing every line and dent in her body. She wore an '*I Love Menudo*' T-shirt with a picture of the Spanish group on it.

"I have to drop all that to the lawyers." Using my head pointing to the bed, her eyes narrowing went directly to the gun as her mouth turned up at the side.

"So, what's the Uzi for, Keith…you playing Scarface or something?"

"That's for the trip. Mel let's not play this game of innocence like you don't know how we eat. If you ever have to use it don't hesitate because people who come for this kind of money will kill you. They're not playing games that's why you have your own gun in the house." We looked at each other.

"So that means you don't want Mofango?" she replied.

I smiled. "No, baby I don't want your Mofango this morning."

"Keith, I don't want to live like dat."

"I know baby, we almost out of here. It's almost over, I promise…okay."

"Okay, Papi," she said with a cute accent as she turned at the waist, swinging her arms side to side and looked at me seductively.

"You want to play before you leave…like a quickie?"

Davi came running in with Julissa chasing behind him. She had on a full pajama set that hugged her body. I tried not to look at her so I wouldn't envision her jumping out of her clothes. She was a bigger version of Mel.

"What the fuck…get outta here!" Melinda yelled.

"Davi' I'm going to beat your ass!" Julissa yelled as she cornered him by the bed.

"Oohhh, look at the money. Can I get some, Keith?" Davi asked while trying to dodge Julissa.

She caught him and grabbed him by the arm, then looked at Me and Mel. "Sorry!" Her face was polite as she turned to Davi looking angry. "Get your ass over here!" She handled him by his arm. *Pap!* "Didn't…" *Pap!* She smacked him hard on his ass. "I…" *Pap!* "Tell…" *Pap!* "You…" *Pap!* "Don't…" *Pap!* "Eat…" *Pap!* "My food in the fridge…" *Pap! Pap! Pap!* "Don't be eating my stuff, Davi!"

I knew it hurt because he flinched with every hit, but he took the pain like a G, Davi was tough.

"Okay…okay…Tia…I won't no more…I won't…won't do it no more!" he said.

She reluctantly let him go still maintaining her attitude starring at him. His baby face turned cold when he got some distance away, This family was trained to act.

"Until you put something good in there that I like to eat again!" he said and disappeared out of the room with Julissa chasing behind him.

"You better punch him…he getting too big for a spanking!" Melinda yelled after her sister, then picked up the bowl full of Mofango she was mashing while walking out.

I looked right into Ciera's eyes and started speaking to her. "That whole house thing will be done by next week, CeCe. We out that's what the money is for." Her eyes darted to the bed. "Next week we say bye-bye Harlem. We're starting life fresh and leaving this behind." She definitely smiled at me.

I don't do the baby talking thing to her and hate when others do it. The phone rang, the television was playing and for some reason, I was on edge and a little nervous over nothing in particular as I looked at the phone. Then to the money out in the open, even in my house this apartment did not feel safe. I put CeCe down, she crawled to the television that laid on the super clean-scrubbed floor and watched the *Smurfs*. She was so small her body filled up only two square tiles. She stopped on all fours and put her face right into the screen.

I lifted her gently and slowly by the legs and arms, she stretched them out flailing them, trying to understand being lifted up. The phone rang again and stopped after the third ring. I put her down on her baby blanket that she loved to lay on, some spaces away from the TV. She then relaxed while blowing her lips at the screen enjoying the *Smurf's* sing.

My beeper went off, there was a lot of work for me to get down since I was back. I saw Scottie's number with 117-117-117 following it. On the first ring, I picked up the phone and heard my lawyer's calm voice.

"Hey, Keith have a good vacation?" he asked.

"Yes, I did tha…" Before I could get another word out of my mouth, he cut me off.

"Good…good, so I'm on a heavy schedule today, prioritizing things here at the office. We're handling your dealings since I have the last touches of paperwork on my desk in front of me. Now for the house that will be finalized in two days. I just need some signatures from you and of course, the money and Al is asking for a retaining fee. He says you can drop it here as well."

"Fine…fine, I will be there at four."

"So, to be clear, do I tell Al that you're handling his retainer now as well?"

"Yes, you can."

"Good, see you soon." He hung up.

I covered the safe sitting in the back of the closet with the boxes of new clothes we bought. It held four-thousand dollars I'd saved as well as the end deal for the vitamin store. I grabbed a baby blue bag, stuffed the money from the bed into it and the loaded gun on top of that, then zipped up the bag tightly. Outside Guy was wearing a Doo-Rag under her hat as she hustled down the block alone. Mama was nowhere to be found. I had to teach Guy that she couldn't be wearing things that the police would easily be able to identify her in or she would be right back in jail. I crossed over to Scottie on the corner by the pay phone and beeped my personal O'Jay driver, I was not going through the base anymore for him.

"Have a good vacation?" Scottie asked.

"Hell, yeah, I needed that like crazy. What's going on? The block looks empty."

Welo's crew was only two deep and Ray The Boss had only one person out but there were customers flowing.

"You know I'm just the help. Monk wants to see you at One Fish Two Fish. He's waiting there, right now."

My personal O'Jay driver beeped me back with a 5 meaning five minutes.

"So, all is good?" I asked.

"Yeah."

"Yar handled that situation?"

"Not fully," he said.

"How you doing man, you okay?"

"Same shit," he said making me smile.

"I love you, Scottie. You're not just the help. I rely on you and need you; I really do."

He nodded a yes as he looked around and saw the O'Jay pulling up. We quickly got in, it took ten minutes and Scottie basically said nothing, as I relaxed on the ride for the first day of work. We got out of the cab on Madison Avenue, both of us were on point.

One Fish Two Fish was not packed being that it was still early in the day. There was a bar and an eating area with a live Lobster tank.

Monk was at the bar giving Scottie a look, then his attention turned to me. "So, what do you know?"

"Nothing…you tell me while I listen." I looked Monk over he was not being his usual self.

His beeper went off and he dismissed it in a low tone for no one to hear, "She gotta wait." But I heard every word then he continued. "The block is hot…Fats' is dead, he was killed on Park."

"On one seventeenth?" I asked surprised.

"Yeah," Monk replied with a high tone, lifting his eyebrows.

"Sorry…go ahead," I told him.

"We went to Madison and had a shootout with them niggas and they got robbed along with some local girls. Two of them were shot, now one seventeenth is on fire with the police asking for me. I know because Mama told me she overheard them asking people in stores. And the Cuban store owner told her that yellow cab is looking for me, and I know Guy is out there by herself, so I got my cousin coming, too."

"So, was Fats killed on the same night as the shootout or after?" I questioned.

"No…well I don't know, but I think right before the shoot out."

My mind was rambled all over the place with confusion. He didn't want to talk about it, then I looked over at Scottie. I was not going to ask Scottie if he killed Fats in front of Monk so we all just left. Monk went to his crib to get money he had for me and then we went to Scottie's. The dogs kept jumping on me too happy to see me again.

"Okay…okay!" I said to them, patting Bad on his head as he relaxed next to me on the sofa. I looked at Scottie.

"Yeah, no one saw me that's it!" he admitted.

I had to figure this out. Why was yellow cab after Monk and not Scottie?

"Scottie, what's with this beef now? Them niggas ain't soft we gotta be on top of this."

"They know we not soft now I just need to catch Calvin one time and…it's over."

We looked at each other, I contemplated and reasoned that a coulda shoulda woulda being done was not going to do anything. The dogs ran to the door and Scottie grabbed the gun from his waist. I looked at him noticing his sudden overreaction.

"They may have followed me home," Scottie said. I just stared at him. "I'm not paranoid nephew they may have."

The dogs both looked at me with their eyes low, giving me the '*yes he's been high and bugging out like this'* look, we're glad you're here.

"Go to your room now!" Scottie yelled at them and they left whimpering.

The knock was Monk's I knew because it was the same knock he always used. After letting him in Scottie peaked out the door, then locked it. Monk looked at the gun in Scottie's hand once they faced each other and stepped back.

"Send this nigga to Puerto Rico or something Keith. He needs to relax and he's creeping me the fuck out."

That was actually a good idea after we dealt with this beef. Monk gave me a brown paper bag, in it, was neatly rubber band rolls of money. I put it in a safe in Scottie's crib. I took Scottie with me to visit the lawyers and gave them the money for the crib and retainers fees as I talked to Al about Guy's case. The vitamin store was going through some problems attaining but we were working it all out. I kept Al on standby so the workers could feel remembered when arrested not just pushed through the system with a legal aid lawyer that everyone shares but his own.

A beep came from my connect E who said he would have some bricks for me tomorrow that I needed. Having to see people I ended up at the Lennox lounge after talking to the two lawyers handling things on a clear mind. Scottie, Monk, Guy, Eric Rosario, and his two boys stood with me as we got visits from my Brooklyn cats who were some weight customers that grabbed the last of the big weight I had and my 119th Street people came through too. This was a long day and while conducting business we had a few drinks getting the attention of some girls that joined us.

"Yo' Eric, I'ma have some weight soon. So, whatever you cop I can match with consignment."

"Cool, Keith, but I can pay twenty-five anywhere."

I shook my head in agreement. "I got you at twenty-one if you buying a hundred grams, I'll throw you another hundred." He nodded his head.

Monk pulled me to the side with the others who were drinking and grinding on the girls.

"Yo' that Connecticut chick been on me since you left and she down here asking for you."

"How she get in contact with you? I never gave her your info."

"Yeah, but last time we was up there, I begged her friend and we been fucking here and there. Now they down here saying they need you."

"Where they at?"

"They was at Sylvia's eating saying they going to the movies after."

"Cool hit her up and tell her I will holla at her. In fact, tell her come through and send the O'Jay to get her now…fuck the movies."

The Connecticut chick came through with her crew. Me and her had done business before but we started fucking around. I couldn't do that to Mel, and risk ruining the relationship we'd developed, so I ended whatever we had a year ago. She be selling bricks at forty a key where here it's twenty to twenty-five thousand or even eighteen for buying bulk. I'm lucky to have E giving it to me at sixteen.

She came through, we talked numbers and made a deal for later. She introduced me to her people and left. The night was good, I felt good and handled a lot as everybody talked shit. They got my attention as they started talking about Eric Rosario sending somebody to the Emergency room. We ended up calling three more O'Jays around ten and went to a 145th to Willie Burgers.

Outside of the small place was a line as usual to buy two-dollar hamburgers. The only thing on the menu besides fifty cents toppings was a choice or mixture of two juices: lemonade and punch.

As we were going down 125th *Treach* from *Naughty By Nature* was out wearing a short-sleeve vest, showing his arms when it was cold outside. Cars passed us of all kinds with kids behind the wheels. I was not really interested in owning one, but I liked the Benz 190 that two girls drove past in. We ended up in the schoolyard on 119th Street and all the O'Jays left except my personal driver, I kept him on hold. Ray The Boss was there drinking and shooting dice with four people, two others were playing basketball. Although it was cold outside, Ray had his Maxima's windows rolled down with no one in it outside the schoolyard. Not worried about anyone touching it playing the group Mob Style song that gangsta shit. We fitted right in, all of us were drunk and ended up playing basketball at three thousand a game, us against them.

CHAPTER FIFTEEN
ERIC ROSARIO

We been drinking and riding with Keith for hours now from the club to Willie Burgers and ending up parking the O'Jays one behind the other at the schoolyard on 119th Street. People were in the yard. Ray The Boss was shooting dice with four others and on the opposite end was two big guys balling hard against each other. We turned the music off, got out, and heard Ray's black box Maxima playing *Soul to Soul Back To Life*. Feeling a money getting vibe from the song I walked toward the schoolyard hoping for a big come up on the dice game.

With the rest of my work left and my money together I got five thousand. If I bring Keith sixty-three hundred on this deal buying three-hundred grams, he will give me three on the arm putting me over a half of a key, up there on real money status. He only sells a hundred grams a shot. So, I can't go under forty-two hundred leaving me with eight hundred to play with to make into twenty-one. Eight was my blow money, either blow away or blow up on.

Looking back at Keith, he was paying the drivers as they drove off except his personal one, he kept on standby. Scottie posted up outside of the O'Jay watching Keith catch up to us going into the park. Me and Guy joined the dice game with the others and watched the basketball game, as two ex-college players were going at it. After a couple of rolls, I was only up sixty dollars betting conservative, my money was funny from that Tyson hit, I needed a come up.

Ray started talking friendly shit, enticing Keith. "You caught me for ten-thousand on San Fran winning the Super Bowl. I'll put up ten to your twenty-five on the NBA Championship ahead of time, that Detroit repeats this year, Big Willie."

"Bet, if you give me a bet that Magic gets the MVP for my five to your ten," Keith responded coming closer to the dice game.

"I got Michael Milken money you ain't saying nothin' that's a bet," Ray said.

"Who's Michael Milken?" Guy asked not impressed.

"Money talk you wouldn't understand," Ray answered.

"Cool, bet my little bit of money on these dice so I can understand yours when I take it," Guy said pulling out a stack of cash.

"I hear you, I'ma take all that, blame it on your mouth. What's up with you, Eric Rosario? You want to understand my money, too?"

"I'm not betting on no NBA months from now, but I got a hundred on your roll," I said, and Ray threw the dice cracking us as everybody payed him. Fuck my jackass got caught in that moment. "A hundred," I said paying him from a stack I had, then counted out seven hundred and sixty dollars and put the rest away.

"Don't hide that re-up money, Big Willie," Ray said smiling.

"A hundred," Guy said, and the others called out their bets to Ray.

When Keith started walking away from the dice game Ray spoke to him again. "So, you act like you can ball or something, Keith?"

"As good as you, Boss. What's up?" Keith said coming back, he was in an aggressive mood today, like I'd never seen before.

"I'll play with four of these drunk niggas, right here, right now a thousand a man. As long as you playing, we going to win," Ray said shaking the dice in his hand and rolling them with no point coming up.

"Bet, we got five right here, too. But everybody has to down a forty, first," Keith told him looking at who he was going to play with.

Ten of us down a forty ounce of Saint Ives beer each then started playing ball for money, us against them. Both sides had a real ballplayer from college. Ray had Paul Green and Keith had

Raymond Nebbles both were over six-two, and both had left college to get money. Paul got work from Ray The Boss and hustled in Binghamton New York and Raymond got work from Keith and went to Syracuse New York. I knew Ray longer than Keith and felt odd playing against him.

The money being betted made it real with all of us playing hard, respecting the fouls called out. Being scratched up and pushed but no one took it personally. I was playing in new sneakers, and they were getting marked up, but fuck it I'ma boss now. My boys and others on the sidelines laughed at us especially when one of Keith's Brooklyn people fell. Bets were made on individual hits or misses in the game. I heard from a player after a shot was made.

"That's two-hundred." And when he missed. "Down to a hundred now."

I was asked to be on my miss because I couldn't shoot when asked again by a different person, I felt some type of way almost taking the bet. But I remembered how I let myself be pushed into the Tyson bet and declined. It was cold outside and getting darker, so we made adjustments after losing the first game all of us went to our T-shirts to see our teams better in the dark and Keith sent the driver for Davi. I was the smallest on the court before that, playing hard and physical on every play. People kept coming into the yard to watch and when Davi came Julissa was with him getting a lot of attention with her thick body and cute face. We played, seeing the people on the sidelines bundled up in clothes.

Monk made jokes and yelled to Keith. "You can't play no ball you like giving your money away." He was laughing harder than usual watching Keith play. Keith got the ball and Monk said aloud. "Watch this!" To some of the girls that came into the yard to see him and the ball freakishly jumped out of Keith's hands. "That's his no-look pass!" Monk yelled laughing.

We broke even winning the game Davi played. Keith and Ray doubled up betting two thousand a man then changed it to three thousand a man for the last game as Keith told us if we win this one everybody gets five hundred each. I don't know about everybody else but I needed that and Davi definitely wanted it. So,

I took bets that went against Davi's hit's as they bet on his miss fifty a shot, underestimating him because he was a little kid who did not shoot much in the first game, but I knew better.

The sidelines were crowded with about twenty spectators and others coming in. I noticed Stacy from my building waving at me, of course, everybody else noticed. Outside the fence, Druggem pulled up in his black Volvo station Wagon behind a red 300 Z that had Welo sitting inside of it. Money was all around, good looking girls, gold chains, and music playing from a handheld radio someone had brought, it was insanely Harlem.

We lost and Keith paid fifteen thousand to Ray, but I won four hundred after Davi made four more shots, then he missed betting two people on that. Putting that money with the money I could blow it started looking like something toward that sixty-three hundred I needed. That game was tough for both of us and they barely won. Tee and Chito stood by on the sidelines. I grabbed my Gap sweater and leather jacket, then put them on. I felt the .32 automatic weighing it down. The cool air that was hitting my skin went away and warmth grabbed my body making me realize the alcohol was still alive, Chito passed me another forty.

At the dice game, we bet together, winning three in a row. The dice was going our way, Welo, Druggem, Puerto Rican Ramel, Steamer, Fat Wayne and a little kid came inside the fence. They shook hands, gave a few hugs and changed the whole mood. I could feel the tension in the air. Having different crews together in the dark of the night was always tense. For the most part, we'd all grown up together or knew someone related to the other and it was like that through most of East Harlem.

I watched the interaction between Welo and Keith keeping my back turned to them. There was not much I could see with everybody trying to get an ear full without really trying. The only thing I heard was Fats' name and shit is hot and we got to calm the block down. Really not caring for Fats, I would still like to know who killed him. Welo and Keith were both opposites of each other, Welo was plump dangerous and flashy. Keith was slim, smooth and laid back.

People played three on three basketball for money taking either Paul or Raymond the ex-college players against each other. More cars pulled up from other neighborhoods. They were more interested in girls and life in the yard. Cop cars passed us regularly which made sense since the precinct is across the street from the school. The night was dark and alive as another dice game was going some feet away, from ours.

"Aww, shit yar know what time it is? Pay your rent baby, it's the Landlord. Don't hide, or you'll be sleeping in the streets," he boasted walking past our game with money in his hand onto the other dice game where was Guy was betting.

My girl Tiffany and her cousin from Carver Projects popped up looking real good. Too much was going on at once, so I did not want her to stay. I had the money in my hand and took a sip from my beer that was in the other hand.

"What's good, Tiff?" I said.

"You, I know you not going to be here all day, right, Eric?"

I knew she meant night. "No, go home I'll meet you there at two on the dot when your mama is asleep."

"I know you gambling so I won't mess with you. See you tonight, be safe, okay." She gave me a kiss that triggered her words be safe clearer in my head.

"Oh, here take this," I told her, putting my blow money in my jacket pocket and gave her the gun as some people watched.

She took it and walked away, her cousin looked back and saw me watching Tiffany from behind. She smiled then started giggling in Tiffany's ear. At that very moment, a fight broke out and I saw the Landlord walking away.

"Yar going to jump me? Okay…okay!" Then he left, only after one roll of dice.

Guy walked off from our game and as she passed us, she didn't say a word, this kid from Johnson projects yelled after her. "Fuck that cunt she needs to let me fuck her pretty ass and stop wasting that tight pussy!"

Guy had already left so she didn't hear him, which was probably a good thing. People were taking girls to the back of the schoolyard one by one more than likely getting head in a corner or by the steps. Like a movie, even the music went with the theme. The radio played *Bell Biv Devoe Do Me Baby*. Every person not from the hood was trying to talk to Julissa and she went over to Keith. Welo was boasting about DC and how he got shit out there in a frenzy. He was inviting anybody to go and warning them about the war. Since they didn't like us, and we didn't like them and if you stayed for a month you would come back with a car. He was always trying to get me back on his team but there was too much killing around him.

The dude who was arguing with Guy walked off toward the 3rd Avenue exit. I was about to make a bet when from the side of my eye I saw fast movement come by the Lexington exit. I dropped my forty and it smashed on the ground and quickly started running. Chito and Tee also took flight, instantly following me without a thought or questioning my decision to run.

The police were running into the fenced yard fast and we heard sirens and saw the cars pull up on the Lexington exit. People stood their ground not worried and were thrown to the ground. Street post lights were shining in the dark like stars in space as I ran knowing Chito had cracks on him. My heart jumped into a scare seeing the other exit, I was running and covered by cops. Then heard stomps and the rustling around of police equipment that only came when they ran as two officers were chasing us. We were running hard, my speed picked up and a smile came across my face. I felt a rush of intenseness take over knowing they couldn't catch me in an open run. I peeked back, then slowed down and reached for air.

Chito yelled with a laugh. "Too slow, you don't want it." We all laughed as they continued to chase us.

It felt like we were playing Manhunt and I did what I would have done if we were playing the game we grew up on. I ran toward the cafeteria part of the school, its roof was only one story high, and since kids we'd been able to climb it quickly. It was like we'd trained for this moment. We ran after the cops thought they had us cornered, I skipped a few steps, jumped on top of a handrail with my left hand on the wall and pushed off forward to a gated window. I grabbed the window with my right hand then left and pulled myself up and was on top of the roof instantly. Tee and Chito did the same, the cops were behind us but unable to get on the roof.

I looked back to see them looking up at us. I saw Vuggio watching us from a distance in the yard. We ran across the roof hearing sounds of our feet crunching on the little black rocks spread across the roof top. I never knew why they have them, but I used to love throwing them in handfuls as a kid. Chito and Tee both grabbed a handful and tossed them over. I ran back doing the same thing and started laughing, then ran away again. The roof led to the other side of the block on 3rd Avenue and we hung off the lip jumping down hitting the floor running.

Blat! Blat! Blat!

Three shots from a small gun was fired and I hit the ground. Chito and Tee jumped behind some cars. I checked myself quick to see if I was hit, then I was up and running again toward my block. I didn't look back as I ran, deciding not to stop till I got there. When we reached the front of 1990 my building, we watched feeling they weren't coming around here. Sirens were heard and the cars, both police as well as regular ones, were all gone. Chito started making sales and Tee went to get some packs, he had in his crib. Some people who escaped from the yard started coming telling us about the events. It was one of those remembered things that don't happen too much. A dice game happened as the losers from the schoolyard were now piling up trying to get some get back money.

Clicking a little I left to go to my crib for more packs. On the elevator ride up I knew I needed to sober up. I had thousands on me, and I couldn't let my moms see me drunk or let her see the money. I hid my money in my socks and waist on the ride up to the 31st floor which made me sweat. I wiped my face and ate some candy so I wouldn't smell like beer. Getting off the elevator I headed down the hall and went right inside my apartment. The door was already unlocked and open, my mom was waiting there on the couch.

I watched the last ten minutes of The Honey Mooner's it was a good one where Ralph knew every answer to who made what song on a game show for big money and as he got to the final question, they played a tune for him to name the author. The tune was one *Ed Norton* always played over and over, annoying Ralph warming up before he played anything. So, Ralph stuttered saying what came to his mind, *Ed Norton.* He got it wrong when they told him sorry, he'd named the wrong author of that and anything they said she knew a song and the author to it until they threw him off the stage, it was funny. When it finally went off, I snuck out of the house.

Dudes from Washington projects were in the dice game when I came downstairs. I saw them around but didn't really know them. Chito and Tee came to me with a snack box from King Corporal.

As they finished one of the Washington projects cats said, "They got young fiends pitching over here and getting food for them."

"Yar niggas be easy, plus, it's hot out here let's not beef," I said, being bothered when people talked about Tee.

"Fuck hot yar be easy," one of them said.

"Yar don't want it," Chito said in his accent and with a smile like he was joking but was dead ass serious.

The group of five laughed as others from our hood laughed with them while they repeated his bad English. They continued to roll dice and I was ready to smash the forty on the one with the biggest mouth's head. Until Tee pointed to Ms. Carter, walking past and her daughter froze, and we stared hard.

"Hi, Ms. Carter," someone said from our hood, she ignored him but continued to watch the three of us.

"Hi, Ms. Carter," I said.

One of the rude cats replied, "I would hit that, right there," in reference to Ms. Carter's daughter.

"Word!" another one commented.

"Me too!" another one answered.

"Hell yeah!" another agreed.

"I'll fuck the mother with that dusty nigga's dick," came from them and finally got Ms. Carter's attention as she held her daughter's hand tightly.

"We can't even walk and not be disrespected where we live," she remarked.

Tee showed hate on his face which was unusual for him as he went into 1990. Ms. Carter was about to turn the corner but stopped and looked back. "A bunch of punks letting their own block be run by other punks," she said with a disgusted look on her face.

I dropped my food and put my forty down on the sidewalk. I went to the corner she'd just turned and grabbed the steel garbage can, I emptied the trash out of it, then dragged it to the dice game. I swung it over my head and hit Loudmouth over the head with it until he fell out. Chito dropped one of them with a punch and hit another as they started fighting. I was hit and sent falling to the ground getting jumped. As quickly their group responded fighting us and everybody else that was shooting dice, jumped on our side since they were from our block or close to it.

One of them ran away, then two others ran to him leaving two of them laid out. One wasn't moving but he was still breathing as he curled up into a ball. Tee came out with a gun in his hand the curled-up kid got off the ground and ran in a different direction than his boys.

Tee aimed at them and I yelled at him, "Nah, Tee let them go…let em go!"

They were gone, we hid the gun under a car tire across the street while others continued playing dice leaving the unconscious kid on the floor. My snack box was smashed up and stepped on, and it made me hungrier. Warrior who lived on the twenty-eight floor went through the laid-out kid's pockets and took his sneakers off his feet along with his jacket. Then his sweater and tossed it to the side, he awoke, got up and ran past me. I swung, hitting him solid dead on as he fell out again. We left him right where he was.

After two minutes a girl came to see Warrior and asked, "What's up, with that dude laid out on the ground with his clothes off?"

Someone said, "E.R. did it."

"Who's E.R.?" she asked.

"Emergency Room?" Warrior questioned laughing.

Somebody called the cops they came with an ambulance and took the kid. I noticed the time and started walking to Taino Towers to see Tiffany. Everybody else just hid stuff and scattered until it cleared not wanting to leave this night to pass. A five-minute walk had me inside building 230. I walked into the first set of doors, feeling hot as the drunkenness was wearing off. The security guard looked at me, I recognized him as Shawn an older creep who liked to talk and trick on young girls. Ignoring me and not opening the door, I buzzed the intercom very lightly so the buzzer could buzz, then laughed at my thoughts. Tapping it in a short buzz again the guard looked my way.

"Fuck you looking at?" I asked, he turned his head as the door buzzed open. I entered passing him.

He got his six-foot security uniform self-up now from his chair. "Sign in!" he said.

"Fuck you, bitch nigga, open the door next time!" The elevator was waiting for me being that it was so late no one was using them.

I got off on the 19th floor, Tiffany was in the hall waiting for me in a T-shirt and panties with a sleepy look on her face. She held a finger up to her lips and motioned for me to be quiet and follow her. As I did, I watched her ass twitch naturally in money coined panties and felt my drunk trance, the world was great right now.

All the lights were out in the apartment and she held my hand leading me to her room. Then she moved her hand to touch the lump in my pants, laughed and shushed me. I undid my pants and dropped them down to my ankles as she laid in the bed watching me. Then I took off my leather jacket and Hoodie, threw it to the floor and moved over to her like I had on shackles. I slid her panties to the side and entered her as I held her waist. I pumped fast and wrapped her legs around me as I watched her tits under the light. Her T-shirt moved around loosely, I felt her warm skin hit against mine, my body warmed up from the light chill. She started feeling it, pushed her body hard matching my strokes. I came into her trying to put my body through her until I finished.

She got up as I laid down pulling up my pants. "Stop getting in the bed with outside clothes on," she said leaving the room

She came back a few minutes later with some food she'd microwaved. I ate it without really tasting what it was being that I was so hungry. She left and came back with a wet rag and washed my little man off. I laid back relaxed as I felt her warm mouth on me. I knew she wanted more sex because I'd come so fast the first time. I pulled her to me and got on top of her taking off all my clothes then I undressed her until she was naked, and we did it again.

Early the next morning, I snuck back into my crib and got ready for school. I walked down the steps to the 27th floor and picked up Tee. Who didn't like to miss school, he was book smart and we all loved that about him. The building was different outside in the daytime as people went to work and school in different directions. The light was going into the indents with no blind spots, a totally different place it felt like. I wore a Levi light blue jean suit, a dark blue hoodie, and a dark blue Scalee hat, I was ready for school.

Shawnty and Meat Head from Wagna projects went to Graphic Arts with me on 49th Street and 10th Avenue. It was dominated by Brooklyn students. A gang called the Decepticons fucked with people, but we had our own thing going on. Once me and Kenny from Foster both were wearing North Face three-hundred-and fifty-dollar coats got jumped and we were beating them, which gained us respect from Steel and Taco Man plus, Sticky Fingers…I would never be forgotten.

Tee walked to his school and we took the train using our school passes, all of us had knots of money in our pockets. I made enough last night for my work and an extra three hundred I could blow. Outside Meat Head hid his bun because there was a metal detector in the school, plus, we had truancy cops inside. School was fun, I checked into homeroom class then print class and played the lunchroom most of the day. After attending a math class, I found a dice game-winning fifty dollars before security broke it up.

On the way back, we rode the train and saw a girl fight. Some kids were dancing for money and they were good. I got out on 25th Street. The train station on 25th was like a fashion show, everybody was dressed up it seemed. I wanted to get back and finish the last two packs and be for ready for Keith. Chito was sitting down and told me Tee left a gun under a car tire, he pointed toward the car. Shawnty came back to the block with me giving him the last packs to do. He fucked with purple city up the block but said he just wanted some quick bread before his shift started there. I sat on the concrete slab next to Chito as Shawnty hid one pack and served customers from the others. Yellow cab was passing by then and turned the corner. Not too many people hustled at this time but there were two others out not worried about Yellow Cab.

They came back around and jumped out on us. Vuggio came at me as I stood with my hands against the car waiting to be searched. I didn't have anything to do with anything, but that didn't stop him from grabbing the back of my neck, throwing me to the ground and cuffing me.

Chito was searched by Chuck Norris his partner we called him that because he looked like the actor Chuck Norris. Shawnty got caught up with the crack and placed in the back of a car. After a moment he told me to get up, as he lifted and placed me into a different car.

"Check under the car tires!" Vuggio yelled.

After ten more minutes which still seemed like forever, I heard, "We got it!"

They released Shawnty at the precinct while I remained in the cell.

CHAPTER SIXTEEN

GUY

Eric Rosario was so thirsty to shoot some dice he left his O'Jay for Keith to pay like a little kid. I was about to go home feeling nice off some weed, me and Monk had smoked earlier. Instead, I decided to chill with Keith, he said he was picking up some money from Raymond Nebbles who was playing ball. Once Keith leaves I'ma be out too.

I left my .25 automatic with Scottie, he just nodded at me as he took it and put it in his car. I walked behind the rest of them into the yard pulling my hood over my head. Ray The Boss had the dice in the yard. He be taking all bets allowing big come ups off him or I could lose small money to him, I'ma try my luck.

While betting on the line a few times my mind was on my aunt acting up and not wanting to go home tonight. I thought about moving out, the only obstacle was she depended on the money I gave her. Keith and Ray were talking shit to each other as usual.

"I got Michael Milken money you ain't saying nothing that's a bet," Ray boasted.

"Who's Michael Milken?" I asked not really caring but getting into the game wanting to shoot some dice.

"Money talks you wouldn't understand."

"Cool, bet my little bit of money on these dice so I can understand yours when I take it," I told him pulling out some bread ready to play.

They started talking a lot of shit and ended up buying forties to drink and started playing five on five basketball drunk as hell. Monk lit up another joint, so I gave him ten dollars to smoke with him.

"Where your mouth been?" he asked.

"On some nice joints not like them chicks you be hitting," I told him passing the blunt.

Me and Monk smoked as we watched them play basketball and the night felt relaxing. Being that money was on the line, they were calling Phantom fouls when a shot was missed not wanting the blame on themselves for losing the game. Their coordination was off as they scratched and pushed each other. It was starting to be funny and even the nice players were off a little because of the beer.

"This is the type my mouth be on," I said as two girls were coming straight to Monk. He gave them a hug and introduced me to a cute girl named Cindy.

"Maybe my wife one day if she acts right," he said.

Girls came in, Julissa was looking good, but I would not try and hit too close to home. My lifestyle didn't mix with people that's going to worry who you know. First-time girls be with it as long as it's not out there. So as much as I would like to deal with her, I wouldn't even play myself, but she looked good.

That Stacy chick was looking sexy, her waving to Eric Rosario was just her letting it be known she wanted somebody to trick on her. I'm not really in that zone, right now. She was looking right and had an appeal, but she was just not my type. Her attitude had no innocence to it. People were coming in the yard and I started up a dice game myself. I had bank and was taking bets I was coming up. They started another dice game after the basketball game ended. I was thinking about leaving.

"If I take all that money what you want to do for it?" This tall skinny kid said referring to the stack I held from the bets I made.

"What…take what?" I said looking at him.

"Nah, man not like that. If I take it on the roll, count that out let me stop the bank."

"Nigga call out your bet, and if you want to cover the bank drop your cash on the ground and see if it covers mine. The first bet is to you."

"You kinda cute shorty. What's your name?"

"You betting or not? Yo' everybody call out your bets it goes from him to yar whatever is left."

"My bad, you just mad cute I got three hundred."

Other bets were made that I had covered with twelve hundred in my hand. I was about to throw the dice then I heard him.

"Aww shit yar know what time it is. Pay your rent baby it's the Landlord. Don't hide, or you will be sleeping in the street. Who got that bank?"

"I do. What you got?" I told him wanting to throw the dice already.

"Oh, shit this is how it goes now. This that new shit fuck it her money green, too. The Landlord don't discriminate everybody gotta have a roof. Bet ten dollars."

"Bet ten to you, three-hundred…sixty…a hundred, eighty, eighty and seventy!" I called out.

I pointed to everyone who made a bet and rolled the dice, A four came as the point. Landlord ran to grab the dice and the kid who bet three hundred cut him off before he grabbed them.

"Slow down nigga, you just got here and you betting ten dollars. Fall back, get your ass out of here," he said grabbing the dice first.

"Whaattt!" Landlord said in a high-pitched voice, squinting his eyes in disbelief. He put his arms behind his back and made fists out of his hands.

"Whaattt, you better ask somebody. I'm the Landlord baby we can handle this thing me and you…fuck the bullshit."

Another kid swung as the Landlord started weaving it, throwing his hands up ready. Then the taller kid threw two punches, the Landlord weaved dancing back and forth.

"You can't fuck with the, Landlord baby. Fuck yar, I'ma go get some rent somewhere else yar fucking around," the Landlord complained and walked off. "Yar gonna jump me, okay…okay!" he yelled as he exited the yard.

The taller dude looked at me. "See if you had a man like me with your pretty ass, we coulda avoided that," he commented.

"I don't need no man, I get pussy, too. You rolling to the four or not?"

"Here take my hundred, I don't even want to roll now." He tried to pass it to me.

"You bet three, my man."

"My bad." He counted out the money holding on to it.

"What's up with your number? We can be a good team."

"Keep your money you slowing up the game. Just go bounce homeboy. I don't get penetrated, I penetrate. That what you want?"

"Fuck you, bitch! Nobody wants your boney dried up pussy anyway. I just wanted you to suck my dick because I know you can suck good that's all you do, right?"

"Roll or bounce?" I said

He threw the money on the ground and I picked it up.

"You got a nice little ass under there," he said.

I ignored him, the next person rolled the dice to the four and paid me as he lost, and the next roller won and got paid. Everybody was rolling and ignoring him.

"Let me hit that once, I'll change your whole perspective."

I looked at him. "Chill you crossing lines…let's get this money." Everyone was looking at me.

"My bad!" he put his hand out, probably just wanting to touch me to see how I felt, and I was not letting him get nothing.

"Call you bets." I said

As I bent down to get the dice, his hands touched my pussy and ran down to my ass from behind. I jumped turning around to see him as two others laughed. He did not deserve a fight where he would probably win. I was fed up and walked away. There was nothing to say to nobody. I never fucked with nobody, that nigga is dead.

Scottie was posted on the cab and saw me coming from outside of the yard. I got inside the O'Jay as he stood silent. I took off my jacket, Doo-rag and hoodie, then put my jacket back on. Scottie came inside and handed me my gun.

"You need help?"

"No, I got this."

"Don't run, you'll look like a bystander. Just walk away after."

"Okay," I said after Scottie's schooling.

"Walk past the precinct," he continued.

"Okay," I said once again and left.

I got out of the car, waited on 119th Street and Lexington on the opposite block of the street. My hatred got stronger as I thought about him touching me and laughing afterward. I saw his face laughing again and again. Then I saw my mother's boyfriend tell me it was okay…telling me it's just like the candy he gives me, and we don't tell mommy about it. My eyes locked in on him and after five minutes he started walking toward the side exit on 119th Street.

My nerves were grabbing me, as I held onto the gun inside of my jacket pocket. When he left the yard, police were rushing all over. I felt like it was an excuse or a sign not to do it. They ran directly into the yard now running around people. He stood watching from across the street and I cocked the gun still in my pocket and walked toward him.

Spectators were watching the raid, and there was a chase inside the yard between the cops and Eric Rosario, that got the attention of the onlookers. But I was watching his every breath from my side view, and after the chase was lost by the police he walked away. Then I followed behind him.

I walked fast as I turned the corner onto 3rd Avenue catching up to him. "Hey, cutie! Where you going?" I said.

His thirsty ass looked back seeing my hair not even knowing it was me. "With you, or you with me. Where you wanna go?" he replied.

"You kinda cute shorty what's your name?" I said mimicking his voice, then he looked at me strange. I pulled my gun out before he had the chance to change his facial expression. "That will be the last time you ever touch me you sick fuck!" I pulled the trigger twice.

Blatt! Blatt! His face showed hurt as the bullets entered his torso, but he did not fall so I pulled the trigger again. *Blatt!* This time he dropped. I was still angry and walked over to him. I smacked him with the gun breaking his skin. I saw blood and stopped, then stepped back and walked off quickly back the same way I'd came. Down 119th Street right into the spectators who were still watching the police searches take place. Cops were running in the direction I'd just left.

I kept going as I walked toward the precinct entrance. I heard the sirens and continued walking as I held the gun inside my coat pocket, once I reached Park Avenue Scottie was there with the car waiting. He took the gun from me and put it inside the car, then told the driver to leave with it.

We walked headed toward the Westside and he finally spoke, "Tell me all about it and don't leave out nothing."

CHAPTER SEVENTEEN

WELO

I shoulda never came to the schoolyard while it was packed like this. The police came running with guns drawn, putting people in groups, searching them. Now I'm about to have my hands up on the fence like everybody else.

"Come on, Welo, you slipping," I mumbled to myself. If they put a bullshit case on me with all the money East Harlem and D.C. is pushing out that will slow this paper down.

The cops were chasing that pimpled faced Eric Rosario and his little crew in the middle of the yard. They were dusting the police in the chase and having fun doing it. One of them even did some maneuver making the cop look silly as he tried to grab him and missed. They got away by climbing a roof. The diversion and darkness were used by many to rid themselves of anything illegal so they could toss whatever it was to the ground.

Cops were going after Eric Rosario as they reached up to climb after them when rocks came over hitting them in their faces. They attempted again and again, and rocks continued to hit their faces. The police back up and started pointing guns toward an empty roof. That kid had balls, I want him back on my team before he goes to jail, I need more hustler in D.C.

"Everybody face the fence, put your hands on it and don't move!" three cops yelled at us.

"Ain't nothing here but money, officer," I spoke holding my composure, but was feeling anxious the same way I do every time a cop has control over me. I felt it diminished to a few jitters as I saw my crew around me. I was glad I'd told them before we got here to be clean and it paid off.

"Turn around and all of you put your hands on the fence now," one of the cops repeated.

We did as two cops came over and started searching two of my boys.

Blatt! Blatt! Cops became alert and started running toward where the shots were coming from including the ones that gave us orders. *Blatt!* A third shot was heard.

"Shots fired…shots fired, from third avenue on one-nineteenth street!" Came over the radio.

"Shit that's where Eric Rosario and his crew had gotten away to, they probably shooting in the air acting out," I mumbled to myself.

"Gun…gun…gun!" Came from my right.

I turned and saw them grab somebody off the fence some distance away. Then they threw him down to the ground and he was kicked a couple of times. He tried to toss his gun while the cops were distracted by the gunshots. They had me cornered I could never let this happen again. The gunman was taken right outside of the fence and tossed in a police car. While the searches continued and sounds of radio's and police with flashlights spot checking the ground all around us in the yard had everyone completely occupied.

"Look at the fence before I take you in for the cracks over there," the cop said in my ear from directly behind me, referring to some yellow top cracks on the ground some feet away from us.

His hand was in my back pressing my two-hundred and sixty-pound frame forward. He was too light in the ass and I was able to hold myself in place. He took off my hat, then emptied the shit out of my pockets. He took my four beepers, my wallet, five dry cleaner tickets, three packs of AA batteries, my keys, and some condoms, then squeezed a pocket that had a bulge of cash in it and left me alone.

"Hand me your coat without turning around," he ordered, putting pressure on the center of my back again. I took it off and passed it back to him. His voice grew with concern and was extra loud. "Place your hands high!" I did. "Higher and pull your feet back more. Don't move not even a little bit," he said.

The attention of all the onlookers and other cops was on me as he felt some weight in the coat thinking it was a gun and had me upset.

I smirked. "Whatever man hurry up so I can go. I have things to do, money to count, and lawyers to pay."

"Well, right now, you don't fuckin' move!"

My boys started laughing together and I joined in with them knowing we were all good. He stepped back off of me, reached in the coat pocket that was the cause of the weight and pulled out a Ziplock bag full of quarters that he musta held upside down because they all fell out onto the ground and some rolled away, down a white painted baseline. I could see to my left that went to home base. I looked down and saw behind my legs jellyfish candy he'd poured onto the ground out of my coat, that dropped in bunches into a white painted box with the number three in it, third base. The small red candy glowed off the light reflected from streetlights that hit them. His foot stepped on them while he patted over my coat a final time and then tossed it on the ground.

On me again, he pulled out the money from my pocket with a jerk. "Put your hands down and turn around," he told me.

I did and saw him push my coat to the side with his shoe as he stepped on the candies not caring. My hat was on the ground and contents were placed inside of it from my pockets. Then my eyes went to his instead of the money in his hand.

"What's this?" he asked.

"Play change!" I said and my boys busted out laughing again.

All their property was in front of them, coats with money in it and shit on the ground. He placed my cash into my coat and wrapped it up.

Vuggio came to our group and silence fell over us. "Get all of their names and addresses. Whoever can't prove who they are, take 'em down to the precinct to be identified, and give me his car keys. I'ma search it myself."

"Yes, sir." Was the only thing heard.

Vuggio looked at all of our faces, then stopped in front of Ramel and Druggem. "Look around hard for any guns near here. I saw one of these two throw it there, so if you find any put a star next to his real name when you write down their governments," His last comment was to Ramel. He walked away taking my keys with him down the fence past others as they were being searched.

Keith was talking for little Davi after he was searched and playing all innocent. They were trying to take Davi in for some cracks they said he tossed to the ground. Vuggio ignored Keith and went to other groups then to my car, that pissed me off. I should kill Keith, in case I decided to later I'ma keep tabs on him, so I won't have to do it on the block.

"Get the fuck outta here and take your shit," the cop said in a mustard up voice after minutes of looking around for guns.

I looked in his face and smiled, then looked to the ground at the quarters, stomped jellyfish, coat, and hat laying there by third base. My people took their possessions and I reached down taking the contents out of my hat, put them back in my pockets and my beepers back on my waist. I grabbed my hat off the ground, tossed it toward a white spray-painted line that was the pitcher's mound. The cop's eyes followed it for a second then back to where I waited for his gaze to return and I smiled and opened my coat taking out my money as some bills blew away with the wind. Not acknowledging him anymore I turned my back and walked toward my car where Vuggio was searching.

"You left some money and other stuff," I heard from behind me.

When we reached the outfield, which was also the basketball court Steamer yelled, "Buy you some binoculars so you can catch the motherfuckers throwing cracks on the ground officer of the law." The cop was picking up the cracks when I looked back. "Oops," Steamer said letting some bills fall out of his hand and blow away passing the cop.

The group started laughing. "Those gotta be ones," Ramel said.

"Stop frontin' Steamer you going to be hustling all night to get that back up," Druggem joked.

"We drive new cars, eat steak and get pussy every day like it's our days off, of course, they hate us. Everybody relax before they take us in for some bullshit," I told them.

Vuggio finished searching my car and handed me the keys as he left headed back to the yard. I could tell he was pissed by the perplexed look on his face.

"If people getting hurt, I'ma just start putting cases on you people that'll stick," he told me.

"Well, I can't help you, sir. I can only assure you that I have no idea of any of it," I replied, then got into my car along with Ramel and drove off.

I dropped Ramel off at Johnson projects and told him to be ready in one hour along with those other two kids we'd picked up. I went to my garage and switched cars, I was now driving my red BMW, then I went to my grandma's crib in Taino Towers. As I rode on the elevators up this woman kept staring at me.

"I know you?" I asked.

"No! Do you want to?" It was only me and her on it, she was sexy dressed in a conservative way, but I was in a hurry.

"Maybe another time, time for me cost a lot."

She put her hands behind her back and when the elevator stopped and opened, before she walked out, she reached her hand back and touched my chest fingering my chain.

"Next time don't waste the moment," she said and left.

I showered and changed my clothes when I got to my grandma's apartment. I looked at my beeper then made some calls and beeps. I'd seen that elevator woman around before and she was now stuck in my head. I was hitting this hot chick up on the beeper and her little brother that hustled for me in the Jefferson projects was hitting me on another.

Exactly an hour later, I went to pick up Ramel and the two new kids. We were bringing them to D.C. for the first time. The drive was quiet, allowing me to think the whole ride there. I had twenty keys up here with six of them out being pushed in spots. A lot of Harlem cats that were coming out there was loud, thinking they could do whatever they wanted then leave headed back to Harlem like it was a different country, especially that Po' cat. I'm just going to keep getting my money here and leave without being on front street.

I was tired and hungry but before we ate, I had to stop at this spot. Different people kept beeping me from there, so I had to come through. It was a female lawyer's crib who'd got turned out by the drugs and lifestyle. She was smart and slick but all I needed was her apartment which was the perfect location.

We parked a block away and watched customers and others going in and out of the building. After five minutes or so, I got out and they followed behind me. My beeper went off, but I had no quarters, so I didn't even bother looking at it. The actual apartment was on the 3rd floor, while they pitched on the 2nd floor landing. The lookout slash gunman watching from outside gave me a nod as we passed him entering the building.

As we walked up the stairs Ramel told the youngsters, "Y'all be ready at all times. Those guns are not for holding the work, it's real up here. These DC and Baltimore cats will shoot at us just because we from New York over a beef that may not be ours."

I watched them as he spoke knowing the guns, they carried were their first ones and they'd never shot anybody before. We passed the hustler on the 2nd floor serving people and went up to the 3rd. I knocked on the door three times and waited three seconds before it opened. Physcho held a .38 at his side pointing it downward. The smell of weed was strong, his face showed he was high but still had a calm effect that it gave off to people. Physcho's crazy looking eyes made him seem odd fitting his name. We all walked past him into the small living room and the door closed behind him.

Ramel became angry. "Nah, leave it open we outta here soon. You wait on the first floor and you right out there by the steps on the landing where I can see you be on point."

Both kids listened to him and left, while Ramel stayed by the door, their faces were serious. A young girl was sitting in a chair by a table that had a lot of crack on it.

"Yeah, so what's up, Ramel…you goodie?" Physcho asked.

"Yeah, but you got too much bullshit you not handling making us come out here. What's up, you want to go back to pitching or keep running this shit?"

Physcho looked angered and Ramel looked at the gun in his hand, then back at Phycho unfazed and showed it.

"Fuck, I'm going to do? I keep telling you this lawyer bitch is doing shit with them B-More niggas. Yar think I'm slow or something while she thinks we all slow," Physcho replied.

On cue she entered the room yelling, "Welo, this shit crazy! This nigga be getting head right here by these little girls in the fuckin' living room. Having the crib smelling like weed while handing out work. He trying to start more beef out here, disrespecting people sisters and daughters!"

"They ain't little girls you just want to suck my dick wishing you was them. When you see it being done but your head is too lazy for me. I keep telling you I'm a fast, sloppy, Harlem pace nigga not no slow, love me D.C. cat."

"Everybody relax just fall back." I calmed the situation and took her back into her room.

I didn't want to stay long but I had to fix this shit. Her white face, and slim body sat on the bed in front of me. When I first met her that's how she gave me head in her office.

"Welo, you got to put someone else in charge or this shit going to crash," she informed.

"First off, don't tell me what I have to do. Secondly, I know he's not your type but he's tough and smart enough to handle this spot. You don't understand about the personnel part of this business? It's about maximizing the full potential out of others talents."

"So, because he fits a profile you going to let him…"

I cut her off, "Listen, and look at me, this is a fuckin' crack house. You should move out, I'll pay for it, but this shit is not a church. You eat off of this, too. So, it's time you moved out before it get crazy. You still get your cut without being on the scene."

She looked at me uneasy like she felt I was being cold to her and she'd done something wrong, like a forgive me look.

"Look let him run this place, you eat not even being here and we all win. You good?"

"Yeah, you can stay. I just need to be around you."

I wanted to but I was hungry more so than horny and had lots of shit to handle. "I'ma hit you up later, be ready."

"Let me just put it in my mouth, Welo!" she said pulling her hair back.

"Later, be ready, for now, start looking for a place to stay, come here get up." She did obediently, I pulled her pants down just to her thighs and fingered her, she was wet. "I'll come get you later," I said liking the idea that she was horny for me. Her head is slow and okay, but she takes it in her ass after arousing me.

"Okay," was all she said as I left.

Ramel had a bag of cash in his hand and was waiting to leave.

"Physcho we going to talk later for now just hold it down," I instructed.

"Got you, Welo."

As we exited the apartment the kids walked ahead of us, down the steps then outside but the lookout was gone and as soon as we all come out of the building gunshots started ranging out.

Blatt! Blatt! Pop! Pop! Pop! Blatt!

"Shoot…shoot!" I yelled, dropping to the ground. "Get them, niggas!"

The kid that was next to me was hit already and on the ground. The other shot over a car, along with Ramel firing away. The sounds were noises of shots and the things they hit. I had my back to the car looking at the two of them fire, now I only heard their shots being fired. The young kid held his gun up and pointed it like a pro as I got up. Ramel went back to the kid that had been shot, shot him in the head and took his beeper, then we ran to the car.

"She set us up!" Ramel said as we pulled off.

"You right, I got her don't sweat it."

CHAPTER EIGHTEEN
DETECTIVE VUGGIO

I didn't want to wake up, but I couldn't sleep, and my phone kept ringing disturbing me, so I had no choice.

"Hello," I said looking over at the clock, it read 11:20 PM. I'd been sleep for only two hours.

"Detective Vuggio this is the desk sergeant at the Twenty-Fifth, Officer McCoy. Your suspect wanted for questioning; Monk is in the school park."

"Okay, send some blue and whites and hold him till morning."

"We also have a person of interest wanted by the T.N.T unit. Keith of One-seventeenth Street. They want his full name and address if possible, without tipping him off."

"You can send the Vice Squad detectives they can handle that."

"Sir, we also received three unanimous tips that weapons are in the park. Our detectives are saying these are people of interest that we need profiled and may fit descriptions to violent crimes committed. With our new comp stat and broken window policy we are adapting, this is a great opportunity for this precinct to have our best out there."

"Okay, okay, I get it. Send for Officer Bengal from my squad. Have the blue and whites on standby and tell the Vice Squad detectives to keep an eye on the situation. I'll be there soon!"

I quickly said a prayer, got out of bed and got dressed, then left for work. This was an Intel operation that could fill in data for everyone making the Joint initiative work. I'll let my team sleep in tonight since they had a homicide suspect to pick in the morning by the name of Wallace Bell, known as Balley. His profile was on my dresser. He'd killed a person in front of witnesses, so it was an open and shut case that they could handle without me. It took fifty minutes without being stopped by traffic to get to Harlem.

The Vice detectives set up blues and whites in position to roll. Detective Shell met me on Park Avenue with binoculars and told me he could no longer see Monk in the yard.

I spoke into the radio so that everyone on standby could hear. "I need you to keep everyone in the groups they're in. Do not mix them up. Arrest anyone you find with anything illegal. But let me know who they are with, give all this intel to Officer, Bengal. When searching a group larger than the officers present, have one officer observe and ready to help, watching those not being searched. Let's be smart and aware. Safety is first, be ready in thirty seconds."

I walked up to Lexington Avenue in the same clothes from the day before, work was becoming my life. The Keith description was not anyone I cared for, but Welo and his crew were. I knew he'd ordered the murder of Glock who beat him in a fist fight. I have a description of the shooter that no one in the yard fitted so far.

"Go it's a go!" I said into the radio.

Officers ran into the yard as marked and unmarked cars rolled up. The kid crew from 122nd Street started running as officers chased them. Others were throwing stuff all over hoping not to be seen. I entered the yard behind cops and scanned the ground for guns but only drugs were being tossed. The kids got away after they climbed on top of the roof. It looked like they were laughing. One looked directly into my eyes. If my team was here, we woulda caught them on 3rd Avenue. They began to hit officers in their faces with rocks. That made me want to go after them, but I decided not to. I had too much to process and I saw my prime suspect that I wanted to detain.

Officer Bengal came next to me as officers were searching suspects and gathering information. "Go to every officer and get the intel I asked for," I instructed then pointed to a heavy black man. "Make the arrest of that heavy guy right there, he's from Jefferson projects. Put those unclaimed drugs on the ground on him. They call him, Chubbs, he fits the description of a shooter from a case four months ago. Let's put him through the system on light drug charges and I'll get the witness to come in before he's released to see if he can be identified."

Officer Bengal took over the search of Chubbs and two females near him.

I called over Detective Shell. "That guy right there street name is Ramsey, he's a suspect for homicide in Carver projects, but we have nothing, put those cracks…" *Blatt! Blatt!* I was cut off by the sudden ring of shots fired. I pulled my gun out. "What…are they crazy?" *Blatt!* Another rang out, it was from a small caliber pistol and close by.

Officer Bengal radioed in, "Shots fired coming from Third Avenue."

I ran in that direction getting angry. Someone was shooting seconds away from us and only a few feet away from the precinct. As I turned the corner, I saw that the officers had someone on the ground.

"Let me see your hands!" a cop told him with his weapon drawn.

"I'm shot this shit burns," the person laying on his side said while bleeding.

"Hands out," the cop said with authority being ignored while the man held his wounds. Another officer in front of me pointed his gun at the bleeding suspect from a distance.

I tapped his shoulder then he lowered his weapon, "Go search everybody you see, go…go!" Then I attended to the bleeding man. "Who did this son?" I asked searching him quickly.

"I don't know, I was walking, and shots came, "he lied.

"You're stupid, you will get killed next time. Who did this?" I finished frisking him, he was clean of any weapons.

"I don't know," he repeated.

I looked up 3rd Avenue, knowing the school was behind the supermarket, those kids up on the roof must of came this way. My radio barked, "We got a gun."

Detective Shell came and I asked him to take over this shooting scene as he radioed for an ambulance and officers assisted him. I hurried back to the yard. I saw the gun offender who I knew to be a small dealer named, Capone.

"Don't push him through the system, hold him for me," I told the arresting officers. Tomorrow I will get those kids from 122nd and Lexington Avenue. Capone was from there as well. "God, I wish detective Blanch was here with me," I mumbled seeing someone else of interest. I radioed to Detective Shell, "Respond back to me after you find out where the shooting victim is from."

"Roger that."

This was a lot to sort out and Welo's crew had Players in it that I wanted addresses for, Ray The Boss was definitely on my radar.

"Sir, I found a nine-millimeter gun," a blue and white told me showing a sweater with the gun in it.

"Where?"

"In this sweater by the wall next to no one." He pointed.

I looked at everyone's face being detained close to where the gun was found and saw Sam from Foster who was out of place here and also a suspect in a subway murder. "That guy, Samuel Jenkins book him for it."

"Yes, sir."

I walked over to Welo and his crew telling the blue and whites what intel I wanted. My mind was on what I had planned as the arrest was being made. I took Welo's keys as he was being searched and walked away.

On my way to Welo's car an officer was observing a different search.

"Arrest that little kid next to that man and if he vouches for him let the kid go after they give proof of who the man is and where he lives. If he does not vouch for the kid arrest him for loitering." I pointed out Keith of 117th Street, my mind was running full speed, fuck rest.

Welo, Danny Rios, had money in his trunk. I didn't bother to count it. I will inform the T.N.T unit of it. The car and dry-cleaned clothes in the back smelled new. These guys lived this short fast life not making it to their thirties, not experiencing enough life to even make changes.

My radio interrupted my thoughts, "Shell to Vuggio, the shooting victim's home address is Johnson projects."

"Got it, thank you," I said and went back to my thoughts for a minute. Those kids don't have dealings in that area that I know of, so far, I saw no retaliation as the motive.

In the precinct my work continued. I had witnesses picked up, line ups arranged and called Detectives about the cases as I drank coffee after coffee and handled the paperwork. Officer Bengal gave me a list of eight groups, Welo's, Ray's, Keith's, Capone's and one saying: *Running Kids* from 122nd Street on Lexington Avenue, with descriptions along with other groups as well.

"What about the females in the yard, what do we do with 'em?"

"Search them and let them go."

Antonio Vega also known as Tone had a light rap sheet, a gun charge dismissed, and another gun charge that he did a year in jail for along with a loitering charge all on 122nd Street. He was cuffed and sitting down when I came in and sat in front of him.

"So, you want this gun charge, or you want to talk? One chance you know who I am."

"Can I walk from here…after?" he asked

"Don't work like that son, but if you have the goods, I will help you."

He smirked not looking away. "Can you lose the loaded weapon and give me a plain weapon charge?"

"What you got let's start with that. I can only help you from there, and yes if you tell me enough of what I need that will be done."

He couldn't wait to talk, "Those dudes that got away…"

"Yeah, what about them?"

"That's Eric Rosario, he's the guy responsible for all the violence on one-twenty second."

I looked unimpressed. "Dates…actual events I need them."

Capone thought for a second, "The day Tyson lost, a kid was placed in a coma and other people were hurt. That was him, he hit the guy with a table."

I knew that incident, but this seemed like he hated the person he was talking about. I continued listening to him for hours and got information for the 23rd precinct. I believed Tone did not want to tell things he knew close to home except for Eric Rosario. Who was in his way somehow and he wanted to eliminate him, but I cared for none of that. Capone insured me Eric kept a gun outside every time he was out under a car tire nearby. With only a power nap in the precinct, I worked through the night. The next day I met with my team after their shifts. I wanted Eric Rosario off the streets, so we went to pick him up. He was spotted easy and we found the gun as the informant told us. Eric Rosario was a hard ass. He refused to say a word, so I overcharged him with drugs so we could confiscate the money he had on him. Plus, the gun and misdemeanor assault on three police officers for the rock incident, he just rubbed me the wrong way.

CHAPTER NINETEEN
CINDY

"Chantel, you better not leave me when we go inside. I'm telling you!"

"I'm not…I'm not, he better have somebody cute with him though."

"Whatever, Chantel, you not leaving me by myself." I held onto her arm as walked to the school. She was just slightly bigger than me.

"What…you scared he going to get you alone and put his thing in you? Ah…ha…"

"Stop playing I'm not giving Buddha none, he's a player. Until he shows me, he for real he can't even sniff it."

"Yeah, right, if he wants to lick it you going to be like…huh." She opened her legs with her pelvis out in front of her walking and laughing.

"Don't even play me like that."

We walked into the school yard together, holding each other. There were a lot of people around, some of them were good looking females. I wondered if Buddha dealt with any of them. We walked up on him as he talked to a cute girl next to him.

"This is the type my mouth be on."

'*She's cuter than me*,' I thought but she dressed like a boy.

Me and Chantel both looked at him and he was smiling, showing off his cute, chubby cheeks. Then he gave me a hug smelling like weed.

"Cindy this is Guy my homie," he said.

"Well, who you got for me? I need a Harlem slide off for when I come down here with her," Chantel told Buddha.

"We got all kinds. What you want a money nigga…a big nigga…a ballplayer? This Harlem, baby!"

"She wants somebody to be nice to her," I said.

"No, I don't I want a combo, Buddha. Get me an order of big hands and money on the side to go."

"Chantel you better stop." I was getting mad because I knew she better not be like that for real.

"Anyway, how you doing, Guy? My friend is rude."

"Hey, Guy, that's a cute name and you cute, too," Chantel said to her.

"There you go some action," Buddha said.

Guy looked at Chantel then back at the game that was getting a lot of attention, while ignoring Buddha's comment. I liked this girl.

Buddha held me. "I don't be doing this affection thing in public but since you giving me some tonight, you're the exception to the rule," he said.

"Yeah, right you better use your hands tonight."

He grabbed me from behind and I felt his dick poking through his pants on my ass. I pushed back on him to feel more and felt it grow. Buddha was laughing and had others laughing as he stood behind me making me feel like I was his. A couple of people kept coming to talk to Chantel, but she liked a Spanish kid who never looked at her. Buddha said his name was Chito. I felt danger all around me for some reason, but it was for Monk if he stayed here something was going to happen to him.

"Let's go, Buddha, take me home."

"Hold up wait till…"

"Wait nothing!" I cut him off. "Seriously, I got school tomorrow and I want to go home."

I pulled him and the three of us left headed to 3rd Avenue. He called a cab company from a phone booth and we waited only five minutes for the car to arrive. We stopped at a Chinese restaurant on 2nd Avenue between 122nd and 123rd called May-May's. People were shooting dice right in front of it.

Somebody called out to Chantel, "How you doing, you got a minute for me?"

Chantel looked back and said to me, "I'ma talk to him till we leave."

"Go ahead, I'm right here," I said, watching her from inside the small place through a large plexiglass window that exposed the whole small store with only one small table and two seats to it inside.

People waited outside and the little Chinese lady everybody called May-May knew them all. She yelled out their orders once their food was ready by name. As they retrieve their orders, they held conversations as if they were friends and she gave them nods but no real responses. We ordered six orders of wings and gave May-May six dollars, for eighteen fried wings.

"May-May the shit, right?" Monk said smiling. "Better not be no cat in here." He held up the bag and she just nodded then we left.

Chantel said bye to the guy she was talking to. "That was green-eyed, Tone." She told me with a joyful smile.

"You open on them Wagna niggas, huh?" Monk asked.

"He a cutie is all I know, and I got his beeper number too," she said smiling from ear to ear with her eyes closed.

We dropped Chantel off and Buddha walked me home. When we got in front of my door, I told him, "If you stop playing and be real. We can do something, but I'm not your play pussy."

"I got you, I'm not even going to play myself like that I see you special," he told me.

"Okay, so, you telling me there is no one else?"

"If I say that can I get some, right now?"

"No, stupid be serious…I'm not playing."

"No, I'm not saying that, I'm saying give me a minute to tell you that but don't fall back on me yet. Okay?"

I looked at him in thought for a moment, taking in what he was really trying to say to me. "Not okay, but we can work on it." I gave him a wet kiss.

"I told you, I'm not into this kissing or public affection thing."

"Shut up, stupid." We hugged and he walked away, then I called him back. "Wait come here." He turned around and walked back over to me. "Let me touch it," I said.

Without a word he unzipped his pants, putting my hand inside and I felt it grow, it was big. His eyes were on what I was doing down there. I went from his face to what he saw too. I put my hands on his balls, then the tip pulled it back and then held it. It grew longer than the length of my palm. I'ma ask Chantel is that big because it scared me a little as I let it go. I left him standing there as I made my way inside the house.

"Oh, word it's like that?" Monk yelled behind me.

From behind the closed door, I said, "Goodbye, hubby."

CHAPTER TWENTY

ERIC ROSARIO

Somebody was telling or they'd been watching us. I heard Vuggio say check the car tires when he put me on the ground in handcuffs. They didn't see who'd put the gun there because they didn't know which car tire it was hidden under. They just knew we put guns in the car tires. No matter what he was taking me in. He had me in cuffs before finding anything. Fuck we lost the Nine.

I sat in a cell alone in the precinct thinking. Shawnty was let go, which wasn't surprising. Vuggio be wanting guns not drugs. Shawnty did not know the gun was there so my quick thinking of anything bad on him vanished. I was just happy he got let go and wasn't going to be caught in this bullshit. All the other prisoners arrested was taken out for further processing to the bookings an hour ago. Why was I here?

It was dark and silent, only footsteps were heard. They sounded clear and was approaching the cell I sat in. They stopped and I felt a presence standing over me.

"So, you want to talk before we start the paperwork?" It was Vuggio.

I didn't even look at him, I just stood facing the wall. We were separated by the bars. Tee's father always said if you're ever arrested don't try and be smarter than them by running your mouth. They do this more times than you, just be quiet and let them do what they gotta do.

"You're in a lot of trouble for assaulting cops in the park last night. We also got you for a gun and drugs. We taking that fourteen hundred you had on you, it's confiscated as drug proceeds. Any time you have a drug charge, my friend, we take your money."

I coughed and took my eyes off the wall, then looked to the floor only seeing him through my peripheral. It was a fake cough, but I almost told him, you know those drugs were not mine. I wanted to ask him what he was talking about, assaulting officers. Did some cop get hurt while they were chasing us? I assaulted no cop, then thought about the gunshots. Did a cop get shot, and they're blaming me? I looked up and saw him looking at me.

Tee's father was in my head, "*Keep your mouth shut.*" So, I did.

"I'll tell you what. Let me make it easy on you, Welo and Ray The Boss…just tell me what you know about them and the drugs go away. You keep your money then we can go from there. Everybody knows I won't make a deal and not keep it."

One of my bad habits hurt me. I liked to keep money for dice games or buying stuff off the streets and didn't want to miss out on it. Now I'd fucked that package up. I shook it off and thought about who talked to him before me? And who would after.

"I arrest people all the time, I arrest people that hurt kids like you. Kids that commit violence and think they are the only ones that have a gun or can swing their fists, or a table until they find themselves hurt." I heard him but I wasn't listening. "Fine with me, no deals for you." He left.

Being arrested was a crazy mind game, we were treated like cattle. I spent six hours in the precinct going in and out of the cell, getting fingerprinted, searched and questioned to now riding to Central bookings to do it all over again. I sat in the back of the paddy wagon, with my wrists cuffed to a chain, connected to a longer chain, that connected sixteen people mostly men except about three who were young like me. We were crammed in the back of a truck with steel enforced walls that made it tighter. Most people here were busted on drug charges and some were talking about their case. New clothes and jewelry were all around along with the bummy and smelly, custies.

We hit a bump that made all of us bounce high off the steel bench and land back down on it hurting our asses. I heard others cussing and complaining as we hit another bump. The older men were telling us what to expect. Hearing them talk about their cases took our minds off the bumps. I was tempted to ask about mine to this older cat who had a lot of answers for others but decided to stay quiet. When we made it to Central Bookings it was like a farm and we were the animals. As soon as we got off the van, they took our personal property and our shoelaces, and placed them in an envelope. Then they moved us one by one to the next cell.

After that, they took our fingerprints, then to the next cell, where they took our mugshots. All during this process, I saw new people coming through after us, headed to the same cells. We left and others ahead of us were telling us what cells we were going to and what to expect. We began mixing in during the process, every cell was shaped differently, but they all had toilets and one sink with a metal bench that ran across the wall. At times I saw people nodding off to sleep one minute then standing up the next like a damn zombie. Being so tired from this process and the precinct wait I wanted to nod off myself.

I was ready for them to move things and get finished. People who were arrested from New York City were processed here. The last cell for Central Bookings was a holding pen that was crowded with at least forty people, as soon as they put me in, and the guard left a fight broke out.

"Give me them fuckin' sneakers nigga." The man who looked about twenty-six said, beating up a younger kid who was probably about eighteen.

The kid submitted and fell to the floor covering his face while getting punched. His new uptowns were taken off his feet and a pair of old dirty Reeboks were thrown at him. I waited to see what was next as all the shenanigans were interrupted by the guards showing up outside of the large pen. The veterans lined up fast for the food about to be given out. The kid on the floor began putting on the dirty sneakers in a slow, shameful manner, refusing to look at anyone. He was defeated and reduced to lower standing in his own eyes.

I got on the end of the line and watched the robber as he kept his eye on his victim not wanting to become a victim himself. The kid got off the floor and looked down at his feet as he walked to the very end in disgrace. A C.O. was staring into the cell checking everyone visually and spotted the kid with all new clothes and bummy sneakers. He appeared out of place and slightly bruised in the face, so the C.O. pointed it out to another C.O. who looked at him intentionally up and down.

"Hey, youngster, you cut or want another cell?"

"No!" the kid said with an attitude he'd developed.

The C.O. then started giving out sandwiches, putting them between the bars to be taken by the moving line. I looked at the dirty Reeboks on his feet and started feeling angry, but I moved up in the line to my turn and took my food.

"Cop and go," the C.O. instructed, using a term we used for selling drugs in the streets.

It was like we were the customers now. I found a spot on the steel bench that was crowded shoulder to shoulder then tore open the plastic that wrapped up two sandwiches. I placed one on my lap and balanced it so that it wouldn't fall. The bread was crumbling in my hand hard, around the ends. I took big bites trying not to taste it, making faces while I ate. The second one I peeled back the bread and saw the bright pink meat that was bologna.

A man saw my disgust and told me, "That's called a cop-out sandwich."

Everyone in the cell laughed and another guy replied, "Yeah, once you get tired of eating it you going to cop out quick."

I got up, went to the toilet and flushed it down. At the sink, I pushed hard on a button to get a drink of water. The first attempt was hard, but I pressed the second time and a low drizzle finally flowed out. I slurped the warm water that had a clear tint of rust in it, it gave me another nasty taste to add to the one I already had.

The guy who'd taken the sneakers was looking at me. All my clothes and sneakers were new, and my Uptowns were crispier then the ones he'd just taken. I balled up my fists and felt my face get tight, I was ready to fight.

When he finished chewing his food, he got up off the bench and said, "Yo' E.R. what's good, what they got you for?"

I recognized him from Wagna projects, now that he'd spoken to me. He was related to a friend of mine that I went to Junior High 45 with. I remembered meeting him twice not really having any real convo, but we talked. The rest of the people in the pen was in conversations and our seats were swallowed up causing us to stand.

People were sleeping on the floor and I thought to myself, '*That will never be me.*'

"I'm good they got me on some bullshit I didn't do. A hammer they say they found and some other shit," I told him.

"Yeah, that's all of us, I ain't do shit either." He laughed and gave me a hug as others watched.

We talked again his voice was loud over the others it was clear he wasn't letting his arrest faze him. He was still confident and proud. Which gave me some kind of hope since I was starting to feel low. I'd been dealing with all of this for more than a day now. As time was passing more people started going to the floor to sleep, some even slept under the steel benches, curled up with their arms tucked inside their shirts for warmth. We talked for what seemed like hours and the cold that left off the steel cell bars and brick walls I could feel in my bones.

"Why you call me, E.R?" I asked.

"I heard how you be doing them niggas on Lexington. Every beef you be having they end up in the Emergency Room and people were like you know that's, E.R."

An annoying loud sound interrupted us. It was the steel keys banging on the steel bars awaking the people who slept.

"Listen up!" The C.O. yelled. "When I call your name step out, say your birthdate and address." He started calling out names, that evoked some nervousness in me.

People walked out of the cell in groups after being called and were escorted by a C.O. that waited for them to a court part. Some inmates were so slow they were forgetting to say their birthdates and addresses. Which caused the C.O. to start yelling at them, I told myself to be ready for that. When they stopped calling names I did not know how to feel. I wanted to get called but did not want to face a judge, I did not want to accept this. The pen was emptied out to half and conversations immediately came back to life.

Me and my friend took two spots on the bench next to each other and kept talking until I finally fell asleep. After a while, I was just not able to stay up and it seemed like he woke me as soon as my eyes closed.

"I'm out they called my name. Hold your head see you on the island," he said.

I was tired, hungry and felt alone. The cell was now crowded again with mostly faces I'd never seen before. Most of their conversations were the same questions that we'd all asked. I stretched out and stood up, then my seat was swallowed up as I leaned on the gate and sat on the floor. After another bologna sandwich meal that I didn't eat, I called my moms on the pay phone in the cell. I told my sister, Angie, where I had money hidden for my bail and to have mom waiting at court for me. After the call, I went back to my spot on the floor and just stared at the faces around me.

Clang! Clang! Clang! Clang!

The key sound was aggravating. I opened my eyes due to the loud noise, I jumped up from where I was laid out on the floor.

"Alright, listen up! If I call your name come out saying your birth date and address," the C.O. said and started calling more names.

"Eric Rosario!"

Recognizing my name, I moved forward. I felt wobbly and weak, I was tired in different ways and sad with frustration as I walked out, just glad to be moving on.

"Birthdate!" the C.O. yelled at me angrily.

"Oh, two-eleven-seventy-three."

"Address…what are you stupid or something? You can't hear?"

"Nineteen ninety Lexington Avenue."

"Follow the C.O…listen everybody that comes out say your birth…"

I didn't hear the last of the sentence as I was led away along with another group. In this pen, people were more alive. Some paced and a few slept. This pen was different, it had two tiny men booths that we could enter on our side and the lawyer could on his side that was separated by two windows. A kid came out and the lawyer called another to go in. A lawyer came dressed in a sharp suit to the other booth and a black kid got up knowing it was for him as he entered from our side. He had a private one and wasn't being represented by legal aid like the most of us. I told myself not to sleep but I did anyway. I awoke to my name being called, by a lawyer and got off the floor.

He spoke first, "Okay, Mr. Rosario, you have a prior drug sale pending in front of Judge Slezzinger and some serious charges now." I waited, wanting to hear what they'd charged me with. He looked at me and asked, "Do you speak English?"

"Yeah…yeah, I do. I just want to know what I'm here for."

"What…you don't know?"

"Just tell me already please!"

"Well, the top charge is penal law two-sixty-five a loaded gun possession. Then you have two aggravated assaults on police officers. Then a drug possession charge with the intent to sell. So…"

"Wait…tell me about the assault, what they said I did?"

"Oh, okay, we only have the felony complaint for now." He then read down the paper mumbling to himself. "You hit two police officers in the face with rocks."

"This is bullshit…where…when?"

"I don't have time for this they will be calling us to court soon."

"Listen just tell me where this happened…what they…" then I realized it, they saw us tossing rocks over the building. We were throwing them just to be throwing them kid shit for fun at nothing.

The lawyer noticed my hesitation and said, "So, that's a misdemeanor."

"Please just get me a low bail as low as you can, and we can talk later."

He asked a few more questions and left. I sat down and a fight broke out again. Both guys were swinging away, and the guard came, broke it up and removed them from the pen. My name was called, I was taken to the court part and put into another cell. This one was small with only three others in it and for the first time no toilet and sink. They called one of us and he left us waiting only four minutes and came back with the C.O.s. I noticed they were not city corrections guard but state C.O.s wearing different uniforms. All four of us were nervous and quiet.

They finally called me to court, I was escorted by a C.O. and immediately saw my mother and Tiffany in the audience behind a low wall, that separated the spectators and the court. Another C.O. with a holstered gun had his back to them and was waiting for me with a seat pulled out in front of them for me to sit in and face the judge.

I heard a clear crisp voice say, "Docket number ninety-one-six-six-five-two-four-four-one, Eric Rosario."

All else was just noise to me. I sat next to my lawyer telling him my mother and Tiffany was in the audience. He looked back at them to make sure. The air was cold and clean, the judge sat higher up than us in a huge wooden desk, bigger than any you would see in life. I remembered Tee's father telling us they did this for intimidation tactics. It was natural animal instincts in the wild to have, fear, as we looked up at him.

My lawyer said something about family support, and I was in school, but I was so tired I just wanted to sleep and eat then I heard a date, this caught my full attention.

The judge said, "Bail is six-thousand."

The gavel banged awaking me, and I felt someone under my arm as I was being helped to my feet and escorted out. I waited only a minute in the small cell I was escorted back to the cell I'd left and back to the one before that, then to a different one. Now I saw some of the same faces from before who'd been processed already and returned.

My friend from earlier yelled out to me, "E.R.…yo' E.R., what's your bail?"

"Six, I'll be out soon," I replied hopefully.

"Well, if they don't got it on them you going to the island with me."

CHAPTER TWENTY-ONE
TALL-TALL MAN

The weather broke and it was still a little cold as I sat at Rucker's Park on 155th Street watching the team practice with a couple of onlookers seeing the action. They were pretty good as one of them caught an alley and dunked the ball on a break and my heart sunk feeling heavy looking at my leg in a cast. I pictured that Little Kid's face and mine drew tight. He destroyed my life and my family's hopes for me to play ball or at least finish college.

I could hear him laughing, saying, "That's the kid who plays ball!"

I felt pain in my leg just thinking about the incident. A group of people was walking past me with that money kid Alvin, talking fast to them.

He looked back and glanced at my face. "Shit ain't you that college kid, that used to fuck with, Rick?"

"Yeah," I simply responded.

"Damn, you can play ball, B. Wanna rock out with this team when you heal up? I got talent here to beat the Nike team, plus, take the tournament. Ain't nobody fucking with us. So, what's good?"

"Nah, I…I can't play no ball," I said the hurt and pain in my voice was evident.

He looked confused and told his people, "Yo', yar bounce over there, I'll catch up to yar." He sat, we talked for a while and I explained everything to him. "I know the exact niggas you talking about. I don't like them anyway. You just gave me a reason. I'll send my people to get at them," he told me.

"It's not going down like that, this is personal. I need to do this myself," I informed him.

"I hear you, B, that's why Rick fucked with you. I hear you and I'm still here…I'm right here anything you need just let me know, B."

It was funny because I always thought he had something to do with Rick's death. Now I didn't think so since he seemed to be repaying him.

Before he walked away, I said, "I do need a favor now that you mention it."

Later that night, I was home with my grandmother, she was in the living room and I was in my bedroom holding the gun Alvin gave me. I'd never shot one in my entire life. As I unloaded and reloaded it, I kept seeing them beating me. I held onto the gun, feeling a tear run down my face. My mind was racing as I sat alone in my room staring up into the ceiling.

"Why…why me, God?" I cried out. "Was I that bad?" I tasted the salty tears and saw my career fading away right when it was supposed to start. I did my best to do good all my life. I skipped out on selling and using drugs and went to school when I was supposed to. What the fuck happened? It's like I just woke up a drug addict with a busted leg, out of school and now holding a gun. I mean I even walk with a limp now like an addict. I used to see addicts and not even think they had a regular life.

"Oh, God, why me…why me? This can't be, nah this ain't right!" I got so angry the sadness left. "I don't care if he is a kid, he's gonna pay, I'ma handle this shit. Fuck…fuck…fuck! The doctor said I will never be able to jump off this leg or walk the same ever again."

I must have fallen asleep because I awoke to my grandmother bringing me some orange juice, toast, eggs, and bacon. She placed it on the dresser, said nothing and just left the room, leaving me to my thoughts. As I laid in the bed, I was no longer sad, just angry as all hell. There would be no more crying. I laughed picturing what I was going to do. Then I got up, so I could get ready to leave and get the cast taken off. I also needed to get ready to handle the motherfuckers who'd done this to me.

CHAPTER TWENTY-TWO
KEITH

My personal driver, Thomas was with me on Long Island making the house come alive. I knew Thomas when I lived in Brooklyn and he just happened to be an O'Jay driver in Harlem where we developed a better relationship. We were like family now; he was never one to get into trouble and was just a good guy.

I watched him in the kitchen through an opened counter space next to the Bell Atlantic lady, she came a half hour ago and he took her around the house, as she installed telephone lines in all the bedrooms, the living room and now the kitchen. She did look cute in her uniform her hair was tied up in a bun and she was working on one knee by the wooden counter with tools in her hand. Thomas stood by her talking and as she looked back over her shoulder smiling at him, he got closer, that's when I walked away.

The cable man called me into the living room, turned on the television and I started singing the words with the puppet characters that appeared on the T.V.

"Worries for another, let the music play!"

As a Fragile Rock preview played on HBO the cable man spoke, "I thought it was just me, but I like that show too."

We both laughed, I did like that show and gave myself a mental note to watch it with Ciera. She was home with Abuela and Melinda. Melinda said she was going to be out shopping early today at the Baby Gap. So, I took this time to handle some business and set the house up to surprise them later. He handed me paperwork to sign and I thanked him with a twenty-dollar tip and walked him to the front door. It was ten in the morning now and I had got a lot done. We picked up twenty keys from my connect E, at six this morning after I paid him three-hundred, forty thousand for my last load, the keys were upstairs in a trunk with cleaning items, bathroom supplies and a few other things we'd picked up at stores.

I had Thomas pick me up this morning in a Caravan instead of the town car. So, I'd look like an average person doing average people shit. I even installed Ciera's baby car seat in the back-passenger seat. I told Thomas that she would be coming later, although she nor Mel was not going to be here today. I had the blue baby bag filled with baby stuff and the Uzi under it all looking like an average Joe. If the police decided to pull over people, they'd have many to stop before getting to us. Many get caught on stops that just be straight harassment or stereotypes. I used those same stereotypes to be exactly the opposite as a way of avoiding them.

There was a knock at the door, and I placed the baby bag around my shoulder letting it rest on my hip, the O'Jay driver was relaxed, he walked from the kitchen looking in my direction with a big smile and a bop in his step.

"I got the seven digits," he said pointing with his head back toward the Bell Atlantic lady working. "I got the door too…I got everything."

He headed to the door without any thoughts but of us being people moving into a new house, in a new place, not knowing he'd just transported earlier enough drugs to give him twenty-five to life if caught. Not knowing that people would kill us for what was upstairs. He was just a cab driver helping me move and that is what made everything seem that way, him not knowing.

I could tell he was enjoying the move as his own as he opened the door. A man stood there saying he was a mover from the furniture store. I walked over and looked outside and saw his truck parked next to our Caravan with the furniture store's logo that I shopped at and relaxed a little when a BMW with

Connecticut plates pulled up and parked behind the vehicles. I greeted the mover expecting the BMW would be here at this time.

Two other movers waited by the truck and watched the female driver and two males leave the car. The movers stared hard as she passed them coming to me. I watched them watch her which told me they were really movers acting like regular men, doing a job and not focused on anything else. Their eyes trailed up her body from top to bottom, eyeing her high heels that went up to her pants. Her pants looked painted on, she had curved legs that led up to the tied-up coat tightly around her waist covering an hourglass shape underneath. Her coat opened up in flaps around the neck showing a flat, solid, gold necklace with diamond stud earrings on a small Latina or white face. A face that wore light make-up, she was elegant to them and they said nothing verbal but everything with their eyes, she was just good business for me.

She walked up to me and gave me an exaggerated hug, then looked at me as she let go.

"Meet me by the television, I'll be there in a few minutes," I instructed.

"Okay, whatever, you say, Keith," she said, and her two friends followed behind her.

Thomas looked at me confused with a lifted eyebrow. "It's nothing like that just wait right there by the stairs. I need you to do something," I told him, then turned to speak to the movers. "You can start bringing in everything now. I'll tell you where it goes after it's all in."

"Sure, no problem is that the wife?" the mover asked.

"Nah, if the wife was here your friend's eyes would have popped out of their heads."

"Wow, what a life," he said smiling and turned headed back to his truck.

"Thomas, wait by the steps and don't let no one go upstairs…no one!" I stated.

He just nodded and sat on the steps watching the movers as they started bringing the furniture in. We began moving the sofas and couches to the living room and the guests put it to immediate use. Seeing the VCR, I noted I needed to buy some more kid tapes for us to watch. I directed a few things upstairs to the bedroom and went up there to oversee things until everyone went back down and Thomas stood by the stairs with the Bell Atlantic lady talking. The empty house now had two rooms that were nearly completed with new furniture.

In the living room, my three guests were all seated and watching TV. I walked the movers to the door, tipping all three of them a hundred each. The Bell Atlantic lady took that opportunity to leave as well. She gave Thomas a hug and I tipped her fifty dollars. When she left, he looked back at me smiling, this was a good day for him, reminding me to pay him and get it out of the way. Where he usually made thirty dollars an hour to drive, I counted out a thousand and gave it to him for the whole day.

"Good, looking, Keith. I really appreciate this man, I don't be seeing no thousand together at once," Thomas stated.

"You deserve it, bro, you do a good job," I assured him.

"Anytime Keith, you don't know how much you help me." He gave me a hug.

In the living room, I did not want small talk as Thomas came in behind me in a joyful mood. "Keith take off that baby bag already Ciera is not here yet."

I put on a phonie smile like the bag meant nothing and placed it by the TV away from the couches.

"Being a dad is twenty-four hours a day, Thomas." I sat closer to the bag, then anyone else and told Thomas, "Go find us a Chinese store or some fast food and give me the bill. I'm hungry!"

Thomas left without questioning, happy to do his job he was paid for.

"I see you busy making a home, Keith. So, we can be fast since you don't like me no more and it's all business with you."

"Yeah, that's all good, but I'm here alone. Why don't you tell your people to wait for you outside?"

They looked at me, one of them I knew from when I was out there hustling. She was looking around the place shaking her head up and down. Then she faced me as she finished surveying everything. They stood waiting for her to say something.

"Go ahead, wait in the car. I'll be ten minutes, Keith wants me to himself," she ordered, seductively looking into my eyes as she spoke.

"We here if you need us," one said, and she just nodded as they left.

"So, what's good, Keith? How's your little Mel and life?"

"Good…good!"

"And that dangerous security you have by the name of Scottie, he still protecting you?"

"Till death do us part," I said thankful to Scottie for showing me how to rush people with short answers.

"I'm surprised we doing business here," she admitted.

"The safest place I could think of."

She stopped the questions and went into her purse, taking out neatly stacked bills held together with rubber bands. I saw a small handgun inside the bag also.

"Don't hurt yourself. What's your help for if you gotta carry?" I asked.

"Keith, please, I know what's in that baby bag of yours. You fool many, but I know your slick ass. Shit, it's probably that same ass Uzi you like to have when you're alone." She smiled a real smile and that shit got to me.

My beeper went off for the second time since we'd been talking, both times it was Scottie.

"Keith, you not finished with me that fast, are you?" Her flirting didn't stop.

She would learn nothing would come of it. I didn't think she understood how my love for Mel was more than she could ever love herself.

"We B-I only baby girl, let's never confused that. If you can't flow with that, the next time just send the dude you came with today that I know. You have my word his safety is backed by my guarantee."

"Maybe there won't be a next time." Her face did not move after that comment, only her lips as she stared at me.

I cocked my head ready to respond, thinking on her reply, needing her B-I to continue as part of my retirement plan, but nothing was worth more than Mel.

"Fine, Keith, I'm messing around, you win." She touched her earlobes slowly then took the money in her little hands that rested on her lap.

She walked over to the brand-new wooden table and placed the money on it. The sight was worth a picture, it just looked good, a beautiful, tough woman placing a stack of hundreds on a brand-new wooden table, then her purse dropped, and she bent over at the waist to pick it up, showing the imprint of her pussy in the tight material hugging her body. She stood up and turned to look at.

"Two keys, please," she said.

I did enjoy the sight of looking at her. I didn't think there was nothing wrong with a few harmless peeks, but my mind stayed on safety mode.

"Wait here just a minute," I told her picking the money up off the table and walking past her. "I'll be right back." I walked out of the living room, then came back in with her eyeing me and walking towards the TV.

As I grabbed the baby bag, she laughed hard, breaking her persona. I kept my composure as I walked away laughing, too. I went upstairs in a hurry to get this done. In the chest, twenty-keys were all wrapped individually in saran wrap and I took out two eyeing the eighteen giving them a quick count and placed the money in the space the keys were just in, then rushed back downstairs getting to her and placing the keys on top of the table.

"What no scale?" she asked.

"For real you want a scale?"

"All business right, Keith, we need to be right."

I went back up the stairs this time taking the Uzi out of the bag, cocking it and placing it on top of the stuff in the bag leaving it unzipped. She'd just irked me a little and I wanted to not let other emotions keep me from being on point. I hurried back up the stairs, retrieved the scale and a small mirror, then ran back down into the living room. I saw her coat off and her bag next to it. I placed everything on the table. The triple beam scale couldn't weigh a key at once you had to break it down. I was mad at myself for not bringing a digital scale with me to the house.

"May I?" she asked.

"Of course, go ahead."

She put the scale weights on zero to see if it balanced out. Of course, it did, of course, she knew it would and she stepped back looking bored and said, "Forget it, if it's short I'll bill you later." She took the razor from her purse and unwrapped one key, then began chopping a small piece off. Then chopped that piece that was about three points of a gram into fine dust on the mirror. Her hand went into her bra, she pulled out a bill, rolled it into a straw and sat in front of it taking a snort of the white powder into one nostril after the other gesturing for me to try it.

"I'm good," I refused.

She closed her eyes for a second feeling and tasting it then said, "Wow, Keith, I guess you really did change. This shit is good, it feels like a vacuum is sucking in cold air up my nose." She then wet the tip of her fingertips with her mouth and wiped the coke off her razor tasting the Coke once more and put the razor back into her purse.

"Uummm!" she said very low. "That's good Coke, Keith."

As I escorted her out, I thought to myself, *'Someone else is gonna have to make the sales with her. She herself is not a problem but with the Coke my other love that I gave up, it's too much.'*

I made a profit of sixteen thousand that fast when we got to the door, she turned back to me.

"I'll see you next week so we can arrange our next buy," she said, I nodded, and she left.

After closing the door behind her, I went to the phone to beep Scottie and give him the house number. Plus, beeping three others and ignoring some that I would take care of later. I put away the scale and small mirror that had some Coke left on it on top of the refrigerator. I was placing the furniture exactly how I wanted it when another knock came at the door.

I let Thomas back in, he was carrying bags of food and singing, "Nobody beats the Biz nobody beats the Biz!" He was smiling and clearly in a good mood after meeting a new good-looking woman and making a thousand dollars.

I joined in with him feeling good myself, doing the dance of Biz Markie as we walked into the kitchen. He played a tape in the big radio; he'd bought in earlier. It started playing *Rob Base*: '*It Takes Two*' to make things go right. He did that dance, too. I was not a dancer, but I tried it after he showed me again. I surprised myself once I got it right and fitted it to the beat. We were in the groove when the phone ringing stopped us. I picked it up and Thomas took the food out onto the counter still singing the song. I was feeling happy as shit that I'd really gotten out.

"Keith," Scottie's voice came on the line.

"Yeah, what's up, Unc?" I asked.

"I saw, Melinda."

"What you doing downtown, Scottie?"

"I'm staking that nigga out?"

"So how you…" I froze in my thoughts for a moment.

"Yeah!" He stayed silent on his end and me on mines.

I felt my heart drop and pain replaced it. My thoughts went to what he'd told me without him telling me. I could feel my pulse by my ear from holding the phone tight to my face. My heart was beating loud and fast, fear came like I couldn't remember having, then a rage built up and my face tightened. I could see her smiling face then I could see her naked body and I closed my eyes.

"Are they together?" I asked.

"Only she went into the building, I've been here since eleven this morning," he said.

"Okay…okay wait there till she leaves and when she does beep me all zeros. Don't let her ass see you," I instructed.

"Okay and if I see him?" Scottie inquired.

"Walk away."

"Got you." The phone went dead.

I must've been stuck on the phone for minutes after Scottie hung up because I heard Thomas' voice bringing me back to reality.

"Keith, sit down…sit down for a minute and try to relax. What happened?" Thomas asked taking the phone out of my hand, hanging it up, then he walked out the kitchen to the couches and sat me down.

"Call your base and get a town car to meet me on one-seventeenth street."

He got on the phone and did exactly that. When he got off, I beeped E.R., Monk and some of my other homies with 117-117-911-911 with my Harlem number behind it on their screens.

"Mel, what the fuck, baby? What the fuck? Is this you saying your goodbyes…what the fuck?" I realized I'd said it out loud and went to the baby bag, taking out the Uzi. I shoved it down my pants then relaxed as Thomas kept his eyes on me. "Get the car ready, I'll be out in an hour or two. In fact, drive around and call me in an hour."

He walked out without a word spoken, no questions asked as usual. I needed to focus and started putting things away, then I saw the Coke on top of the refrigerator.

CHAPTER TWENTY-THREE
ERIC ROSARIO

The bus ride to Rikers Island made me nauseous, our rusted gas smelling bus hit every little dent in the street making us bump up and down sometimes real high and falling back down on hard plastic seats. I felt sick and ready to throw up, luckily it was late with no real traffic slowing us down, only a red light here and there.

'Why the hell did I get arrested?' I thought opening my eyes after being awakened by a light bump from the bus, preventing my face from trying to rest on a dirty window, while being cuffed to another person.

A slight relief came over me as I saw Riker's Island's bridge. I was wanting a bed badly and needed to sleep. Bump after bump I gave up the idea of napping and looked through the wired glass window backed up with a rusted gate on the outside as the Island came into a good view, looking tiny. There were multiple jails on it surrounded by fences all different from each other. We were going over a river and behind us on my right was an airport, being in the Queens area I guessed it was the JFK. Inside the bus was coming alive with conversations around me about which jail they thought they would go to as they have so many times before, even predicting where others would be going.

A five-percenter like Tee's father was talking louder than everyone else. "This was created just for us. This is modern day slavery manifesting into existence. We are fools for selling poison to our communities and killing each other. It's all a part of their plot to keep the Black Man down." He got louder with some stopping their conversations to hear him speak. "Knowledge of self is the key to open the door for us to get out of this mental prison that leads us to the physical one ahead."

People looked at the approaching jails in silence.

"The black man is…" A man next to him cut him off with a louder voice.

"If you believe that shit! The fuck is you here for?" he asked cuffed to a kid looking right across the aisle to the other man's face.

"To teach, to teach the eighty-five percent who are deaf, blind, and ignorant to the facts of life," replied the five percenter.

I remember Tee's father said they are not Five percenters, but God's of the nation and that five percent is just the number they represent.

"Yeah, yeah, I hear that bullshit. But what did you do to be on this bus and how come you can't get off it, G.O.D?"

We hit a bump that made everybody say, "*Shit!*" As we came out of our seats and fell back down into them.

I tasted bile in my mouth, I swallowed it then ignored all the talk, trying not to throw up, luckily, I had not eaten much of anything for days.

Two C.O.s were with us; one was driving the bus and the other was seated next to him divided from us by a locked gate. As we got to the end of the bridge one turned around facing us.

"Listen up to what jail you're going to!" he yelled.

The bus became silent as he started naming people and their correct jails. I was told I would go to the four building by others on the bus. It was for adolescents, kids sixteen to eighteen that were charged as adults but were really not adults, just kids like me making it to the wildest place on Rikers Island.

The C.O. was calling names of kids my age, "And Eric Rosario you five are going to C-Seventy-Four be ready to get off when I call it."

The most cuttings on the entire Riker's Island happened there. I had to be on point, nobody was going to do shit to me, with Brooklyn cats deep in here and Latin Kings the Gods. I'm not going to let nothing get me hyped for this. I fought my sleep as conversations picked back up.

I heard the God say, "My Spanish brothers you are also of the original man. In the beginning, there were two million Natives in which you call Indians today, who were your ancestors. The white man gave them the name Indians..."

We dropped off two people at the North facility, one of the jails on Riker's, then C-95 another one hearing names called and people rushed off the bus. We came to a stop and I was feeling so sick to my stomach and wanting to sleep.

I heard them say, "C-Seventy-Four let's go!"

I'd forgot that was my stop until the guy cuffed to me stood up making me realize it was my turn. I walked off the bus, down the small steps as the kid said his address to the C.O.

I said, "Nineteen-ninety Lexington Avenue."

We walked past him as the air hit me then into the four building. The officers that drove us here took off the handcuffs, and the five of us all rubbed our wrists in a small space were we all cleared a metal detector before entering a bigger room. Inside three black C.O.s looked tired and bored; they were all resting on the desk. One of them came around grabbing the cards with our information on it from our driver's and directed us to one of the many pens that faced each other on two sides.

I went straight to the bench to rest while others stood, and they began taking them out one by one in no real order. I rested for maybe two minutes then they called me last and escorted me to a shower room. Where I was stripped, searched and put with the others who stood in the first cell. Since others had made it to this cell before they now occupied the benches, leaving me the floor that I now sat on. I watched everyone and saw no threat and closed my eyes.

Clang! Clang! Clang!

Not knowing how much time had passed, if any but the annoying sounds of keys hitting the bars came followed by someone yelling, "Get your setups, let's go!"

We left the pen and got a rolled-up blanket. One kid unrolled his and inside the wool blanket was two sheets, a pillowcase, a green cup, a tube of toothpaste, a toothbrush and a wash rag.

"Don't go to sleep we need your info!" a C.O. yelled to us.

One by one they called us to the desk verifying the information I gave for the I don't know how many times, then gave me an orange ID with my picture, name and ID number 349-90-3266 the numbers that now represented me.

"If yar want to eat don't sleep," I was instructed.

I didn't want no sandwich, but I was so hungry. I stood up as the pen opened and we went out each getting a small box of cereal and small milk that tasted like the best meal in the whole world but did nothing for my hunger. I got an hour of rest that felt like ten minutes as the pens kept getting new people, disturbing me.

Then finally I heard, "Eric Rosario!" My name was being called from the outside of the pens, by a C.O.

"Yo'," I said happy something was happening to me.

"You going to mod nine," he said then called another kid telling him the same thing.

"Fuck no, C.O. I'm not going there!" the kid refused.

The C.O. now came up to the bars. "Yeah, you are. What you scared of murder mod nine?"

"Nah, I blew it up there already, I'm telling you, I'm not going," the kid sounded adamant.

"Well, you going in five minutes," the C.O. finalized and walked away.

"Fuck you…you think I'ma joke?" The kid was up on the bars yelling out to the C.O.s getting no response, then he paced the cell back and forth and kept going back to the bars yelling out to them. "Alright…alright, ignore me then. You fuckin' ignore me then!"

I stood up alert, watching him as he went to the back of the pen and squatted slightly, then put his hand in his ass taking something out. He looked around the cell, then in a flash, he rushed this kid with one swing slashing the kid's face, tearing a rip and opening up the victim's cheek.

The dude froze not understanding what had just happened, holding his face and then out of shock ran to the front of the pen and started yelling, "C.O…C.O….C.O.!"

The cutter wrapped up the object quick, squatted back down and put the thing back up his ass and then yelled out, "I fuckin' told you…I'm not going to mod nine!"

C.O.s ran to the pen.

CHAPTER TWENTY-FOUR
MAMA

"Your honor can I speak please?"

"Yes, you may."

"I don't know where those drugs came from. I did have…I had those two pipes; I get high your honor they call me Mama. Everybody knows Mama gets high and I want to stop so if you can help me get a program, your honor, I will get help, but that cop is a liar…"

"Enough, this is not a trial Ms. Carson and you're felony possession was not indicted so instead of wasting this courts time, I will offer you time served with misdemeanor probation of three years for the possession charge to run concurrently with your other four pending misdemeanor charges. Two of them you never came back to court for, talk it over with your lawyer."

"No! No, your honor, Mama trust you. I want that!"

"We will call you on second call."

Bang!

She banged her gavel and they took me out of the courtroom to a small cell across from a bigger one that the men were in.

My lawyer came over to me and said, "So, of course, you want it, right?"

"Yeah, Mama wants that. The probation people will help me get an apartment."

"Yeah, well, they can get you help to get it. We will call you out soon." Then he walked away.

I noticed that I'd gained weight, Mama was eating everything, and I slept for days going through the system than to Rosie's. Now Mama was going back out. Last night I washed all my clothes so I could leave clean and made sure I slept with my leather jacket so no one could take it. I knew to be strong and ate every baloney sandwich they gave me in the pens.

"Second call for, Linda Carter."

The C.O. came and took me back out to the court.

"Do you have all four dockets there?" the judge asked the older person. After they called out some numbers and said some things, I heard the judge say, "So, it's trespassing charges, two assault charges and drug possession all to concurrent to time served and three years' probation?"

"Yes, your honor," my lawyer replied.

"Yes, your honor," the D.A. followed up.

The judge named all the charges one by one over to me asking how I pleaded to each one.

"Guilty, Mama is guilty your honor." The judge asked if there was anything I had to say? "Yes, your honor. You going to be up there judging people. I'm telling you right now that Vuggio is a liar and going to be messing up people's lives. Mama telling you your honor, the cases are going to come up and he's going to lie."

They sentenced me and I left out of the courtroom.

CHAPTER TWENTY-FIVE
KEITH

I was cooking up five keys making the five thousand grams of Coke into six thousand one-hundred and eighty-four grams of Coke. I could have easily made a couple of hundred more with the purity of it by whipping the Coke harder as it cooked. They once said Melinda had me whipped, I remembered as she popped into my mind. I saw her pretty teeth behind her smiling face and shook my head quickly erasing the image. I can't be distracted right now; I did not want to make a lot of work but rather get better quality from it. A bomb for the come out and this was looking good I couldn't wait to get it tested. That made me think about not seeing Mama for a while. No one would even care about her besides me, yet I don't even know her real name.

Mel was the name Melinda told me when we first met, she had just got out of a relationship with her abusive boyfriend Calvin, that was her story his was she cheated on him with me. I just have to move on for now and get her out of my head. On our way to Harlem, Thomas was driving me with the cooked-up Crack packed separately in bags. One, one hundred-gram pieces of rocks, one eight gram and one four gram all in different Ziplock bags, then six keys packed in saran wrap with the triple beam scale all in the baby bag and the gun on my waist.

Melinda spoke in front of me, "I just want a little bit." Her eyes were in mine.

But I didn't know if she was looking at me or at him, her eyes were staring straight. I was bugging out like it was really in front of me. As I felt my hand on the handle of the gun, I pulled away. Thomas looked at me seeing or feeling the sudden movement I'd made, then his eyes went back to the road.

"Why Mel…why? Was this real?" I asked myself but quickly shook my head to get those thoughts out of my mind. I had to concentrate on my work. "Come on, Keith, just keep busy until you see her." I coached myself. "One thing has nothing to do with the other. Focus Keith…focus!"

We stopped on 117th Street and I went to the store and bought a couple of Very Fine fruit punch juices. I opened one and the bottle cap came off making a popping sound, I drunk it and was loving the taste. I looked at the foam type of label on the bottle for the ingredients.

As I walked out of the store, I heard someone say, "Papa…Papa?"

I turned and saw Mama and it made me smile. Her face looked worried.

"They locked Mama up. Vuggio put me through the system wanting to just know your name. They wanted your name, Keith and Vuggio told me he would let me go because all they had was my stems…" She hugged me for a quick moment, as I held her, she pushed me off and continued to talk. "…I had cocaine residue in my stems. When I told him no, he put me through the system for drugs. Papa that motherfucker coming he put drugs on me, but I knew he wouldn't come to court because Vuggio only wants guns. So, I went to the grand jury and he did not show up as I copped out to misdemeanor probation."

"Well, you here now Mama, relax I was missing you. Next time know the house number by heart," I said looking at her relieved.

"Keith, what's wrong?" she asked.

"I'm fine, Mama…I'm fine," I lied.

"Papa, tell Mama what's wrong?" she urged.

"Later, Mama…later, I'm dirty and we got a lot to do." I was about to hand her the four-gram pack to taste for me, but she looked clean and healthy.

She stared at me waiting to see what to do next. I watched the town car pull up with the other driver Scottie didn't like and Scottie walked fast to me just moments after.

"Keith, we gotta talk," Scottie said.

"Mama, wait in the car. Scottie let's go inside," I said.

Monk came up the block, saw us and came in the building behind us. Then we all went into the apartment to my room since the apartment was empty.

"Buddha take this brick one-seventeenth is yours. Don't call me for nothing. Do whatever you want just give me twenty-seven back." He took the brick and I took a bag out of the closet and gave it to him to put it in. "And if you got any beef call, Scottie. Don't call me for anything besides giving me work, money or needing more work," I instructed.

"You got it, Keith. It's over for you, huh?"

"Almost but the block is yours starting now! Take the car and use Mama to run errands while you bag up. Pay her in cash only. I'll collect the rest of the work money from, Guy. You go ahead and bag up, beep me when you done. And send Mama back in the car, I'ma take her out."

"Got you, Keith…and here I got Calvin's beeper number from a girl I know," Monk said taking out a piece of paper, he gave it to me, along with a hug then left the room.

I handed the paper to Scottie, "So, what's up, Scottie?"

"That cab nigga, I don't trust him. He was just at Calvin's building, too," Scottie informed.

"Scottie, not now man, handle Calvin if you see him but don't fuck with nobody else the cab could be being used by anyone," I told him.

"Watch this cab, nigga, nephew."

"I'll get another one, Scottie. I will tell Thomas to find us someone else. Driving Monk will be his last job for us." Scottie nodded in agreement. "Here take this, Scottie." He took the eighty-gram bag from my hand and exited the room.

I saw the baby crib and it motivated me to get rid of the Coke and I started beeping others for the weight. After making a few sales and giving out some consignments. I was left with three and a half keys, leaving the cash I made and one brick in the house. I took two bricks with me and was about to leave when the phone rang.

"Hello," I answered.

"Hola, Tio, I have Abuela here. She says to ask you is it okay if she keeps Ciera overnight here in the Bronx?" I knew that voice was Melinda's ten-year-old little cousin.

"Yeah, of course, tell her I'll pick them up in a car tomorrow morning," I replied.

"Okay, Keith, I'll say it and bring me a gift." Then she hung up before I could answer.

I felt good that they were going to be away for the night, I felt safe. Melinda's naked body was smooth, her face was smirking, saying, "Who are you Scarface or something?"

But she was not talking to me. Her face changed to the expression of sexual pleasure. I left out of the apartment with speed. I got into the caravan's front passenger seat.

"One-nineteenth street on Lennox Avenue, Thomas," I instructed.

"You got it, Keith." And we drove off.

I got real lucky with this spot as the building once had four different crews hustling in and out of it. I had a couple that sold drugs lightly for me then ended up selling weight to two of the crews. Uniting the two of them to use the couple's apartment and swap out the shifts between them. I promised they never would have to buy drugs again just pay the couple every shift one-hundred and fifty dollars and what they owed to me when they finish, and work would always be there. I also gave the couple an ounce of Coke every month. It's been over seven months here and the other two crews were no real competition for us. One sold Coke so we really didn't care. We parked in front of the building and I rushed inside.

I walked up the steps, passing the 2nd floor Crack and Coke spot, then to mines on the 3rd floor. I knocked on the door and an instant reply, came back.

"Put your money in the slot."

The entire key face came out with space for money to be put in. "Wow, clever," I said to myself. "It's Keith," I said aloud.

As two more customers came behind me with money in their hands, after a moment the door opened, and I recognized the hustler letting me in. I stepped inside passing the doorman who went to work serving customers behind the door. He closed behind me a narrow hallway and lead me to the living room. the female of the couple was there.

"Good, I need that Z, Keith," she said.

I had a Very Fine fruit punch drink, but it was not cold the way I liked it. So, I went to the kitchen and she followed me.

"I got a better deal for you. We changing up everything beep big Al and Joe so we can talk," I instructed as I put the Very Fine juice in the freezer, then went back to the living room and watched her go over to the phone on the kitchen wall and dial some numbers.

"Well things changed around here!" she yelled out to me.

"That fast huh, what's the change?" I said.

"I'll let Big Al tell you."

"I need, Joe, too," I reminded.

She looked at me listening to her phone, dialed in codes, then said, "I'll let Big Al tell you." Then she left out and walked into her bedroom, leaving me to myself.

I could see the man by the door making sales, he sat on a chair looking through the peephole and took money exchanging Crack vials through the locked hole. I did not want to be here long. I took the baby bag off me feeling the Uzi on my waist as I sat down. It was not smart Mama had just told me Vuggio asked about me. My alibi for Fats' murder was solid, I was in the lodge with proof. A gun charge right now would be foolish and so would being stopped by him.

"Stay on point, Keith," I told myself.

Big Al must have been in the building when he got the beep because he came up quick. When he entered the apartment, I heard his loud voice with authority shooting through the house.

He was about forty years old and stood at a big six-three height. "What's up, Keith?"

"Well, I rather have you and Joe together making changes to better both of you," I said cutting right to the chase.

"Yeah, what kind of changes, Keith?" he asked.

"The kind of changes that make more money for yar."

"I like more money and just so you know there has been changes already. But tell me about this deal," he said keeping his eyes on me.

"I want to give you weight instead of work. I want to give you both a brick at a time and pick up the cash later. The same as before but now you do your own bottling and pay me for the weight. Keeping more profits when you're finished and the same goes for, Joe."

His eyes blinked hearing Joe's name. "At what price?" he asked.

My beeper went off it was Mel, she was home.

"Keith, at what price?" He asked again.

"At twenty-five, you can pay me after you're done."

He blinked again making me uncomfortable as his face looked unhappy with the number. The door opened and two people came in.

"Yar, wait in the kitchen!" Big Al yelled to them from the narrow hallway as they walked past us into the kitchen then back to me, he said, I'll buy my own work, Keith. If you can let them go at twenty-one, I'll buy two at a time from you but if not, I'll go somewhere else."

He took control of everything, but this made me happy. I would lose out on some money but him paying me for it up front was good business especially with me not having any involvement besides the sale.

"You got it, Al…no problem."

A tiny smile showed his delight, as he got up and walked to the other bedroom the couple rents out, it looked like it was his now, the female of the couple came over to me.

"So, you got ounces for me and my man? You owe us," she said.

"Yeah, I…" I was about to say when Big Al came back cutting me off.

"No, he don't I got this. I told you get the fuck out of here." She got up and left as directed. Big Al dropped the money on the table. "Count that, Keith."

"Nah," I said and took out two keys for him from the baby bag. "Want to weigh it?" I asked

"Nah," he said.

I took the Uzi out and placed it in the bag back in its place.

"Nice Keith, let me buy that off you before you hurt yourself."

I looked at him towering over me. If he wanted to ambush me there was nothing I could do, but I felt no ill qualm behind him.

"Here it's yours, a present for our new agreement." I took out the clip and passed it to him.

His hand on the gun made it look smaller then what it was when he picked it up.

"You good with me, Keith. Never worry about my end, we have a solid deal."

"Good to know…now I'm out," I said, and we gave each other fives.

I left thinking how I did not want to carry it all anymore and just made a stronger bond with one stone. I called the house and Melinda answered.

"Hello," she said.

"Who's in the house, Mel?" I asked.

"Well, hi to you, too, Keith. It's me, Davi and Julissa. Why?"

"Okay, okay, meet me at the steak house on eighty-six street and third avenue. We going out to eat."

"You okay, Keith?" she asked, and I just hung up.

When I got back outside, I told Thomas the address and we left as Melinda kept beeping me again. The drive there was fucking with my head, so I counted the money all the way there. I waited at the steak house for an hour ordering drinks and getting tipsy. Thomas parked in a garage some blocks away and waited in the pool hall between Lexington and 3rd on 86th Street. I told him we would meet him there later.

"Keith, why you acting funny?" Melinda asked when she finally showed up.

"I'm good just been a busy day, Mel. Let's get our trays."

We went online, grabbed trays and started going down the line. I picked up some desserts and ordered at the register. "Steak done…done…well done, with baked potatoes and put cheese on top of it a lot like three slices each."

The cashier rung me, and Mel's order and we waited there.

"So, Davi and Julissa are in the house and Abuela took the baby to Tia's casa. Can we stay in a hotel tonight, Keith?"

"I got a better idea, Mel…" I stopped short; I was confused. I wanted to bring her to the house…our house…but then again, I didn't.

"Keith, what's wrong, you acting funny."

"I'm acting funny! Mel, we good I got a big surprise for you tomorrow, just relax I had a tough day." I looked at her and she stared at me. She made her eyes bigger like she was pestering me to say what was really on my mind.

"I love you with all I got. I love you! You and the baby are everything," I said. She straightened up and listened with real concern as I continued, "I do all I can for us, and tomorrow you will see the surprise. I'm just tired, Mel…" they called us for our order.

We took our food and went upstairs to a table to eat. Her face showed love to me. I wanted the truth and had to find out. I was getting angry just thinking about it.

"Let me ask you this and I want nothing but the truth from you. If you can't give me the truth just be silent and let's eat. Then when you're ready we can talk about it," I said.

"Yes, okay." She was looking in my eyes, I was not crying but my eyes had to be glossy.

"Where did you go today? And please if you love me, tell me the truth." I felt a tear come out the corner of my eye. I wiped it as my face tightened and anger flooded me thinking of her naked with someone else.

My heart picked up pace as I watched her face fade into concern, then a light of confusion with much thought. She chose her words carefully before she spoke.

"Before I went shopping, I went to my friend's house, but I know you don't want me over there. So, I just stopped by while her kids were at school. What you having me followed, Keith?"

"No, I don't have you followed, Mel. But lots of people know me and are in contact with me about a lot of things. You know what's going on, you know people talk to me. Mel people will kidnap you for money! Kill you to get to me, you can't…" I noticed I was raising my voice, so I lowered it. "…you can't be going over there especially to that building with the guy you cheated on me with." Right there I knew I'd messed up and would never know the truth now. She knew that I only knew she was in the building but maybe not.

"First of all, Keith. Why can't…" and I cut her off.

"Because your ex and me both want each other dead. They shoot at me and I shoot at them. But the question here, Mel, the question is were you with him?"

She looked shocked, "Keith, I'm telling you the truth. No…no, I was not with him. You believe me, right?"

"Melinda, let me tell you what I know. One…" I said holding up my finger looking directly into her face. "You was there and two you know you were not sa…" she cut me off.

"Where Keith, be specific where was I?"

"Mel, you were in the building," I raised my voice.

"I was in my friend's house!" she replied louder; people were looking at us now.

"Let's just eat we're getting too much attention, Mel."

She took what she thought was a big bite of her food. She was angry and red in the face, as she stared at me. I was hungry, I ate a chunk of potatoes with cheese on it, then placed butter on the potatoes to melt while it was still hot. I ate good thinking about everything. I would never truly know what happened, not now anyway. My beeper was peaceful being that I handled a lot of B-I. This was working out on the exit plan. Mel was still looking at me as I tasted my strawberry toppings off a strawberry shortcake, it was good.

After we ate, we walked in silence to the pool hall. It was up some flights of steps and if we were not mad at each other, I would have grabbed her ass on the way up. Thomas was there with the Bell Atlantic lady smiling, this made me smile, too. He made me think of having a good day.

"Mel, look at me." I grabbed her arms as we faced each other. "We going to put this behind us if you promise me you will never go over there again without letting me know. I don't want to hear about it. We got a life that's better than this and about to be better than what we've ever had."

"Keith, let's talk 'bout this later, okay. We're here and you're right."

"Thank you, Mel. We have a big day tomorrow you will be major happy. It will change our lives."

She gave me a light smile then grabbed my hand. "Tell me, Keith, tell me the surprise…tell me." She showed her true smile.

"Nope, I'm not telling you, let's play some pool and enjoy today. Tomorrow we will enjoy tomorrow."

Thomas saw us and his face lit up. We went to them as they held pool sticks in their hands.

"Let's play me and my girl against you and Mel," Thomas said.

"Your girl, huh? You a sucker for love that fast?" I laughed giving him five.

"He can't help it," the Bell Atlantic lady said looking different in regular clothes.

We played for about an hour, then went to the movies to see *Home Alone*. The vibe was good for all of us, we were enjoying each other's company. After the movie, we walked down 3rd Avenue feeling the night air. I had my arm over Mel's shoulder, and she had her arm across my back on my waist and we watched the other couple ahead of us.

"Keith, do I have to dress up, tomorrow?" Mel asked.

"No, baby, we have to pick up Abuela first anyway." She had my heart but I'm nobody's fool. This shit ends now.

"Are we bringing, Davi? I don't want him outside so much, let's take him."

"Yes, he's coming, baby."

I will give Scottie one day and if he don't get him I'ma call my Brooklyn people, maybe even E.R. We walked all the way to the garage and Thomas went and got the car. It was late now, and my beeper went off. I got into the car as he pulled it out of the garage. My beeper went off again.

"I'll deal with it when I'm home. I hope Mel is telling the truth," I mumbled to myself low so no one could hear me.

CHAPTER TWENTY-SIX
SCOTTIE

This motherfucker just dropped off Monk and now his car is in front of Calvin's building again. Keith said it's nothing. But what would he say if he knew the cab was here again, the same day, right after leaving our people? Fuck it, I'ma stick to the plan and if I don't catch Calvin, I'm going to rob his workers. I'm getting something out of this shit. I lit up a woolie and smoked while walking up Madison Avenue. I was walking around the block but this time I paced back and forth then it hit me hard.

"Damn, Keith you made a bomb, this shit strong." I looked at the blunt as it was smoking at the tip and pulled on it again.

The cab driver came out of the building and walked toward his car. Fuck it, I'm going to check this motherfucker out. I walked over crossing the four-lane street of Madison Avenue and reached his cab before he did.

He paused when he saw me. "What's good, Playboy?" I asked.

"Oh, shit Scottie what's good? You live over here?" he asked.

I leaned back on his car. "Something like that, drop me off at one-twenty fifth on the Eastside." I pulled out fifty dollars and handed it to him.

His hand reached out by habit knowing he did not want to take the money, but it was in his hand. "Cool…cool, Scottie get in." He went around to the driver's side as I surprised him getting in the passenger side.

"You mind?" I asked showing him my unlit blunt that went out.

"Sure, Scottie go ahead."

"Let's let bygones be bygones, sorry about that Long Island thing," I told him.

"It's nothing, Scottie, we good. Where to?"

The smell of Crack took him by surprise and his face scrunched up.

"Go up one-twenty-fifth, I'll tell you where to stop."

As we drove it hit me strong again. I rolled down a window blowing out the smoke to not give him bad energy off me. I was not in a violent mood but a good one feeling the scene on the drive and seeing everything like really seeing it as it passed me then I started thinking. I still had to get rid of the gun Guy shot that kid with, it was in the house. Guy stayed over that night and told me how she shot him till he fell with the low caliber gun, but she did not want to kill. She only wanted to hurt him, we ate, and she slept on the couch. Guy is a cute, little dike bitch; I like her heart.

"Keep going up there."

We were at the end of one-twenty-fifth.

"Scottie, that's a dead end."

"Yeah, go ahead in there."

We were on the very end of the Eastside driving into a deserted area that looked out to the East River. It was dark outside, no one could see us from anywhere.

"Get out let me talk to you."

"Scottie…" he said

"Shut the fuck up! I did not pull out my gun. I did not raise my voice. Just get out so we can talk."

He did and I came out after him. The East River smelled and there was a mound of natural salt three stories high just sitting out there. This little strip was used by people in cars sometimes parking and getting head or fucking. I walked over to the edge as he followed behind me. I turned and looked back at him, noticing that he was a big guy, then looked back out over the river.

"So, this what we going to do. I'ma ask you questions, and I only need real answers. If you lie…you die."

"Scottie, what is this? You know what go ahead ask away."

I had my back to him listening to his presence and tone. He coulda easily push me in the river or at least tried to anyway.

"Do you know who, Calvin, is?" I asked.

"Calvin, from where?" he asked.

"Do you know that after we left you on Long Island some kids followed me and Keith trying to kill us?"

"Nah, man I didn't know anything about that."

"Why two times today you were on Madison on one-hundred and six?"

"My aunt lives in fifteen-ninety, she called me back to finish putting her bed together that I started earlier which got interrupted by work."

I felt good, that high was nice and he was not scared or nervous from the sound of his voice. I turned and looked at him, he was not scared but I could tell he was confused, and I wanted to roll another Woolie.

"Let's get in the car, let me just roll this up then you can drop me off."

"Whatever, you want, Scottie. You got me for an hour if you want."

Inside the car, I rolled up a blunt and just wanted to go home. I had work on me and needed to take Bad and Luck for a walk and get rid of Guy's gun.

"So, you don't know, Calvin?"

"No, Scottie I don't."

"Cool, I believe you, it's nothing."

The sound of the river inside the cab was soothing. I went into my pocket and searched for a lighter. I found Calvin's number and looked at it.

"How strong is your vibrate on your beeper?" I asked. "My shit don't even faze me when it buzz."

"Mine vibrate good. I be using it to wake me up when I sleep. Duracell batteries are the best to use for a strong vibrate," he said glad to be helping me.

"Let me see it," I said.

He passed me his beeper like nothing, and I put the paper next to it as I checked the numbers on his screen list that beeped him to the one on the paper. I found a match; he was confused as he sat there watching me.

I passed him back his beeper and looked at him. "Didn't I say don't lie to me?"

"What, Scottie, I…"

I grabbed the back of his head and smashed his face into the windshield repeatedly as his face started bleeding. He got off a hard punch and I tasted pain realizing how strong he was and how much bigger than me he was. I pulled out my .357 Magnum and he grabbed my hand instantly controlling it.

"You die tonight," I barked.

"Fuck you, Scottie. You die tonight… and we robbing that crib so fuck you and Keith," he said pushing me down in the seats getting the best of me, punching my face with the other hand as he held a good grip on my gun hand.

I was swinging back up at him, but he was hitting me harder than I was hitting him. He was stronger than me and in a better position than me. I was so mad I banged my face into his face hurting myself and hurting him. The second time it felt like I hit metal, but he was stunned, and the third, the pain was worse as blood covered both of our faces and he loosened his grip, I pointed and pulled.

Boom! Boom! Boom! The three flashes lit up inside the dark cab. His bloody face lit up every time as I controlled the powerful jerk of the gun. He dropped on top of me. I struggled to get from under him. He was breathing hard and making an unusual sound. I crawled backward on my elbows and fell out of the car. Then I got up, pointed the gun and squeezed.

Boom!

I hit his back as his body seemed to lift off the impact and not move or be heard again.

I picked up paper bags, paper plates, and trash off the ground placing it in the back seat of the cab. I lit it with my lighter. I went farther collecting more paper bags and anything off the ground that would burn. I placed it in the seat making a decent fire. Then I opened his glove compartment, lit the paper in there and looked for anything that would burn as the fire grew and the smoke started getting darker. The smell changed to the burning of plastic material as the seats caught fire. I stepped back from the cab as it burst into big flames and walked off fast.

Four blocks away I stopped a cab, but he instantly drove off making me realize I was bloodied up. So, I walked real fast as the streets watched me, people in cars were looking, everyone kept their eyes on me. I was bugging or they were really watching. I stopped, acting like I was taking a piss to see who was looking at me, then moved on.

"I have to get off the streets and get home," I mumbled to myself.

I gripped the gun in my black army jacket pocket that had two shots left. I was going to use them if I was stopped. It shoulda taken me fifteen to twenty minutes to rush home but I walked to 124th Street then straight down to Lennox Avenue making a few stops like I was pissing to see if I was followed or watched. I passed 117th Street. I remembered what he said and walked toward Lexington Avenue, rushing in confusion of what to do. I stopped a cab that allowed me to get in. I had to get home, clean up and get a bigger gun with more bullets.

CHAPTER TWENTY-SEVEN
JULISSA

"Who is it?" I screamed at the door it had better be Davi. He was supposed to have been in the house. Everybody was out and his badass knew Melinda or Abuela was not home.

I went and opened the door and fell backward from being pushed. As I hit the floor with my back, the pain shot through my legs. I looked up to see Davi with tears in his eyes. He was angry and being held by two men with masks on. They pushed him into the apartment, and I started yelling at them.

"Get the fuck out are yar stupid or something!"

A gun was pointed to Davi's head. "Shut the fuck up!" They barged in closing and locking the door behind them.

"Get up and move," the shorter one said.

Davi had his fists balled up and I did not want nothing happening to him. I got off the floor then we all walked into the living room.

"Where's Keith's room?" The bigger one asked smacking Davi to the floor with his free hand before I could even answer as I flinched not believing this.

"Stop!" I yelled out. Davi got up fast about to swing and I grabbed onto him. "It's over there, it's over there. You don't have to hurt us please get what you came for and go!" I told them pointing to Keith's room while holding onto Davi.

The bigger one said, "We not playing no fuckin' games do as we say and we in and out. The boy comes with me, you stay right here." He grabbed Davi by his shirt and pulled him away from me.

"Davi just let them get what they came for don't fight. No, le pele!" I cried.

Davi stood silent and as he was being dragged by his shirt into Keith's room. I prayed and hoped he didn't lose his temper and try to fight back. The shorter man was silent and just stared at me holding a gun. His eyes went up and down my body. I heard things being tossed around in Keith's room.

"Get over here and turn around with your hands out. Let me make sure you don't got no gun on you."

I came to him in my T-shirt and sweatpants, knowing he knew I had nothing on me. I heard the room being trashed and searched. The gun was pointed at me, I couldn't see Davi and I wanted him safe. I wasn't just thinking about me.

"Mister, please, I told you where Keith's room is."

"Just do what I say and relax," he said.

I put my hands up and turned in front of him. Then I felt the gun pointed into my back. Not long after, his hand was on my neck and he started breathing in my ear.

"You're a bad bitch!" His hand went down to my breasts as he pressed his body against mine. The gun was off my back, I felt his cold hand under my breasts, then they moved down my stomach and went into my pants.

"You a nasty motherfucker. You know that, right? What you can't get no pussy out there?" I insulted.

"Keep it up and I'ma take yours so just shut the fuck up!" he barked.

"No…no, don't do that please that's nasty don't!" I pleaded as I felt his dick grow on me.

I couldn't think what to do with his hands past the drawstring in my sweatpants, it loosened easy and he was comfortable with this.

I faced him. "You going to have to fuckin' kill me."

"How about I kill that little runt?"

"Fuck you!"

"Get on the floor you pretty bitch, now!" he yelled pointing the gun.

I moved slowly with tears in my eyes. Then I looked into his eyes. "I swear you going to die, motherfucker." I prayed in my head. "*God, please take this man's life. He don't deserve to live or have children. He needs all traces of him gone.*" I smirked at him and sucked my teeth. "Go ahead do what you want. You going to get yours. Dio Te vas a co hel." I closed my eyes and laid on the floor.

I felt him coming toward me, then really felt him feel on my ass as he kneeled over me. He grabbed on me, I looked back and he was watching me in a trance.

"Stop you nasty motherfucker!" I felt the gun on my back as I faced the floor again. Then I felt him tugging at my pants and I cried out louder. "No…please…no!"

Blatt! Blatt!

I flinched holding my face but felt nothing.

Boom! Boom! Blatt!

Shots were being fired in the house. "Oh my God, Davi no…no!" I was screaming not caring about myself as I got up and pushed the pervert.

He dropped his gun down in shock by both the gunshots and my sudden aggression. The bigger man came running out firing into Keith's room.

Boom! Boom!

He ran to the door with bags in his hand, unlocked it and ran out. I pushed the pervert and smacked his face. Then kicked the gun away, he looked toward the room and Davi stood by the door taking shots at him with his eyes squinting as he held the gun with two hands.

Blatt! Blatt! Blatt! Blatt!

The perv ran as the shots missed him but followed him hitting the spots where he ran from all the way out the door, seconds behind the first guy. Davi ran to the room getting another gun and went chasing behind them, until I grabbed him.

"No, let them go…let them go. Get all the guns or anything illegal and take it upstairs to your friend's house. We leaving and the police gonna come, let's go, Davi."

CHAPTER TWENTY-EIGHT
SCOTTIE

I got out of the cab with Bad and Luck on Park Avenue. We were rushing toward Keith's crib after hearing faint gunshots. A guy was running towards me taking his mask off, carrying three bags. He raised his hand and heavy shots rang out at me.

Boom! Boom!

I pulled out my sixteen shot 9mm. *Pop! Pop!*

I returned fire as I crossed to the other side of the street out of his way. Bad and Luck wouldn't be in his sight. Welo's crew saw the commotion as people started running for their guns. Luck was tapping his left paw eager to take off.

"Relax boys…stay…stay!" I ordered.

The shooter had the drop on me as he pointed his gun in my direction trying to get a clean shot at me. When I saw another one running out the building, then I turned my dog loose and told them, "Get him…get him…get him!"

As they took off, I knew the shooter would see it. He reacted by turning his head toward the dogs and letting off one shot. *Boom!*

I jumped up and let off, *Pop! Pop! Pop! Pop! Pop!* I aimed directly at him when he aimed back at me, he got hit and fell then got back up quick.

Boom! Boom!

He shot at me, I ducked as he ran away. This guy was the real deal. I went to Keith's building and Luck was shaking his head with a grip on the man's arm, trying to rip it off. The guy was yelling out to me and hitting Luck.

"Call him off…call him off…tell him to stop!" he pleaded.

I wanted a better view and looked for Bad, then saw him bleeding in between two parked cars. He wasn't moving, "No…fuck no…noo!"

A car pulled up and stopped, then Keith got out and I heard the sirens wailing.

"Scottie, get in the car…get in the car…call Luck off!" Keith instructed.

"No, Keith! No…Luck, neck…neck…neck!" Luck let go of the man's arm and went for his throat. The man threw his arms up as he was bitten and tossed while Luck tried to get his neck.

"Scottie, go now get the fuck in the car!" Keith ordered louder and ran towards his building.

I got up, but before leaving I petted Bad for the last time, then yelled out, "Luck to me…to me…now!"

Luck came to me, I looked in the man's face and took aim. *Pop! Pop! Pop! Pop!* Then me and Luck jumped into the car and drove off. Luck had blood on him, I had to think fast. "Stop the car now!" I yelled.

Thomas stopped the car between Park and Madison and there was an empty lot there. I wiped my prints off the gun and tossed it under a car. "Luck go over there wait for Scottie…wait for Scottie…stay!" Luck ran into the lot while looking back at me. "Go in…go in…wait for Scottie!" He went further into the lot disappearing into the darkness. We drove off and as we turned down Madison the car was stopped by the police.

We were searched and questioned, they took our names and let us go. The small pockets holding the Cracks saved me again. Thomas drove us around for ten more minutes then back to the lot where I left Luck at.

"Luck to me…to me!" I yelled out in the dark lot and no one came. To me, Luck…to me!" Then he came running into the car and we drove off.

Thomas took me to my apartment, and I went upstairs. When we got inside, I escorted Luck to the bathtub, ran the water and washed the blood off him. I looked at my face in the mirror and noticed I was crying.

"That motherfucker…this shit ends now!" I growled.

CHAPTER TWENTY-NINE
ERIC ROSARIO

'You might be cooling, you might be wilding, but you won't be smiling on Rikers Island.' That song played in my head as the ten of us were escorted by a C.O. through the halls of the four building, known as the worse jail on the entire Island for cuttings. I was going to Mod nine the worse housing unit in that building. Wanting sleep was no longer my main concern. Us new jacks carried setups under our arms only having that as property. People who had been here dragged their belongings behind them in wool blankets across the floor. I tried to look out of the windows while we walked passing them all around us on both side of the hallways made the same with each one having about eight small rectangles of glass windows most replaced by fogged up fiberglass that opened together by turning a knob at the bottom of course only one out of twenty had a knob to be turned.

Even if opened, you couldn't put your hand out, there was a dirty screen of metal covering it. Adolescents passed us walking alone with passes in their hands on the opposite side of the hall as we headed in the other direction. Each one made it their business to look at us with a serious face, a look they all shared.

Like a checkpoint the C.O. standing by a metal detector told us, "Everybody clear the Mag."

One by one we all cleared it, then moved on stopping at an opening in the hall that leads down some steps as the escorting C.O. called out, "Mod eight will set you straight, let's go!"

I hated when they used the lingo inmates was using like they wanted to be us. We waited as four others from our group went down the steps with the C.O., another young kid with a mug on his face walked past us to the Mag showing his pass and clearing it then moved on. Our C.O. came back and escorted us to move it along down the hall.

He stopped us again and yelled, "Four main houses of pain… let's go, don't be scared now!"

I hated this guy, he had floor cards with our pictures and information on it in his hands. As he went with two inmates, he came back with two fewer cards and we moved on through the halls that looked the same everywhere with the exact same windows. Clearing another Mag, I was feeling sleepy. I saw a light skinned kid, my age with a scar on his face walking the hall alone. This gave me a strong feeling in my gut to protect myself and my anger took over me. I was not going to be punked, he looked at me and I looked back. He gave me a nod and I did the same. A feeling hit me, it was like everybody's vibes were connected and alert.

A female C.O. that had a nice body got the attention of many. The adolescent with the scar stopped and talked to her like two people in the streets as our group moved on. It felt good to keep moving along after everything I'd gone through these past couple of days that I had to wait in cells. All the adolescents walking the halls had intense looks like they knew what they were doing.

"Murder Mod nine you three…let's go!" he said as one kid waited in the hall.

We followed the C.O. down some steps into a metal tunnel added onto this building. As we walked in, we heard the hollowness echo from under our feet. It leads to Mod Nine, that was actually two trailers connected to the tunnel.

The C.O. yelled, "Mod Nine three coming!"

Another C.O. came out taking our three-floor cards from the escort now leaving us. There were two sides North and South both had large plexiglass windows with adolescents faces in it looking out at us. Most of them were wearing Doo-rags and again

I saw that look that made them different from people our age. They all looked like they knew what the whole world was about. They were not kids wanting to play but needing to survive.

The C.O. spoke loudly as he eyed what we wore and how we looked. "Anybody want P.C.?" We all said no, then he looked at the orange floor cards in his hand. "Eric Rosario?"

"Yeah," I said, he caught me looking over the adolescent looking at me."

"Your address and birth date."

"Nineteen-Ninety Lexington Avenue…two-eleven, seventy-three."

"Northside," the C.O. said then called out the other two names and they responded the same as I did.

As I walked into the Mod the windows were different. On the left side was a day room with plastic colored chairs, three heavy plastic tables, a TV that only a few people were watching and to the right was four rows of fifteen beds lined side by side next to each other from the back of the Mod to us. Directly where we came in from behind us was the Bubble. The thick plexiglass window had one C.O. watching us from inside of it. He left our side to watch the Southside. On the wall of the Bubble in between the plexiglass was two phones being used. I wanted to get on, so I just looked at it. I started feeling like I was being watched by the adolescents like they knew everything I felt, needed and wanted. I took my eyes off the phone and got that same feeling I had when the female walked, everyone was alert.

The beds farthest from the Bubble against the wall was the in-crowd. They had mattresses and wool blankets piled up on their frame making big and comfortable beds. The faces that watched was talking to those that owned those beds now as we came in. we walked to the back, I needed to sleep and nothing else mattered. The phone would have to wait until after I got some rest. The CO sat on a chair in front of the Bubble reading a paper.

All three of us walked to the back and saw three empty beds with no mattresses just metal frames and a locker. I heard some snickers being made, I was crazy tired, so I laid the wool blanket out over the metal frame and two white sheets over that then put my toothbrush, toothpaste, green cup and wash rag into the small metal locker. Then finally laid down with my jacket over me like a cover to rest. That feeling came, my eyes opened, and I saw the C.O. walk out.

The guy with a set up like me was about to sit on his metal frame until the third guy who came with us that still had his property rolled up in his blanket said, "Nah, yar bugging I need a mattress. Somebody giving me one of them shits."

"Who got em?" the new jack said deciding not to sit, getting courage from the other guy.

"Man, you don't see all those over there piled up under them?" He pointed to the other side of the dorm letting his finger move across the air, pointing from bed to bed with multiple mattresses knowing everyone saw him.

My eyes were now wide opened, I looked at the two middle rows of beds, every one of them had single mattresses, but some had multiple blankets making their beds look comfortable.

"They got mad mattresses. I'm getting at least one for now!" The kid was clearly experienced, being purposely loud so everyone else would hear him.

I looked at others in our row, almost all of them had no mattresses and I laid down. I would figure this out later after some rest before I moved stupid, so I closed my eyes.

"So, what's up…who giving me a mattress?"

My eyes opened and watched him walk across the two middle rows of beds as the other new kid followed him towards the in crowd.

A small kid standing about 4'11 jumped off his bed. "Yar, don't want none of these I'm telling you."

The dorm was at attention, a bigger kid the size of a grown man jumped off his bed, "If you want one of mine you can fight me for it."

Other's peeked their heads from their beds. I looked toward the Bubble; the C.O. was looking from side to side. The middle row laid watching but the entire back row was getting out of bed except the last four beds that their mattresses were at least five high with blankets tying them together. The two of them were now in the back row and the experienced one was leading them straight to the big guy when one of the in-crowd people, spoke.

"You, Nut from Bed Stuy?"

"Yeah, that's me. What's goodie?" the Vet answered.

"I'm Tyson." They looked at each other and smiles broke out.

"Oh, shit, Tyson. You my cousin's man! What up, Ty? I ain't seen you in a minute yar still together, right?" The Vet said with a look on his face like '*he betta say yes*'.

"Yeah, that's my other half." They slapped hands and pulled each other into a hug. "Yo' this people right here. This is, Nut my family," Tyson said. He called out to the others on his row and then to the four who stood in their beds. "Yo' Fuquan, Gotti, this my boy, Nut!" They had earbuds hanging over their shoulders that were taken out of their ears when the two walked over. "This my people you heard." He continued talking and received nods from each one of them.

The small kid spoke up again, "You good, Nut?" He slowly walked, passing Nut. "But who's this nigga right here that came with you like he ready to fight for something?" He walked directly up in the new kid's face, looking him up and down. Then looking up to him, he was so small anyone in the dorm could probably beat him with ease.

The new jack tried to speak, "I'm…

The smaller kid interrupted, "You ain't shit…you ain't nobody. Go to your fuckin' bed before you get hurt!"

"I don't got a bed, I need a mattress."

"Fuck your mattress!" That came from the biggest kid who now walked over to them.

Fuquan spoke in a low voice and everybody paid attention, "What you need my man? We got you come back here."

The new guy walked off to the very back to Fuquan who was laying down relaxing. The new guy touched one of the five mattresses under him.

"Oh, that you gotta put some work in for that. You wanna put in some work?"

"Whatever, just give me one!"

Fuquan hopped off his bed, he was dark, tall and had gold fronts in his mouth top and bottom, with a flat top fade and two fresh cut lines on his right side.

"Hero, get him a mattress."

I closed my eyes and stopped watching trying to think. Moments later, he was next to me with a mattress on his frame tying sheets on his bed. I got up and knew if I did not get a mattress I would not be respected. Because I got up, I was already in position to be noticed.

A kid with no mattress on my row, two beds away from me said, "You Harlem, right?"

"Yeah," I said tiredly.

"Where at?"

"One, two-two," I replied.

"What's that, Wagna?" he asked pissing me off because he was a sucker with no mattress talking to me.

"Nah, Lex. How about you, where you from?" my voice was getting strong when someone in the middle row spoke up.

"A Harlem nigga…they gonna take all his shit!"

The kid I was talking to ignored the disrespect being said to us. But I heard him like a background noise being faded out, caring about nothing he was saying.

"Manhattan keeps on making it. Brooklyn keeps on taking it. Manhattan keeps on making it. Brooklyn keeps on taking it!" I heard someone chanting.

I looked back. "Ain't nobody taking shit from me. I don't know what Harlem nigga yar used to!"

The small troublemaker named Hero was instigating it as sounds of laughter was getting louder.

"Oooohhh…speak up. Who said that? Tell Harlem to his face!" Hero said

The middle row kept quiet then Hero said, "Fall back Harlem, just fall back. You want to use the phone?"

At first, he threw me off, but I did want to use it. "Yeah." I was upset with myself for showing eagerness. I fell right into their trap.

"Go next on any phone that opens, you got six minutes." Then he yelled out to the phone direction. "Harlem got next!"

Another kid that had the phone logbook nodded his head. I slept hard after talking to my moms and being told I would bail out any time after twelve tonight or early in the morning. My mind was still on a mattress though. After falling asleep on the metal not knowing how long I'd rested, I heard screams and the sounds of feet squeaking on the floor that made me jump up.

"Aaaahhh…aaahhhh…, bitch ass nigga who the fuck is you? Who the fuck is you?" Yelled a person bleeding from his face.

The new kid that was given a mattress earlier ran to the back of the dorm with a razor in his hand toward Fuquan. As a kid that came back from court, had blood on his shirt and a cut on his face. Not afraid but confused and bleeding. He was trying to put together what had just happened to him.

"Word, Fuquan, you gonna do it like that?" The bleeding kid said.

The C.O. walked into the dorm. "Yar, did this on my shift? You couldn't wait…you couldn't respect my shift!" The C.O. said.

Then he pulled the emergency pin on his talkie which made everybody in the dorm scramble to get ready for what was next

"What's going on?" I asked.

"The turtles are about to come and flip this place. He pulled the pin." The kid that was cut went to his bed on the in-crowd row. "And yar, fuckin' took my shit while I was in court. I fuckin' get back from court and yar sneak thief me!"

The C.O. yelled while keeping his distance, "Come on, let's get you to the infirmary…you bleeding!" He walked toward the C.O., grabbed a broom and went after Fuquan.

"Handle that nigga," Fuquan told the new jack standing like a soldier by him.

He attacked the broom holder. All eyes including the ones in the Bubble saw the broomstick swinging away hitting repeatedly over the soldier as he tried to get another cut-off, swinging his hand with the razor in it, but the stick was rapid until it broke then punches followed. When he dropped the broken stick, the razor holder no longer swung but held himself trying to keep from getting hit. A direct punch caught him so hard he dropped the razor and held his face, then laid down on the floor. The biggest kid then punched the cut kid and they swung punches at each other as Hero grabbed the razor off the floor. Loud footsteps and the vibration of stomps could be heard growing louder with every step.

"Put your hands on the wall!" I got up and the C.O.s was rushing. One got directly in my face that fast. "Hands on the wall…you're not special!"

All the C.O.s were big, some wore riot gear, with helmets and sticks in their hands making us look like kids for the first time. The gear they had on made them look like turtles. My hands went up and I faced the wall as others did the same. They put plastic wrist restraints on the cut kid and the big kid who was fighting and left Hero alone. Property, chairs, everything was being thrown around and onto the floor by the C.O.s that came in.

"Everybody turn and face me." I turned off the wall and saw a white shirt talking. All the C.O.s had on blue shirts; he was the captain. "This row put your hands on your head, lock your fingers and go to the day room." It was my row and we all did as we were instructed. "Doo-rags off!" he yelled looking like he was avenging the violence himself.

Turtles were positioned directing us to the day room. All the clothes that were drying on chairs or clotheslines were on the floor along with dominoes and cards. The tables were flipped over, the room was searched before we got in there, two C.O.s dressed in riot gear was waiting on us.

"No fuckin' talking, I will buss your fuckin' head. Line up here one behind the other!" We lined up single file. "Closer!" he said. I was up near a person. "Closer!" I was touching someone lightly in front of me and behind me. "Closer, I want yar butt fuckin' each other!" We were piled up close. "Another line right here, closer get fuckin' close. Don't act like you don't know!" The white shirt in the dorm directed row after row into the day room to the C.O. directing them into tight single lines. We stood in silence with our hands locked behind our heads.

The Captain walked in once we were all in there. "Yar want to cut people? Okay, let me show you how we do. One through ten let's go to your beds now!" A group of ten was taken out of the day room. After waiting ten seconds he called out, "Eleven through twenty to your beds now!" That was me and I walked out behind others with my hands still above my head and fingers locked.

A C.O. put his hand over my locked fingers and asked, "What bed you in?"

"I'm in twelve!" I said. He escorted me out of the day room to my bed.

Kids from the first group were naked in front of their bed and a C.O. was searching their clothes, then as they got dressed, they searched their property while tossing shit to the floor.

"Where's your mattress and property?" A black C.O. asked while chewing gum. He looked bored and smelled like a bottle of perfume.

"I just got here," I said.

The C.O. searching the bed next to me said softly, "They probably will cut him next. Let's pack some of them up to another house."

I was tired and just wanted to get past this. I followed the orders given to me as I got naked down to nothing and turned bending over so they could look in my ass, then I put my clothes back on and was escorted to the bathroom. People who were searched already stood waiting for this to end.

"Why the fuck you throwing my clothes on the floor?" A kid yelled.

The captain said extract him and the turtles went to him with shields, put plastic cuffs on him and took him out. The rest of the turtles left, and we left the bathroom back to the dorm. Once we returned you could see, cookies, sodas, cakes, deodorants, and soaps, clothes, books, and sneakers were all over the place as people started picking up their property and organizing stuff back into their beds and lockers.

My stuff was just laid on the metal frame, I saw mattresses piled up at the back of the dorm. My heart speeded up, no way I was going to sleep on metal tonight. All I wanted was what I was supposed to have. I looked around and my face tightened, these motherfuckers thought I was scared. I walked to the back of the dorm and felt eyes on me. Everyone was busy but knew where I was going. I grabbed one it was so thin I grabbed a handful then reached down and grabbed another one. I dragged the two of them to my bed. As I did, I felt as glaring on my back. The looks were all different, some were surprised others had admiration and the back row was giving me daggers in my back. I didn't care I made it to my bed and threw one on the metal frame, then put the sheets on, tying it at the corners.

A fight broke out with two middle row kids. One took the opportunity to snuff the other, while I had the dorm's attention. He was punching him constantly; blood was on the victim.

The C.O. came running in record time. "Break that shit up…break it up yar want the squad back in here, right now! You motherfuckers making me look like I can't run my house!"

Fuquan and Gotti went to the fight and told them to stop and they listened.

"One of them has to leave yar send him to the Bubble." The C.O. left out the house with one inside the Bubble watching.

"You pack the fuck up and go to the Bubble before we blow your face off. The fuck is you doing snuffing somebody?" And the winner went to gather his things and walked to the Bubble.

The big adolescent that had left out came back into the dorm receiving laughter and hugs as he passed everyone. I gave the other mattress to the Harlem kid who'd spoken to me earlier. He looked reluctant to take it.

"These Brooklyn dudes are deep, and they going to try and get at you," he said in a low tone. "They like to wait till you go to commissary if they think you got money. Then take everything you got!"

The dorm was busy with people talking and putting their things away. An open bed on the in-crowd row came from the kid who'd been cut. Nut took his stuff and dropped it there, the soldier took the middle row kid's bed who was told to leave.

The small kid Hero looked at us, "You not keeping those we will be there to get them."

I was getting mad and responded, "The next person that comments on me let's just shoot five I don't want to talk!"

The entire dorm was fixing their areas up, but attention was paid to me standing up to them.

"Relax Harlem, you good"

This got me thinking they were just waiting for me to go to the store, I was about to bail out but for some reason, this all seemed important to me.

An argument happened with Fuquan. "That slot time is not for you, I'm splitting it up," he told someone that was from his row.

"Fuck you!" the kid replied, and a fight broke out.

Fuquan was hit then back up and Hero tried to cut the kid who'd punched Fuquan, but the kid was ready. He knew how they operated, another kid tried to cut Hero with a razor, and it was two against six. A chair was tossed at the two, then back at the six. One of the two with the razor ran toward Hero, trying hard to cut him while trying to grab him as he ran. I could see all the hands, but I knew Hero had a razor too. Swings of the razor were missing back and forth, the two now separated from each other and the one with no razor was fighting with the big adolescent down with Fuquan. He was beating the big guy, others got punches in, but the loner was moving fast and not getting grabbed.

As they were holding themselves and getting the better of the six, they forgot about the new recruit, Nut. Nut came over and cut the kid who was fighting the big adolescent. Once on his arm then lightly on his face. Nut jumped the other guy making him fall with the razor in his hand. Hero cut the guy on the floor as he got up swinging. He picked up his razor and started chasing Hero again right past me. I saw the fresh cut on his face clear to the inside of his mouth.

The squad came running in, after going through that same process of stripping, showing my ass and being searched again. Some were extracted out refusing to go through this again. the house was a mess again, we were told to stay by our beds after our search as the deputy of security Bally who was respected by inmates wanted to speak to us.

He was heavy but not fat, six-two with a walkie talkie in his hand that kept speaking. He wore a blue shirt like a C.O. with gold stars on his shoulder indicating rank. He had all our attention.

"Because you want to act out, I'm going to restrict Mod Nine from the population so you won't spread this nonsense you're doing. From now on no passes will be given. You will leave only by escort anywhere you go. When Mod Nine goes to recreation you will go alone."

"Aww, this shit crazy!"

"This is bullshit!"

"He bugging out!"

Comments were expressed as Bally watched faces. When he looked in those directions silence followed. His radio came alive asking for him, he spoke back into it continuing with a loud clear voice.

"I'm going to put bolted down chairs and tables in the day room and yar can eat in there not even able to go to the mess hall. Yar can eat in there this is too much." He paused doing a three sixty and looked around at all of us. "These cutting are childish! You can't tell me all these people need to be cut! I know this is jail but it's my jail, not yours. I run this shit and yar cutting each other won't help your cases. You are not cutting snitches you cutting anybody for any reason you can find!"

Hero spoke up, "Bally, what's up with the VCR so we can watch some videos. And some real recreation we be having Rec at seven in the morning and don't be getting the gym. I know you run this shit, but we need ours, too."

"Look at little man," Bally said looking at a paper he had while continuing to talk. "Miguel Snuggs, yeah, I know your name. fighting…a homicide and asking about movies. Don't you make enough movies around here?" The dorm busted out laughing knowing the slang of making movies. "Yeah, I know who you are." His radio called for him and he talked into it, "Ten minutes."

Then he turned back to us and continued, "I know all of you and this won't help you get home. When you start acting right, I will look into what yar want but as of, right now, yar on the burn!" People were trying to talk to him. "No…no…no, you get no time from me acting like idiots and not even gangsters with all these senseless cutting in my building. Whatever happened to fighting? Yar too soft, I know little man over here ain't fighting nobody but got people scared because of his razor game. In fact, come here." Hero went to him. "We strip search you again? You coming with me." And they left.

I couldn't stay here if bail did not happen, I wanted to call home. I walked over to the phone and asked the kid on it for next. He looked at me like I was crazy.

"It's slot time my man."

"So, what that mean?" I asked.

"It means you have to wait until tomorrow to get your six minutes!" The big adolescent came to me. "You been acting like you live since you got here. Slot time is for people who put in work."

Gotti came over to is. "Let him get on the phone maybe he busting a move or something."

I got mad at both of them, I knew Gotti was trying to set me up and big man was trying to scare everybody. I got on the phone and my moms told me it was all done we were just waiting for them to get me out. Before I could say bye to my moms the big kid was back.

"Six minutes is up!"

I told my moms bye and smashed the phone on the floor causing it to splintered into pieces. Then hit the kid with punch after punch. He threw some back hitting me that I ignored while I was still swinging. I rushed into him and he threw me to the floor. I got up as his fists hit me in the face. He was trying to toss me on the floor, but I held on and kept punching. I felt another hit and went down to the floor.

"That's it's…that's it…stop before I let him hurt you!" The C.O. was inside with us, I noticed for the first time.

"Fuck you!" I said.

The C.O. left the dorm and the big kid started smiling. We kept fighting and as much as he was hurting me and throwing me around, I noticed his face was bruised up. Gotti came and stopped the fight. That night was long and although I had a mattress it was hard to sleep. Early the next morning I was called for bail.

CHAPTER THIRTY
LITTLE KID

It was flowing with customers for everybody who came out today, even now this late at night. It was almost time for my shift to end, but I was staring down the line of custies waiting on me as my back leaned against the building. I made it a habit to stand this way so they could see me, and I could see them. I was on point and kept my eyes on the lookout since Vuggio had come through the block three times today. One time he jumped out and searched people for guns. He found Cracks I tossed on the ground and just kept them. I told Steamer about the loss when it happened so he wouldn't take it out of my PC tonight.

I slowed down serving customers on purpose. "Next!" I called out.

The fiend Nubs came to me off the front of the line with three dirty ass dollars. He had a curly afro, was about my height which was short for a man, he looked white, but was Hispanic and all of his fingers were halves like they'd been burned off at the joints. I opened my hand with Cracks in my palm for him and he picked one up with two nubs like tweezers as the corner of his mouth curled. I hated it when he touched my skin, but if I handed Cracks to him, he would drop it and I don't want him standing around looking for Crack on the ground. He stared at a bottle of Crack, then switched it for another one from my palm. As he touched me again, I got angrier, he was about to drop it to switch but I closed my hand.

"Get the fuck on, Nubs. That's it, shit it's too hot out here for you to be picking Cracks," I fussed.

"Give me the first one, just give me the other one I had first," he replied.

"Next…get the fuck outta here, Nubs, before I smack you!" He gave me the creeps. As he walked off, he was staring at the one bottle of crack he still had. "Put that shit away, Jackass!" I yelled, he looked back at me and walked faster.

I leaned back on a car in no rush at all. Why should I care about how many bottles I sold? I got paid the same anyway. Earlier today two of my hundred packs came up six dollars short and that shit will come out of my spread money tonight. I looked down the block near Park Avenue and saw the new kid making sales. I nodded my head for the next custie to come and move along. It was a girl that be out here parlaying, she was getting dirtier by the day. She handed me nine dollars, as her hand touched mine, I became upset again. I hated fiends touching me, but her hand was warm. She looked in my eyes, her eyes were mesmerizing, and all this combine gave a horny feeling.

I looked at her lips wondering how they would feel knowing almost everybody got some head from her even Welo before I came to the block. But she didn't look like she did before, she did not look like she did last week. They all talked about how she would make you disappear in her mouth. I hadn't had the luxury of putting my dick in a girl's mouth yet. I wanted it bad, but I noticed her dirty clothes and felt nasty just thinking of her that way. I gave her three bottles, she walked away shaking her small ass. My lookout came off Lexington Avenue, I froze and was getting ready to toss the drugs thinking police was coming.

"Hold it down, I'll be right back, Cee." He told me and went behind the parlay. He said a few words to her then she followed him into Keith's building. He was an ass and would not leave the bigger kids out here to hustle without a lookout but did shit like this when I'm hustling.

The last of the Cracks from a hundred pack I started was loose in my pocket. I counted twenty-eight without taking them out.

"Next!" I served a custie real slow.

One time I got no spread money for the night and owed twenty-one dollars. That's when I knew some of the packs were being shorted and Cracks were ending up in somebody else's pockets for their PC. But I fixed that by counting out every bottle in every pack before I pitched it. Somehow, I was being shorted in a different way now. It had to be the custies, their asses were slick too. I looked at the line and nodded for the next custie who came with the money in his hand. I snatched it, counted it and put it into my pocket, then passed him his Crack. Welo told me to be on point, maybe he's teaching me. I'm making money for my shift and bottling up; it was a hassle putting all the Crack into thousands of bottles, but he gave me a thousand dollars every time I did it and a thousand dollars when I watched others do it.

"Next!" I yelled serving another custie. No matter what I needed my spread money and all this money counted.

"My change?" the custie I'd just served said standing there with me.

I hadn't noticed him because I was so caught up into my own thoughts. "Nah, exact money, keep it moving," I told him.

"I gave you ten dollars and you gave me three treys."

"Yeah, so you get three bottles. It's hot out here bring exact money next time. Next!" I yelled as the next custie handed me six dollars.

I gave him two bottles the custie who complained walked off. From across the street, I saw one of Ray The Boss' people buy a new Red Line bike from a custie and hand him a couple of bottles for the bike and rode it up and down the block. He had on some new Nikes that I'd never seen before.

"I'ma buy a pair of those tomorrow," I told myself.

Monk had just bought the Accord, I'ma get me a car for the summer. I just got to ask my moms to put it in her name. It was getting cold and real dark outside. I looked up the block seeing no cars parked facing us with people sitting in the front seat. T.N.T don't be rolling late and Vuggio had come through already I just wanted to get home.

"Next!" a white custie came with a guitar.

"This is brand new just give me five bottles for it," he offered.

"What the fuck, I'ma do with that bullshit? Man get the hell off the line," I argued.

"Okay, just give me two," he continued.

"I'm giving you one minute to get off my line before you get fucked up out here."

The new kid on the other end of the block who was wearing bummy clothes was moving his line faster than mines making sales without looking around. Keith's crew was flowing more than us lately, I'ma tell Welo about that shit, too. My lookout came out of Keith's building and walked straight over to me with the parlay and the old man who buys Crack from the top floor, both waiting in front of Keith's building for him to cop for them.

He rushed to me skipping the line of custies that waited. "Give me ten for the old man you know he about to freak off."

I counted out thirty dollars. I took my time retrieving the Cracks. "Hurry up nigga, you had me out here looking out for myself. Shit it's hot out here."

"Nigga, give me the bottles!"

I counted out ten, gave them to him and he must have used the old man's apartment to parlay with the girl and returned the favor by skipping the line for him. After going to them giving them the Cracks out in the open like he had a license to sell drugs. He posted back up on Lexington to do his job.

The next custie did not look like one and was a big dude, he handed me a twenty-dollar and I gave him six bottles. "Next!"

"My change homeboy," he told me not walking away.

"Exact money," I said to him.

He looked at me. "You got it twisted my man. I ain't no Crack head just give me my change or another bottle or something." He was not moving at all as he kept his focus on me.

The next customer was not approaching with him there. My work was almost finished, and this big guy was holding me up. He could probably beat the shit out of me, so I got off the wall.

"A yo' Steamer…yo', Druggem…Stagalee!" I yelled out.

The lookout Steamer and the new kid all came rushing, he looked at the sudden rush of people that were coming toward us with no fear. I swung with all my might hitting his chin dead on doing nothing his recreation didn't make him do. He pushed me down to the ground, but I was unfazed and focused on those coming to me. A kick came to his back making him move forward but not fall, punches came and another kick to his back. He knocked the lookout to the ground with a punch. Steamer hit him with a guitar breaking it on his head. I got up swinging, the new bummy kid was tossed down hard to the ground as others began coming including custies beating on the big man who was winning. He fought moving toward Lexington but not off the block. Not afraid he was positioning himself to fight with no one able to match him. I walked off and went to get the guns we kept stashed.

I ran back to the action and handed one gun to Steamer while keeping mine by my side as I inched toward him. The big man noticed this and walked off our block looking back as he made it to 3rd Avenue by McDonald's. Laughter erupted and some of the small kids on the block that jumped in were hyped with jokes.

As I made another sale, I told Steamer, "I'm done that's it and it's almost time for me to go."

"Finish another pack first. Shorty got a line waiting on him, knock them off and we all out of here. Why that nigga was flipping like that?" Steamer asked.

"He tried to jerk me on the money, thinking I was alone. So, why can't we let the new kid finish off, Steamer? Why I gotta do another pack?" I asked.

"Look the pack will go fast stop bitchin' Cee! I should make you pay for the guitar I just bought and broke on that big ass nigga."

"You bought that shit for rec, that ain't coming outta my PC."

The stash of packs was closer to Park Avenue and Steamer went to get me another hundred pack. I sat on the steps that led up into one of the tenement buildings across the street from the big church on the block closer to the Park Avenue side of 117th Street. It felt safer here for two reasons, one it was further from Lexington where the cars come down from and if they came the wrong way up the street from Park you knew to run. Second, it had a cement wall that covered both sides of you instead of handrails. I sat down on the steps counting out the hundred bottles in the pack with Steamer right there waiting on me. I nodded my head and he sat back on the car and called the new kid over.

Feeling shielded from anyone that was not directly in front of me, I stood up with my upper body now being seen above the wall and called out to the new kid's line.

"Next!" A custie passed his money up to me.

I had the whole pack out serving him right out of it. I handed bottles down to him, with the new kid in front of me making sales we were moving the line fast. Steamer counted out some money and leaned back onto a car as the kid served.

"Next!" the kid yelled.

"Pay your rent baby you know what time it is. The Landlord is here baby."

I took his money, counted out twenty-one dollars and put away the cash.

"What's wrong with this nigga…taking so long to count the money?" Landlord asked Steamer who ignored him. "It's all there shit you should be giving me double for having me waiting. I'm the Landlord baby, you better ask somebody."

I was passing him his Cracks when loud gunshots rang out at us. I ducked and dropped his Cracks on the steps.

Boom! Boom! Boom! Pop! Pop!

I could feel the scratching sounds of bullets hitting the surface on the other side of the cement wall as the new kid fell and Steamer went down crawling behind a car. More shots came hitting the cement wall meaning they were trying to shoot me. Shots kept hitting the opposite side of the wall I was behind making me flinch with every hit. I pulled out my gun and dropped the pack of cracks including loose ones that fell on steps where Landlord was ducked down.

"Give me the gun little nigga. Give me that shit or buss a move," he said in a high pitch.

I looked over the wall and saw the two men coming closer, one was taller than the other and taking careful aim at me.

Boom!"

I aimed my gun back and shot over the stoop as the gun jerked slightly my eyes blinked with every shot.

Pop! Pop! Pop! Pop! Pop! Pop!

I wanted to shoot Tall-Tall Man, I ducked back behind the wall. Steamer came out from in between the cars letting off shots at them. The new kid had blood on him.

"It's hot…it's hot…aahhh shit it burns…I'm hit!" he yelled.

Steamer stood up and looked down the block. I stood up with the empty gun pointed over the cement wall, I didn't see the shooters just our block people taking stashes and going inside buildings.

"Let's go! Get the drugs and money from him and go to Madison on 119th Street." The lookout came and Steamer told him to stay with the shot kid until the ambulance arrived.

The fiend Landlord was looking at the Cracks I dropped. I looked at him and he said, "Don't sleep baby don't sleep, I'm the Landlord." Then he walked off.

Steamer went and got the rest of the stashed Cracks. The kid was grunting and complaining about how much pain he was in. I took the rest of the drugs and money off the kid, then me and Steamer ran off the block with all our guns, drugs and money. We walked to 125th Street and 5th Avenue finally slowing down feeling safe. Steamer was wearing two rope chains and all new clothes but seemed rugged no matter what he had on.

"Yo' Cee, can we go to your house and get all this shit together?"

"Yeah, my moms is at work."

"Damn, I wish she was home," he said laughing.

I did not think it was funny, we hauled a cab and went to my crib. As we walked up the stairs Steamer was behind me. I opened my door with my keys and my sister, and her friend were sitting next to the stereo in two chairs listening to music. She looked at me like I was interrupting something important. However, when she saw Steamer the anger she had quickly vanished, and she started fixing herself up. Usually she would beef but instead, she stood and smiled.

"What's up, Cee, you need us to leave?" she asked.

"Uh…no," I said slowly and a little puzzled by her tone.

She was looking at Steamer and he was looking at her as we walked past the girls. We sat on the couch facing the television with them to our backs.

"Come on let's get this done," Steamer suggested.

The music was playing, and I pulled out money and Cracks from my right pants pocket knowing this was my work and dumped it all out.

"This is my work let me count it out. That nigga Landlord was close to my Cracks when I dropped them."

Steamer started taking out stacks of money in rubber bands and putting them together in piles of fives on the coffee table in front of us. I counted out my work and work money putting it neatly together on the table adding up to three-hundred dollars combined. From another pocket, I pulled out another stack of money mixed with loose Cracks and dropped it on the table. I reached in my pocket grabbing a bunch more while Steamer took off his coat and moved the gun to the front of his waist.

"This that kid's work," I told him.

I spaced it apart from what was mine on the table. I had at least ten more left I could feel. There was an urge to pull it out but since it did not come out the first time, I just left it feeling a little nervous. We finished up with the new kid being sixty dollars short, but he did not care or even question it since his mind was on something else.

"Let me use the phone to beep, Welo," he said.

Before I could answer my sister said, "Yeah, there's a phone in the kitchen. Come on I'll show you." They left to use the phone.

There was thousands of dollars in front of me as I adjusted the gun on my waist and took off my coat, I heard a voice behind me.

"What's that?" she said.

I looked back over the couch seeing the face. "My gun," I answered.

"Can I see it?" She came over to me and I passed it to her like it was nothing.

"Is it loaded?" she asked.

"It was but I used em," I told her.

I could tell she wanted to ask more question but didn't since Steamer and my sister had reentered the room

Before I was able to feel anything about that in a cute voice I heard, "Corey why you don't say hi to me?"

"I do but you be ignoring me."

"So, I'm not ignoring you now. These are nice!" She came around and sat next to me then started touching my jeans. I felt every finger on my leg. "Can you buy me a pair of these?" They were Levi denim and I just wanted her to keep touching me. "I like them with the jacket," she said.

I felt myself get hard. "Yeah," I answered, thinking that was just spread money to me.

Her hand moved off my leg and I found myself counting out money from my pocket then I felt her hand on my dick.

A slow song was playing in the background and she leaned over me with her chest touching my back and said, "Cee, you like me?"

"Yeah, I like you," I answered.

"So, let's go tomorrow and you buy me that Levi denim jean suit." She kissed my earlobe and I could smell her sweet gum candy breath.

"Yeah," I said real low forgetting what she'd asked.

"Can I have a hundred dollars for some door knockers?" She stood up watching me count money.

I noticed I was now counting Steamers money that was in fifteen hundred piles.

She then walked to the kitchen, "Wait, I'll be right back." She skipped away.

I pushed all of Steamers money together and quickly counted out the Crack bottles I kept in my pocket from the kids work, it was nine. I placed that in my work pile and took out twenty-seven dollars cash from the cash pile and put that in my pocket. Everything was in order and she came back out in her bra with some water.

"It's hot, drink some water." She sat down beside me.

I drank some water then she kissed me putting her tongue in my mouth. After we broke away, I looked toward my sister's room.

"Let's go to your room, Cee, they doing them." She took off her bra and I saw her hard, small nipples then she ran to my room knowing where it was.

I followed her and closed the door. She was smiling and laying on my bed with her pants down to her ankles looking at me.

"Oh, yeah, Cee that hundred you got it?"

I counted out a hundred dollar and gave it to her. Then I took my pants off and sat next to her. She bent at her waist and put it in her pockets that were at her ankles, I watched her every move. She kicked off the pants while she laid back on her hands, then took off her panties that said Tuesday on them. She took my hand, put it on her hair in between her legs and it felt wet as my fingers started going inside. She closed her eyes and laid all the way back. My heart was beating fast and I started moving fast. She opened her legs, then I pulled my pants down to my knees and got on top of her with my shirt on. She guided me inside of her, and I started pumping fast. She was taking off my shirt while I pumped and when she held me, I started coming and was finished as I laid on top of her.

CHAPTER THIRTY-ONE
MONK

The Cross Bronx Expressway had only a few cars on it and most of them were speeding past me. It was eleven at night, I was driving 55 miles an hour to pick up Cindy and her friends in my new dark blue Honda Accord. They were going to a disco type club and she needed some money. I turned on the radio and Biz Markie came to life singing his hit song.

'*Oh, baby you, you got what I need, and you say she's just a friend*!'

I might just wife Cindy, her mom is cool, she is cool, looks good and smart. It was not luck that took me out of the schoolyard before the police ran up in there but her. I knew Vuggio was just waiting to grab me up when she basically saved me, I'm definitely going to wife her.

Last week I tricked off, buying her a beeper, some Reeboks, got her hair and nails done, got my nails done for the first time, then we saw Ghost on 86th Street on Broadway and finally I hit it only to find out she was a virgin. That thing was good, too. As I drove now, I was still thinking about how good it actually was.

Commercials came on the radio, so I turned it down low as I saw the small buildings of the Bronx cluttered together with Graffiti on every wall. I was looking out over the rail, seeing a place totally different from Harlem. A calm feeling came over me as I drove in the coolness of the night. My mind had time to think about the block clearly. I left two people pitching with enough work to last them till morning. Vuggio has been on a mission with shootings after shootings going on so I only kept one pitcher out during the day taking precautions not to risk two people getting caught up.

Welo kept his full crew out and was not one to fuck with. His crew was banging out shots back and forth with some dudes yesterday. I hope Keith never gets into beef with him, Keith would probably just leave, and Scottie would probably kill Welo. Then Keith would come back with more beef making me a target. He left me the block but took a big loss when they robbed his apartment, I don't know what he's going to do.

My name has been in the police's mouth because I'm on the block way too much. Shit when Keith gave me the first brick, I was taking all the PC going hand to hand myself using workers only when I slept or went to see Cindy. Scared to be out on the block I pitched from inside Keith's building as the work was so good it sold itself which brought the custies inside looking for the Red tops to cop. Hugging the block was my thing but that's a rap, I can't be out there like that no more there is too much tough guy shit going. One thing Keith taught me by his example was to be smart and stay away from violence.

As I turned off the Expressway in the Bronx, I stopped at a light, turned the music up and heard *Vanilla Ice's Ice-Ice Baby* then turned it back down. I need to buy some tapes and needed to hurry up and get where I was going so I could smoke. I was way up in the Bronx and Throgsneck Projects was coming up. It was said to be wild, but I didn't play into beefing and didn't wear gold to be getting robbed. Another good thing I picked up from Keith was that money was better than anything you could buy. I drove around the projects and saw people grouped in places and even sales being made. I drove past her building and found a space to park.

Some girls were together outside dressed up for Friday night. They were looking good but not dressed like Harlem chicks. Their project buildings were taller and more spaced out than in my hood. As soon as I got out of the car my beeper went off, I was glad to have something to do to not look at the girls out there. I walked past them to a phone booth, it was just a phone on a pole but the whole booth was intact. I was surprised because the Bronx was usually run down, but way up here was in good shape. As I grabbed the phone, I looked across the street outside the projects onto a grassy field elevated with dudes playing catch with a football. I heard laughs as they tried to catch the ball that disappeared into the night's darkness and dropped down from nowhere hitting the ground. It was tossed up again this time someone caught it when it came down. The catcher looked at me and the rest of their eyes followed his. Ignoring them I dialed Cindy's beeper putting in 07734 which would show up as '*Hello*' on her screen then I beeped her again with my number so she would know I was here.

My beeper went off it was to the phone on 117th Street. I called it back, my cousin who was pitching answered on the first ring.

"Yo'…yo' who this?" He was louder then he needed to be.

"It's me fool. What's good yar need me or something? You just hit me up," I said.

"This Monk, right?" he asked with a serious tone.

"Yeah, nigga, you just beeped me. What's good?"

"Okay, just being sure it's you. That E.R. nigga wanted you, he left a new beeper number for you to call. He said it's important stuff. You want it now?"

"No, I don't have a pen just beep it to me. Everything else good?"

"Yeah, we good." And he hung up.

I ignored the other numbers on the beeper screen and walked back to my car with E.R. on my mind. He hustled hard and was like a young Scottie and Keith mixed together. He took a big loss by being arrested, maybe he needed to pitch to get his money up to buy some work. My beeper sounded with his number on it.

"I'll call him later," I said to myself.

As I continued walking to my car a girl from the group started talking loud enough for me to hear her. "He can't even handle this!" she said.

I looked over at her catching her eyes as she turned her little body to show herself. I got inside my car and looked at myself in the rearview mirror.

"Damn, Monk, you fly as hell!" I told myself.

I turned up the radio and smiled as I heard the announcer say a new song from Soul to Soul. I stepped out facing the group of girls, I wanted to smoke but didn't know how the police rolled around here. I leaned back on my door and listened to the words play.

'However, do you want it…however do you need it…however do you want it… the beat was smooth and the girls in the projects put their hands in the air sticking their asses out and started laughing while cutting looks at me especially the same cute, little, brown-skinned one with Classic Reeboks on. Behind them, my girl came out with two of her friends all smiling and speed walking to me.

Chantel yelled out closing her eyes and shaking her head, "That's my song!"

They walked past the other girls who were vying for my attention not paying them any mind. Cindy's two friends came first, they slapped my hand five as Cindy followed right behind them.

Cindy gave me a hug and kissed me with her eyes closed. She was happy to see me and the car since it was her first time seeing it.

"We in there tonight, yar?" she said with a big smile, her eyes showed she was truly happy.

"They don't play music like this in the club we going to tonight, Cindy. I just want you to know that!" said her friend Chantel.

"That's okay, we going to have fun," Cindy responded.

"I just want to relax to a different scene tonight and be around a different crowd. That's why I picked this one for tonight," the one I did not know spoke looking at them seeking their approval.

"We going to have fun yar," Cindy said smiling.

She laid on me and started singing the song knowing the words. She looked into my eyes and I felt her happiness. Her warm body against mine was making me hard. My beeper went off, but I ignored it as not to ruin the moment. All I wanted was to figure out where we could go fuck, right now. I couldn't help but remember her cute little sounds and how tight she was, this only made me grow harder.

"Your mom home?" I asked.

She put her tongue out letting the tip of it touch her top lip. A cute but not sexual thing she does when she's thinking.

"No freshy," she said turning her body dancing to the music.

She was swirling her butt on me. "Well, let's take a drive alone before I take yar to the club!" I told her leaning my upper body over to her ear so only she could hear me.

She turned back facing me and did the tongue thing again, as she looked at me with deep thought, then said, "No." She leaned forward on me, putting her small fist under her chin with her elbows between her chest and my stomach.

I grabbed her ass with one hand, then she put her face in my chest.

"Where the fuck you think you going?" A dude grabbed the girl's arm that came with Cindy. He was yelling loud over the music, blowing my whole mood.

She pulled away from him. "Who the fuck you touching? Don't touch me, nigga!"

This the type of shit I be trying to avoid. I wanted to get the fuck from there and go somewhere so Cindy would let buss her ass. I'ma kill it this time. Other dudes were with the loud dude.

I said smoothly, "Yo' where can I get some weed around here?"

I lightly got off Cindy and walked around the car, then got in ignoring the scene being created. I opened the passenger door and Cindy got in with me. The girl was screaming loud shouting threats. Chantel got in the backseat as *Humpty* started playing on the radio station. My eyes caught the eyes of the raging boyfriend, I slightly adjusted it to my girl avoiding his stare.

"So, they sell weed over there?" I asked pointing past the dude.

She looked. "No…no, but I know where, though. We got to drive around the block just hold up a minute, Monk."

She was confused by my question at this time and I was trying to tell her, it was time to get her so we could go. My eyes were now ahead, and my hands rested on the steering wheel, I was ready to go.

"Get whoever the fuck you want bitch!" the raging boyfriend said.

They were arguing at full force and I was really ready to just go but Chantel had her door opened in the back waiting for the girl. Cindy was looking at them, I backed up the car slowly as much as I could. I got stares from the girls inside and with their eyes, on me, I turned the wheels ready to pull out when she finally got in.

"I'm not fucking with you no more! What you going to do, huh…what? Beat me up because I don't want you? You go ahead beat me, you still not fucking with this no more!"

Me and everyone else was looking at him for a response including his boys.

He was mad as hell. "Word, alright, you want to play me. I got you…I got you, go ahead!" He walked off looking hurt and angry.

As she got in my car, I was so happy to finally be leaving. Cindy gave me directions around the block. We stopped where a couple of guys was chilling. Why the fuck we stopped here I have no idea and was starting to get a little agitated.

"Give it to me," Cindy said. I gave her two hundred in all singles. She laughed giving me a light kiss with her warm lips on my cheeks. "No…no, Big Willie. The weed money, we here. You wanted some weed. But I'll take this thank you very much, Hubby." She lifted her ass off the seat and put the money into her back pocket.

"How much you want he got dimes?"

I had forgotten I said anything about the weed spot and gave her forty dollars. I had three bags of smoke on me already from the bus stop spot. In Harlem, I'd check this shit out and see what it was about.

"Happy Land going to be popping tonight. You sure you not going with us?"

"Not my style but a hotel with music playing after and some talking is more like it."

"Oh, boy, I see where your mind is…forget it." She got out of the car with the money and closed the door. She looked back to see if I was watching.

As I watched her, I felt stares of my own, I looked back at the girls in the car.

"What?" I said.

"That's all yar be wanting," said the one I didn't know.

"Not at all, we be wanting some other stuff, too." I was saved by the song playing.

They forgot me and went right into singing and waving their hands like they were taking over by *En Vogue.*

"My first mistake was I wanted too much time."

They moved their bodies with their eyes closed, like they were in a trance then I cut the music off.

"Save that for your man, don't be erasing all the newness out of my car and all that."

But they kept singing even with the radio off and knew all the words.

"Happy Land here we come, let's go, baby!" Cindy got in and kissed me. Then she placed the bags in my hand. It looked like some good dark chocolate weed.

"What no pit stops for us?" I questioned.

She did that thing with her tongue on her lip as she looked at me. "You can wait, I'm going to make it real good for you."

The girls in the back said in unison, "You going to get the total package boy!" They started giggling.

I was looking outside at the attention I was getting and drove off. I parked in a spot still in their projects. We rolled up two blunts together and smoked in the car. Cindy was smoking for the first time as my hands rested in her lap and felt on her while she pulled on the blunt. Her friends in the back were smoking and paying us no mind. When she passed it to me, I pulled on it and held it while feeling her small hand on my dick. When I get her this time after hitting it slow, I'ma go all out, knowing she won't be able to take it. Maybe I could drop her friends off first? When I looked over at her, her tongue was on her lip and she looked at me like she knew what I was thinking.

"Okay…okay you got it." I drove them to Happy Land.

As I drove back to 117th Street I was smoking a bag from the bus stop, first I passed 117th checking it out. I parked two blocks away and came to 117th beeping E.R. on the Lexington Avenue phone booth. I put 117 in his beeper. I saw my cousin out there making sales to some night stragglers. E.R. did not call back but instead came to me in minutes to the phone booth where I waited.

"What's up, Monk? I need you!" he said.

"I can't be out here on the block; next time I beep you just call me back. Come on let's walk." We went to 116th Street.

"Yo' I got a weight sale waiting, right now. Can you get some bricks from, Keith?" he asked.

"If we got cash we can get as much as we want. What's the PC?" I asked.

"Well, what can we get it from, Keith, for? I'll give you a big profit but not fifty-fifty…this my sale."

"All money is good money E.R. What we paying so we can figure this thing out?"

E.R. looked at me and smiled. "Twenty-eight…he wants two."

"Good money, I'll ask Keith to give it to us at twenty-two."

After calling Keith and getting an O'Jay cab E.R. did not want nobody to meet his custie. So, I got Keith to give me two keys for twenty-two each that I would pay him for later. We made twelve-thousand and E.R. gave me five, it was a good night. March 25th, 1990, my first key sale ever.

"Tomorrow, we going to see *'Do The Right Thing'* at the movies. You wanna come?" E.R. asked me.

"Yeah, hit me on my beeper. Want me to drop you off at your block?" I responded.

"In what?"

I pulled out my keys and opened the door to my parked car, E.R. busted out laughing. "What's so funny?" I asked.

"You frontin' nigga. We been riding around in an O'Jay and your whip, right here. Then out of every place in East Harlem we standing next to your car."

I laughed with him and said, "I don't know how to drive to Long Island." We left his block.

It was after four now, I was waiting for Cindy to beep me to pick her up. But there was nothing from her. E.R. got out of the car and that Stacy chick got out of a cab and gave us a look, she looked good. The money I had on me got me nervous. Keith's forty-four stacks plus my PC and pack money I picked up, I drove home to drop some cash off. Scottie beeped me and I went by his crib still not seeing any beeps from Cindy. I was getting mad waiting on her, I ignored two beeps from girls and she probably took a cab home already. If she don't hit me up I'ma call one of them back or swing by 1990 maybe Stacy will be outside.

When I got to Scottie's crib it was dark everywhere all I could see was the table with sewing needles and thread on it.

He seemed very relaxed. "You good?" he asked.

"Yeah, all is regular, everything is Ivory," I answered.

"Give me five-hundred," he told me just like that.

I kept a stack on me after dropping off all that money I had earlier. I gave him half of it for whatever he needed it for. I saw three guns laying on the kitchen counter.

"You need me?" he asked staring through me.

"Nah, shit is smooth, right now, Scottie."

He kept his silence and just stared. I took my cue to leave, Scottie was always quiet, but this just felt more eerie than ever. I walked to the door noticing there were no dogs. Oh, shit I forgot one of them got killed. Being that they were Scottie's true family I had no words for him and left.

I slept good once I got home, the next morning after washing up. I got dressed and checked my beeper, there was nothing from Cindy. This shit was crazy, that's why I don't be getting serious with these bitches. My father was not home last night, I opened his bedroom door and there he was laid out with his clothes on. He must have been out drinking somewhere last night. He was a good dad when I was a kid. Now he just couldn't pull himself together after my moms died, he was not able to give up the Vodka.

I drove to 126th Street and Lexington my little breakfast spot and ordered some sausages, grits, eggs, and toast with a side of orange juice. I sat on the spinning stool while the two men worked fast on their flat stainless steel big hot plate with a pile of freshly made home fries, over to the side waiting to be ordered. They were filling orders for customers who mostly needed their food to go. The store was tiny with eight stools to sit on and no room for any other customer.

One of the cooks looked at me and said, "What no lady friend last night you eat breakfast alone?"

"I'm getting money, Papa. Can't use the little head all the time."

He told his partner in their language something. I think they spoke Albania and they both laughed and served an awaiting customer.

"What he say?" I asked, wanting to know why they were laughing.

"He say he always think with his big head down there!" he replied serving a person some coffee.

I laughed with them. "I got bitches for days, kiddo. Give me three more orders of the same to go."

"Okay, Big Willie you got it. You got bitches?" Hearing him talk like that when he don't speak so much was funny.

Guy was waiting in front of Keith's building when I drove pass checking the block. She probably knocked on his door wanting some work, and no one answered. I parked two blocks away and came to the block through Park Avenue. When I entered Keith's building my cousin who'd been out all night and Guy followed me as customers waited on them outside. I saw Welo's crew cross over on our side to serve them.

We walked into the hall out of the exit view and my cousin pulled out his pack money and gave it to me. "This is mine and that other nigga you had out here money. He just left it's all there, though, I counted it." He gave me piles of cash in bundles with mad singles.

"This thirty-two hundred, right?" I asked.

"Yeah, you took the other money last night."

I nodded knowing that already.

"I'm out and it's clicking this morning, but I need to sleep cuzzo."

"Cool, go ahead, I'll see you tonight," I said counting his money hundred by hundred and folding it over in piles.

He hugged me and left the building with his pockets full of PC. As he left the building some customers came in. I gave Guy five packs and an order of breakfast forgetting I had ordered for my cousin who'd left.

She smiled more surprised than happy. "Good looking, I did not eat all morning."

She opened a pack and served the three custies then sat at the bottom of the stairs and started eating her food. Knocks on the entrance door were heard as Guy sat eating and looking at me with caution. She took her gun out her waist and put it in her jacket pocket so it would be accessible. We heard the knock again; I became nervous since I had a pack on me and thirty in the car. I peeked and saw four custies waiting in between the door wanting the Red tops. I let them in, served them and as they left three more came and I served them as well.

"This is stupid," I mumbled to myself, I had to get out of here. I turned to Guy as she continued eating her food. "Yo' I'm out, hold it down."

"I got this go ahead, Big Willie."

The old man from upstairs came from the elevator's direction and went to Guy, he bought a whole pack off her. As I went outside custies wanted the Red, Keith had made a bomb. I looked up the block and saw Welo's crew making sales. So, I pitched the rest of the work I had. Guy must have finished her food because she came out and custies rushed to her as she made some sales. I noticed the white bag with the food inside of it hanging off her wrist. I walked off to my car.

I needed another worker, I started feeling frightened of more than just the police, but I was making so much money, I needed to start carrying a gun. On Madison Avenue I beeped funky Dee, we called him that because his name was Darrell and he did not use deodorant. We used him to hustle at times, he called me back and I told him to come through, it's money here. Then I sat in the car only for a few minutes when Guy beeped me. I knew it meant she needed more packs this made me even more nervous.

I went back to Keith's building and Guy gave me five hundred dollars. I gave her ten packs this time and she ran out of the building to make more sales. I stepped out and saw Welo's crew again on our side making sales. I went to the pay phone on the corner, knowing I shouldn't have been there and beeped Scottie. Customers were flooding the block as Ray's people came. The kid from Welo's crew went to his side and the phone rang.

I picked it up. "Come through tonight, I need you to post up out here." He was quiet for a minute, my beeper started going off and it was Keith.

"I'll come at eight but I'm not staying."

"Okay, that's cool." He hung up.

A custie walked up to me on the phone and said, "Yo' I got six hundred tokens for half price in Cracks. What's up?"

"You got it on you, right now?" I asked.

"Hell yeah, fresh from the robber. You want it or not?" He was a tough looking man with a material type bag in his hand.

"Yeah, let's go to Park Avenue."

After that transaction, I sat in my car and my beeper went off. It was this shorty from Carver, but I had shit to do. Cindy still hadn't hit me up. Guy and Funky Dee made sales fast and I needed more packs, so I had them come to my car with the work money. I gave them what I had left and took the work money home. I had thirty packs in the car now and kept getting deals. I bought walkmans, new sneakers in boxes, video game cartridges, even baby gold jewelry. It was one of those days and I parked on Madison on 117th deciding to stay close to the block. I looked at the block, I saw cars set in position then T.N.T rolled past. I got in my car and drove off.

This was some bullshit and I went home. I parked in front of my building. Two young kids from the 3rd floor who always asked to hustle gave me a high five each.

"That's your ride?" asked one of them.

"Yeah, you like it?" I asked.

"That's the new Accord, it's okay."

I laughed. "Okay, huh, yeah alright yar want to make some bread?"

I sent them both with packs of Reds to pitch together and told them to watch out for T.N.T and stay in Keith's building. I just wanted to finish another brick. Hopefully, they don't get caught but they were under sixteen so it wouldn't be shit for them anyway. Plus, T.N.T wasn't coming back, I hoped. I fell asleep upstairs and woke up to my beeper ringing full of hits but none by Cindy. I forgot to call Keith earlier and did it now to his house phone.

"Who's this?" A cute woman's voice said.

"That's how yar answer the phone there? Damn, make me not want to call no more. It's me, Monk, hola."

"Oh, hey, Monk it's Julissa sorry about that. Who you want, Keith?"

"Well, I'll take Keith, but I was calling for you."

"Yeah, right, little nigga maybe a couple of more years, some more class and some years in the gym then you can be my husband. Hold on let me get you, Keith." I heard her yelling out to Keith and heard Abuela in the background.

"You heard, Monk I shot a gun and saved Julissa."

"What…who this? Davi, what you just said to me?" Then the phone dropped, and I heard Julissa in the background.

"Estupido, gayate and get in the room now!"

Then Keith picked up. "Hello, Monk."

"Yeah, this is me. You got a full house going there, huh? I got to spend the night one day if you keeping Julissa there."

"Yeah, the real life after life, you good?"

"Yeah, I got this Keith, shit is all gravy."

"Good…good, but you going to have to do without, Scottie. I'ma send him to Puerto Rico for two weeks or so. I'll have one of the Brooklyn people stay in his place and hold you down."

"Cool, Keith just give him my beeper."

"Yeah, I will, when you're up we gonna talk. Be careful and you should carry or have someone always carrying."

"Yeah, I've been thinking about that, I will."

"Alright, Monk, I'm gone, hit me later."

"Later, Keith." We both hung up.

I saw Guy later; she did not get caught up in the sweep, but funky Dee did on his first day pitching she told me. She finished all her work and so did the two new kids who stood out hustling. I met them on Madison Avenue not wanting to be on the block. My cousin came back taking packs for his shift and I went back home. I fell asleep again I counted out the money in stacks of five thousand and picked up Guy from 117th. I drove to 1990 so we could go see the movie. It was crowded when I parked right in front of the building and walked over to E.R. and his crew.

A conversation was going on in the crowd and I heard someone telling E.R., "Shit, I'm not going nowhere that I'm locked in. Didn't you hear about that fire that killed all those people?"

"Nah, what fire…where?" E.R. said.

His boy Tee said, "Yeah, last night eighty-seven people was killed. The cops found out it was a jealous boyfriend who started the fire."

"Word, damn that must have been some good pussy!" An older dude with them said.

Tee continued, "They say he chained the doors from the outside."

"Yeah, them Bronx niggas be on that beat there girl up if she don't fuck with them no more type shit," I stated.

Tee said you right that's where it was in the Bronx. He burnt down that club called Happy Land.

CHAPTER THIRTY-TWO

CINDY

"I can't breathe!" I was saying but no one was listening to me.

People were pushing past me going in the direction of the entrance. I tried to follow but other people came running back toward me, smoke was everywhere, and they just disappeared into it.

I was frozen with movement all around me and started crying. My throat was dry, the air was hard to inhale. I was gasping, and screams came from all directions. The alcohol feeling in my body was fading as the reality focused in, I did not believe or understand what was going on. I took small steps toward the back of the club and away from the pushing crowd, I'm going to die.

My friend Chantel ran to me speaking fast but I just cried, and she held my hand. I was smaller than her, smaller then everybody and nobody helped me, but she stood by me, a crowd ran back toward us.

"There's no way out, the door was chained from the outside!" they screamed.

Music was playing behind all the commotion. People were moving in groups not being able to see in front of them. Their hands were extended out like zombies walking as smoke erupted everywhere getting heavier, panic broke out. I kept walking to the back of the club step by step leading us. Feeling Chantel's hand in mine gave me hope as people ran past us in two directions from the entrance. A big guy ran into me, throwing me back, hurting me, then someone ran right into my arms breaking our grip. We reconnected our hands and it was broken again as people were running right through our arms. I cried harder and fell to the floor. I felt her hand on me, I got up and we stood closer to each other and held hands tighter. The music stopped and loud screams rang out.

"*Fire! Fire! Fire*!" People were yelling all around us.

Trying to breath was difficult, I got knocked to the floor, but got up with Chantel crying and holding onto me. We were not running around like everybody else. The coughing was everywhere so I calmed myself down. I couldn't take the smoke and I couldn't see. I took off my sweater and hot air hit my skin, I covered my face and breathed through it.

Chantel cried out, "Let's try and…" her voice was lost in the noise around me.

I held her close to me and said, "Relax." I said this like four times.

I was trying to speak directly into her ear as more smoke filled my mouth. I quickly put my shirt over my mouth and nose showing her how I was breathing. She took off her shirt exposing her bra and skin, she placed the shirt over her face and nodded her head up and down. She breathed with her eyes wide open. Our eyes met each other for a moment until the smoke-filled mines forcing me to shut them, as I still held her close while other people kept running past us.

"I don't want to die…I don't want to die!" I told her in a muffled voice through the sweater.

"So, let's not die…breath slow!" she said muffled through the shirt.

I couldn't really hear but understood by her gestures as her shoulders went high up as her chest filled up and my eyes closed tight.

"Just look at me," she said and kept speaking to me moving the shirt off her face with her lips on my ear.

She was speaking to me as hands were touching me that was not hers, trying to feel their way around, I slapped one off me.

"If they're running back and forth the same people and can't get out. We can't get out either. So, let's stay calm and breath…look at me breathe!" I heard her in my ear.

My eyes burned so I shut them and stayed facing her with our hands holding each other's arms. We stood there getting glances of each other. My eyes were burning, my throat was dry and hurt like a hard object was in it. I was swallowing dryness nothing went down except more pain. So, I stopped trying and the tears helped me to peek here and there feeling them clean my eyes then heat came over me like a wave forcing my eyes open to see that I was not on fire.

The fire must be close to us it was more than hot and starting to make me sweat. The air I took in was choking me and Chantel tried to talk, I could not make sense of nothing and was choking to breathe in. Her crying voice was saying something, and she pulled me down to the floor with her.

"Better," she said, and I breathe through my sweater.

Then I felt a kick to my head, and I cried while holding her. She cried as we laid on the floor with our shirts over our faces breathing slow, holding each other. I got kicked in the eye and cried harder then felt my earrings being snatched out of my ear. I let the sweater drop off my face and she put her hand to my face making me hold the sweater up. I couldn't open my eyes, I couldn't breathe, the heat was over me, I must have been burning. I felt her and another kick to my back. I felt but saw nothing it was all dark, I couldn't feel her hand…I felt nothing I heard nothing, and my sight went black.

I pushed up off my hand getting upright and took a deep breath. I was confused as I breathed in hard deep breaths, I woke up in a hospital to my mother holding and shushing me.

"It's okay…see she's okay. My Cindy is a fighter and a drug dealer. What you doing with that beeper?"

I smiled, thinking about the beeper and said out loud, "Oh, snap, Monk!"

My mother said, "Who?"

Then I thought about my friends. "Chantel, where's Chantel!"

A nurse came into the room, right over to me and touched my head trying to ease me back into a laying position, but I didn't let her.

She said, "Just relax and lay back. Relax you are a lucky lady."

I half smiled and repeated, "Chantel?"

She looked at me and responded, "We will fill you in but calm down you had a lot of smoke inhalation."

I closed my eyes thinking about what happened and felt my face because it hurt. I felt the bruises and knew I had a black eye as it all came back to me. I cried feeling the tear on my earlobes.

CHAPTER THIRTY-THREE
ERIC ROSARIO

It was three in the morning, Chito and Tee met me on the twenty-fifth floor of my building, they were both ready for anything I had in store for them. I felt strong as we stood together in the empty quiet hallway full of closed apartment doors. After me and Monk got back to Harlem from Long Island, I beeped them three times each and they both came quickly.

"We have to bottle up and start pushing this work, right now!" I said to them pulling out two big Ziplock bags of hard-cooked Crack from my waist.

I spent six-thousand-six hundred of my seven thousand PC I made with Monk right back with Keith buying three-hundred grams and getting three hundred more on consignment the most work I'd ever had in my life.

"Where we going to do that? It's late to be finding a place to bag up." Tee said, his voice carrying through the hall, as he looked at the work I held.

We all felt exposed and walked in unison out from the long open hall into the four-elevator waiting area.

Speaking in a low tone, I said, "Fuck it, Tee go to your house and get two plates and a bowl for us. Chito, you go to the twenty-four-hour smoke shop and get a pack of razors, a lighter and twenty-hundred packs of 019 blue top bottles, oh and some snacks." I gave Chito the money I was still not sure where we were going to bottle up, but I was not going nowhere until I knew.

As I leaned back on the elevator door, I felt gushes of wind from the other side, shooting up the shafts, then it hit me.

"Tee bring candles or a flashlight, too!" It was grind time.

After they both came back, we went inside the incinerator that was in the elevator waiting area. It was the size of a closet and smelled like piss and trash. The dim light above was just enough to see the chute on the wall. Me and Tee sat on the floor facing each other and Chito's back was to the door, as he held two flashlights above us directed on the plate, Tee had laid out in between me and him. We took out the stuff from the paper shopping bag Chito came back with and started setting up. We pulled the covers off the razors and opened up some chips and soda, then folded the brown bags neatly, they'd come in handy for us to use later.

I pulled the 019 vials and tops out, I ripped a small piece on the corner of the plastic it came in and poured them right on the floor, keeping the plastic intact. Then I took out two rocks from a Ziplock bag and placed one on Tee's plate and one on mine and we started. The chopping of Crack was noisy to us, especially when the razor hit the plate and for a moment it was all we heard.

"I left my door unlocked I have to sneak back in by six before my moms wake up," Tee said.

I nodded and kept chopping the Crack into little rocks that I knew would fit into the vials. I liked to put two good sized rocks in each vial for the base heads that smoked the pipe and the last of the dust that's left I put into vials for the wool heads that liked it in their blunts. After chopping I placed the rocks two at a time in a vial and capped them off with my Blue tops, I dropped the finished product into the bowl and Tee did the same, until we finished all the loose ones on the floor. I counted them out into a brown bag to be sure it was a hundred as Chito took the bag and left us to go pitch it, then opened another pack. It was so late and quiet I heard the elevator doors open from inside the incinerator room.

Chito's voice came to us, "I'm out."

Then quiet came back, replaced in moments with the sound of chopping Crack. The flashlights were now on the floor pointed at the plates, lighting up our faces with it as we bottled up. I counted another hundred vials from the bowl, into the brown bag and gave it to Tee. He put it in his pocket and continued to chop. Time was lost and I was in a zone with a plate of already chopped Crack, I moved fast, taking the Crack putting it into the vials it became one move to me as the Cracks piled up in the bowl. I took plastics that the empty vials came in and put in forty vials now filled with Crack into it and melted the tip of the small tare with a lighter smashing it together with my thumb and finger feeling a light burn that happens every time. Me and Tee froze in motion as we heard the elevator door open, someone got off and the incinerator door opened hitting Tee's back. Chito stuck his face in looking down at us in the same position he'd left us in.

"It's clicking out there and there's a custies for a thirty-sale waiting on the third floor, she wants a five-dollar short," Chito whispered loudly.

"Third floor you said?" Tee asked while getting up to leave.

"Yeah, it's the crazy voodoo lady," Chito said switching places with Tee. He started chopping away at the crack as Tee left to pitch.

By five thirty we'd done four hundred vials with Tee and Chito switching places back and forth doing packs. The paper shopping bag had a pile of sealed packs and work money rolled in knots of hundreds. The floor was junky with loose empty vials, empty soda, chips and candy wrappers laying all around us. Tee was bottling up and Chito was out pitching when he broke our silence.

"It's time for me to go before my moms gets up," he was loud now.

"Yeah, I got to go soon, too. Go 'head we'll catch up later," I told him as he got up. "Hold up, take these and when you wake up you can start again." I gave him ten packs of Blue top Cracks.

As I was sitting in the incinerator alone, the block must've slowed up because Chito did not come back right away so I continued, Crack, vials, top, bowl, Crack, vial, top, bowl and a noise from behind me made me jump and turn with the razor in my hand. I laughed in the tight room as I could hear the trash continuing to fall down the chute in the wall behind me. Someone on a higher floor threw their trash out this morning it was time for me to go. When I got up, I was stiff like crazy and heard my bones crack. I was hungry as I tasted the candy bar, I'd eaten a while ago. I left the incinerator with everything in the shopping bag, I waited for the elevator and when it opened Chito was on it. I got on and we rode back down.

"Damn, I thought you fell asleep on me. Fuck what time is it?" I said.

"Ain't no more custies coming, right now, but I can't go home until after eight. It's seven now," Chito replied.

I reached in the bag giving him four packs. "Take these since you staying out in case it picks up. But I gotta go home."

He put them in two pockets as the elevator moved quick not stopping on any floors.

"I'm going to the breakfast spot on a hunnit and twenty-six first, I'm starving," Chito said.

"I would but I don't want my moms to catch me outside, finish what you can, and I'll see you tomorrow…well today on the block."

It was daylight outside, and I beeped my older sister to let me in the house. She better have her beeper on vibrate, too. When I went home my other brother and sister was sleep along with my moms. I hid a ziplock bag in her room while she slept, hyped up my mind was racing. I was about to make thousands, not wanting to sleep I turned the sound off the TV and played Excite Bike on my Nintendo to relax.

I must have fallen asleep because I woke to my sister saying, "Tee is at the door…wake up!"

"Where's mommy at?" I asked.

"She took the shopping cart and went shopping just now."

"Wait did she see me asleep in my room?"

"I don't know, you know she checks. I'm going back to bed," she said and left.

I was so hungry I could feel the inside my stomach. But seeing the shopping bag right in front of me I got scared. I went to sleep without hiding it and was lucky my mom did not snoop in here like she usually does or my ass woulda been in trouble, I had to move the drugs. Owing Keith popped in my head, I wanted to give him his money fast. The PC is going to be over fifteen thousand when I'm done, and I'ma buy more work and blow up getting all this money. That was all I cared about as I grabbed the bag and left.

Tee was dressed in his same clothes just like me.

"How many packs you got left?" Was all I said when I saw him.

"I got four and it's clicking again," he said on the same page as me with a smile on his face.

"I'ma go to Don Poe's house, right now. When you finish those just come through there."

At Don Poe's the room he be renting was empty and I gave him ten bottles to bag up. After I set up all the stuff out of the shopping bag and pulled out the triple beam scale. There was a knock at the door, he stuck his head in pissing me off. He looked in and saw the Ziplock bag out next to the triple beam, plate, bowl and empty vials on the glass table that was on the same frame I used to hit that guy with at the Tyson fight.

"I got a friend with me who wants to spend two-hundred. You got a deal for us?" he asked, I could tell he couldn't believe how much drugs I had out.

"Yeah, I'll give you two forty packs for two hundred, that's forty dollars off for you." I'd basically just given him the PC somebody would make.

"You don't got no weight for me?" His body was still behind the door as he continued looking at the work I had.

"You bugging, Don Poe. You want it or not? I got shit to do, get the fuck outta here."

He came in and sat next to me. There was nothing that said gay about him, he just was and once in a while the way he spoke revealed it.

"Oh, and thanks, I never said thank you for the Tyson fight thing." He looked at the table as he spoke.

"That was nothing. You want the packs or not?"

"Yeah, I'll take it since you can't do better. And just so you know this is a bomb all the customers talking about the Blue tops."

I was uncomfortable with him in the room without me having a gun, but his comment about my Blue tops gave me a jolt of happiness. I took out two packs and gave it to him, he counted out money like an old timer, feeling on each bill with two fingers making sure it was only one bill and that they were not stuck together. Then he placed it down on the table one bill at a time. I just waited till he finally passed me the money and counted it out fast as he started walking out.

"Don, how much you gonna charge me to rent the room by the month?" I asked.

He looked back. "Month, I make a lot of money off this room in spurts. That's like renting a hotel room out like an apartment. Nah, can't lock this down, Eric."

"Don't me Eric, it's E.R."

He looked unimpressed and I wanted and needed a place.

"If you keep that traffic in and out of here with different people it's just a matter of time before the Po-Po come running up in here."

His face showed interest like I revealed something he'd been thinking.

"You know what you right, I'm not even going to play with you." The gay came out again, so his eyes went up in the back of his head and he counted on his fingers while making a noise. "Mmm…mmm…mmm…pay me upfront for the month, two thousand."

"A thousand in work," I said.

His eyes went wide open and his face changed again. "Ha, okay, seriously this is what I'll take." I stood up. "Give me a hundred bottles and a hundred in cash now. And every Friday give me a hundred in cash and forty bottles, and this room is yours with keys to the apartment door and everything."

"Deal, go get me the keys and I'm putting a lock on this door."

He walked out and I counted out what he asked for.

Tee dropped off money and left with work. He brought up Meat Head from Wagna that goes to school with me, he saw the set up I had as I bottled up.

"What's good, Meat Head?" I asked.

"You, it looks like. You know where I can buy some grams from? My connect got locked up."

I didn't want to give out Keith's number to anybody. "How much you paying?" I asked.

"Twenty-five a gram like everybody else. What you got it lower than that, Big Willie?"

"How much you want?" I said agitated ready to finish here already but did not have a problem helping a friend.

"A hundred, I got twenty-five hundred on me now. I was about to go see the Papi's on Broadway."

If I sold him a hundred, I would have less work to double up on, but I can get more from Keith. I would make a quick three-hundred dollars for just this, I weighed out a hundred as he watched the scale. Then we made the sale and he left. After hours of bagging, I had to go eat. Chito and Tee were out pitching and I also had Karate George out, too. When Chito came back I left him in my room. Cuchi Fritos on 125th on Lexington was one of my spots, for five dollars I got a huge plate of rice and beans with beef stew, another two dollars got me a large Coco drink from those containers that look like a waterfall inside it. The size cup you get could fill you up alone.

There was a man bagging outside and I bought him a plate and he sat with me as we ate. I ordered two more plates to go for Tee and Chito, feeling myself, I ordered a potato that be in the window heated under the light bulb crisping the fried skin and some fried plantains with the garlic sauce. Eating all of that than drinking the last of the Coco had me full and I couldn't move.

It was now five in the afternoon and others were out hustling with custies lining up by Tee as Karate George ignored them. I stood looking out for them for a while then I heard a familiar female voice.

"Le me alone, I dos botha nobodae." The drunk lady was outside with a beer in her hand wrapped in a bag. I sat her down on the concrete slab and sat by her watching out. After they made sales, I went to the smoke shop and bought more bottles and tops then walked to third Avenue and bought the doorknob lock and another regular lock for my room.

We hustled all night and customers that ran out of money started bringing things to sell us, now that I had a room I bought a TV, a VCR and ten VCR tapes of good movies, it was a long day and when eight o'clock came me, Tee and Chito was in the room relaxing while George stayed out pitching.

"We still going to see *Do The Right Thing* tonight?" Tee asked.

"Hell yeah, it starts at eleven so I'ma nap for a minute." Tee was counting out his PC and I gave him and Chito two packs each. "That's to keep for yourselves."

Tee put it away and said, "I'ma go home so I can sneak back out with yar later. I'll meet yar in front of the building at ten."

When he left it got quiet and I fell asleep then was awakened by a loud banging on the door that caused me to jump up. It was Karate George needing more work. I was glad he came because it was ten-o-clock now, so we locked up our room and left headed to the front of 1990.

CHAPTER THIRTY-FOUR
TEE

After leaving Don Poe's house I headed home. When I got in front of 1990, the block was alive with people and hustlers out making sales. Capone was about to make a sale until the custie changed direction once he saw me.

"You got blue, right?" he asked.

"Yeah," I said.

"Give me eight," he requested passing me money that I quickly took.

"Hold up, I got you," I told him.

Capone looked upset and walked off as I watched and waited for the traffic to stop moving. At the same time, my hand was in my pocket poking a finger into the plastic pack of Cracks in there making a hole. I moved putting my back to the wall of 1990. The custie followed me as I counted out eight bottles with my hand still in my pocket. The custie was way too anxious and looked impatient not knowing I was ready to serve him. I put out my hand to slap him five and he was about to speak then felt Cracks in his palm. He smiled and counted them visually. Others flocked to me and I served them while the traffic was still not moving. I did not want a car to roll up on me with Cracks on my person.

"You got blue?" a dark-skinned man with dirty jeans asked.

"How many you want?" I asked with loose Cracks now in my fist to move fast.

"Two." He was served and gone as another came behind him and another behind him.

"Five," said a lady that be prostituting on Park Avenue.

"Eight," said the man who be fixing cars for cheap.

"Three," said the twenty-five-year-old girl that did not look like a custie. She dressed nice and came from New Jersey a week ago not able to leave this trap.

"One." I looked up seeing Sly. She had hidden beauty with a sweet attitude all this time the streets never broke her innocence.

The flow of custies kept coming and the work E.R. had just given me was done in twenty minutes. Others that was out, were moving their drugs slow as Blue tops became in demand. Finally, I was about to go upstairs knowing I'd served so many people so fast anyone watching would know what I was doing.

"Teddy up…Teddy up!" a call came putting us on point.

Two blue and white police cars were coming with the traffic as adjustments were made by hustlers. They stopped and jumped out on the block as I tried to walk into the building a gun was pointed at me.

"Hey, asshole get your fuckin' hands on the wall."

The four cops put eight of us on the wall and searched us. All the drugs had been stashed already so they came up empty and left like nothing happened. I walked into my building and Karate George was coming out looking like he'd just got high.

My elevator ride was quick and as soon as I was in the hallway, I began tucking my money all over me to not to be seen. Then as soon as I entered my apartment, my mom started fussing.

"How come when I seen, Ms. Carter, she telling me you out there selling drugs?" my mom fumed.

"What…Ms. Carter, told you that?"

"Ms. Carter, said you be outside at night with that high-yellow boy."

"Ma, she probably saw me with him but not at night. You know Eric is my friend."

"I don't care about no, Eric! You better not be selling no damn drugs boy!"

"I'm not selling no drugs, Ma. I'm not stupid if I was selling drugs where all the money and new clothes at?"

"Stupid or not if I find out you selling that stuff, you have to get out of my house. Ain't no dealers in here."

Her and my sister sat on the couch both looking at me. My mother started getting up with difficulty being a heavy woman but more so tired and was not going to sleep until she knew I was home safe.

"Next time you come home so late ain't going to be no food for you neither." Her back was turned to me as she walked to her room, leaning from foot to foot while she spoke.

My sister acted like she was concerned in front of our mother, but really was just waiting for her to go to sleep so she could sneak out, too.

I was in my room checking my three thousand-four hundred dollars stash hidden in the dirty clothes hamper. I decided to keep a little over a hundred to spend later freely.

"Oh, shit, Terrance you and E.R. getting money like that?" My sister was tall and over my shoulder.

She scared the shit out of me. I felt like I'd done something wrong. "Get out of my room. What's wrong with you? Knock next time!"

She put her finger over her mouth. "Ssshhh…you going to wake Ma up."

"Seriously get out," I calmed my tone a notch.

She left only because she wanted to go out and not wake our mother. I noticed her tight jeans and light makeup she had on. My sister was not cute but not ugly and because she was tall, people were afraid to approach her. But when they did, they went hard. I was not putting the money back, I decided to keep it on me until I figured out where to put it. Not that I had any reason to think she would steal. I just didn't want any possibility in any way and I wanted to have peace of mind something my dad taught me. He was part of the Nation of God's and Earths telling me his job is to always teach.

My house chores were the bathroom and garbage, so I did that as I heard my father's voice in my head while I thought about the money.

"The white man loves black men that sell poison to each other for doing their jobs destroying ourselves."

I saved all my money and wanted a business. I figured if I could save fifty thousand before I go to jail, I would have a business to live off when I got out and never have to sell drugs again. I scrubbed the sink, shower, and toilet in that order and wiped down afterward. My father said his teachings were a steppingstone to a better life and sacrifice for a greater end is a plan worth its pain. I don't know if that was an excuse, I was using but selling drugs was what I knew. If there were doctors around maybe that's what I would have become.

"Come on, Terrance let's go already," My sister whispered clearly to me behind the ajar door.

I finished cleaning and walked out passing her with the trash and headed to the kitchen trash and put it all together by the door.

"You don't need me go ahead," I said now walking to the living room, putting the TV on, getting a quick glimpse at the news.

"Yeah, right, you might wake mommy up by mistake. Turn that down some more."

After five minutes we left together, I gave her a hundred dollars, me and my sister have always been close with each other. I took the trash into the incinerator and hurried to get out remembering being cramped in their earlier. I dropped the trash in the chute and got out fast. Outside was packed, people were all getting ready to go places for Saturday night. The sight of beer in bags being held and an occasional scent of reefer in the air just passed my nose.

I heard my father's voice again, *"We act like walking billboards giving free advertisement with everything we wear."*

Name brand clothes, gold chains, and earrings were on everyone. After a while E.R. and Chito came along with his people from school, old timers from the block, my sister was with Stacy and other females were out all getting ready to go somewhere or just hang here in front of the building. E.R. called two O'Jays that was on standby in front of the building and the *Leave Me Alone* lady came out with her daisy dukes on in the cold, immediately whining to us.

"Le me aloe I doe botha nobodae," she said.

E.R. gently guided her to sit down on a cement slab not to be messed with by people from our building.

Swoosh! Swoosh! Pang! Pang! Pang!

Before I knew it the BB bandit was hitting us up as people ran covering their faces.

"Le mae al lo, I doe badda nobody." The leave me alone lady was up and panicking with a sad face.

At one time she probably was a beautiful woman, now she had a drunken sad face stuck on her. E.R. tried to sit her down, but she whined to him that she don't bother nobody. Everybody was moving back and forth across the street looking up to see. This time he was caught. It was said to have been the Voodoo lady's nephew, Aaron who I'd suspected. People looked up as they were coming out from cover. Things were going back to normal with a few yells up to his terrace apartment on the fourth floor.

"I'ma fuckin' hurt you Aaron, you muthafucka!"

"Your ass is our you better not ever come outside!"

"I'ma sick my dog on his ass!" An older man named Jasper said.

Then E.R. yelled out, "Wait till I catch your ass, I'ma…" I stopped him.

"Don't put him on point he will duck us," I said.

I wanted to tell him don't threaten him in front of everybody but knew E.R. would not listen to that. So, E.R. started telling everyone to fall back he would get him. So, my logic did work.

Dice games between the older cats started and everybody was the same again. Monk pulled up in his car and Guy got out. She was beautiful, her face was model perfect with features small like they were drawn. She was fly wearing blue leather pants, with a Pistons jersey over a black hoodie. A Doo-rag under her Pistons hat and the small Timberland's on her feet revealed her feminine side. She caught me staring and I quickly looked away.

"How many you want, Tee?" Monk said fucking with me.

"How many you want, Big Willie? You get a car and don't know how to act." I gave him five and nodded to Guy as she walked past ignoring me.

E.R. said, "We out."

"Lea me aloe, I doe badda nobody."

"Fuck is this?" Monk said making a face.

He and Guy looked at the lady approaching us in shorts. E.R. lead her back to sit down.

"This too much over there you got drunk ladies bothering us! Talking about leave me alone, and customers selling work." He pointed at me and laughed. Stack a Joe who stutters was next to us laughing as Monk continued, "Fuck you laughing for with your stuttering ass? If you were on one-seventeenth street you could never make a sale." He began mimicking Stack a Joe. "How…how…how…many you want." Monk was slapping the side of his face a thing Stack a Joe does to get words out of his mouth. "Shit by then I woulda served your customer."

"I get…get…get bitches, though," Joe blurted out smiling and continued, "I…I…I'ma fla…fly ass nigga, too."

"Yeah, yeah, we get it." And more people laughed.

My eyes stopped on Guy's face, she was looking at the girls on our block and I couldn't stop looking at her small features that were perfect.

"Tee, let me get some of those powdered donuts you ate," Monk said, and I licked my lips as he laughed, and Guy did, too.

Then others getting the joke also laughed. They were not even dry because I put Vaseline on them before leaving the crib.

Welo pulled up in his red BMW and Little Cee got out. Welo stayed in his car and talked to my sister as Stacy stood next to her then left quickly.

Cee came to us.

"What's good, Cee? You got more powdered donuts?" Monk said as Cee licked his lips and everybody laughed.

"Oh, yar got jokes over here?"

Stack a Joe replied, "The…the…that's yar seventeen street cats, wit…wit…with all that playing! We getting money over there!"

"Money…where yar whips at?" Monk said.

"Clown," Stack a Joe responded with a serious face.

We laughed again as he used only one word. Guy saw me looking at her and gave me a look that killed my stare. She had me thinking about the wrong things. I'm on the block with all this cash on me and plus she a dyke. We were talking about the fire and when I told them it was the club Happy Land after I saw it on the news, Monk's playful face changed worry and he quickly walked to a pay phone.

A group of four girls was passing and one kept looking at Chito. "What's good, with yar?" E.R. said and they stopped.

In minutes E.R., Chito, and Stack a Joe were talking to them. Meat Head and Kenny High stopped another group and started talking to them as one girl sat waiting alone for her friends.

Cee was next to me and Guy was not too far waiting for Monk to come back. Monk did and knew a girl talking to her, she was up on him close ignoring Meat Head. The one girl left out not being talked too had her back to us.

Cee said, "Go ahead, Tee, I got a girl."

I inched toward her when I heard someone tell her, "So, you want company while you wait?"

I was beaten to the punch as I looked at my beeper feeling embarrassed, I glimpsed at Cee who was laughing at me.

As I got closer to the conversation I heard, "No, I mean yeah, you can stand here it's not my property," the girl said smirking looking at Guy while looking around probably never having a girl talk to her with sexual interest before.

My father's voice played in my head, "*The devil will use any weapon, even encouraging homosexuality as a tool to depopulate us.*"

Their conversation continued as Guy spoke, "You cute."

The girl gave her a *'yeah right'* face responding, "Are you kidding me you're cuter than me."

"Well, it's all about you, right now, I'm Guy. What's your name?"

"I'm Latonya! What kind of name is, Guy? Is it because you a girl that like girls?"

"Well, no not really. My moms said I was named after a king during a Holy Crusades."

"The Holy what?"

"The Holy Crusades, but I do like girls…I like you."

The girl smirked again, and I walked off.

Another cute girl was coming to the block fast and she stopped in her tracks. I noticed her looking at Monk and the girl he was with as she hugged on him. Then I remembered her, it was a girl Monk was with at the schoolyard.

She walked up to Monk and started yelling at him, "Are you for real? I was in the hospital almost dying. I left to let you know I was not dead and you here with a girl! Are you crazy?"

Drunk and high off weed laughs, ooohs and aahhs and uh-oh was heard all around.

"Cindy, I just beeped you like six times and called your house and hung up when your moms answered," Monk replied.

"Beep me…beep me! What are you talking about? You got a girl on your arm, don't tell me about beeping me."

"You…you ga…got any powdered donuts, Monk?" Stack a Joe said, and people laughed.

Cindy was in tears as she said, "Fuck you, I hate you, don't ever call me again!"

"You buggin', right now, Cindy. I'ma talk to you later, when you feel better."

"Monk your soft ass better never call me or even dare come to my hood or you will get fucked up!" Spectators showed no mercy and did not help the situation as laughter kept going. Cindy walked off and Monk rushed behind her.

"Sa…sa…sa, Cindeee, I'm right here when you ready," Stack a Joe said.

"Teddy up…Teddy up!" The warning was late as unmarked cars curved to our block.

Two yellow cabs and a blue Sedan came screeching to a stop and the gun squad was out with their guns drawn.

"Fuck I got all this money on me!" I grumbled.

They had about ten people on the wall, they cuffed E.R. and Monk and placed them in the back of the unmarked cars. They arrested Steve who had a gun but left me alone. Vuggio and two officers were looking under car tires and kicked over the garbage cans kicking the contents that came out of it searching for guns. After a few minutes, they uncuffed E.R. letting him go and left. Monk had nothing on him that I saw as people started leaving the block saying it was hot.

Cindy was gone and Guy asked E.R. "What about Monk's car?"

"We gonna have to send somebody to the precinct to get his keys," E.R. told her.

The show did not stop, we got in the O'Jays and was finally headed to the movies.

CHAPTER THIRTY-FIVE
SLY

It was getting a little cold now and late, I was bundled up in sweaters. I pulled the outside one around me tighter and tucked my ears in my scarf. I walked up to Lexington and saw someone leave after being served.

"Hey, do that kid got Blue?" I asked him.

"Yeah," the man said.

I went to get online behind three other customers. I was licking my lips constantly only becoming aware that I did it because a smile came to my face as I saw the kid serve Blue tops. My smile did not stay though I found myself constantly licking my lips. I started getting excited, I knew what I was going to get for these three dollars I'd hustled up. Someone was always here selling it and I got to pick out the ones with rocks over the shaved crumbs. It was like a name brand product I felt guaranteed.

At six this morning I was out waiting for a date about to give up with no one around. Then I caught a break with the janitor from my building. The second break came when we found out the Blue tops were out that early. He usually wanted sex but was so high I just played with him a little then we kept getting high in my apartment until his money ran out. After him, I hustled up some money one date at a time and went to Lexington to cop the Blue all morning.

"One," I said aware that I was licking my lips.

The brown-skinned kid serving me looking into my face with recognition. I remembered him from last year when I still had a nice ass. He gave me money to have sex but now he didn't even look at me long. I know he was not one of those hustlers that do that because he never did it again. He was just young and horny, and I looked good then.

Since it was only one, I went into the tall building and was followed by another kid I knew who just kept quiet as he stood next to me waiting for the elevator. I knew what he wanted and knew he didn't want nobody seeing it. It dawned on me that this was not even my neighborhood and that's two people I dated before. Seeing his eyes catch my movement, I noticed I was licking my lips again.

We both rode the elevator and got off on the fourth floor.

"We good, baby girl?" he asked.

"Yeah, but I want money. I'm not getting high after this. I hope you don't mind." Wanting to buy the Blue and not smoke whatever he had I lied to him.

He looked upset. "How much?"

"Twenty-dollars."

"Fifteen," he said.

I nodded and walked knowing he had lots of money, he just didn't want to spend it on me. He followed me into the staircase. He stepped up two steps and pulled his pants down, his dick was already hard. I dropped down and put my mouth on him, then closed my eyes as my head started bobbing up and down fast. I grabbed the back of one of his legs to keep my motion. I was thinking about getting high, not really focusing on what I was doing. It was just like breathing to me, my body could do it on its own.

For some reason, my mind went to Tall-Tall Man that I'd met and his promise of coming back for me but then I pushed it out of my head. I took back control of it and sucked hard to hurry up. The noises excited him as he was about to cum in my mouth. I felt him tense up, I moved back my head and saliva ran across his dick. I jerked him off quickly while holding the base of it tight. I looked at his face, he was in my control, his body jerked then froze up. He thrust outwards holding the rail tight, I jerked him faster as he spilled out onto the steps until there was no more coming out.

"Why didn't let me come in your mouth?" he asked.

"If you woulda gave me twenty I woulda."

"Come back, later on, I got you with twenty-five and do it the same way."

"Okay," I said.

He gave me twenty dollars and I smiled. As he left my smile did, too. I just wanted to smoke. After the high I sat in the staircase for five minutes thinking about my check coming on the first, I needed a break from this. The staircase door opened scaring me and it was the same guy who came back. He gave me twenty-five dollars upfront.

"Sit on the steps," I told him.

He did what I told him after pulling his pants down and I went down on him then started spitting on his dick.

"Nah, what you doing…you bugging out."

"Trust me, just hold on," I said.

He looked at me with an angry glare, I just smiled but was really afraid of him getting angrier. I looked down and he was moist with my saliva. I jerked him fast making sure I went from the very bottom and pulled it up, then down with a light force so fast he blinked and jerked lightly. I watched his feeling take over as his eyes closed and hips raised. He made a noise and came shooting a thick load over his pants.

I was scared at first, people used me as an excuse for any problem they encountered.

"I'm sorry. You want me to suck it again?"

"Nah…nah, that was good." He started cleaning himself then walked away.

The people over here were nice, but I will still be one point and definitely remember him, he was a good trick. I left the building and outside I didn't see no one with the Blue. I panicked, as I walked away.

"Blue tops…Blue tops!" I heard someone yelling.

He was a grown man wearing karate pants and looked like he gets high himself. I went to him seeing a customer buy one and again I smiled seeing the Blue tops.

"Let me get seven for twenty."

"Sorry baby no shorts I'm just getting by myself."

"Okay, give me eight," I said giving him twenty-five with a big smile. "Only rocks please."

He laughed and picked out rocks for me. A fight broke out and I got scared. It seemed like the whole block was yelling at one kid.

"There he go, right there!"

"He shot me twice!"

"He hit my sister!"

People were swinging on and hitting this kid that fought back and pulled out a knife slowing everybody down. They continued to yell at him.

"You better move outta the building nigga, you getting your ass beat every day."

A tall girl spit on him. "Fuck you!" she said, and the crowd was trying to move on him, but he was fast swinging the knife. A figure with a hood covering his face ran into the crowd pulling a gun.

Pop! Pop! Pop!

He shot the man with the knife. Everybody scattered in different directions and I was stuck in shock recognizing the dealer that was in the staircase with me. He looked down at the one he shot and fired again.

Pop! He hit him in the head then ran off.

The dealer that had just served me said, "Get outta here!" and he ran off.

CHAPTER THIRTY-SIX
VUGGIO

"Sir, we have a call for you from your C.I. twenty-two-eight."

"I'm coming, I'm coming put him on my line two."

That Capone kid has a hard-on for Eric Rosario. I have to put him in his place with this juvenile hatred he has for a peer. I was reading a memo from the Alcohol Tobacco and Firearms, ATF. They were in our district making arrests due to the high rise of crimes with guns. It read the situation in Manhattan just North of Central Park was extreme. Black men in Harlem were less likely to live to the age of sixty-five then men in Bangladesh, one of the world's poorest countries. So, I had ATF agents working in my back yard for statistics from studies.

"Hello," I said into the receiver.

"Detective Vuggio?"

"Yeah, what's going on? We have to talk in person real soon."

"Eric Rosario is out here and pulled a gun out."

"You saw it?"

"I…I seen it."

"What kind of gun was it?"

"I didn't see it up close."

"Where did he place it?"

"I did not see exactly but it's out here. He's with people from all over not from our block. So, they may be holding for him, too."

I did not want to toss a gun case away, but this guy may even be planting one on his nemesis.

"Who's out there?"

"Monk…Tee…"

I cut him off. "Monk, from one-seventeenth Street?"

"Yeah."

"We're on our way."

We parked our two yellow cab vehicles on 2nd Avenue waiting. Knowing that kids knew our yellow cabs the black Sedan drove past 122nd on Lexington Avenue for surveillance first. It was confirmed that Monk and Eric Rosario were out there.

I told my four officers outside our cars, "Our primary targets are two persons of interest. They are to be arrested on sight. You know their descriptions, everyone else we search we let go unless finding a weapon. This is an in and out situation, let's not make it a science project, I have work to do. If you find drugs don't make arrests just confiscate it, we don't need the paperwork. Okay, let's go!" I then radioed to the Sedan to lead us in.

The two detectives were to go after Eric Rosario and Monk. As we moved in, I watched the scene of people seeing the yellow cab knowing who we were. Looking for urgency, fear, or changed movements and especially avoiding my eye contact. A Spanish teen looked as if he was going to run and tried to speed walk.

"You don't move!" My gun was drawn, and I was out of the vehicle. He stood still and was nervous as I got close to him. I searched him and found a gun immediately, then cuffed him.

All of my officers had people they either recognized or detected funny movement, they searched. I watched the performance of my team as they followed protocol with E.R. and Monk, then cuffed them and placed them in the back of the cars. Finding no other weapons and some light drugs, I let Eric Rosario go and left the scene within minutes.

Back at the precinct Monk was questioned but not saying a word. We then charged him with some Gold Top Cracks found on a young dark-skinned kid that stutters. The only thing Monk had on him was five different kinds of weed. The other perp was charged with a loaded weapon and was silent as well. I gave instructions to run him through but we were going to hold on to

Monk because he knows about the murders. I went out with two detectives as the rest of our squad booked our bust. We drove through Wagna being seen, waiting for any reactions or indication of a person carrying a gun. Boo Black was on the list of gun carriers. His back was turned to us and we slowed up to see his reaction as he turned. He did a dance for us as his friends laughed.

"We know he don't have nothing on him today," Detective Snell said.

"Maybe not or maybe so, the same way we play on them, they play on us," I told him.

We jumped out on 126th and Lexington searching Gus. He was another known Felon.

"How you doing officers…having a nice day?"

"Pretty good, if I find that gun you carrying."

"Gun? No guns over here man ain't nothing but love."

"Tell that to the kid who got shot by Lincoln projects."

"I don't know anything about that!"

"Yeah, whatever get out of here."

In our cars, we heard Rosie on the radio.

"Shots fired…shots fired, on one-twenty second and Lexington with a man down. All units respond to the scene…shots fired at one-twenty…"

We were the first ones there and not one person was on the Westside of Lexington except the body. As our cars pulled up, we saw spectators across the street. I went to the kid and looked at his face. I didn't recognize him at all, he'd been shot in the head. I left the scene as other officers arrived and went to search for Capone.

CHAPTER THIRTY-SEVEN
MAMA

Taking hit after hit after hit tasting the white Crack smoke in my mouth but I did not get high. So, I kept smoking. The police came from nowhere and started chasing me, their arms grabbed and reached out for me, I ran with his hands grabbing for me. Another police jumped at me from the side, I jumped, too. Then awoke out of my sleep jerking my body up, seeing that I was in my fire truck pajamas ready to run from the cops.

"Wow, that felt real," I said smiling.

Keith's house was nice, I hadn't been high since I came there over two months ago. My dreams were becoming more real. I slept in a small room meant for storage or something else on the first floor, but it was nice. The smell of Bustello coffee had me go to the kitchen. I saw Abuela in the living room watching a Spanish show. I liked Keith's kitchen, Abuela kept a clean rag on the hook and I started wiping an already clean place making it super spotless now. I poured myself some coffee and took my cup with me upstairs. I passed Abuela's room, then looked into Davi's room. He was asleep and the video game was still on. I turned it off and quietly left off. Then went to Keith and Melinda's room, they were gone so I figured they were at the vitamin store.

I heard the phone ring and ran to the kitchen to pick it up with my coffee in hand. "Hello, who's calling?"

"Mama get your ass off the phone," I was happy to hear his voice.

"Papa you sound like you grew up. When you coming home?"

"I only been away for two months, Mama."

"How much time they give you?" I wanted to know, I liked Monk.

"I got six months and five years, probation, but I only have to do four out of the six."

"Vuggio is an asshole, he put me in there, too, you know." I lifted my top lip and felt disgusted by the thought of Vuggio.

"A powerful asshole, he kept pressing me about Fats and got mad because I don't know nothing."

For the first time, I felt bad for Fats. If I woulda never said nothing he would not have been dead, I did that.

"Mama…Mama, you there?" I heard Monk calling.

"I'm here, Papa," I said snapping out of it.

"Well, you sound good. Tell Keith I said drop five-hundred on my books."

"I will."

"Oh yeah, Mama, get a pen and do this three-way for me real quick."

Monk called a girl named Cindy three times and she hung up on him every time. He then called two other girls, after the calls I went back to sleep. I was awakened by Keith and Melinda returning home.

Keith stood over me. "Hey, Sleepyhead, get up because we going to pick Scottie up and drop Davi off with Julissa. You want to come?"

I felt grumpy. "Keith, why you didn't let me go with Scottie to Puerto Rico?"

"I told you, Mama, he needed to be alone. When I go, I'll take you with me."

I felt funny questioning him, everything was odd, and I was moody. "Monk said to put five hundred in his account."

"If you talk to him again before me get the exact day, he get's out." I nodded.

Thomas, Keith's driver took us in his car. We were a happy family. I got dropped off with Melinda and Davi at 117th Street.

The apartment was now Julissa's. Keith went to get Scottie from the airport. The dealers seemed more discrete with their sales but other than that the block seemed the same. I stood outside as Guy came over to me.

"Look at you Mama, you got big." I was at a loss for words not knowing how to feel. "Red is out…Red is out," she said as two customers came over to her.

I looked out making sure no police were coming. She put her back to the wall and we both watched Ray's people make a sale. I thought about Tall-Tall Man getting beat up and me helping him. The reality is that I was the one who put him in that danger telling that kid, Cee, that Tall-Tall Man took his work, another person I'd hurt. I walked off as Guy made a sale. After being cooped up on Long Island for two months, this was my first time back here. I walked down Lexington passing the schoolyard it had kids playing basketball then I continued to building 1990.

I didn't see E.R., so I went to the back of the building and there he was sitting on a bench with a girl. I walked over to him, and as he saw me, he started laughing.

"What's so funny?" I asked.

He got up and hugged me. "Wow, Mama you look nice."

"Thank you."

"Who's this?" asked the girl he was with.

"My Auntie hold on I'll be right back," E.R. told the girl as he walked with me in the back yard of his building.

"So, Mama what you doing over here?"

"I just wanted to see you."

"Well, I'm doing okay." Eric said.

"You be careful, it's getting bad around here. The police locked me up, too, ya know." And I felt the arrest as I said it.

"I know and now that I'm getting money, I got more friends and more enemies."

"Let me get some money!"

He laughed, then pulled out a roll and without even counting handed it to me. "No, that's too much, you didn't even count it."

"That's only fifty, it was from loose bottles I had don't even worry about it."

E.R. brought me, him and five other people some food from a lady who set up a tent with two long tables of cooked food. The plate was ten dollars and you could pick out whatever you wanted. I had rice, Barbecued ribs, and mac and cheese with some sweet plantains. We all sat in the backyard of 1990 and for a minute everyone just enjoyed their food.

"This shit good," Tee said.

"You not lying," Chito responded.

After eating we went in front of the building and across from it. E.R. stayed in the backyard as everyone else went back to hustling. I walked off, passing down 125th Street, going further and ending up in Lincoln projects.

"What you need, lady?" I heard someone ask.

"What, you talking to me?" I said.

"How many you want?"

I did not think about getting high, but the money was a nagging presence I felt. It needed a purpose and could not just be on me.

"Give me two for five," I said.

"We got nickels over here do you want one."

"Yeah, no wait…give me two," I said and was served.

I went into a building then realized I had just bought Crack. My mind cleared up. Like, I know I bought it, but now I saw and felt it all. When I did buy it, it was like it was not me, but my brain did it on its own. I walked back out.

"Fuck no pipe," I grumbled. *'Wait, am I deciding to get high? Maybe I need help. I'm just doing things and it's not me. Is mama crazy?'*

Park Avenue was close and girls were out as usual trying to catch men. I walked to Park Avenue going under the metal train tracks over my head, I saw a group of three girls I didn't know.

"Anybody have a stem for sale?" I asked. The three of them looked at me strangely. "I said who got a stem? I'll pay five dollars used or not."

"Shit mines worth more than that with the residue," one said.

The smallest of three responded, "Show me the five dollars."

I was about to pull out my money and felt like a square. Thinking about the drugs I bought and hoped it was not fake picturing the young man and the clothes he wore.

"Lady, you got five dollars or not?"

"Let me see the stem and call me, Mama," I said.

I walked two blocks stopping by a lot. I went in it and squatted down sitting on a car tire. I felt my nerves rumbling and emptied one of the bottles into the mouth of the pipe. I had no fucking lighter, damn, this may be a sign for me to quit once and for all.

CHAPTER THIRTY-EIGHT
WELO

Driving the new black Celice with Physcho and Tanya that I picked up from a house in Baltimore we were on our way to the White House. D.C. was flowing with more money in the summer than I could ever think it would. The fast influx of money made me cautious, I needed to take it out of D.C. now. Suddenly my chain on my neck felt heavy and I tucked it in. As cars passed me, I looked at the driver, then to the passenger, a strong feeling of paranoia came rushing over me, but I kept calm.

Physcho was bringing in more money since losing the lawyer's crib we vacated. He freelanced on the streets and his number one ringer was Tanya.

"So, I'm giving yar this pad," I told him.

"What, the white house?" Physcho asked.

"Yeah, the white house yar can base everything from there. This way I can relax." I was making some changes a new cash house was the start.

"They sell mad drugs over there you buggin', Welo!"

"They hustlin' outside, you're going to conduct inside business only! Bagging and stashing."

"But you got shit lined up already, my flow is serious, right now."

"Your work will be sold in the same places it's sold now, while you relax instead of running the streets."

"Who's paying the rent?"

"It's paid for another month, then it's on you." He just nodded.

Tanya smiled, then nodded giving her approval. I saw in my rearview mirror; they would definitely not know where the new stash house is going to be. We passed a drug house and my beeper started going off. I think I saw two cops in the car that past us. This car would never come to D.C. again. I parked leaving the air-conditioned car feeling the heat outside, my beeper went off again. It was early in the day and people were out walking as we entered the building. Inside Ramel was watching over three kids who were bagging up work. They came in from New York on the Amtrak just an hour ago. I wanted them to see all the money flow out here to entice them to stay.

"Ramel, pick up any cash our people got we about to spin back to the NY."

"Now?"

"Yeah, now, I keep telling them dudes to never have money with drugs, but they don't give a fuck. So, we got to take it as fast as they make it!"

"Give me the keys man."

I tossed the keys to him and kept talking, "When they get popped on a charge with the cash and want me to bail them out, they bugging. We got rules for a reason." I looked around I had everyone's attention.

Ramel left out headed to the car. The three kids were putting work into little baggies and I gave Cee my gun not wanting anything illegal on me. Then sat and watched them. Not worried if they stole a rock or two. I just wanted to see everything in front of me. Bags of money was in this house to be taken back to New York and Baltimore as soon as Ramel finished his runs.

"There's three keys, right there, Physcho."

"So, what you telling me for?"

"I'm about to boogie out. Fuck you talking about, what I'm telling you for? This is your fuckin' post!"

He looked at me waiting for me tell him what to do. "Get a count when they finish and put it away using what you need until I get back. I'ma give you one of the safes for yourself."

"Oh, okay…okay, I hear you. Here's the last eight thousand, that makes sixty total so we even."

I was trying to give this fuck responsibility and more money, but it wasn't working. I was hoping Cee wanted to stay out here.

"I never counted none of the money you bought me this week, leave that right there," I told him wasting my breath.

I felt like I needed more brain power and looked over at Cee. He gave me an '*I got this'* look, then I walked off, unlocked a door and stepped inside for a second to remember which of the three safes I was putting Physcho's money in. I came back to them with a triple beam scale, rubber bands and five bags of money the same way he gave them to me. They sat at a skinny table with the money he brought neatly out for me to count.

I dumped the money I had on top of theirs making their neat effort moot. "Shorty, help me out by separating all the ones, fives, tens and the rest."

Tanya nodded and started separating the ones first. I put the triple beam on zero to make sure it was perfect, then I placed a pile of dollar bills evenly on the scale. Then added three more, it weighed five hundred grams. I weighed another five hundred and stacked the two together, rubber banding them into a thousand-dollar stacks.

Ramel came back. "This is from Boogie, it's eight thousand." He dropped the bag.

I put it by my foot, and we kept counting out Physcho's money as Ramel left again. As we continued to count, we had sixty stacks of a thousand each total. I went and got out what should be a hundred and forty thousand from another safe. Everybody was working, counting money and bagging work except Physcho who lit up a blunt.

"Get them some beer from the fridge make your people comfortable," I instructed.

He smirked back at me. "Now I'ma flunky?" he asked and went to get it.

"No, you're a boss," I yelled after him.

Ramel made a trip picking up money and had to go back to the same place to drop off more work, which was not what he does. Work was being pushed so fast, they needed more. It was too much money in one place.

"I had to knock Shawn out," Ramel said.

"What, why the fuck you do that?" I asked.

"Because he don't listen. I told him to stop leaving the door open to the crib. He be too comfortable and when I came back…"

I did not even want to get into this now I had to move this money out. "I'll deal with that when I get back," I said cutting him off. My beeper went off again, everything was going to have to fuckin' wait.

Ramel came back from his last run. "Guess who's coming in, right now?"

I was almost ready to go; the chopping of Crack was heard and Physcho had that stone weed face. We'd already counted out two-hundred eight thousand and had another that was supposed to be a hundred even when she walked in. She was wearing a new dark blue pants suit, had a nice leather bag over her shoulder and her blonde hair was done nice, she looked good and professional.

"What's up, Missy, how you been?" I asked her.

"Hey, Welo, I had to stay low. They still found me at my mother's house and were asking questions," she replied.

"Questions about what?"

"About who runs the drugs and who did the shootings."

"What did you tell them?"

"Come on, Welo, I'ma lawyer, they can't get me to tell on myself. I understand anything I say about you would incriminate me; I'm not going to jail."

"Smart girl, that's why I like you."

"Can I talk to you alone, Welo?"

"Nah, talk with us all."

She looked nervous but wasn't. I knew she wanted to get high. Losing her apartment, hiding out on the streets and being questioned by the police she was in a jam and wanted to stay high since she was running out of options.

"I need some cash and a new set up," she said,

Ramel pulled out his gun. "We going to play with this bitch or handle her?" he snarled.

"What's wrong with him, Welo?" she asked looking confused. "I did not tell the police nothing." She backed up into a wall and no one moved but her and the room grew quiet as everyone's attention focused on what was going on.

I spoke to her ignoring Ramel. "I know you did not talk or I woulda been in jail…but you set us up!"

"How…why would you say that?"

"Because he did bitch. What we going to do, Welo!" Ramel snapped.

"Welo, wait, I'll do anything…*anything*!" she pleaded.

"Ramel calm down." I looked at him standing by the door. "Let's start with who tried to kill me? And if you're smart you won't lie."

"Welo, I…I have no idea…"

I cut her off, "You got one chance!"

"It was, Cabo, but I didn't know." Silence fell over the room; she threw me off, he was nobody.

Physcho spoke up, "That nigga trying to come up. I don't trust her Welo she could be lying."

All eyes were on her as she looked at Ramel then back at me. "He told me you killed his cousin Chewy, that's why. He said he did not really care about him, but you were taking all the money. But I did not help him." She was scared and I believed her.

I did have Chewy killed and Cabo don't buy weight off me no more. "Because you're not a rat and that's hard to find, you get one shot to prove your loyalty. And you don't have to take it, you can choose to leave and take your chances with life or rectify yourself staying here."

"I'm with you, Welo. Tell me what to do…tell me."

The four kids from New York were looking at her now. Physcho and Tanya were waiting by the money, Ramel stood with his gun still out.

"Get ass naked, don't say a word and let anybody do whatever they want to you until I leave and we even. After I see you're loyal to me we good."

She looked around as her face changed and started looking strong. Her thirsty look of wanting Coke was evident, too. She was high class and you could never talk to her like that.

I made it clear again, "You don't have to do shit, you can leave. I give you my word either stay and be exonerated or leave and be exiled."

"You know what I want first, Welo." Her voice was heavy and in control, she now ignored Ramel and his gun.

I nodded. Money was being counted again and drugs were being bagged up. She went into the room, sniffed some coke then came out naked.

"Get on the couch on your knees and stay there," I told her.

People stopped what they were doing and looked at her thin model like body, they were not used to white women and here was a naked, high class one.

"Yo', keep fuckin' working I'm trying to get out of here. Ramel go ahead and make that last run I got this," I ordered.

The sound of chopping Crack went on but the looks at the pretty, high-class lawyer on her knees continued.

Physcho told her, "Open your legs let me look inside that thing." She did as he asked, and he put his fingers in her. She closed her eyes and dropped her head, then came back up with a smile. "That shit got me horny," he said. She pushed her thin white ass back. Physcho then unzipped his pants and put a condom on with a smile. "Back up," he instructed as he moved her back holding her ass. She was bent over the arm of the couch and Physcho entered her. "She wet like crazy. You a freak lawyer?" He was going in and out of her slow.

He smiled and looked at the workers while trying to work her. He slowed down, then put her on the floor on all fours, then he put his leg exaggeratedly over her ass cheek on one side and under on the other, he held her shoulders and pumped hard in her. Her face changed into a look of pain and pleasure.

Tanya pulled her pants down to her ankles and waddled over to her. "This is going to be my first time with a girl," she said smiling at Physcho.

Tanya picked up the lawyer's face and held it between her legs, her knees were bent as she humped lightly.

"I see why she was special to you, Welo," Cee said breaking the silence.

The lawyer was on all fours and began directing her lips over Tanya and as a rhythm started between the two girls, Physcho's stroke into the lawyer became harder and began disturbing them. Tanya now feeling it, held the lawyer's face that moved out of position with every thrust. Her face showed his entering her was a lot for her to take. Her eyes were closing with each stroke. She took her hands off the floor getting up from all fours, leaned up and held Tanya's ass. She was licking and moving while being banged by Physcho. Physcho slowed down pumping and the lawyer was pushing her ass back with her head in motion. He couldn't hold himself any longer, he pulled out trying hard not to cum. But he came jerking himself into the condom. By the time Ramel came back, Cee was having sex with the lawyer.

CHAPTER THIRTY-NINE
KEITH

Thomas pulled up into a waiting space in front of the airport's exit, it was crowded with cars picking people up. I rolled down the window and looked up seeing the planes I was hearing. The sky was cloudy and bright blue. I took a good drink from a Very Fine fruit punch juice as we waited in the car for a half of hour until Scottie finally came. He was dark and looked stronger than usual. He opened the door and got into the back seat.

"Look who came back blacker from Puerto Rico. I thought you'd be more Spanish now," I joked smiling at him.

"The Crack there is better than yours. You should holla at them," he said.

Thomas was shaking his head as they gave each other dap. I laughed knowing Scottie would get high out there. I sent him away from all the heat not to get sober.

"Thomas let's go," I said.

His face became serious as he drove off knowing where we were going. Leaving the airport ground was like a maze. Thomas followed all the signs as he drove us out.

"Here I got you a present," I said passing Scottie a brown paper bag.

Scottie grabbed it not looking excited until he looked inside it. His eyes opened wide and a grin came across his face, then he looked up at me. "Nephew, you surprised me."

Smith and Wesson introduced the .40 S & W cartridge and I got Scottie two of them along with two boxes of bullets, some stores did not even sell them legally yet, but I had a good connect. We were on our way to see Calvin now. I passed Scottie a different bag, this one had a .38 Revolver that I took from his house, a scarf and two glass bottles filled with gas stuffed with a cloth. We drove with the traffic as it moved smoothly. We were all in our own thoughts and quiet for the duration of the ride back to Harlem. New York was New York but Harlem was Harlem and as we got close to the hood, you breathed the difference. We drove down Madison Avenue, Thomas dropped us off and left headed toward the other side of the projects. Me and Scottie walked and saw teens playing in the basketball courts, some girls were in front of the grocery store with the usual people going in and out of it, same ole regular shit. I looked up saw two pair of sneakers hanging from a light pole and although I'd seen it all my life here and in Brooklyn, I still never knew why people did that.

Calvin's building came up and we went inside. I followed Scottie straight to the staircase and we went up the steps seeing graffiti on walls. Calvin pushed his luck way too much. On the 3rd floor, we came out of the exit and the hall was empty with apartments on our right and left sides. Two elevator doors were closed in front of us and a small steel chute that was the incinerator sat alongside the wall of the hall.

Scottie grabbed the steel handle, pulled it open and lit the cloth that hung from the bottle letting it catch good before dropping it down the chute. We waited for twenty seconds as he inhaled then dropped the other one. A couple of minutes later we smelled some burning and went back into the staircase, and up to the fourth floor where he lived. All the apartment doors were not marked so I did not want to look at them all trying to figure out the order and we just stood there. Not saying a word, our faces looked both ways than to the incinerator as light smoke started coming out of it. I grabbed an empty cereal box that was on the floor and opened the incinerator up to keep it open as the hall filled with black smoke.

Another minute passed and I began banging on doors yelling, *"Fire! Fire! Everybody, please leave the building now!"*

Scottie waited in the staircase exit with a scarf over his face.

"There's a fire, everybody get out of the building now!"

People were leaving their apartments running, some wore scarfs or shirts over their face. Straight to the exit they ran passing Scottie on their way out. I went down outside with them and waited. Thomas came back around, and I got in the car watching and waiting to hear the gunshots. Fire trucks began coming and Scottie came out. He shook his head as we watched from the car, people were waiting to see where the fire was and what was going on. Firefighters went inside and after ten more minutes I was getting upset, then I saw him. He was alone as he left the building and I saw his heavy breathing. I pictured him breathing heavy over Mel as she was enjoying him.

Scottie was focused as he watched him through the window.

"I got him meet me on fifth avenue," Scottie said before getting out of the car.

As we drove off, I still had the urge to put a frown on my face. I needed to be smart and just sit back while Thomas drove calmly. We parked and waited, time passed like ten minutes but was really two and counting as I watched the time. Then I froze seeing Calvin walking out of the projects toward us. He past us and went into the other half of the projects. I got out of the car feeling the 9mm I had as I followed behind him.

"Where the fuck is, Scottie?" I asked myself.

He was about to go inside another building. I looked around no one was paying us any attention, regular shit. People were into themselves and I took out the gun. No one was seeing me, I felt my heart, I saw Melinda and thought of Ciera. If I get caught, I will be another man in jail. Calvin turned around and reached…

Pop! Pop! Pop! Pop! Pop! The shots were loud, I aimed quickly but he was already down.

"Nephew let's go!"

Calvin had his hand on a gun that he did not get to pull out. Me and Scottie walked away fast.

CHAPTER FORTY
WELO

Coming down from D.C. with the lawyer, Ramel, and Little Cee too much was going on. Putting Physcho in place to handle shit there was a rushed decision that I had to make. Corey getting locked up hurt me a lot and let me know I needed more thinkers on my team. I shoulda used someone else to kill that fool in Jefferson projects. But Corey was perfect, he was the right one, but his coke habit destroyed him. Now he's facing twenty-five years in jail.

Dean is out in Jefferson projects pushing work with no problems. The shootings have stopped, and they know not to fuck with us. So, Corey did serve his purpose. Moving this money home was the gratification behind all this. Still needing some brains out in D.C., I have to get E.R. to get this money with me. I should put little Cee in Jefferson and Dean in D.C., I'ma see.

"Yo,' E.R. let me holla at you for a second." He was next to a few dudes posted up in front of the building. He walked confidently over to me and our eyes met.

"What's good, Welo?"

"You, you ready for some big weight?"

"Nah, I'm plugged in something nice, Welo. I'm good, B."

"I see you playboy, still forgetting, Welo?" I wondered who he was getting work from? Not letting him see he had me upset, I continued talking, "If you ever need it, I got it. We can talk numbers when you ready, E.R."

"I hear you, Welo. I'm feeling my feet, right now." He looked at the lawyer in the back seat.

"You got a crib over here?" I asked him, and his look changed into a slight agitation.

"Yeah, why you asking?"

I pointed my head, giving a slight nod without looking back at the lawyer then said, "This is my lawyer from D.C. she's staying for a while. Just hold her down with you for a minute, till I make some runs. Then I'll hit you up on your beeper to pick her up."

E.R. looked at her. "Fuck you talking about, Welo?"

I smiled. "She don't know nobody, I need her off my hands for a minute, just hold her down."

"How long? I got shit to do too, Welo."

"Like two hours or so, let me know. I can drop her off somewhere else."

He looked at her again. "Cool, I got her ain't nothing," he said like he was doing me a favor.

I then yelled out to E.R.'s friend who I'd used before, "Yo', Tee you want to get a couple of dollars bagging up real quick?"

Tee walked over smiling. "Yeah, I will," he said and got in the car taking her seat as she got out.

As we drove off Ramel laughed.

"What?" I asked.

"You, your funny leaving her in the hood like that."

"I just want E.R. to see there's a whole world out there with us. Get him open on some white pussy."

"How you know she gonna fuck him?"

"She out of her comfort zone and gonna want to sniff some coke, then the book will write itself."

"You going back for her?"

"For what? Let the streets keep her ass!"

CHAPTER FORTY-ONE
TALL-TALL MAN

Money came good all this week as I watched my Crack spot serve customers. Never will I get high again, I sat in my blue Honda watching the streets thinking about my life. Customers were leaving the block and others were coming to buy the five-dollar bottles that were stuffed to the top. It was not a career but a kick start to get out of the hood. Maybe even finish college and be able to pay for it.

Alvin hooked me up with coke and a spot to run. Being so tall I became popular real quick with other dealers, allowing me to push drugs real fast and make deals but I felt so alone. Trusting no one while dealing with many people, I felt empty and needed someone to trust besides my grandmother and little brother. Alvin was definitely not to be trusted, I still think he killed Rick, then I thought about Sly.

As I drove off my block, I decided to see her, it was close to eight at night and warm. I drove down 8th Avenue enjoying the lights from the opened stores on both sides of the streets. An old lady dragged a shopping cart of her belongings. A group was standing on the corner selling drugs. Two girls raced each other, passing men and women. It was Harlem, people were out alive doing their thing. Everybody living their life and loving it. I drove up a 125th leaving Lennox Avenue then 5th passing into the Eastside. The color of people went from all black to a mix of Spanish and black outside. East Harlem had a different feel to it.

I made it to Jefferson projects where she lived if she hadn't lost her apartment yet. It was a fifteen-minute ride, I was glad to get here as cop cars past me and I hoped they wouldn't pull me over. I got out of my car and the projects sat on both sides of me.

Groups of females on Sly's side inside the projects, sat on benches with their children out, playing under their watch. I parked, enjoying the love of family. Inside her building two people were waiting for the elevator, they looked back feeling me tower over them as the male spoke.

"You should be a basketball player. You ever think of that?"

"Maybe, I'll give it a shot one day," I told him.

"Sorry, I hope, I didn't get you mad. You probably hear that all the time," he responded, he must have noticed some agitation in me.

I heard him but did not want to talk about basketball no more. That was a past life, and he turned facing away from me. Maybe I could still get in there somehow, maybe not playing but in some other way. The elevator door opened, we all went inside, and two more girls ran in before the doors closed. The girls wore tight jeans and light jackets, summer was here. I got off before everyone else and walked to Sly's apartment. Not knowing what I was really doing there, just that I could help her, then I knocked.

She did not answer, so I knocked again and started feeling kind of silly. This girl was a Crack addict, she'd lost her dignity and any worth she had was probably gone. Yet, she was so innocent and maybe just needed a little help. The hall made me feel uneasy, as I recognized it from when I was getting high. The last time I left here was the last time I'd had any hopes of playing ball. I wanted to leave this was stupid. I knocked again, and the door opened as a young kid spoke with authority.

"Who the fuck is you?" he snapped.

I wanted to beat the shit out of him just because he fit the same profile of kids that ended my career. He was young, proud and cocky just because he could be for now. Then Sly came into view, she looked, then ran to the door, past the kid and gave me a hug.

She felt so fragile and warm, I thought about what she was doing with this kid. My mind was in a bad place, seeing her on her knees pleasing him then realized how ironic that was knowing she was trapped in a pattern of pain. My mood switched and I started feeling angry about how she was being abused by the streets. I looked at the kid then back at her. She lifted her face and I could see that it was clean and clear. A scarf covered her head, her eyes looked enslaved with getting high, but she held a sweetness and a mix of sexuality with innocence. My new street instinct was telling me this was her ploy to entrap people. To entrap me to spend money on her but she truly was a hidden prize. A diamond in the ruff, she held me again…she held me to save her.

The kid stood watching and said, "What's this, Sly?" he asked. "I need like ten more minutes."

"You can stay for an hour just lock the door she's leaving with me." Sly was buried into my chest and the kid looked at me wondering who I was to her.

I imagined what he thought, he saw a strong, powerful man that towered over him, wearing new clothes, caring for a woman who he probably had his way with many times. Like she was alive for his life and had no other purpose. Sly was under my arm as we walked to the elevator, her eyes searched my face and I looked forward as I heard the door slam behind me.

"They bagging up drugs I need to be there when they finish so, I can get paid," Sly said looking at me. She did not get it fully yet.

"Fuck all that shit, I told you, I was coming back for you and here I am. Are you ready to give that bullshit up?"

She answered quickly, "Yeah, hell yeah, but let's not let no money get away!"

The elevator opened, I led her in and stared at her, but she stood in front of the door. There was a black bar that made the door open when it touched her. There was a slight burn mark on her attractive lips, it comes from smoking a hot pipe.

"I hear you, but we have to leave I'm getting bad vibes."

"I…I need to get something from my house," she said as the doors closed and the black bar touching her made the doors retract and open again automatically. I then knew she wanted a hit of Crack; I knew because I was the same way for only a short time.

I hurt for her. "Are you really ready? I'm not dragging no trash and not looking over my shoulder. So, here's a chance for you."

She stepped inside the elevator and the door closed. "I knew you were coming back for me." A tear formed in her eye, it stayed there then finally fell. We had to be on the same page.

"I knew I was coming back for you, too." The elevator was moving down and we could hear it in between our voices.

"I'm ready just don't give up on me." The door opened and we had enough words as we exited the elevator, then out of the building with her under my arm, we walked in silence. Her head was down, as we past people but mine was up. I stopped in front of my car, she smiled but said no words and we got in.

CHAPTER FORTY-TWO
WELO

The Taino apartments had the Spanish aroma of rice and beans mixed with cooked coke. Julio's eighty-four year old mother liked to cook lots of food. I liked to eat it whenever she did, afterwards she usually stayed in her room watching soap operas or sleeping like she was now.

"Yar good, here or need me to babysit your asses? I need fuckin' hustlers, not kids!" E.R.'s homeboy Tee was here with Cee and two girls all sitting in their T-shirts at one table. They were bagging up Crack that Julio cooked up hours ago.

"What up…what you need me to do?" Cee asked.

"I need you to finish bagging that then give me an accurate count."

"I got that," Cee said.

"When you finish, I won't be here. Just give it all to Julio after and take a thousand bottles to Steamer."

"I got you," Cee said.

I nodded, then walked off to Julio's room. The old gangster sat on the bed watching a movie called *'Killer'* with the volume up high. The television sat on top of two milk crates close to the bed and another shoot 'em up movie called *'Hard Boil'* sat on top of the VCR waiting to be watched next. He was into it, then he noticed me after a few seconds.

"Oh, chit, Welo, you leaving now?" His English was understandable.

"Yeah, I'ma bring you five more bricks to cook up…" I hesitated not ever wanting him to hold too much work. "Like in two days, I should have more work for you to cook," I told him.

His hand reached out to pause the VCR, then he got up. He was a little man, a gangster in his time and still dangerous. He wore a colored button-down shirt, his hair looked wet and was brushed to the side, he held a creepy stare, but in all reality, Julio was a hidden gift.

"That work out there is going in the safe for pick up. Just keep track of who you gave what to like you do."

"Yu no it bae-by, this shit here is solid." He was reliable, I thought about using him to kill Keith but this place and other stuff he does was situated.

"Cee, is dropping Steamer a thousand bottles so put that on Steamer now."

He looked dead in my eyes and nodded. "So, what's up wit' them little chicas out there?" That was Julio's downfall, young girls.

"You going to have to miss out on them, I need my good workers."

He nodded, I went to the safe by the window and took out a nine, then checked the clip it was loaded.

"You know I gah the too, Papi. You don't have to use that. Julio got you!" His eyes told me how true that was.

They all would do as I asked. I could tell the girls to entertain him. I could have him kill, Keith. But I wouldn't use him for shootings and couldn't let him bother the girls. I have to protect them to protect me. In the living room, Julio came out with me. His attention was focused quickly in front of him. I followed his gaze to the nipples of girls in T-shirts. For some reason, his thirst made me aware that the gun I carried could be my downfall. I left out of the apartment without it. I waited in the elevator and had time to think. Ramel was waiting for me downstairs and we had shit to do. Ten bricks had to reach D.C., I had a combination of weight sales and workers up there. Jefferson projects were simpler, a consignment of two bricks was dropped off. The profits from there were higher than selling it because Dean does not pay upfront. His advantage is that he gets to never use his own money and I'm fine with that. I think I'ma start clearing that block out and get all the money. The elevator came and I got on.

As it rode down two flights, a Spanish girl got on looking at me, cutting her eyes away. I had no time, right now but she then licked her lips as she looked up at the numbers that represented the floors. They moved as the elevator was passing, then her eyes went straight to me, and held a stare before breaking it back then she turned back to the numbers that stopped on twelve. The doors opened and an older black man got on as I got off, and she followed suit.

"You setting me up for something. What's up?" I asked her as the elevator door closed and left the hallway.

"You, you're up, you're Welo, right?" She was confident and looked at my chain seductively.

"Yeah, who are you?"

"I'm Vicky, they call me Fresca Nena."

"I heard about you, Fresca."

She then put her hand lightly on my gold piece and moved them slowly.

"So, I hope you heard good things about me?" She then stepped back with her hands held behind her back and looked at me.

"Yeah, I did but, right now I'm rushing off. So, take my beeper number and hit me up in an hour. We can hook up then." I pushed the elevator button ready to leave as I turned my back to her.

"If you know about me, then you know I only need one minute in there," she said, and I turned to see her walking to the staircase exit door. She pushed it open and held it for me to follow and I did.

Fresca Nena was what I needed. She gave me some crazy head and lived up to her rep. She excited me with a mystery that was different, and it was over quick, she was like the hoods,

Cleopatra. I left her with my pay attention to beeper number. As I finally made my way outside it was chilly and getting dark. I felt wrong, leaving Taino's always did that to me. I thought of anything I could be forgetting.

"Where we going?" Ramel asked.

I looked across the street to my car and felt uneasy. Then from the oncoming traffic came two cars speeding fast. Two men wearing badges were coming from the opposite direction of the cars, the fuckin' cops.

Vuggio had a gun in my face, yelling, "Turn around, put your hands up and don't move!"

As soon as I turned, his hand was pushing me towards the wall. The cold concrete on my hands added to the discomfort I felt as he searched me. Instantly they found a gun on Ramel, cuffs were placed on him and he was rushed into a car.

"You don't carry yourself, huh? One day you will yar always do. Get the fuck out of here!" Vuggio told me and I walked off to my car.

There are rules for a reason. I waited in my car for an hour before I went back upstairs. The game never stopped, inside the apartment, I saw Cee watching over them as the chopping sounds of Crack kept going. Julio sat on the couch now looking at me, but I knew he was viewing the girls the whole time.

"Welo, what's up?" Cee asked.

"Relax, keep doing what you doing," I told him.

I went into a room and called my New York Lawyer. I told him the events that had transpired and gave him Ramel's name. I needed to know if this was a random bust or if I was being watched. More than likely it was Vuggio being Vuggio and we got caught slipping. I took the gun out of the safe and walked back into the living room.

"Tee!" I said going out of the room coming toward them at the table.

"What's up?" he asked in an '*I'm ready what you need*', tone.

"Forget that and come with me." I passed him the gun to carry and he put it in his waist without question.

We drove around East Harlem for twenty minutes with Tee in the passenger seat making sure no one was following us. Most girls we passed gave looks in our direction. Tee was not like other kids, he seemed focused. I had to handle my business. We got on the FDR and drove down to the Lower Eastside in downtown Manhattan. I parked and left Tee in the car, it was bad enough he's going to know I keep work down here. I came back with twelve raw bricks of coke.

Back on the FDR, we came back to East Harlem. I parked in Wagna projects and let Tee walk two blocks, carrying two keys to drop off to Cee in Taino Towers. Cee had to take that to Dean now since Ramel got locked up. When he came back, we drove to D.C., I played music on the tape player during the ride up. I wanted to take the gun from Tee now because if shit popped off, he may not be a shooter, but I did not want to get caught with it. I was tired now as we drove into D.C. the scene changed to a different type of hood, but it was still ghetto. We drove to the new stash crib, nobody but Ramel was supposed to know about the new stash crib for D.C. but since Tee would never come out here it didn't matter.

Once inside I dropped the keys on the table, the place smelled new. I felt he was seeing too much and wanted to put them back in the bag and take them in the room, but it was too late for all that. I'm just going to take the gun from him.

Bang! Bang! Bang! I felt shots enter my body painfully and anger rose in me as I turned to see his face holding a look of fear.

"Hold up, hold up nigga are you crazy?"

He aimed squinting one of his eyes. *Bang!* He hit my neck, I felt the air go inside where he hit me, and my breathing grew hard. I had to live, I held onto my neck and movement around me was fast. Pain shot through my mind and I relaxed myself lying face down. I had to get through this, I hurt, as cold air went through the holes in me. I tasted the blood as I swallowed, then found myself breathing in air slower. The movement around me was a blur. I stood still breathing and pausing, holding my breath as it hurt when I breathed. My beeper went off, it was loud and awoke me. The blur movement stopped, it focused in front of me into a face. *Bang!*

CHAPTER FORTY-THREE
KEITH

The grin on my face stuck while I fast forwarded a cassette tape in the living room getting it to the part I wanted. Melinda, uncle, auntie and two kids a boy and girl came over from the Dominican Republic last night. They all sat in the living room this morning with Abuela watching television in Spanish. I went upstairs with Ciera in my arms, her small hand was in a fist, waving in a playful mood. As she smiled at me, cute sounds came from her, right before we entered the bedroom.

"Shhh…mommy sleeping," I told her.

I quietly placed Ciera in the crib as she stood up holding onto the wooden bars watching me. I went over to the stereo, placed the cassette into it, the music came to life and I started singing along to Babyface.

"Noooo…oh…one…does it like me…I…ah, know for sure. You got the whip appeal on me…yeah, however, you want it."

Melinda woke up with sleepy eyes, pulled the blanket over her nose and watched me as I kept singing.

"It's alright with me…you got the whip appeal. So, come on and work it on me."

Mama came running into the room with her pajamas on. She jumped in front of me and started singing the words on cue, "It's bet…ter than love…sweet as can be…"

Then Davi came in and started singing with us, "Oh, you got that…you got that…you got that…"

We all sang together in our different voices. Ciera was now rocking her body with small bounces showing her little teeth coming through. Everyone was in their own zone singing to the song. As the song ended Melinda stood in the bed watching us with the blanket still drawn, then we heard Spanish music being turned up louder from downstairs. They probably didn't like us playing the music so loud and making noise, so I turned the tape off. Sounds of people approaching came as we watched the door. Melinda's uncle came I singing loud to the song playing in the background.

"Quien sinte…quien sinte…quien sinte…Abusadora…Abusadora…Abusadora…Ahhhbusahhhdorr a!"

Abuela came in dancing moving like I'd never seen her move before, Mel's auntie and kids joined them. The Spanish music had a beat that made you move. Melinda got out of the bed dancing in her panties and T-shirt with a good Spanish rhythm and her uncle was impressed looking in awe. Then he outdid her with a fast spinning whine that looked so cool, it was timed to the tune as I tried to copy it. Davi picked up Ciera and danced with her in his arms. Mama was in it and this went on until the last three horns blared in the song.

Watching everyone made me think of keeping our family safe. The vitamin store was doing good. I went backward losing too much money with the robbery. I needed to move this coke faster. Now that I'm in the background I get less money for the work I push out. So, I need more Avenues to move it faster. Calvin's block was up for grabs now Connecticut had to be used. I'm playing a different game and it was all about placement.

"Da…Da!" Ciera said out loud and everyone looked at me.

CHAPTER FORTY-FOUR
TALL-TALL MAN

It's been three weeks since I took Sly from her apartment and she hasn't left out of my place since. While I was going in and out handling things for us, Sly was battling her Crack addiction. After returning home, the first few nights I didn't know what to expect. Sometimes she would awake in bed and other times she'd be in silent tears struggling in her own solitude. It seemed to be getting worse, showing in everything she did. Every minute the urges to get high tore at her and she became more reclused.

I comforted her when I could and kept food in the apartment that she liked. It was the one thing she enjoyed. Some nights I waited for her to sleep before I slept, not trusting what she would do. Leaving her every day was a true test. The choice to stay or leave had to be her own to make for this to work. One day I thought she would just be gone. Thoughts started to come that this was a waste of time.

Until the day she woke up with a smile on her face. That day we talked together, we ate together and even showered together. Our conversations grew in depth through the coming days making us closer. It was the whole table of questions of favorite color, favorite food, and lucky number type of conversations. She started eating heavy and asking for specific food, she even began cooking. I woke up to served breakfast, yet, she never left the apartment.

Today 7th Avenue in West Harlem was strong with attitudes. It was sunny with people outside looking proud and content. A group of young girls walked ignoring the wino we called 'Red' as they passed him. Their attention went to a couple of men that got out of a cab, wearing expensive things but seemed edgy as a police car passed. The men ignored the girls as they rushed around the corner to handle their own business. The wino watched an older lady that had two young children holding onto her shopping cart full of groceries. He changed his entire aura while asking her for change. A Crack addict with dirty clothes rushed past going somewhere fast. I wanted Sly to come outside it was about time.

I went back upstairs and entered my apartment it felt like home. The streets were filled with people's gimmicks and inside here became tranquil. Sly was in her panties, a T-shirt and a scarf covered her head. I bought her some new things but not another scarf. It reminded me of her past that I wanted to be rid of. I looked at her noticing she'd gained a few pounds quick and kept the place spotless like hers.

"I'm taking you out today and getting your hair done. I want you to throw that thing away."

"What this?" she asked holding the top of her head looking at me. "It's just a scarf and I like it why should I throw it away?" she asked.

"To me, it's like the people, places, and things, thing," I told her.

She smiled and changed the subject, "Look at my butt it's getting big, right?" She turned her torso while facing me, I went to the bedroom and took off my shirt as she followed.

"Okay, counselor, people, places, and thing. I will get rid of the scarf," she said as I sat down on the bed pulling the end of the mattress up grabbing a stack of money.

"I wasn't upset about that, I need you to put some clothes on Sly, so we can go outside and shop a little, right now!"

She went behind me, held me around my neck and whispered into my ear. "You got it, you're my knight in shining armor." Her kiss on my cheek was warm and odd being that that was the first time she'd ever done it.

I was starting to question what I was doing this for. My feelings were so strong for her, but Sly was a hard fiend who's been doing all type of things in these streets. I have to slow down with this emotional thing, I'm helping her as a friend. As Sly went to get dressed I got my gun. We drove to 125th Street and parked the car. We walked up and down the streets going into the stores buying things. I noticed her little ass had grown and shown in the new jeans she wore getting the attention from others. We walked back to the car and dropped the bags into the trunk. Then we drove to a Spanish salon on the Eastside of Madison Avenue called Megalines. Inside I sat in the waiting area, reading a magazine that was on the table.

She sat in a chair getting catered to by beautiful Spanish women. Since I was the only man in the waiting room, a Spanish woman asked me was I a basketball player and I said no then got up and left.

Once I got outside, I went to a grocery store and bought some Super bubble gum and a soda then walked around the block. Not knowing what I was doing I knew to be happy things were not bad. Sly was complicating things for me but she made me feel comfortable around her. Back in the salon, I sat down for only a few more minutes until they were finally finished with her hair. I watched from the same mirror as she stood up and looked at herself. I was shocked, Sly transformed into a beautiful model just like that. A tear dropped out of one of her eyes and she wiped it quickly. I stood up and stared at her natural beauty.

She walked over to me. "You like it?" she asked.

"You look great. I mean you're the prettiest girl in here and I mean it," I said honestly.

"I feel funny," she said in a low voice.

"Well, you don't look funny," I told her.

After I paid for everything we left, it was late as we drove to her neighborhood in Jefferson projects to get some of her personal belongings to take back home. I parked not far from her place and kept looking at her as she remained silent.

"You okay?" I asked.

"Yeah, it's been a while and this place seemed so far away. Like it was not me anymore, but here I am," she said.

"This will be the last time you have to be here, okay."

She nodded looking around, I thought I knew what she was feeling but I didn't. I fell into that trap for a week. Whereas she'd lived that life for years, doing things that she would probably hate now that she was sober.

"You don't have to go, we can do this another time, or I can go do this myself you know," I told her.

She looked into my eyes then forward at her block that she saw from a new perspective and got out of the car.

"Thank you, you saved my life," her voice was strong. She was strong as we started walking.

"We can do this another time," I told her again.

"No, now is fine and let's talk about something else," she replied.

"Okay, your butt is getting big," I said.

She smiled but this time it made me want to see her always smile. She was strong, she was beautiful, and she made me feel good. This could be a good thing for us.

People were out in the projects and I was on point eyeing everyone. Even though it was dark I noticed eyes were on us. I adjusted the gun on my waist to get a feel for it. No one was hurting me or her. Then I knew what it was, they were staring at Sly. We got in front of her building where a few dudes were. They all took double looks and one could not help it but say something.

"That's Sly?" he asked her not being sure.

"Yeah, it's me! Hey Ty," Sly responded.

"Woowww!" came from one kid.

"Oh shit," came another in a smirky laugh.

A few more comments of surprised remarks came. Ty then said to me, "No disrespect B, but we just not used to her looking like that."

"Don't sweat it," I told him as Sly looked in my face.

I tilted my head and we moved on into the building taking the elevator up. We got off on her floor when we got to her apartment the door was locked. We went inside and nobody was there, I guessed the kids were in and out of here still using it.

"Let's get whatever you need and get out of here. I got a couple of things I need to do."

She froze up, her face became angry and tears fell from her eyes that quick. I reached to hold her, and she pushed at me, but I held on and she pounded on my chest.

"I heard you on the phone last week. You going back to college. And now what…what happens to me?"

"Sly, it was a surprise, they offered me an assistant coaching position. I was going to tell you as soon as we got back."

"You're a drug dealer now, you sell drugs!" her voice was vicious, and she pulled away from my arms.

"Sly, I'm here."

"No…no you're not, you just want me to suck your dick. You think you can just have your way with me, then live your life. Well, don't wait just go now! I don't need your charity!" I remembered being angry and wanting to get high as she kept fussing. "You want me to suck your dick, go ahead and pull it out. I'll suck that shit good and you can go." I remembered wanting an excuse and knew she was fighting her demons wanting to get high. "You want to fuck my mouth, you want to fuck my ass now that it's fat again? Whatever you want to do, do it and go."

If I left, she definitely would just fall apart and get high. I tried to hold her, but she pushed me away having strength with meaning.

"Go…go…go…go!" she yelled.

"Sly, this is not what you want," I told her.

"Oh, so now you know what I want? You don't even know what you want. What you're going to live with me, be with me, protect me? You know how many men I've been with, huh? You don't want me, you can't help me!" she was screaming now. Her face was so sweet, yet her pain was so deep. She waited and the silence was louder than when she screamed.

"I do want you; we can do this."

"No!" she yelled.

"I need you as much as you need me, Sly."

"No, you don't, all yar do is use me. You're nothing but another drug dealer just like I'm nothing but another fiend."

"I came back for you, Sly because I was alone and you…"

"No…no…no!"

I walked over to her and said, "We can both leave New York together and not be another drug nothing. They offered me a paying job, no more drug shit, this is not me. Look at me, this was not my life. Remember when you met me, I was wearing clothes too small that did not fit looking stupid? I was a vick this is not my life! They beat the shit out of me, knocking my career right out of me…this is not me." I held onto her and she did not push me away. "Just like I promised, I came back except I won't be a rich basketball player. I'll be a regular Joe working a regular nine to five getting a check."

She looked in my eyes and cried falling into my chest. Her arms were inside mine and she wiped her face with small fists.

"Let me think about this, go home and give me…"

I cut her off, "No, Sly!" I said loud and angry.

"You seen how them guys were looking at you and will play on their lust to get you high. You have to make up your mind now, I'm not playing!"

She held onto me. "Don't let go," Sly said burying her face into my chest.

CHAPTER FORTY-FIVE
LITTLE KID

I thought they were going to kill me. Welo died two days ago and I found out now, but that was how he moved, on his own. I met with Welo's four lieutenants from 117th Street at the Taino apartment. Julio sat listening to them asking me what I knew. Once I proved to them, I was not in D.C. when he died, and I left him alive while still handling his business the questions changed. Now it was all about collecting what was out there. The four lieutenants seemed to be in a power struggle of taking over not even caring who killed Welo. This went on for another half hour.

"I'ma pick up the money from Physcho and drop him off another brick to push," Steamer said.

"How we know he did not kill, Welo?" Druggem asked.

"We don't, but if he don't pay then it's him," Gee replied.

"I been up there before, too, Welo ran it the way he wanted, and we need to make changes to run it to work for us," Fat Kevin said.

"His girl in Baltimore got the red BMW, a couple of bricks and money. We need to get all that down here and let her keep some money," Gee said staring at everyone.

"She can keep most of it! But let's give his mom's some cash, we can't forget her," Steamer added.

"Yeah, you right. Plus, his mom's may have some bricks for us to take off her hands. In fact, I'm sure she does," Kevin implied uniting the group with good information.

"So, Cee does Dean got money for, Welo?" They all looked catching me off guard.

I knew their relationship with Dean was not approachable, Jefferson projects alone was foreign to them.

"I doubt it, but I'ma check with him," I told them feeling fear inside.

"If he does, we will split that five ways and give you an in on it," Steamer advised, and the others nodded in agreement.

They were not getting a dime I already knew how I was playing that out. They kept up with this agreeing to stay together and split everything between the four of them.

Julio finally spoke, "I go to D.C. we killing somebody, and anybody who has sumthing to do with Mi hermano's death will die."

All eyes were on Julio and after a few seconds Gee spoke, "Maybe it's time one-seventeenth only has one color."

"Let's get this together first then think about shit like that," Steamer suggested.

They told me I was in charge of the whole bottling up process, plus a four day a week lieutenant position on 117th Street from three to twelve. They agreed to not deal with Dean no more or Welo's other lieutenants in New York but keeping D.C. Julio and his rent would stay on payroll. The gun I had on my waist felt like part of me now. When I first came here, I bought it for protection but when I thought they were going to kill me the gun I carried made me more afraid. Julio pulled me to the side while the rest of them were talking.

"Give me five thouzan and a girl and I say nothing." He looked at me, I was puzzled. "The two keys Dean got, lezs work together."

"Five and a girl, you got it," I told him.

I left them and went to May-May's just around the corner on 2nd Avenue. A dice game was being played between some Wagna project cats, two guys I knew from school.

"I see you, Cee getting this money," said one of them commenting on everything I had on being new.

"Regular Harlem shit yah know," I told him as I entered May-May's.

I ordered the most expensive Chinese food on top of the menu, Lobster lo mein. Outside the bets were made as the game started going on. Two of the kids from my school asked me to play but it was not my thing and I had things to do.

May-May yelled out, “Lobster lo mein, yo orda ready!”

I went in to get my order, I ate my food while riding in a cab to 117th Street on Lexington. I passed 1990 not seeing my boy, Tee. E.R. was out there with a good-looking older girl all over him. I looked at my beeper and the last time my girl beeped me was when I gave her a hundred dollars. The cab stopped, I paid him and stayed inside. We had a pitcher out making sales, Ray The Boss had a lot of people out on our side making sales, too. I took the cab to go see Dean and get my money.

I beeped Dean and waited for him as an older female looked at me. She had one of those grown women bodies that were thick in all the right places.

“Hey, shorty how you doing?” I asked her.

“Shorty, you the shorty. How old are you, Little Kid?” she asked.

I was about to say fifteen and would be lying. “I’m old enough to take you wherever you want to go.”

She smiled, then it turned into a laugh that got me angry. “Little Kid you need more than some new clothes for my attention.” She walked off switching her nice ass.

I found myself walking behind her watching it move. “There’s nothing little about me. You can bet that I handles my business.” She stopped and looked back at me. “My name is Cee, and people know who I am,” I told her.

Dean called out to me as she looked over my shoulder at him. I looked back seeing him rush to me. Her face suddenly changed.

“Let me take your beeper number, Cee but don’t be coming over here looking for me. I’ll hit you up when I want you, but don’t be telling me no stories about how you ain’t got it when I call.”

"We can do whatever you want as long as I hit that."

"No problem." She wrote down my beeper number just as Dean reached us.

"What's up, Dean? Talk to your little friend he thinks he in my league." She walked off and we both stood watching her ass.

Dean knew about Welo's death and said he would give me the money. As long as the numbers would stay the same on the bricks of consignment to him. I agreed telling him it was for our ears only. I was to pick up some money in four days. I walked through the projects feeling good. There were some more girls ahead and I wanted to see them up close. I needed girls to bag up.

Pop! Pop! Pop! Pop! Pop! The shots were all around me and one hit my leg. I yelled out something and fell holding myself then took out my gun. The girls saw me and started running, I looked and saw Tall-Tall Man coming.

CHAPTER FORTY-SIX
SLY

"This will be the last time you have to be here okay," his voice was calm as I nodded my head in agreement.

I'd prayed and prayed leaving everything up to God until this point. Being awaken inside myself seeing Jefferson projects reminded me of what I'd left behind. Stress and worry ran through me, aware that I looked nice made me feel uncomfortable because I was not myself. People would look at me different.

"You don't have to go; we can do this another time…" his voice trailed off in my head.

I thanked him then told him to talk about something else. Not wanting to hear from him right now, I was trying to figure things out.

"Your butt is getting big," he said bringing me back to reality with a smile.

I did feel better physically and did look better, too. I liked him for that thought and got out of the car confused yet wanting to stay positive. I walked close to him as he towered over me. Funny tingles came from inside, I didn't need his comfort anymore. I was home, coming here made me uneasy, but really, I was uneasy all along being who I wasn't. The projects began relaxing me, inviting me to stay with no worries, no judgment.

I sat on every bench here before, I got high in these buildings. People were deep in the projects all around doing different things. I knew what each of them was up to. Who was hustling, who was going to get high, who was going home or going to see someone? My mind raced into hustle mode, feeling for my scarf but it was gone. That life was gone, and I held onto him as he walked next to me. We were almost there.

"That's Sly?" I heard snapping me out of my thoughts.

"Yeah, it's me, hey, Ty," I said recognizing the voice and wanting to be regular.

His eyes were stuck on me and the other people with him was making comments, enjoying me with their eyes. I did not know how to feel, and things were moving in flashes. All their voices and faces became blurs to me, and we moved on into the building. When he finally got upstairs my apartment door was open. He shielded me but I could probably protect him here more than he could protect me. We went inside and it was empty. He spoke and all I heard, or saw were blurs. I saw Corey having sex with me against the wall, thrusting hard into me with force making me feel good like I was not a Crackhead. Then he left me to never come back. Now Tall-Tall Man looking taller in my apartment came to me, holding me like he cared. I was losing it, I started hitting him, he was going to leave me, too.

"I heard you on the phone last week. You going back to college. Now what…what happens to me?"

What he said became a blur while I was remembering being slapped by one of those kids' downstairs. I owed him some money, he made me suck his dick and I still owed him money.

"You're a drug dealer now, you sell drugs!"

"Sly, I'm here!"

"No…no you're not you just want me to suck your dick. You think you can just have your way with me then live your life. Well, don't wait just go now! I don't need your charity! You want me to suck your dick, go ahead and pull it out. I'll suck that shit good and you can go!" I was yelling at him.

He was going to use me and leave me. Nobody wanted me, nobody. They wanted me downstairs though. I shouted at him to fuck my mouth, fuck my ass, I just wanted him to do whatever he needed to do and go. He tried to hold me, and I pushed him back not interested in the bullshit.

"Go…go…go!" I yelled.

"Sly, this is not what you want," he said trying to game me and I only got angrier.

I yelled and yelled at him and the angrier I got the more hurt his face was. I saw he was hurting for me.

"I do want you, we can do this," he said.

No was in my head and all I could say was, "No!" to his face.

"I need you as much as you need me, Sly."

"No, you don't, all yar do is use me. You're nothing but another drug dealer just like I'm nothing but another Crackhead." He tried to speak. "No…no…no!" I yelled and he came closer to me.

I wanted to get away so bad but felt him and was now listening as he talked. He was holding me with his words and his arms. He was a force field, he was sincere. I could go away with this man, away from here or be abused in these streets forever. I wanted to get high badly like never before and the dealer knew it and wanted anal sex from me. I was young again and scared. It was when I first got strung out.

I told him no over and over, but he wanted to fuck me in my ass, and I let him hurt me to get high. I was in his brace away from the dealer hurting me from behind. Safe again, my mind flashed back to the kids downstairs and what they wanted. This could all happen with him. I just needed to get high one more time. I wiped my eyes and calmed down.

"Let me think about this…" I started but he cut me off.

"No, Sly!" He was so angry, he cared so much I held onto him.

"Don't let me go," I said.

After packing a few things, some paperwork and pictures that I showed him with a smile. I was feeling better. He sat watching me collect my things when I went to my room, I found a scarf in my drawer. I walked past him with it on my head, he jumped up chasing me as I ran into the room being cornered. He snatched it off as we looked into each other's eyes.

"We have a life ahead of us, you will be free of this. I did it and you're stronger than me,"

"Enough of this sad stuff, let's get out of here and move on," I told him.

We headed back outside; it was dirty to me now. I was never coming here again and when we leave New York I am never coming back. On his way to the car, he started acting funny.

"Are you okay?" I asked but he ignored me. "Uh, hello are you okay?" I asked again.

"Yeah, yeah I'm fine," his voice was different, but I just wanted to go.

We got to the car and he let me in then walked around to the driver's side, put the key in the ignition and turned the car on but didn't get inside.

"Just give a second, I'll be right back," he said.

"Hurry up, I want to go," I told him.

"Okay, just a minute, Sly," he said reaching over giving me a kiss on my mouth. It felt good, no one has kissed me on my lips since high school. Then I felt it.

"No…no don't go I won't see you again," I said seeing him walk away.

"I'll be right back," he said and left moving fast.

I watched him going toward people then deeper into the projects until I didn't see him anymore. It may have been forty seconds that he was out of my sight when I heard faint gunshots. Sirens came fast that was right in the area. I even saw an unmarked police car heading in that direction. I got out of the car and ran; crowds of people were around looking in the direction I ran toward. I wanted to see what they saw. There was someone shot a little kid. There was someone else shot and still struggling with the police. It was him; he was in cuffs but resisting.

"Nooo…nooo!" I shouted.

People looked at me as I ran to him and cops stopped me. As I watched him struggle, I fought them. Then started screaming, I wanted to die, I wanted to hurt them, I wanted to hurt him for leaving me.

CHAPTER FORTY-SEVEN
DETECTIVE VUGGIO

A file on my lap had the pictures of Miguel Cruz. His visage was unfamiliar to me. He was a skinny, young, Spanish male who was wanted for robberies and cutting at least three people with a razor. Two here in Jefferson projects, We called him The Harlem Slasher. This was detective Smalls case and I was familiarizing myself with it. The report showed people in The Harlem Slasher's neighborhood were eager to give information to remove him from the streets. His last victim's statement read: *A couple was robbed giving up their money and he chose to cut the male in the face after the fact. A real creep.*

I was viewing the projects from inside the car while being recognized by some teens across the street. They were sitting in front of a building glaring in my direction. Two of them were small drug dealers and one probably had a gun. It was tempting for me to jump out for the collar, fortunately for them, I was waiting on the Slasher. They walked off into a building I noted. The next time I encountered them, I'll know their console, they will run to.

Detective Smalls watched intently from his view seeing the other side of the projects.

"So, we know the Slasher is coming through here?" I asked him.

"His modus operandi dictates it, Sir," Smalls said looking at me.

"Just say M.O.," I told him.

"Yes, Sir," he said laughing, then turned to surveillance toward his area again.

It was true, our biggest weapon to take someone off the streets was to follow their M.O…modus operandi. I laughed in my head.

"There's circumspection we have to take with Raphael. He's a microbe patient," Smalls said.

Microbe was the term we used for a drug attic that had a mental disorder. They could be dangerous and extremely unpredictable. We had an unmarked car on 3rd Avenue waiting and watching and another in route driving around the entire projects. We also were seeking out a young black male named Dean that dwells in these projects. He was known to carry weapons and tips had been coming in about him.

I remember Dean from almost a year ago after he was shot for the second time in their projects. He told me he got hit by a car while he laid in the hospital bed with bullet holes in him. I knew he was a hard ass then but appreciated the humor.

"Hey, Vuggio look," Detective Smalls said, directing me to Tall-Tall Man walking fast.

He fitted a description of the shooter we'd been searching for. A young kid from 117th some months ago was shot by a tall, black, fit male. We checked everyone fitting that description for a lead and came up empty-handed.

"Shit he pulled out a gun…call it in!" I said.

Detective Smalls used the radio. "Car two…car two, we are pursuing an armed suspect. He's Tall-Tall Man wearing…"

I was out of the car with my gun drawn as Tall-Tall Man started firing at a little kid.

Pop! Pop! Pop! Pop!

"Freeze!" I yelled at him some feet ahead of me.

He turned and I fired one round hitting his shoulder. His gun dropped as he fell back onto the ground. I ran over while keeping him in eyesight.

"Don't fuckin' move or I'll shoot you again motherfucker!" I told him. As I looked further up the block over to the little kid, I saw him flash a gun as he dropped down behind a car. "Put your hands behind your back!" I ordered paying attention to my apprehended suspect who was shot. I radio it in. "I need an ambulance here we have a gun wound to my suspect."

He laid on the ground grunting lightly. I secured the weapon first, then looked up seeing the little kid get up.

"Don't move, stay right there!" I yelled to the kid as officer Smalls pulled up in the car.

I pulled my collar up handing him over to Smalls. Fuck, then I saw Dean run away from the little kid with something.

"Don't move…both of you, stay there!" I yelled to startle them, about to go after Dean, but our collar saw the kid he shot at and went wild lashing out.

Our unmarked car came.

"Get the kid and Dean," I told them.

They went in pursuit stopping at the kid, but Dean was gone. The man in cuffs was vigorously defying us. Even with his hands cuffed behind his back he continued to struggle.

"It's over, relax you're going to make it worse for yourself."

"Aaahhh!" he yelled as we pushed him back down to the ground. "Aahhh!" his yells came with hard attempts to get out of our hold, being so tall and strong he got up with us still on him.

"I'ma kill him!" he yelled.

The radio began barking, "We have another victim in need of medical assistance, a gun wound!" the little kid was shot.

"Let me go, I'ma fiuckin' kill him!" He would not stop.

Our third vehicle came as the officers responded quickly forcing him to the ground. I radioed to the officers that held the little kid.

"Put him in cuffs too and search him thoroughly." We had the situation under control until a lady came screaming.

"Nooo…nooo!"

A detective grabbed her, and she pushed him making him fall back as she advanced toward him. Blue and whites got to her throwing her on the ground with force, The female struggled and did not give up.

"What the hell going on with these people today?" I asked myself.

We finally got the bleeding Tall-Tall Man into a police car as the little kid was driven away in a patrol car. The female was taken in by the blue and whites to be booked. The bleeding Tall suspect was put into the ambulance minutes later as he calmed down not seeing the kid, he wanted dead so badly

At the hospital, the kid was cuffed to the bed and patched up. His wound was not threatening.

"So, why did he shoot you?" I asked him.

"Who shot me?" the kid responded.

I thought about Dean. "Kid you're playing a silly game that will only end up two ways. Both bad for you."

"Why am I cuffed?" he asked.

He was underage so I really couldn't ask him anything without his parents or a lawyer. After calling his mother, I had detective Smalls wait on her to see if the kid would talk then. We booked the Tall man on assault, criminal possession of a weapon and assault on police officers. The woman was sent to Bellevue hospital for psychiatric evaluation for twenty-four hours, then let go. I wanted Dean badly, he dared to take a gun and run in my face.

CHAPTER FORTY-EIGHT
GUY

My bed was a lustful rollercoaster ride as she laid naked on her stomach. Her face was on the opposite end of the bed than mine. The back of her small toes was in front of my face leading down a path of sexiness. It went up her legs, rising higher to her butt then dropping down a curve in her back, it was nice. I laid with my head propped up on one elbow sideways looking down her body.

"I'ma call for an O'Jay to drop you home in Brooklyn," I said.

Her pretty brown face popped up and looked back with a smile.

My small toes were farther from her face then hers were to mine being that she was longer than me.

"Okay, you have to pay for it though. I ain't got no money on me, Guy," she said positioning herself up on both elbows as her ass jiggled. She stayed on her stomach being over conscious of a light belly I could tell. I wanted her for the second time this morning but was not going to seem thirsty.

"I got you, first we gonna make a stop at this breakfast joint I like, then I'll ride you home. The car is paid by the hour anyway," I told her.

Her face was older and beautiful by years over me. She was looking from a backward side glance stopping at my light bush than to my face. I liked seeing her see me, last night she was a little timid with her eyes to my body.

"Nah, you don't have to do that, just pay him here I don't want to be a bother," she said.

I lifted my leg up, petted her ass real slow with my feet, purposely letting her see a clear view of me exposed. I used my big toe to go in between her cheeks feeling a warm spot.

Her eyes closed then opened. "Let me touch yours with my fingers," she said.

"Go ahead," I told her even though I really don't like that.

She sat up with her face right over my lower body giving me a nice tingle inside seeing her lips close. I laid back spreading open my legs lifting one knee, knowing what she was seeing. The sit-ups I'd been doing made my stomach flat, my legs looked strong and my tits were small and heavy. Her fingers felt small inside me since I was wet and ready wanting her mouth again. I looked up to the ceiling.

"This is the first time I put my fingers in someone else's," she said still inside me touching around my walls now. "And you got a pretty one," her saying that changed the good vibrations I had into shivers, her fingers seemed to become rough now.

The thought of his fingers in me, I shook out of my mind. I didn't want his thing to come next. I looked at her, she smiled making me want her mouth, but it didn't come, I thought about last night. I was pumping fast with my fingers as she came in jerks under my control. I watched her face and body tremble in a lustful good experience making us one, wanting the same thing. I positioned myself over her mouth, her lips moved tasting me. I snapped out of it, that was last night fun and her mouth was not on me, but her fingers were in me speeding up. She was irking me; I closed my legs trapping her hand.

"Let's get dressed," I said horny for her mouth but agitated by her fingers resisting the urge.

Still being agitated I needed to move on. She looked puzzled watching me get up. I walked with her eyes to my ass and got my clothes out of the dresser along with my gun. I plopped down on top of it, I had shit to do.

Scottie wasn't home and usually, he'd be in his room at night. It was comfortable having a room here way better than being at my auntie's. I remember when I was small, and my aunt's husband went to jail for selling Crack. Everything got harder in the house, not just money but everything. When I started getting money, she began leaning on me. Then depending on me, I didn't like being around her anymore because she changed after he left.

We washed up and I was brushing my teeth. Luck would usually be in here with me. He got real attached to me after Scottie once said that I reminded Luck of Bad. I wished Luck was home so I could scare shorty a little bit with him. After we dressed, she looked good in clothes and we were ready to go. I got some money together from out of the room. Her eyes went around seeing the fifteen pairs of new sneakers lined against the wall, the small stereo system on a dresser, the new bed covers and new lamps. My room was different than the apartment she'd came in. Not taking nothing from Scottie's stuff but it was just fly in here.

I changed my jacket twice then my sneakers to match when the phone rang. It was the cab waiting downstairs.

"The cab is here you ready to go?" I told her tying up my kicks.

"You can stay Guy, just give me the money," she said acting a little funny.

"What's up, you don't want to walk outside with me? You don't even know nobody around here!" I told her.

"No, it's not that, you could walk me I just thought you had things to do that's all. Dag don't act like that, Guy."

"Shorty, you turning me off, right now…just be quiet." First, she rejected breakfast, and I knew I was hungry. Then she told me to pay the driver knowing she didn't want me to even go downstairs with her.

"Come on, let's go, Guy. Walk me to the car," she said.

Man fuck this bitch; I'm not going out like that. "You have fun last night?" I asked her.

"Yeah," she said.

"So, why you…come here," I told her. She came obediently. "Turn around for me." She did and her ass looked nice in her jeans. She felt shamed letting others see her with me that's what it was. I felt her ass slow then slapped it lightly a couple of times watching it move back into place. "Get the fuck outta here!" I walked towards the door and opened it.

"What…why you acting like that, Guy, what's wrong?"

"You're wrong, get the fuck out before I get mad."

She looked at me and walked past into the hallway. "I don't understand," she said.

"Yeah, that's the problem," I told her.

"Well, can at least get the cab money?" she asked.

I wanted to say no, but who was I kidding? It was a sex thing, why do I care about her insecurities? I had my fun.

"Here and lose my number," I told her passing thirty dollars for the O'Jay.

"I'ma call you, don't act like that Guy. I'm still going to call you and you better answer," she said.

"You do that! But right now, just get the fuck out of my face."

Scottie got off the elevator with Luck as she was leaving me. Luck came running down the hall in full speed, passing her. She pushed herself against the wall afraid.

"Good boy, Luck…good boy!" I said petting him, he was excited.

Scottie stared her down as she past him to get on the elevator and left.

"That was nice," he said as we all entered the apartment.

"Yeah, but she phony," I said.

"Why you say that?" he asked.

I was shocked with his concern and cocked my head back. "She thinks she's too good to walk outside with me, but I don't give a fuck."

"Probably just shy, you know, Welo is dead, right?" Just like that, that was how Scottie was.

"No, I didn't."

"Yeah, so stay strapped you know pussy Monk ain't thinking and we don't know if it's a takeover or what."

"I stay strapped, Scottie."

He nodded and went to his room. I left out with a .32 semi, instead of my new .25 auto I bought. I walked up Lexington, the weather was nice outside. When I got to 117th Street a blue and white past through slow looking at people posted on the block. Ray The Boss was out there talking with one of Welo's lieutenants Druggem. Custies was flowing to pitchers that were out.

"Teddy up…teddy up!" I heard and another blue and white rolled past slowly.

It was hot out here, so I rushed into what we called Keith's building. I knocked on what was now Julissa's apartment and Monk opened the door. I needed some work; I was glad he was running things. Scottie may call him soft but not being in constant beef was good for making money. The apartment looked different, it was roomy and empty like.

"You heard Welo got killed?" Monk said.

"Yeah, I'ma try and get all this money now. They looking weak out there," I told him as Julissa came out of the kitchen with a bowl of food.

"What up, Jay?" I said to her.

"Hey, Guy, you looking good today," she replied.

"This is what I'm talking about, I want in," Monk said as we ignored him.

Julissa looked plainly sexy in her Tee and pajama pants.

"Let me leave this hammer under your couch," I requested of Julissa.

"Cool, just don't forget it okay," Julissa agreed.

"Hell, no I won't I need mine on me. Wait…is Davi around you know he be finding them shits!" I said seriously.

"No, he out with his friends and have to go back to Long Island tomorrow night," she said sitting down eating her Spanish food.

That was how she stayed so thick eating that heavy food all the time. Her body was just too sexy to ignore.

"Yo' you heard this nigga got popped with like two keys, right?" Monk said.

"Who?" I asked.

"Welo's lieutenant Kevin, he was driving one of Welo's cars and got stopped and searched," Monk informed.

"Damn, I coulda used all that and ate real nice. They falling apart already," I said.

"He was mad cool, that's fucked up," Julissa said.

"Yeah, well that's going to be some time he facing," Monk stated.

"You giving me a dollar today?" I asked Monk.

"No, why would I do that?"

"Because it's hot out there and I'm your number one ringer like you was Keith's, that's why," I told him.

"I'll give you the same fifty cents and after every ten packs, I'll give you a pack to keep let's start there," he told me.

"Give me the eleven packs and I'll give you a stack, but I'm staying out all night and I want a dollar after twelve."

"Damn, you thirsty, I got you," Monk said.

Outside I had two packs on me, and the rest was hidden in the garbage ready to get pushed. Monk already had some kid out here and everybody was flowing with sales.

"Red is out, Red is out!" I yelled and a dirty fiend that smelled came and bought two.

I could feel the heat come off her. A woman with tight clothes was next, then Nubs, the Landlord and the old man from upstairs it was flowing. I watched up the block for the police. My court date for my open case was coming up, another arrest would hurt me bad.

Ray The Boss called out to me from Welo's side standing next to Druggem.

"A yo' B let me holla at you," he said.

I heard him but was in no rush. I felt nervous to cross over like police were watching everything. Keith always said act like they always watching you and you won't slip.

"Guy, let me holla at you for a second," he called out to me again.

I put away my money and walked across the street. My awareness intensified as I felt the gun on my waist while I walked making it to him.

"Just so you know that kid from Johnson projects you shot came through here yesterday."

Confusion and awareness hit me, people knew that I did it, and I gave that fool a chance. "Word, did he stay long?"

"Nah, he was on the corner of Lex posted up with another dude. After ten minutes I walked over telling them all beef on this block is all of our beef. So, he better find someplace else to post up."

"Thanks for the heads up, Ray."

"Ain't shit, you ready to roll with the Green? We ain't playing no fuckin' games."

"Nah, I'm good but good looking."

He nodded as I gave him dap and walked off. After getting money for some hours, I checked my beeper seeing shorty hit me up twice. It was getting late, so I walked home to drop off the money I made. Scottie sat on the couch sewing some shit. I knew he was high. I went straight to my room with Luck tagging behind me. I put the TV on and napped a little then fell out. Waking up in my bed fully clothed bothered me. I picked that up from my aunt to not let anyone even sit on the bed with clothes on. Shit, it was past eleven at night, time to get that dollar a bottle money.

The night was usually safe to pitch, no T.N.T, blue and whites were called for the creep shit going on. Vuggio chasing guns was the problem. I went and knocked on Scottie's door.

"What?" he said.

"I'm taking, Luck out," I told him, and silence came from behind his door for a few seconds.

"Go ahead," he said, and we left.

The night went slow but the dollar a bottle made up for it, getting paid double than normal. Welo's crew was out but seemed weak. Ray's people seemed strong. Scottie was right Monk better be paying attention to what's going on. After hustling for three hours, I called the O'Jay company on the pay phone and ordered them to pick me up in front of King Corporals.

I walked there and the cab pulled up shortly after. I put him on hold as my time was running. A few custies and dealers were inside ordering snack boxes moving quick. I ordered three boxes then got in the cab after they came. I rode by some weed spots from Wagna projects and stopped at a store getting junk food and Dutches. I gave the driver a snack box and some pulls as we rode around the Eastside smoking with Luck laying on my lap.

After I went back to Scottie's, I smoked again in front of the building before going up, I wanted to be super high tonight. I was enjoying the night; it was cool to have Luck next to me. This block had a slow Crack flow and the hustlers were older selling drugs for themselves.

"Guy, right?" One asked walking over to me.

Luck stood at attention knowing the man as well from the area. "Yeah, what's your handle?" I asked him.

"T-Money," he said.

"What's up, T-Money?"

"Ain't shit, Guy, I just wanted you to know we got that killer weed, right here. Next time you blow it down," he said.

"Let me get two dimes and see what you working with."

After buying the weed I went upstairs. If this is good, I won't have to ride to Wagna no more. Opening the door with Luck by my side I saw a naked fat lady bobbing her head up and down on Scottie's dick with fast speed. Her big ass was in the air and Scottie held a gun in his hand with the rest of him uncovered. She stopped looking sweaty and exhausted.

"Fuck are you doing keep going bitch," Scottie said.

She went back taking Scottie's thing into her mouth as it disappeared. Luck looked up at me, waiting to see what I would do. I dropped a snack box next to Scottie as they ignored me and went to my room. I rolled a blunt and smoked it as I counted out money and cleaned up my room. I was busy, it was not until I looked at Luck that I realized I was getting things done but moving real slow.

This weed was good, I was super high and felt good. Getting into my panties I went to sleep while watching a video on VCR. I woke up late the next day picturing Scottie getting head. Eww, it was a nasty sight burned into my brain. My shorty was blowing up my beeper, I also saw my aunties number too.

Luck was with me and I was afraid what I would see if I walked out of the room, but we did. No one was out there but it was a mess with Red Cracks on the floor. I past the living room, ate some cereal and fed Luck some food. It was late, around two in the afternoon, Scottie was not home. After a shower, my mind felt focused. I was not going to hustle no more in the daytime, not until after my next court date.

I cleaned up Scottie's mess and walked outside leaving Luck in the house with three hundred and a gun on me. At the schoolyard on 119th Street around 4:00 pm a dice game was out, and some music was playing loudly. I'd just missed a basketball tournament game for an all girls' teams. Ray sponsored one of them. It was alive and jumping with people. A slow looking kid named Chucky was dancing with a crowd around him. I smoked a bag of that new shit and just watched falling back on the fence.

I must have zone out, time was moving and then I saw Julissa moving fast toward me crying.

"Oh, my God, Guy…oh my God!"

"Calm down, what happened?" I asked.

She couldn't get it out all she said was, "Keith, Keith…nooooo!"

CHAPTER FORTY-NINE
ERIC ROSARIO

I woke up and felt it, heard it, then saw her mouth going to work on me real slow. The straight hair and white face with make-up was foreign and looked nice. Even after all this time she's been here, it was still different…she was different. I felt ready and was preparing to let it all go. She must of knew it and speeded up her sucking and bobbing just a little. I came hard in abundance, it was great. Now it was time for her to go. I buttoned up my pants and looked at my beeper.

The lawyer lost her way somehow ending up in East Harlem and staying in my stash spot. Now getting me up with a smile this afternoon. Probably thinking of me as some dumb kid to manipulate. She was not my problem to solve. I walked over to the safe.

Don Poe complained about her being here all this week. We were fucking all the time, he even walked in on us in his living room once. She had one leg oddly folded on top of the couches arm rest, hand on the wall and slightly bent over with me pounding away. All that was okay because I usually made her leave at night before I went home.

Last night I stayed over going in and out from the stash spot to the block hustling. A new kid from my school named K High started pitching yesterday and we showed him the ropes. Never make sales in the open. Go into the indents to not be seen by police. Don't keep work on you and if you do stash it in your nuts. The block was hot, and you will be searched. Don't let the fiends switch bottles. Ask them, if they want rocks or shaved. Yell Blue is out to any custies that pass by. We taught him while we drank

Saint Yves. All night we hustled, and K high made his PC. More pitchers were a start that I needed to step up my game with.

The lawyer sat watching me. I walked over to the safe still in thought. Ignoring her for now. Opening it, I did a count of the money and packs. I was drunk last night and wanted to see how we did. It looked good with more money than Crack packs in the safe.

I'm going to make Chito and Tee my lieutenants so I can fall back from being out there. I want to graduate high school next year then go to college and become a CPA. I need to beat my open cases first. Trial was a scary thing, really a joke for us to try and win, guilty or not. If I adjourned the cases long, and because of my age, do good in school, maybe I can get probation. If I catch another case, I'm going to prison for sure. The new kid was out making sales to custies. I really needed to go home, my moms is going to kill me.

"You ready?" I asked her.

She looked at me surprised. "Can't I stay? I don't feel like going outside, right now," she told me

I was not used to talking to a white woman, to a lawyer at that. "I don't own this apartment, plus it's time for you to leave…leave," I said.

"You throwing me out? That's how you treating me?" she asked, her eyes were an off green I noticed.

"I got to go, get your stuff and let's go," I said.

"That's not even right. Why you acting like that? Let me stay two more days and I'll leave," she said.

"Look just get your shit and get the fuck out…stop playing with me."

She stood up in her panties and started getting dressed. "You New York motherfuckers are foul. Yar, just a bunch of kids playing like men."

"Bitch I don't even know your name, and just nutted in your mouth. Get the fuck outta here!" She started dressing faster.

"Nah, not now, like right now…let's go!" I said while getting her only other outfit she had here and rushing her out of my room.

She picked up things that were hers and held them in her arms. In the living room, Don Poe sat with his legs crossed next to an older custie watching me rush her out.

"About time, Eric. I thought you were getting all Jungle Fever on us," Don Poe said.

She dressed quick and was out of the apartment. I felt a little guilty but needed to go and didn't have time for this. Minutes after she left, I wanted to call her back and give her the two days. That was my lust talking, I left the apartment.

Outside, I had to think of an excuse to tell my moms. I ran across the street to the dry cleaners as a car came rushing to a fast halting stop and scared the shit outta me, catching me off guard.

"Why you running, what you got on you?" the passenger cop said not even getting out of the car. It was Blondie. We all knew who he was. I was relieved it was the police and even better the gun squad. T.N.T will take your ass in and put a sale on you. Putting you with any custies they caught with work, saying they saw you serve him.

"I ain't got shit, Sir," I told him. They looked in my face hard and seemed upset like I'd done something to them.

"Lift up your shirt and turn around," The driver said.

I did real slow completing the turn, but before I did, I heard the car drive off.

Summer was here and it was hot. I mean the block was super-hot with police since the BB bandit got killed. I went inside the dry cleaners and dropped my receipt on the counter. The black family that owned the store lived in the building and knew me. They were the only people I knew that owned a real business in the hood.

The father who was a strict man worked today. He took my receipt, got my order off the rack and placed it onto the counter. I emptied knots of money, two more receipts, and some candy out of my pockets. Then I took off my jeans and sweater giving it to him to take. Then I changed into the crispy light blue Levi denim jeans that were smelling like the cleaners. They matched the blue and white uptowns and new white Tee I had on. My chain that was under my sweater hung off my neck. I was given another ticket for my clothes I'd just given him and paid for it in advance.

Blue and whites circled the block, so I walked fast to the entrance of my building 1990 wanting to go home. I did not even want to be searched or taken in for a fake case. The scary feeling gave me an idea to just quit this all together. I had money now, more than I ever had in my life. Once I make it to college I'ma quit this whole shit. Blue was out, the new kid came over to me.

"I need more work, yar got this shit flowing," he said trying to hand me some money out in the open.

I walked into an indent of the building with him following behind me. Once we were both inside and out of traffic view, I took the money.

"You not going to last long if you don't follow the rules, I told you. You never know when they are watching or from where." I thought about Welo. He was always talking about rules.

"You got that, E.R. let me get some more work. Let me pitch ten more packs," he requested and handed me a thick roll of cash.

I had to go home. "Wait here, I'll send Tee to give you some work. It's going to be like ten minutes," I told him.

"I'ma go eat and come back in five minutes," he said and slapped my hand five.

I went inside 1990, taking the steps running up to the third floor. I counted out his money before I went home, it was all there. My beeper went off, it was Keith paging me 911…911…911. This is fucked up I had to go home. Running downstairs, I went to the pay phone and beeped Tee three times. I knew his beeper was on vibrate being that he was in his crib. Then I called Keith's old apartment and got no answer. The new pitcher was coming up the block. His face registered with danger; a car stopped in front of me. Men with badges dangling off a chain around their necks were out with guns drawn on me. A car stopped in front of him as well.

They put me against the walls in cuffs, dug all in my pockets, placing everything in a brown envelope with my name on it. Then tossed me in back of a van that came. K High was thrown in after me and they rushed off the block. We were driven around in the van and came to a sudden stop picking up another dealer. We picked up a couple more dealers across East Harlem for the next two hours, I had to go through the system again, I wondered what Keith wanted.

CHAPTER FIFTY
SCOTTIE

Keith was hustling hard coming back and forth to the city. He was not in the streets anymore but directly behind the scenes. That loss he took from the robbery disrupted his plans. We were now stronger than ever. Welo was dead and some of their lieutenants were buying small weight from Keith, others from Ray. Calvin was dead and Monk was getting some small weight sales. Keith's way of hustling changed.

In my apartment I watched and heard Luck eating food from his bowl. It reminded me that we were out of dog food. I pulled on the last of my blunt, then put the flame out with my fingers and ate the roach. The high was nice and I was getting horny thinking about getting some wet sloppy head, I got semi-hard. I thought about getting Shirley to do what she do but did not want to see her fat ass in the daytime.

A knock came to the door, Luck was barking and wagging his tail in a way that let me know Keith was on the other side.

I opened the door and let him in. "What's good, Nephew? Why you here?" I asked as he walked in dropping a bag on the couch that seemed too heavy for its size.

"To make sure you don't have no fat girls on their knees in here," he said.

"I was just thinking about doing that," I admitted.

He looked at me for some seconds to see if I was serious and then started laughing. "You nasty, Scottie. Anyway, I came for Guy. Is she here? I want to talk to her about getting out of pitching and selling some weight," he said.

"No, she left out," I told him.

"What you think about her, Scottie?"

"I think she family," I said.

"Me too, I don't want her pitching no more. I'ma set her up in Connecticut," Keith told me, and I nodded in agreement.

He dropped some money on the table from his pocket, it looked to be about two thousand dollars or so. "I'm out, Scottie."

"Where you going?" I asked.

"No, I'm out. After this last key and I set it up for Guy to be in Connecticut, it's over." I nodded yes. He knew how I felt about it. "So, I won't need those anymore." He pointed to the bag on the sofa.

I now knew what was in it. I was curious to see if he put his Uzi in it, too. Keith loved that gun, I looked inside the bag.

"I have to keep something in the house for protection," he said reading my mind. "And take care of Mama she getting high again," he said sadly.

"What did you think, Keith?" I asked.

"I don't know, but she family, too, you know." I nodded. Mama's worth was big to Keith and what he did, she kept him grounded.

He went to the bathroom and came back out minutes later, looking real serious. "I got new weight customers right on Lex," he said.

"That's why you worried?" I asked.

"No, but I'm glad you got me figured out. I heard some people are asking about me, some of them from Madison Avenue," Keith said.

"About what?" I asked.

"I don't got the details yet when I get back, we gonna find out maybe they want some work or something."

"You think it's Calvin's people?" I asked.

"I don't think so, but we gonna find out when I get back," Keith said.

"I'll be waiting for your beep then," I told him.

When he left, I dozed off to sleep for four hours. When I woke up, I had no beeps and saw the bag of guns still out. I took the bag to my closet, put three of the four handguns away. Melinda musta kept her .25, too, because it wasn't there. I checked the twelve shot .380 to see if it was loaded. Then it went onto my waist. I walked out of the apartment, stopped in front of Shirley's apartment and banged on her door just to do so.

She answered quick, "Who the fuck banging on my door like the police?" The door opened fast. "Oh, hi, Scottie what's up?" she said.

I looked at her then passed her fifty dollars. "Buy me some dutches a lighter and beer. I'll see you later tonight."

"Like what time, Scottie?" I just walked off, she better just wait for me.

I was eating in a Spanish restaurant thinking about everything. Maybe I should do my own thing. For a second, I did not feel safe with that thought. Then it was not the thought, I just did not feel safe. It was strange, I felt my gun and knew I was different. Just him talking about leaving changed me. He was more than the boss. I could never do what I do without it being for him. It was not about money or things. My whole job was him, shit I was supposed to buy some stuff for Luck. He needs some food and chew bones, it was getting late, so I'd take care of it tomorrow.

My beeper went off and it was Keith. I started finishing up my food, the beeper went off again 911-911-118-118. I took my last bite of food, paid the bill leaving the money on the counter and walked out. Keith never 911 me with a location behind it unless he needed me there fast, so I left. Outside the restaurant I hurried walking uptown. It was getting dark and if I could hail a cab I would. He was ten blocks away, I looked to the street for a cab as the cars passed. I was moving way too fast without thinking. Not my style.

"What's wrong, Scottie? You're off," I told myself.

I'd forgot the dog food. Keith was talking about people asking about him and I left him alone. I did not even check my surroundings before I walked out of the restaurant. Not looking behind me as I always do before going anywhere. I felt like I lost something inside of me.

"Scottie, you bugging."

Maybe I wasn't, fuckin' Keith got me feeling odd already. To erase the itch I was feeling, I looked back and a gun was being pulled from a waist. I saw no face but reacted pulling out mine. Someone was also running to me from my right side with a gun drawn, too. I hesitated, damn, I fucked up. It was a good setup.

Pop! Pop! Pop! Pop! Pop! Pop! Pop! Pop!

A hard pain worse than anything I knew came. The shots must of hit me in a vital area. I don't know how many he shot or how many hit me. I tried to shoot back but the feeling between pain and my gun was confusing. I could feel my gun, my pain, I saw his face come over me as I fell and looked up.

Pop!

I heard, and felt my head bounce off something hard, it was the sidewalk. "Focus Scottie, shoot back," I told myself.

My gun was in my hand, I pulled the trigger at him and heard nothing. Then I saw my gun on the ground, I was on the ground and my finger was pulling on air.

"Ha…ah…ha…ha," I said. '*I quit,*' I thought. '*Yar not doing shit we quit.*' No words came from me after my laughs, blood came out of my mouth. I saw feet running upside down away. I crawled to get to my gun.

"Fuckin' punks, I'm Scottie you better fuckin' run!" I moved and it hurt bad.

The pain in my head where I was shot gave me a buzzing sensation. My hands felt my side and stomach where I was hit. My finger went in the hole and the pain came alive. Blood was moving down my face. I breathed in then felt for the shot in my neck, it was just a graze but ached.

"I think I done fucked up now, Scottie."

Fuck pain I had to get my gun. I moved with the pain jabbing me, knowing what I wanted. I dragged my body some inches finding my gun and positioned myself up against a car. Looking in the direction they ran I pointed and aimed squinting my eye to the little metal on top of the barrel called the sight. Lots of people were in my sight looking scared. But my targets were gone. The gun was in my hand. I got it, I got the gun, I was ready now. I thought, they were going to hurt, Keith. The face looked familiar and I never forget a face until now.

"What the fuck, Scottie? You slipping!"

Someone came. "We called the police and ambulance, Mister. Just hold on for a minute." I aimed at him, he started running.

"Don't shoot…don't shoot me!" he yelled.

"Get the fuck outta here," I said. 'Think Scottie think. Who was that? Who shot me? Fuck!"

The face, it was Calvin, No I'm bugging. No, no I'm not, it was Calvin, but it can't be. I moved but not enough to make it anywhere. I couldn't warn, Keith.

Pop! Pop! Pop! Pop! Pop! Pop! Pop! Pop! Pop! Pop!

I emptied out the gun as I heard sirens trail off in the distance. The pain was fighting with me, I tasted it. I tasted blood. I laid down…Luck was running to me. Come on boy, good boy. Listen to Scottie.

CHAPTER FIFTY-ONE
KEITH

It was cold outside, but the sun was brightening up the day. The cold then became cool and it felt like the sun was shining directly over me. I looked up and believed the heated rays followed my every move. The crispy new leather jacket I wore fitted me nice, under it was a knick-knack bag of groceries I carried and what it concealed. My mind went to Ciera and I could now see her life moving forward in a positive way. Tomorrow I would be spending the entire day with her and taking her shopping. The feeling of good clothes always gave me a reflection of my life, plus it was a soothing remedy. It felt good, I felt good, except for the light tingle of nervousness.

A Chinese lady stood attentive behind the counter as I handed her my ticket and started undressing out of my clothes. She went directly to the rack finding my order, while I pulled off my jacket and placed it on the counter. Many of the dealers that came here changed out of their clothes for one of their clean fresh setups they left inside. I did it for the total opposite. She found my things and placed them right next to the pile of clothes I took off,

"You put this in?" She asked while looking, assessing and picking through the pile of clothes I'd just took off.

"Yeah," I said, dressing into the worn-out work clothes just given to me.

She looked at the ticket and reached down pulling up boots that were worn and dirty. Her face the entire time was not moved by anything until now as she started looking confused. "Wait, sorry, not clean," she said pulling the worn dirty boots back.

I told her, "No…no that's exactly the way I want them."

She handed them back slowly without any judgment. "Twenty-eight dolla, you still pay," she said.

As I paid, I could still see Ciera's face smiling. I left the cleaners dressed in my construction gear. I was going to throw this entire outfit down to the boots away right after this sale I had lined up today. No more hustling for me, I wouldn't be needing to trick the police anymore. Ciera's face was clear in my thoughts slightly frowning.

"It will be the last one I make," I said to myself and was sure of it, I felt it deep inside.

Then suddenly, I could no longer picture Ciera at all in my mind. It was spooky like I didn't know what she looked like. It was real strange. I shook my head. "Shake out of it, Keith," I coached myself.

In the bag was a key of coke hidden in a box of cereal, there was also two large bags of chips, a small juice and Italian bread sticking out of the bag that I carried in one hand. It was hot out here with the police, so I was taking steps to be safe. Violence was flowing and that made Vuggio run down on anybody he knew that did any type of illegal activity. Even those he knew that just be around and knew what was going on, making the neighborhood uncomfortable. Not my worry after today.

"Make this sale Keith and be on your way."

As I walked, I went over the details in my mind. This was to be my third sale to this dude. A friend had introduced him to Buddha, then Buddha to me. He copped a half brick the first time, then a whole one and now wanted another. I was not worried about him; the price I was giving him he would not want to fuck this up. Now we'd also helped him set up on what was Calvin's block. So, I gave him an outlet with great prices, if anything he would protect me.

"Relax, you thought this out. This sale is safe and it's all final, you're out."

Reaching the pay phone on 118th and Lexington I took out a Very Fine juice that was in the bag, then placed the bag of groceries on the ground between my legs. I put a quarter in the slot and dialed the O'Jay's number.

"Yeah, O'Jay cab service."

"This is, Keith. Can you have a car get me on one-eighteenth and third avenue please?"

"Okay, ten minutes, with your regular driver."

"Good," I said and got a dial tone.

I thought he was asking me, but he was telling me. They must be very busy. I placed the phone back on the receiver. My eyes went to my beeper looking for the customers' beeper number, I dialed it then hung up. His call came back quicker than I thought it would. I felt nervousness in my stomach. Ciera was looking at me, I could picture her again.

"You here?" the voice said into the phone interrupting my sight, and Ciera was gone

"Yeah, yeah, you ready?" I asked

"Yeah, I'm ready, come on up," the voice said hanging up.

I picked up my groceries and waited for the traffic to move. While taking that time to survey the block. Some Spanish women were further down in conversation, an old Spanish man was talking to another, some dudes were walking towards me without a care in the world joking, and two guys were just standing on the block. As I walked towards the building the two guys did, too. This was just nerves; I was a little jumpy. I reached the entrance and heard Ciera crying, I kept walking and passed the building.

I walked up the block speaking out loud to myself, "Man forget this sale, Keith you bugging." Realizing I said it out loud my mind said, "Man just do it already and move on." I turned back to the building but passed it again.

I speeded up crossing the street and went to the same pay phone, I beeped E.R., then right after Scottie. After two minutes I put another number in and the phone rung back within seconds, I picked it up.

"What's up, you here or not, Keith?" It was the sale.

"Yeah, I'm here I'm coming up now," I said.

"You sure?"

"Yeah, yeah, right now. I just want you to be ready to buzz me in it's hot out here"

"Okay, I got you," he said.

I hung up rushing across the street and into the building. I was acting stupid I thought, until the same two guys that came towards me last time was coming again. Inside the building, I pushed the intercom for the sale.

'*At least he'll buzz me in quickly*,' I thought. He did not answer, I buzzed again and again.

He answered, "Hold on."

I began pushing all of the buttons. "Hold on for what?" my mind screamed.

The door buzzed and I reached to open it, but the two guys came in. Immediately, one pulled his gun and my hand reacted on it's own grabbing his wrist and turning my back to him. Our bodies slammed into the wall we were pushing off each other with the gun being pointed away from me.

I was a kid who packed bags and a dealer that tried to stay away from violence. How did I get here wrestling with a gun? I wanted to quit, right now. His accomplice was avoiding the barrel of the gun swinging in his direction, as we moved so did, he. The area was small, the gunman's face seemed familiar, I knew him, but didn't. I recognize his face and was trying to think of a way to reason with them.

"Give them the drugs before this goes wrong," my mind screamed.

We swung hard to the left and I made the gun point at the other guy for some seconds. He dodged the barrel's sight as the pistol followed him, then he put his head down rushing at the two of us struggling with the gun. He got on me and started punching right away. The gun holder got a grab on me from behind, but I kept twisting my body to point his wrist was away from me, trying harder to point it at the other assailant that was hurting me with his blows.

Bang!

It went off once and the glass door shattered as the other guy curled up in fear from a near hit. He lunged back fast and grabbed on to me. "Yo', what the fuck, hold the gun down, B!" he told his friend.

I yanked as hard as I could but their hold on me was tight. We had four hands on the gun pointing it in a downward direction, they were now controlling the situation. Fear touched my stomach, the body behind me was moving to my turns and a hard punch hit me. Then another, and another, it hurt so bad I almost let go of the wrist that held the gun. I was punched in the stomach and could not breathe or hold on anymore.

I yelled, "Hold on, Keith!" While thinking this may not be just a robbery, it was all over if I lose this battle. The pain was stinging blow after blow, wrestling with the hand holding the gun I began losing my grip. I managed to say, "The coke is in the bag, a key of coke, just take it." They did not budge the punches came harder.

"Fuck your coke, Yellow Boy," the gunman said.

"We taking it anyway," the other said.

I was going to die, I lost my grip on his wrist, he was free. Quickly I pushed my body onto his and was grabbed by his accomplice.

The barrel of the gun was pointed at us while we wrestled for position, a clicking sound came, it was the door. Tenants responded trying to buzz me in. It clicked again, I reached for it with one hand and was punched in the jaw stunning me. I grabbed the door and it opened.

A hot pain came. *Bang!* The sound was instant or at the same time, I was hit. The guy near me flinched jumping back as I grabbed the buzzing door escaping the small vestibule. *Bang!* I was hit again this time hearing the sound first, I ran down the hallway.

Bang! Bang! Bang!

The shots missed me as I collapsed on the steps. Hit badly, I could not run anymore. I sat there seeing blood and feeling the pain. I could now pinpoint the exact entry points from the air entering my body through the holes. On the turn came the gunman and I grabbed his wrist weakly that held the gun, he just slapped my attempt away. We stared into each other faces, he looked angry, I knew his face, it was Calvin. Not Calvin but musta been a family member, his brother. A punch from behind made me fall to the floor. The gun was pointed at me and I closed my eyes, but there was no shot, I heard a yell. My eyes opened to a distracted gunman, I grabbed his legs knocking him backward and got on top of him.

"You fuckin' little Crack head bitch!" The other man yelled from behind me followed by a loud shot and I felt it enter, I looked back and saw mama running.

"Papa," her voice came again.

I smiled, everything was just calm and slow now. I felt the burn and it left; everything was going away except my thoughts. I took lots of precautions and played it smart, but in this game, you have enemies in all aspects of it. I was one step away and needed one more moment to plan. In this area and era, this was normal. I was just another story.

CHAPTER FIFTY-TWO
DETECTIVE VUGGIO

1995…

"Car one car one, this is car two, a dice game is starting now, Vuggio!" The Walkie Talkie spoke to me from one of the new faces we have that the dealers never seen before. He was watching 117th street between Lexington and Park Avenue. They were observing from one block away sitting in a dark green four-door Honda, itching to make an arrest.

"Car two, we are here for the two bosses of one-seventeenth street, as I explained to you at roll call earlier. We have information on both suspects to be carrying guns. So, we will not move until we see one or both of those targets. Is that clear?" I told him.

"Yes, sir Vuggio," the Walkie Talkie responded.

I responded back quickly, "And please follow protocol, use the car unit names. Now until we see the prime targets keep the radios clear."

The Walkie Talkie barked again. I felt lightly agitated. "Car one this is car two we have both suspects in question in our sights participating in the Dice game, Sir."

"Car two, confirm that you have both bosses of one-seventeenth street in sight. Boss one, a.k.a Davi and boss two, a.k.a Little Boy Corey."

"Car one, I am confirming, both men in question have been identified. One a.k.a Davi and the other a.k.a Little Kid Corey"

"Here we go partner," I said to Detective Blanch. "Car three follow car two down the Lexington entrance, you will back us up. We will come in from Park Avenue, Units line-up," I commanded in the Walkie Talkies.

"Car two is ready."

Two younger kids now ran the block. They were just as dangerous as the ones before them. Davi was wanted for questioning on two shootings, and Little Kid Corey already had drugs and gun arrests. They were escalating into career criminals.

"Car three is ready."

"Car two pick up Little kid Corey, We got Davi."

"Car two Copy."

"*Okay, team be alert, let's go*!"

The sirens wailed and the cars rolled into the block from two different directions as people began running.

Made in United States
North Haven, CT
13 December 2021